RUNNER

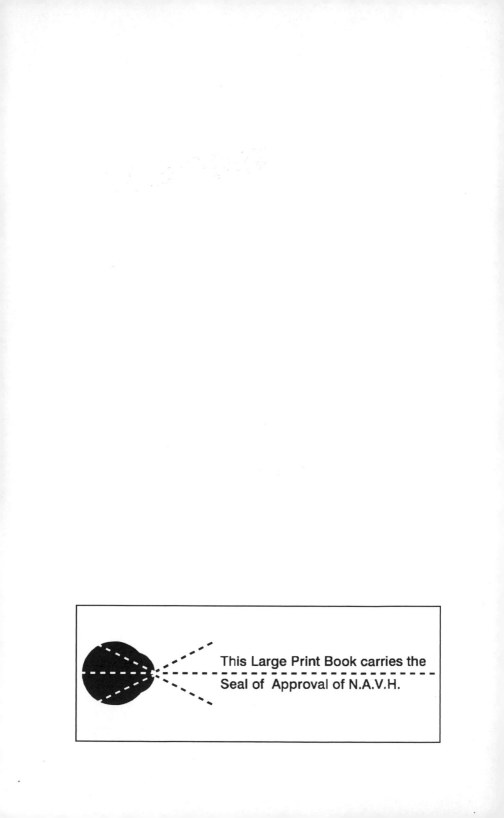

This Large Print Book carries the
Seal of Approval of N.A.V.H.

RUNNER

THOMAS PERRY

THORNDIKE PRESS

A part of Gale, Cengage Learning

GALE
CENGAGE Learning·

Detroit • New York • San Francisco • New Haven, Conn • Waterville, Maine • London

Hog
Gale
$33.

GALE
CENGAGE Learning·

LARGE TYPE
F
PERRY, T

3 1257 01813 9369

Copyright © 2009 by Thomas Perry.
A Jane Whitefield Novel.
Thorndike Press, a part of Gale, Cengage Learning.

LIBRARY OF CONGRESS CATALOGING-IN-PUBLICATION DATA

Perry, Thomas, 1947–
   Runner / by Thomas Perry.
     p. cm. — (Thorndike Press large print core)
   "A Jane Whitefield novel."
   ISBN-13: 978-1-4104-1475-5 (alk. paper)
   ISBN-10: 1-4104-1475-2 (alk. paper)
   1. Whitefield, Jane (Fictitious character)—Fiction. 2. Indian
women—Fiction. 3. Seneca Indians—Fiction. 4. Indians—Mixed
descent—Fiction. 5. Runaway teenagers—Fiction. 6. Teenage
pregnancy—Fiction. 7. Kidnapping—Fiction. 8. Large type
books. I. Title.
PS3566.E718R86 2009b
813'.54—dc22   2008053449

Published in 2009 by arrangement with Houghton Mifflin Harcourt
Publishing Company.

Printed in the United States of America
1 2 3 4 5 6 7 13 12 11 10 09

To Jo, Alix, and Isabel

1

The girl kept half-turning in the back seat to stare out the rear window of the cab, as though she were being chased across Buffalo to the hospital. It made Pete Sawicki as nervous as she was. He kept flicking his eyes to the rearview mirror, but all the way to the hospital he saw trucks, people driving station wagons to the supermarket, kids throwing baseballs beside empty streets — nothing at all that was suspicious except her. He pulled up to the emergency room entrance and got out of his cab to open her door.

She had a pretty face. She was very young, maybe even jailbait, with long light brown hair, eyes that looked gray-green, full lips that seemed to pout as she concentrated on getting out of the back seat of the cab. Pete held his hand out to help her, but she deflected his attention with a look that went past him as though he were gone already.

7

Usually somebody who wanted a cab ride to the hospital emergency room wanted a hand.

She stood and once again her belly showed, stood out from her body under the loose shirt. It was none of his business, but Pete couldn't help seeing the pregnancy as tragic in somebody her age. How could it not be?

"How much?" she said, her hand already moving into her purse.

"Eight bucks."

She frowned. "It can't be."

He pretended to look inside at the meter, and chuckled to himself. "You're right. It's twelve." He took the fifteen dollars she handed him. "Thanks. And thanks for noticing that." He stepped around the cab to his door, watched her walking to the emergency room, and waited until he saw the glass doors slide open to admit her and then close. He got back into the cab, reached into his pocket, took out a ten-dollar bill to pay for the rest of her fare, and put it into the cashbox. Then he drove out the circular drive. He supposed he would head out to the airport and take a place in the line there. It was still early in the day and flights from the west would start coming in soon.

■ ■ ■ ■

At the reception desk the woman in the uniform told the girl to sit and wait, but the triage nurse came out only a couple of minutes later and brought her into an office. The nurse said, "If you've got to be in the emergency room, you picked a good time. Beginning in the late afternoon, things get pretty hectic." The girl recited the symptoms as well as she could remember them, and then she had to answer the nurse's questions. Some were the obvious ones anyone would ask a pregnant woman, and some seemed to be all-purpose questions for emergency rooms. If you answered yes to any of them, you would belong in a hospital.

When the nurse started to stand, the girl said abruptly, "Do you happen to know a woman named Jane Whitefield?"

"I'm not sure. I may have heard the name. Why?"

"Oh, it's not important. Somebody I know told me if I was in this hospital I should say hello for her."

"It's a big hospital. I'm going to have you wait in an examining room. A doctor will be in to see you shortly."

The girl sat on the narrow bed in the small white room to wait for the doctor. She felt stupid, humiliated. Why would anybody ask her to say hello to somebody in an emergency room? Her mistake made her more nervous. She looked at the complicated telephone mounted on the wall. It made no sound, but she could see colored lights along the top, some steady and others blinking — green, red, and yellow. She stood and looked at it more closely. Maybe she could find the right button to make an announcement over the hospital's public-address system. She had a professional-sounding telephone voice. If she could find the right button, she could say, "Jane Whitefield, please report to the emergency room. Jane Whitefield, there is a patient to see you in the emergency room." It would be a huge risk, because they might throw her out or even have her arrested, but she had to do something.

The girl stepped closer and looked for labels on the buttons, then heard a woman's voice talking, growing louder as the woman came up the hall. The girl turned away from the phone and heard the swish of fabric as the woman stepped into the room. The woman was brown-skinned, about forty years old, and seemed to be from the

Middle East or Asia. She wore a starched white coat with a gold name tag. "Christine?"

"Yes."

"I'm Dr. Depredha. Are you in pain? Are you having cramps now?"

"Once in a while they come back."

"Bleeding?"

"I think it stopped."

Dr. Depredha touched Christine's forehead, then took her stethoscope and pressed it against Christine's neck for a few seconds. "All right. Let's get you undressed and I'll give you a brief exam, so we'll know more." She opened a drawer, took out a package, and tore it open. Christine could see it was a gown. "You can put this on, and I'll be back in a minute." She started out, pulling the door after her.

"Doctor?"

"Yes?"

"Do you know a woman named Jane Whitefield?"

"Sounds familiar. Is she a doctor?"

"I don't know. Someone I know said I might run into her here."

One of Dr. Depredha's perfect curved eyebrows gave an eloquent upward twitch that conveyed sympathy, apology, and yet, a businesslike urgency. "I haven't been here

11

long. I'll be back." She went out and closed the door.

Christine's heart was beating faster. She was feeling more and more panicky. Sweat dampened her shirt and nausea was coming on. She had come so far, and she was so frightened. Now that she was here, the place seemed to be a lot of blank, unknowing faces and closed doors, and she had no idea how long she would be safe here. She fought the impulse to step out the door and run, and began to undress. This was the plan she had chosen. She had to carry it through and give it a chance to work. If she couldn't find Jane Whitefield, at least maybe she could stay here long enough to rest.

Dr. Depredha hurried out to the reception area and spotted the big security officer near the doors to the parking lot. As she stepped toward him she saw his head turn, his dark, intelligent eyes see her, and his black face smile down at her. "Mr. Mathews."

"Dr. Depredha. What can I do for you?" For an instant she felt the warm, reassuring attention that he always brought with him. He was about six feet seven and weighed, by her estimate, two hundred and eighty pounds, but his manner made him seem like a doting uncle.

12

She had to speak quickly and just above a whisper. "I just got a patient, a pregnant female who listed her age as twenty. She's showing signs of extreme anxiety. She's afraid. Genuinely frightened."

"Do you need help with her?"

"Not with her. She's perfectly docile. But I have a feeling about this. She acts as though she were being chased. Do you understand?"

He nodded. "What does she look like?"

"Caucasian, brown hair, light eyes. Looks younger than twenty. Her name is Christine. The triage nurse noted that she arrived alone in a taxi."

"I saw her. All right, Doctor," said Mr. Mathews. "I'll begin watching for anyone who might be looking for her."

"Thank you, Mr. Mathews." She turned and hurried back through the automatic doors that led to the examining rooms.

Officer Stanley Mathews stepped to the outer doors of the emergency room and looked out. He wasn't quite sure what he was looking for — an angry parent or brother, an abusive boyfriend, or even some female rival with a gun in her purse. Dr. Depredha wasn't some flighty, overprotected woman who imagined danger. Before she had come to this country she had been

13

in a couple of wars, doing battlefield patch-up jobs while incoming mortar rounds thumped inside the perimeter near enough to bounce the instruments on the table. He'd seen a bit of that sort of thing himself. If she felt uneasy, he felt uneasy. He pushed open the double doors with both hands and stepped outside to see who might have pulled into the parking lot since he'd last looked. Some people had seen enough terror and misery in their lives so they seemed to develop a sense of when trouble was coming. They could feel it.

Jane McKinnon surveyed the room from the doorway. Tonight the hospital cafeteria had been not only decorated but disguised, the windows covered with long drapes and the ceiling hung with clusters of hundreds of white Japanese lanterns of different sizes. The benefit seemed to be going smoothly. People were moving away from the hors d'oeuvre tables and circulating instead of knotting up near the food and drink. The conversation was loud and continuous. The band had arrived, set up, and done sound checks during the late afternoon, so that when the music started it would be tolerable. As Jane moved in among the guests, her tall, erect shape and the light blue evening dress that set off the dark skin and black hair she had inherited from her father made people turn to watch her for a moment. The intense blue eyes she'd inherited from her mother acknowledged them and moved on.

"Jane!"

A man's voice, too close, coming from above her head. Jane McKinnon pivoted to face him, her eyes taking in hands-face-body in the first fraction of a second. It was only Gary Wanamaker, the hospital's director of development. The muscles in her arms and back relaxed, and she managed a smile. Her knees straightened from the preparatory flex that the long evening dress had hidden from view. For some reason she hadn't recognized the voice. She was jumpy tonight, abnormally alert.

His big, fleshy face came closer. "I just wanted to tell you what an extraordinary job you've done in organizing this evening. The fund is past the goal. I've already had three people come up to me to let me know privately that they were making big donations. I was hoping for maybe one gift that size."

"Thanks, Gary," said Jane. "But I didn't do this alone. It was a committee."

"You're the chairperson."

"I made some phone calls, but they did most of the work — Monica Kaminski, Ann Fuccione, Terri Hauptmann, and Sally Meyer."

"No men?" he said. "A sexist committee?"

"We had work to do, so naturally we chose women."

Wanamaker laughed. "Well, you accomplished a great thing. I'll let you know what the tally is as soon as I have it." He looked across the crowded floor of the decorated room, past women in colorful evening dresses toward a short elderly man in a tuxedo standing beneath a long wall of fabric that Jane had helped hang today to transform the cafeteria into a ballroom. "Oh. Know who that is?"

"Mr. Hunter?" she said. "His family owned the old Shippers and Traders Bank."

"Can't stump you on local history, can I?"

"My family's been here for a long time."

He gaped at her for a second. "Oh. That would be true, wouldn't it? Well, I'd better go talk to Mr. H. Thanks again."

Jane felt her husband Carey's hand on her back, and turned her head slightly to look up at him. "Oh there you are."

"I came to congratulate you."

"So you overheard."

"Not in this noise. He told me a couple of minutes ago. You're a fund-raising genius. Of course, I only care about how you look in that dress. Or under it, really. What are you doing in about an hour?"

"Carey."

"Nobody heard me." His voice and expression were exactly as they would be if he were doing a surgical consultation. "Don't change the subject."

"Two hours. After that your chances go up to about a hundred percent." She moved away from him and walked the length of the decorated cafeteria. Ann Fuccione and Monica Kaminski were preparing to lead another tour of the surgical wing when Jane reached them. She said quietly, "Has Gary talked to you?"

"A minute ago," said Monica. "We got the money for the surgical wing makeover. It's been a long time coming, but it arrived."

Ann grinned. "Did he tell you who gave all that loot?"

"Not yet," said Jane. "I'm sure we'll hear. Do Terri and Sally know we made it?"

"I don't know. They were over there, trying to get the buffet table squared away and the coffee service in."

"Thanks." Jane walked across the room, moving through the crowd with an ease that

17

an observer would have thought supernatural, turning her body easily to avoid a crush, then making tiny adjustments to her posture or twisting to get to the next place, never appearing to pause. She stopped beside Terri Hauptmann. "Has Gary come by to thank you yet?"

"Yes," said Terri. "Can you believe it?"

"Absolutely," Jane said. "You were great. The whole committee was great."

"It was mostly you," said Terri.

"We've all been saying it behind your back," Sally said. "You're the best boss I ever worked for. Except maybe Jim. I used to be his nurse anesthesiologist, and he would take me out to lunch every day. You don't do that."

"No, but I will. I'll give you a call next week, and we can all go out to celebrate. It's been fun to work with both of you."

Sally eyed the seven or eight people who were standing politely a few feet off. "Oops. We'd better start our tour."

Jane said, "Sorry. I'll let you go." As she moved toward a group standing along the wall near the counter that had been set up as a temporary bar, Jane felt another wave of uneasiness. She tried to tell herself that it was just the jumpiness from having Gary startle her, but that didn't feel true.

Something was wrong. She must have heard or seen something out of place, but had pushed it to the back of her mind while she concentrated on making the hospital benefit run smoothly. Ignoring the feeling had been a mistake, and she had to find the trouble now.

Jane scanned the big room. She looked at each of the entrances and exits to see which were open and which were closed, who was standing near enough to control one of them, which men and women she knew to be physicians or hospital employees and which were strangers. She recognized many of them, and there wasn't anyone she could spot as out of place, but she didn't stop looking. She hadn't felt this kind of uneasiness in a long time, but it was a familiar feeling. Her breathing was deep and steady, her vision was sharp, the colors almost unreal in their brightness as she moved across the ballroom. Even her skin felt more sensitive, as though she could pick up the electricity in the air.

She skirted the dessert table at a fast walk and picked up a napkin. As she swerved to the inner side of the next serving table, she swept the napkin beside a plate. When she moved on, wrapped inside the napkin was the paring knife from one of the fruit trays.

She kept moving until she came upon Carey, seemingly by happy accident. He was talking with an elderly lady in an elegant black gown with long lace sleeves.

Carey saw Jane and ended his conversation. He stepped gracefully toward her path. She paused and leaned close. "Something's not right."

"What do you mean?"

"I don't know yet," she said. "I hope I'm imagining this, but be ready. I may have to leave in a hurry." She kept walking.

She moved toward the doorway that led to the kitchen, and she knew what she had been feeling. Nothing was happening. It had been at least twenty minutes since anyone had come out of the kitchen. The waiter who had brought the first load of desserts to the buffet tables had disappeared through the swinging door and never reappeared. She had seen a second waiter push a cart into a corner near the dessert table, but he'd never come back. People had served themselves. The desserts that were laid out had nearly all been eaten now, but the trays had not been replenished or cleared.

Going directly into the kitchen felt to her like the wrong thing to do. Somebody could be just inside the door waiting. She altered her course slightly, and moved past the accordion divider that separated the wide cafeteria entrance from the decorated and specially lighted area where the benefit was being held. The wall helped preserve the soft, unreal atmosphere of the party.

Jane held the napkin with the knife in it close to the skirt of her gown and took a step into the hall. She turned toward the outer door that led to the kitchen. There were two men in dark suits standing on both sides of the kitchen door with their backs to the wall. They were strangers, and she had not seen either of them inside the party. They didn't seem to be aware of her, so she looked away, but held them in the corner of her eye as she drifted in their direction. There was something odd about the way they held themselves, as though they were holding their breath, waiting. Were they going to harm somebody coming out of the kitchen?

The floor beneath her seemed to bump upward as though the whole building were taking a breath. Then came the noise, a deep, deafening thud, and as it tore the air the force of the explosion blew Jane off her feet and across the hall into the smooth marble wall where the names of past donors were carved.

2

Sky Woman was contented, living above the clouds with her husband, whom she loved with a fierce, steady passion. There was no time then, because there was no change, and so she was always the same slender young woman who lived in the firmament. She was the one who witnessed the first change ever to occur, because it happened to her. She wanted to get at the roots of a big tree and prepare them as food for her tall, strong husband. She asked him to push over the tree for her, but when he did, the roots came up and tore a hole at Sky Woman's feet, and she fell.

As she dropped from the sky she felt the wind streaming through her long black hair and heard the fluttering of the fringe on her deerskin skirt. She was falling toward the vast and ageless ocean of dark water far below. She knew that this must be dying, and that she would never again see or touch the husband she loved so much.

It took time for her to fall so far, and the animals, who had acute senses, could see her from below. The birds felt sorry for her, so they flew upward to meet her. They placed their soft, feathery bodies beneath her, and spread their wings to slow her fall into a long, gentle glide to the dark water.

Jane Whitefield fought the darkness. She struggled to hold in her mind the possibility of waking, and then to make her way toward it. She felt the pain where her body was in contact with the hard, cold terrazzo floor. She opened her eyes to the sight of the overhead lights flickering and then steadying to a sickly yellow glow as the hospital's generators came on. She could hear the voices of confused people, some moaning and others calling to each other. "Marie! Are you all right?" "Lie still." "Mark? Where are you?"

She sat up, then placed one hand on the wall to steady herself. As she gained a sense of where the pains were coming from and how they hurt, she formed a working theory that they were all only bruises and minor sprains. She got her feet under her and stood. She could hear a clanging alarm and another that made an electronic tone, distant sirens, shouting people . . .

The hallway seemed at first to be full of white smoke. She could see human shapes, some on the floor and some moving half-blind through the haze. Jane sniffed and smelled no burning, only plaster dust. She covered her nose and mouth with the fabric above the hem of her gown and looked toward the door from the hall into the kitchen. The two men were gone. She moved to the cafeteria, dodging a stream of men and women in ruined evening clothes, some of them staggering, a few men carrying injured victims in their arms.

She stopped just inside the cafeteria. For a second she was amazed at the orderly, expert way the party guests were already taking care of the injured, but then she remembered that many of these people in tuxedos or satin dresses were doctors. Where was Carey? She craned her neck to look for him, and then she saw him across the cafeteria. His tall, thin body was so much a part of her world after ten years of marriage that it wasn't exactly the body of another person anymore, and when her eyes found his shape she felt as though she were touching him. He knelt for a second, then stood and lifted a woman in his arms.

Jane saw Carey's eyes find her, and then

saw him grin. "You're all right?" She could barely hear him. Something had happened to her ears. They felt as though she were at a high altitude and they wouldn't pop.

"Yes. You, too?"

"Yes." He kept walking, glancing down at the inert woman now and then, and Jane walked with him. He said, "You saw it coming. Do you know what caused the explosion?"

"No, I was trying to get to the kitchen. There were two men guarding the door. I didn't get that far. Did you see it happen?"

He shook his head. "I didn't see the flash or anything, just felt the force of it. I think it was from the back of the cafeteria. We're moving people into emergency, and I'm pretty sure some of them are going to need surgery right away, so I don't know when I'll be out again. You'd better go home."

They had reached the door to the emergency room, and she watched him step through the automatic double doors with the woman he was carrying, and then he was gone.

Jane moved back up the hall to the cafeteria. Not an accidental explosion, then. A bomb. She fought for calm, to make herself think clearly. This was the only chance to try to see the people who had done it, but the two men she had seen before had vanished. As she passed the accordion room divider she noticed it had been blown off its track. Now that she was closer she could see places where it had been pierced and torn by flying metal. Jane ran to the kitchen and reached for the door, but at that moment the door burst open toward her and three waiters shouldered their way out past her. All three had their wrists bound with duct tape and more tape wrapped across their mouths and around the backs of their heads. They ran into the lobby, moving toward the front of the building. She could see that they had cut or partially pulled off the tape around their ankles. The people with the bomb must have tied them up.

Jane moved back into the cafeteria and stepped toward a group of people who had pulled themselves or crawled to the far wall. Monica Kaminski appeared at her side. Now her shiny blond hair was tousled and powdered with a thin layer of plaster dust. Her milky complexion was red and raw as though she had been in the sun and wind, and the seam of her bright yellow dress had separated at the waist, so it looked like a camisole and skirt. "Are you hurt?"

"No," said Monica. "But I'm pissed off. It's got to be the abortion freaks. I guess shooting one doctor at a time is too slow for them."

"Have you seen any police yet?"

"Yes." Monica looked around. "No. I guess they're just the hospital guards. I want to do something. What can we do?"

"Let's try and get some of these people into the emergency wing," said Jane. "See if you can find a wheelchair, and I'll see who looks most urgent."

"There are always wheelchairs in the lobby."

Monica hurried away toward the hospital lobby, weaving through the people in the corridor. Jane stepped toward the people in the cafeteria. She saw an elderly woman lying alone on the floor near one of the tipped-over tables. She reached her and saw the woman was conscious. "I'm here to help," she said. "Is anything broken?"

"No. I just got the wind knocked out of me, I think."

Jane said, "Can you walk?"

The woman nodded. "I think I can." Jane put her hands under the woman's arms and pulled her to her feet, then took her arm on her shoulder and walked with her to the emergency room. Inside all was motion and voices. Doctors and nurses in dusty evening clothes attended patients in cubicles. There were already people on gurneys lining the walls. Jane helped the woman to a chair. "Just sit and rest for now, while I try to get someone to help." She waved at David Meyer, the chief of pediatrics, and he hurried over, nodded to Jane, and focused his intense gaze on the elderly woman. "Hello, ma'am," he said. "Are you having any trouble breathing?"

Jane turned and rushed out. As she reached the hallway, Monica came by pushing a wheelchair with a man in it who sat very still with his eyes closed. Jane hurried back toward the cafeteria, making her way among the gaggle of confused, frightened people in the hall, when suddenly a hand closed on her wrist.

She looked at the person who had stopped her. It was a patient. She appeared to be a teenager, a couple of inches shorter than Jane, with brown hair. She was wearing a white hospital bathrobe, and Jane could see at the neckline the tiny flowers of the awful pattern of the standard-issue gown. Her expression was anguished. Jane said, "Are you in pain?"

The young woman said, "No. I'm okay. Please. Do you know Jane Whitefield? A woman over there said you might. Do you?"

"Yes," said Jane. "I'm Jane. But look, I

—" She was already turning toward the injured people in the cafeteria, but the girl held her arm.

"Sharon Curtis told me to come to this hospital, and ask for you."

Jane turned to look at the young woman more closely. There were very few things she could have said that would have kept Jane from shaking her off and going back for more victims. Sharon Curtis was a name that Jane knew well because ten years ago she had invented it. Jane's eyes didn't leave the young woman's face. "Why did Sharon send you here?"

"She sent me to a house in Deganawida. I waited for a whole night, most of it on the back steps, but nobody ever came. She had said to try the hospital as a last resort. She said it had been a long time, and you might have moved. But the hospital might know where you were."

Jane's mind was full of conflicting thoughts, and among them was a memory of the day she had left Sharon. She had said then, "If you need me again, you know where to come. If I'm not there, try the hospital where they sewed up your arm."

Jane said to the girl, "I understand, and we'll talk. But right now we're in the middle of a disaster here. Can you —"

"This was about me."

"About you?" Jane put her arm around the girl and pulled her to the side of the hallway so they were against the wall and out of the way. "Why?"

"I got the doctor to admit me because I'm pregnant and I told her I was having some bleeding. I had to stay off the street, where they could get me. I needed to rest, and I needed time to find you."

"They? Who are they?"

"There are six of them — four men and two women. They handle things for a man I used to work for. I ran away and now they've come for me."

"Why would they set off a bomb in the hospital? What does that have to do with you?"

"They wanted the hospital evacuated so they could drag me out and take me back to San Diego."

Jane was frustrated, impatient. "How do you know it's them?"

"I saw one of them here. He was walking up and down the halls in the upper floors looking for me. He was carrying a little bouquet of flowers he had bought in the gift shop, but he was looking in every door. He saw me, our eyes met, and he turned away. When he was gone I slipped out and hid in the visitors' restroom on the next floor. Then a while later there was the explosion. I looked out, and I could see the nurses and orderlies starting to evacuate patients. I ran so I wouldn't be where the six wanted me to be."

"Come on," said Jane. She guided the girl down the hall away from the emergency wing, avoided the lobby, and turned toward the new neonatal center that had been bought with the proceeds of the past year's fund drive. It was scheduled to open in a month, and all evening Jane and the rest of the committee had been leading donors through, showing them the facilities.

When Jane pushed open the door, she was surprised to see that the place had already changed. It was all bright lights and motion. There were hospital staff here, and there were people in bloody evening clothes on gurneys being moved into the rooms. Jane saw that one of the linen closets was open, so she stepped in and took two packaged sets of light green hospital scrubs, then pulled the young woman out through the doors with her.

She stayed close to the young woman, and spoke under her breath as they walked. "Did you leave anything upstairs that you need?"

"No," she said. "I've got my wallet in my

robe pocket."

"Good. We're going to have to leave the hospital while these people are watching for you, so we've got to move fast and change what we can." She hurried up the back hallway past the outpatient cancer-treatment rooms and into a bathroom. Jane took off her evening dress, draped it over the top of a stall, and put on a set of green scrubs.

The young woman said, "That's a beautiful dress."

Jane shrugged. "Glad you like it. You're going to wear it."

"I'm pregnant. I'll never fit in that."

"That's the idea. If they see you from a distance in an evening gown they'll look past you. Slip it over your head. We won't try to zip it. Leave the hospital socks on."

The young woman took off her bathrobe and Jane hurried out. A few minutes later, after the girl had the dress on, holding it up with her hands, Jane returned with a wheelchair. She set the second set of scrubs on the seat and said, "Get in the chair."

The young woman obeyed, and Jane arranged the dress so it looked as though the young woman fit into it. Jane pushed the wheelchair toward the big double doors at the end of the hall beyond the outpatient center. As she walked, she talked quietly to the young woman. "You're somebody who was at the benefit, and you've been treated, and now you're going home. You'll recognize the people who are after you, right?"

"Yes."

"I don't know what they look like, so if you see one of them tell me. You don't have to make a lot of noise or anything, but be sure I know."

"Okay."

The automatic doors gave a quiet *huff* and swung open and Jane pushed the wheelchair into the night air. There were more sirens that she had not heard before. She pushed the chair out into the service road that ran along the side of the hospital, and turned toward the parking lots. As she came within sight of the back of the building she saw that at least a dozen police cars had arrived. She moved into the lot, hoping the presence of cops would protect them, but realized that the cars were all empty. They had simply been left at haphazard angles, and the officers had run inside. There were big knots of people in the lot now, many of them evacuated patients and hospital staff, some of them curious onlookers and others victims who had rushed out of the building. She was pleased that there was plenty of activity to distract the watchers, if they were out here.

She saw that the row of doctors' parking spaces near the building was full. It had been half-empty when she had arrived here this morning with the rest of the committee to prepare for the benefit. She couldn't help noticing Carey's black BMW in its reserved space. She pushed the wheelchair across the lot toward her own white Volvo sedan, looking ahead but watching for movement in her peripheral vision.

She arrived at the car, stepped into the space to the right of it to open the door and let the young woman get in. Then she tossed the package of scrubs onto the woman's lap and closed the door. She heard something behind her — the scrape of a shoe on the pavement — and she half-turned as a man's hand pushed her hard toward the car beside her.

Jane pivoted with the push and set her back against the car. She saw that he wore a dark suit, and recognized him as one of the men she'd seen standing outside the hospital kitchen. He looked surprised that his push had not sent Jane far out of his way, and he seemed to sense, dimly, that this tall, dark-haired woman in the green scrubs wasn't doing what he had expected. He reached into his coat.

Jane's stomp-kick to the side of the man's leg at knee level replaced his suspicion with intense pain as his knee popped and he fell to the pavement clawing and grabbing at his ruined kneecap with his free hand. He struggled to free a gun from his coat and bring it around to aim it at Jane, but that idea had occurred to him too late. Her foot hit the side of his head and battered it against the door of her car, and her next kick propelled the gun out of his hand.

She knelt and looked at the pavement to see where the gun had gone, but she saw something else. There was a second man in a suit sprinting toward her from the direction of the emergency wing, passing the slow-moving people leaving the hospital. She rose and looked over the hood of the next car and saw that there was a third man running into the parking lot off to her right. As he skirted the knot of patients and nurses who had been evacuated, a few stepped aside and stared at him, but none of them seemed to interpret what he was doing. Jane whirled to see that there was a fourth standing on the other end of the lot. It was as though they were moving into firing positions.

Jane ran to the driver's side of her car, got in, and started the engine. She backed up quickly, saw the injured attacker trying to drag his tortured body toward a spot where he must have seen his gun. Jane swung the car around quickly and drove toward the end of the aisle.

She could see that one of the men was moving to the end of her aisle to wait for her. As she drove, he reached into the inside of his coat, as though he had his hand on a gun. Jane sped toward him, reached a spot where there were several empty parking spaces, swung abruptly through them to the next aisle, and cut away from the man.

In a moment she was out the exit and on the street. Jane made two rapid turns and then a third to take her along quiet residential streets to the entrance to the Young-mann Expressway. Then she was on the big highway, moving along at sixty-five, far from the hospital. She said, "Do you still have the scrubs?"

"Right here."

"Then take off the dress and put them on."

—"Okay." The woman tore open the plastic package, pulled the dress off over her head, and quickly pulled on the scrub shirt, and then eased into the bottoms. She folded the dress and held it on her lap.

Jane's eyes flicked from one mirror to the

other, then returned to the road. "Okay. I'm persuaded that you're not imagining that they're after you. Is this about your child?"

"It has to be. I didn't think anybody even knew I was pregnant when I left, but they must have found out."

"Who sent these people?"

"His name is Richard Beale."

"What does he do?"

"He runs a company — business rentals, some residential, some real estate sales, some loans. I was his personal assistant. I quit, and he didn't want me to."

"Why does he know the kind of people who would set off a bomb in a hospital to help them kidnap somebody?"

"Because he's that kind of person, too. I didn't know it when I met him. Now I do."

Jane exited the expressway and drove up a side street. "They must have had a car at the hospital. Have you seen it?"

"I only saw the man in the hallway, and then the other three outside. I never saw a car."

"I didn't either. If I planned to set off a bomb, I wouldn't park in the hospital lot. I'd park on a dark street a block away. Let's hope they couldn't get to it in time to follow us." Jane drove past the lighted front of a small grocery store that took up half of a strip mall. She made a U-turn, stopped behind the building, and said, "Sit tight. I'll just be a second."

She stepped to the pay phone on the wall and dialed 911. In a few seconds she heard the connection being made. She squinted at the tiny face of the white gold watch with the diamonds to time the call. "Hello," she said.

"Emergency. What's the nature of your emergency?"

"I was at the hospital a few minutes ago when the bomb went off. I saw the people who did it. There are four men and two women. The men were wearing dark suits to fit in with the benefit crowd. One of the men got hurt in the parking lot and seems to have a broken knee."

"Who are these four people? Do you know them?"

"*Six* people. Four men, two women."

"Tell me your name."

"Sorry. I have to go."

"Where are you now?"

Jane hung up, stepped to her car, and drove off. She could see that the girl was studying her.

"Just a quick phone call. I had to tell the police the little we knew."

"You shouldn't have done that."

"Why not?"

"Because I can't stay in Buffalo waiting for a trial, and I can't prove anybody did anything. The only person who would be stuck here is me, getting bigger and more pregnant every minute. If Richard knows where I am, he can hire sixty people instead of six."

"This isn't about trials. I'm hoping the cops will see them and pull them over. That creates a record of their names, and it might get them searched for weapons and even tested for explosives. It's hard to plant a bomb without having a residue of certain chemicals on your hands. The main thing it would do is delay them for a day. Nobody knows your name or my name, and the call was too short to trace. Now we're on our way."

"Where are we going?"

"To the place where Sharon sent you — my house."

The car swung north, away from the center of the city along the elevated, curving strip of the Scajaquada Expressway. Jane could always feel Nundawaono place-names in the muscles of her mouth — along the tongue and palate, and behind her teeth: Canandaigua, Conestoga, Schenectady. She reached the stretch of Interstate 190 that ran along the broad, night-black Niagara River — Nee-ah-gah, really, meaning the Neck. It was the long, straight conduit where all of the water of the Great Lakes narrowed to flow from Lake Erie to Lake Ontario and go eastward to the ocean. Jane kept going along the river past the town of Tonawanda — swift water, in English — and then coasted off the 190 at the Grand Island bridge and drove along River Road into Deganawida, the town where she was born. It was named after the wandering solitary prophet — what else could he be called? — who founded the Iroquois league.

When Jane drove the road on the bluff above the river it was more a physical act than mental — reflexes and long habit took the place of thought, and seeing took little attention because her mind was already so deeply imprinted with images of every house and tree and curve that it noticed only the changes. She turned off onto Two-Mile Creek Road, the first street, running between the dark groves of Veterans' Park, and then turned left onto the end of Fletcher, always watching her mirrors to see if anyone followed.

She went as far as Wheeler Street and turned, then continued for a mile or more away from the river, across the railroad tracks behind the long-closed fiberboard factory, and then made three left turns to come back the whole mile to be sure that there was no chance that she had been followed. Finally she turned again and went along the street past her own house, one of a dozen narrow two-story houses built eighty years ago on this block by men who worked in the factories and lumber mills that once existed in Deganawida.

She looked at the tall sycamore in the front yard beyond the privet hedge. Soon the days would be longer, and the sycamore's leaves would spend the summer growing as wide as two hands. She went around the final block and returned to the house, steered up the driveway, and pulled the car into the garage. Both women got out, and Jane closed the garage door so the car wouldn't be visible from the street. Then she went to open the back door of the house. She looked down at the back steps, then bent lower to see more clearly.

"Stay back," she whispered. "Let me check it out first to see if anyone's been here besides you. Be ready to run."

She opened the door and stepped into the dark interior space, smelling the stale air that had been trapped since she'd closed the door three days ago. She picked up the other smells. There was the lemony smell of the wax she'd used on the wooden floors and the chlorine cleanser in the sinks and the ammonia from the window cleaner. But it was a very old house, and she could even pick up the faint scent of the wax that her mother and her grandmother had rubbed into the floorboards and the woodwork for decades, the old paint her grandfather had brushed on for the first time eighty years ago. Maybe there was still, lurking somewhere beneath the paint, the particular scents of her family — her grandmother's corn soup, or the French pastries her mother had learned to make when she was a girl in New York.

As she moved through the house, her senses took in everything. She could feel that the air was as it should be, that the doors and windows had been shut for a long time, but she had to be sure that the house had been that way for the three days since she had been here. She examined all the locks and latches and scanned the panes of glass. Before she walked on the living room carpet she knelt at the edge to see if shoes had left an impression on it. She climbed the stairs to the second floor and looked in each of the bedrooms and bathrooms, but detected no evidence that anyone had been inside.

She stopped in her old bedroom and picked up the telephone to dial the message number. It said, "You have eight new messages." She heard the voice of Sharon Curtis. "This is Sharon, from a long time ago. I'm calling from a pay phone. I'm still well, still safe. I'm sending a girl to you. I hope you can give her the kind of help that you once gave me." The rest of the messages were all the voice of the young girl downstairs. The first began "You don't know me, but —" and the last said, "I'm going to try the place Sharon said to look for you. If you get this message, please call me. Once again, my number is —"

She went back downstairs and held the door while the young woman stepped into the kitchen, then closed and locked the dead bolt before she turned on the light. "It's safe for the moment. Nobody's been in here."

The young woman said, "It's nice here. Cozy. Do you live alone?"

"This is the house where I grew up. My grandfather built it. I don't live here anymore." She pulled out a chair from the kitchen table. "Have a seat. I won't be long."

Jane went upstairs again and dialed Carey's cell phone. She waited through the message: "You have reached Dr. McKinnon. If this is a medical emergency, please call the following number: 555-9852. If you would like to leave a message, you may begin at the tone." Jane heard the tone, and said, "Carey, I'm afraid I have to leave tonight without seeing you. The bomb was planted by a crew of professionals. There are six of them — four men and two women — who have been trying to kidnap a pregnant girl who had checked in for observation yesterday. I'm with her now. One of the men got a dislocated knee tonight, so if you have a way to check with other hospitals, you might find something out and tell the police." She paused. "I love you, and I'm sorry." Jane went down the hall and descended the creaking stairs.

When she reached the first floor Jane stopped for a second to look through the lighted doorway at the girl sitting in the kitchen. She looked exhausted, as if only the fear was keeping her from collapsing. Her light green eyes looked faded, almost gray, and her face was pale. Jane moved on. She opened the door to the cellar staircase and descended into the cool underground. The old walls were made of big stones held together with mortar, but she'd had them reinforced with rebar and concrete a few years ago.

Jane opened the stepladder and climbed it to reach the hiding place in the rafters, the old heating duct from the coal furnace that her father had removed when she was a child. She reached in, pulled out the steel box she kept there, balanced it on the top step of the ladder, and rifled through the items she had hidden there. She set aside a large stack of hundred-dollar bills, and selected four different driver's licenses with her picture on them and sets of credit cards in the same names. She took one quick look at the special sets she kept in leather folders, then returned them to their corner of the box. These were the identities she hoped never to use. One set she kept in case something went wrong. It was for a married couple and had pictures of her and of Carey. The other set was placed there in case everything went wrong. It held papers for each of them with different surnames.

She put the money and her four false-identity packets into her purse, then hid the box, put away the ladder, climbed back upstairs, and entered the kitchen. She could hear nothing but the ticking of the clock on the wall as the girl turned to stare at her. "What do we do now?"

"First we get ourselves something to wear

from the closets upstairs. We can't go any place in scrubs. I don't keep that many clothes here anymore, but I have a couple of pairs of black drawstring yoga pants that are mid-calf length, and I think they'll fit you, and lots of running shoes. If they're too big we'll use thick socks to make them fit. And we'll take a couple of hooded jackets and sweaters. Come on."

They climbed to the second floor and went into one of the bedrooms, where Jane began pulling things from the closet and the dresser drawers. "See if any of these looks as though it might fit you." While the girl picked up some of the clothes, Jane said, "You know, you haven't told me your name."

"Christine Monahan."

"Where did you come from?"

Christine looked surprised at the question. "San Diego. That's how I know Sharon."

"This man — the father of your child — do you think that what he wants is to kill you?"

"Richard Beale. I think he wants to hurt me. I don't know how bad."

"Why does he?"

"I think because I left him. He doesn't like it if somebody doesn't do what he wants. He likes to control everybody around him."

Jane was silent for a few seconds while the two changed their clothes. Christine was holding things back, but she didn't seem to be lying about her predicament. Jane could wait to hear the rest until they were away from here and in motion, but there was something else she had to get out of the way now. "There are some things that you should know before we go any further. This isn't as simple as it was ten years ago when Sharon came to me. It's not as safe. I made a lot of people disappear before I met her, and a lot after her. For every runner there are chasers, and some of them have seen my face. There are people looking for me — people who would do anything to get me in a small room someplace where they can ask me questions. It's possible that the most dangerous thing you've ever done is come here to see me." She paused. "That's one of the reasons why I stopped doing this."

"You're . . . retired?"

"It was never a job, never a business. I simply stopped doing it about five years ago. The last person I took out of the world was me."

Christine said, "Are you saying that you're not going to be able to help me?"

"No. I just need you to know what comes with my help. It isn't all good."

"If I hadn't found you, they would have caught me tonight. I wouldn't be here at all." Her eyes were beginning to fill with tears, but she wiped them away. "I appreciate the warning, but it doesn't change anything. If you're still willing to help me, then I want you to. I'll try to be as easy as I can."

"Don't worry," said Jane. "I'm willing."

"Thank you," she said. She looked at her reflection in the mirror in her borrowed clothes, shrugged, and turned to Jane. "Then what's next?"

"Now we run."

3

Jane drove with an almost animal alertness, looking in the car's mirrors for other cars, stopping at residential intersections with her window down to listen for the sound of engines and to see whether another vehicle was shadowing her on a parallel street. After a few blocks she made a right and headed out of town.

The roads out of Deganawida were stories. Where Main Street left the city it became Military Road, the straight-surveyed road the British army had built between Fort George where Lake Erie flowed into the river, and Fort Niagara, where the river emptied into Lake Ontario. Jane made her way south, heading for one of the old trails that her ancestors had worn into the forest hundreds of years ago. It was the western end of the Wa-a-gwenneyu, the trail that ran three hundred miles from the spot that was now the foot of Main Street in Buffalo to the end of Iroquois territory, where the Mohawk River met the Hudson.

Jane drove eastward for twenty minutes in silence. The road gradually became more suburban, and then the streetlamps and lighted buildings were farther apart. The darkness of houses with windows blackened for sleep enfolded them for longer periods, and the quiet and calm reassured Jane. Night highways were usually deserted, and when they weren't, the darkness and the glare of headlights provided anonymity.

Christine said, "Why were you at that party? Do you work at the hospital?"

"No. My husband is a surgeon. I was one of the people who volunteered to put on the benefit. It's the kind of thing that people expect of you if you're a doctor's wife. It's a good thing to do, and it's part of the role — the disguise." She turned to Christine. "I suppose that brings us to an unpleasant aspect of our relationship."

"Ours? You and me?"

"Yes. When I agree to take you away from your troubles, I'm saying that I know it's possible that someday your enemies will trace you partway and find me. In your case, that's pretty likely. They saw me, and they saw my car. I'm prepared for that."

"You're prepared? How can you be?"

〜 "I mean that if they catch me, I won't tell them where you are. I'll die with that information in my memory, and only there." Jane turned again to look at Christine.

"Oh my God," Christine whispered. "You want me to say that I'll do the same for you, don't you?" Her expression was a mask of uncertainty and discomfort.

"No," said Jane. "I don't want you to say that. If you did I wouldn't believe you, and I would be disappointed in you for saying something that can't possibly be true. I only want you to begin thinking seriously about what you would do. No normal person walks around having made a plan for every bad thing that can ever happen. But if I ask you in four months, or six months, I'll expect that you've thought about it. For most people this kind of secret doesn't exist. For you, as of tonight, it does."

"What if I think about it and realize that I simply can't do that?"

"Then I want you to tell me, and we'll both know it, and we'll have to prepare in some other way to keep our families safe, no matter what happens to us."

The girl didn't know yet. Jane reminded herself that they never knew in the beginning. The reason that decent human beings could go on from day to day was that they didn't darken their lives with thoughts of catastrophe. They didn't even think about dying in the normal ways. This girl was scared, alone and pregnant. It was too much to expect her to be able to keep her mind on anything but that.

Jane would not consider telling her what keeping secrets really meant. In her purse each time she went out, even for the past five years, she carried a pretty cut-glass bottle. The liquid inside looked like perfume, but it was not perfume. It was the extract of the roots of the water hemlock, a plant that grew wild in most of the marshy places of New York State. It was the traditional Seneca means of suicide. To say that she was willing to die without having at hand the means of fulfilling the promise would have made it a lie.

The suburban highway became a country road and the only lights for a mile or two at a time came from the sparse line of headlights behind her, changing as the road left the lake plain and began to meet hills and curves. There were farms now, and old trees with dark, leafy canopies growing close to the road in some places. A few of them had signs advertising stands that would sell fresh corn when the sun came up tomorrow. She was driving east, the direction of New York

52

City. New York was a good place for a person to lose herself, and for that reason it was also a good place to make a pursuer think she was going.

Christine's voice was nervous, fearful. "Why do you keep looking back like that? Is somebody chasing us?"

"I'm looking because it's the smart thing to do. I guess this can be your first real lesson in staying safe. You take as many precautions as you can — not as many as you think you need, as many as you can. The ones that you take early are the most important, because if you lose the chasers right away, they don't even know which direction you went. Later, if and when they find out that much, they have to come after you slowly. Every intersection they pass could be the one where you turned. Every hotel or motel could be the one where you stopped to spend a night. They have to be tentative and cautious, and it buys you time."

"But what are you looking for?"

"I don't let myself expect something specific," said Jane. "I look at what's there and evaluate it. I might see a car that's coming up on us fast. This time if there are lots of heads visible, I would be worried that it might be the people after us. Or I might see that the road behind us is empty and decide it's a good time for us to make a turn — go down the next road and head in another direction when nobody can see us do it. I'm looking for danger and opportunity."

"It's scary. It's not the way I think. I can't wait until this is over."

Jane glanced at her smooth young face, the forehead compressed in unaccustomed wrinkles and the mouth pouting. Jane decided to skip this natural opportunity to tell her the next lesson, the next warning. It would never be over. It would go on until either she was dead or the chasers were, and at this moment the odds were better for them.

Jane said, "There won't be any more stops for a while, so if you want to sleep, you can."

"I'm really not very sleepy right now. I slept most of the afternoon because I had been up the night before. Then, when I saw Steve Demming walking past the door of my room, it was like an electric shock. From then on I haven't been able to calm down."

"Steve Demming. That's the name of the man with the flowers in the hallway? Tell me about Steve Demming."

"He's one of the six, and he seems to do most of the talking, sort of like the foreman of a crew, not like an employer. None of them seems to be a boss or anything. I saw him at the office now and then. Until I was promoted to being Richard's assistant I didn't know who Demming was, and then when I happened to learn, what I learned wasn't even true. I was supposed to cut him a check, and the notation on the stub was that the money was for electrical contracting. Another time I did the same thing, and the check was to one of the others — one of the women — for interior decorating. Every few months, one or another of the six might come by, and maybe they would get a check, or maybe not."

"What about the other five? Do you know their names, too?"

"Yes. Over time, I started to pay attention and remember. The two women are Sybil Landreau and Claudia Marshall. The four men are Steve Demming, Ronnie Sebrot — he's the one you hurt in the parking lot — Pete Tilton, Carl McGinnis."

Jane's telephone rang, and the sudden noise made Christine jump. Then she lifted Jane's purse from the floor and held it while Jane snatched the phone and looked at the number on the display. "This I've got to take." She pulled the car over to the shoulder of the road, got out, and walked to the front of the car before she answered it. "Hi. You got my message?"

"Yes. But I don't understand."

"I'm sorry, Carey. I know I promised, and I really meant it. But something happened." As she spoke she watched the pavement light up as the first of the cars that had been behind her on the road came closer and then whisked past, and a wake of warm night air hit her in a puff.

"I'm grateful for the five years when nothing happened. What's going on?"

"A young girl came to me because somebody I helped a long time ago told her I was worth a try. She ran away from her former boss, and he hired a team of six people to find her and drag her back. They seem to have set off the bomb just so she'd be evacuated from the hospital building, and —" Jane stopped herself.

"And?"

"She's alone, and she's pregnant."

"How pregnant?"

"I haven't asked yet, and she hasn't said, but I would guess five to six months. She's terrified, and I've been taking it slow, just asking what I need to know right now. It was just one of those times when you're only given two choices. I could try to get her out of there, or I could walk away and let those people drag her into a car and disappear."

56

"Okay. You've gotten her out of there. Now what?"

"You know."

"You're going with her?"

"I'll get her to a safe place and get her settled, and I'll come home. It should just take a few weeks."

"A few weeks?" he said. "Jane, you can't just disappear the way you used to. What am I supposed to tell people?"

"I'll have to trust you to think of something convincing. I got hurt, or I went to stay with a relative to get over the shock — anything. Whatever you make up, tell me later and I'll play along."

He sighed in frustration. "So this is the last call for a while, isn't it?"

"Yes. You know how it works."

"I remember."

"I hope you're not mad or hurt or something."

"I'm not happy about it, but what can I do?"

"Nothing."

"That's what I thought."

Jane saw the pavement ahead of her brightening again as the next car approached. It reminded her that while she was standing here with the car turned off she and Christine were vulnerable, and they would attract attention. "Carey, I've got to go. Please understand."

"Be safe."

"You, too." She looked back at the windshield of the car, and saw Christine staring at her. "I love you." She ended the call and put her phone into her jacket pocket, then hurried to the car and pulled out onto the road again. Christine seemed to sense that she wasn't in the mood to talk for the moment. Jane could see she was pretending to sleep, and she was grateful.

As she drove the long, dark highway, she thought about Carey. She kept falling into a circular series of thoughts. She felt guilty because she wasn't living up to her responsibility to him, but she would have felt much more guilty if she had refused to help Christine. She knew Carey's anger wasn't about his own convenience. It was that he genuinely loved her and didn't want her to risk her life. But what was her life if it consisted of little but being safe in the big old McKinnon house in Amherst, probably the safest of the suburbs on the eastern side of Buffalo?

When she had married Carey, she had been very conscious and deliberate about ending the period of her life when she was Jane Whitefield the guide before she assumed the next identity as Jane McKinnon, the pleasant, unremarkable local doctor's wife. She had assumed an identity that she believed would keep the old life away and keep Carey safe. She had kept up her old relationships with family, friends, and relatives, partly because being part of a community made an assumed identity more solid. She had taught the old language to Seneca children on the reservation, served in quiet ways in tribal life and government — the titles that brought unwelcome visibility were traditionally held by males — and had volunteered at the hospital.

One of the assumptions she'd had about marriage was that she would have babies. She had been careful not to let herself get pregnant for the first three years after her last client, until she was sure that some forgotten aspect of her past wasn't about to spill over into her new life, and Carey had understood. When the three years had passed, she had begun to feel that old dangers had become distant. She had told Carey she was ready, and they had stopped using birth control. The one thing she had never wasted much time worrying about was infertility. But after six months, nothing had happened. After a year had passed, Carey had arranged for them both to be examined and tested for physical problems, and they had both been declared problem-free. Still, nothing. After two years of trying, Jane's infertility was unexplained. What was unexplained couldn't be treated.

As soon as she had seen Christine tonight, a hundred contradictory thoughts and feelings had flooded her brain, and she was sure they had affected everything that happened in the past few hours — her concern for Christine, her reluctance to tire her out with pointed questions, certainly. But she felt a hurt, too. She had wanted a child more each month, and when the longing was beginning to be unbearable, who had turned up but a teenager with an accidental pregnancy? It was a cruel joke.

Jane looked at the clock on the dashboard. It was after one A.M. The windows along the road were all dark, and she was seeing fewer cars now. For miles between small towns there were only a few houses placed at long intervals, far back from the highway. She noticed how many of them had big toys beside them — recreational vehicles, motorcycles, boats on trailers.

After a time Christine spoke. "I'm not asleep."

"If you keep trying, maybe you'll doze off."

"No."

"Worrying isn't going to help. What helps is putting miles of road between us and them, and we're doing that."

"I know. I keep thinking about them."

"The six?"

"Yes. I don't know why there are six. When I first noticed them one or two were different people. They disappeared and new ones took their places. But it's always six."

Jane said, "To be honest with you, it's one of the reasons they worry me. It's the largest number who can ride in a car — just about any car. Or they can split into three separate teams and still work twenty-four hours a day — one on, one off. No doubt it gives them a chance to use a lot of different skills at once — a lot of ways to catch us."

"Now there are only five."

"Now there are five," Jane said. Her voice was not as hopeful as Christine's.

"What are you thinking?"

"We know who hired them — Richard Beale. We know their names. When you were in San Diego, why didn't you just talk this over with the police?"

"I couldn't," said Christine.

"What was stopping you?"

"I can't prove they work for Richard. When he did anything he didn't want known, he used to make up a corporation name, get a bank account, use it for a few months, and then close it. But the one who opened the account and had signature power wasn't him. When I worked for him, a lot of the time it was me."

"So if the police connect these people with a crime — the bombing — when they trace the money to the person who wrote the check or withdrew the cash to pay them, it will be you. Your name, your fingerprints on the checks."

"A lot of the time, I said. Not all of the time. But it will never be Richard."

Jane turned to study Christine's face. "Didn't this strike you as an odd way to run a business?"

"What did I know about business?"

"What *did* you know?"

"I knew what Richard chose to teach me. It was my first grown-up job. I was sixteen when I started, and Richard told me what he wanted me to do. He didn't make a fuss over any of this. He didn't say something like 'This is illegal so don't tell anybody.' And I figured that the presidents of Microsoft or General Electric certainly didn't sign all the checks for their companies. They wouldn't be able to do all of them in a lifetime even if they did nothing else. So why should Richard? So I did what Richard said was my job, and I was secretly grateful that he was patient enough to explain how to do things. And also relieved that he didn't know I wasn't actually eighteen, which is what I had said."

"How long did you work at his company?"

"Three and a half years. Not all of it was working for him, though. The man who hired me ran the apartment rental business for Richard. I was actually looking in the newspaper ads for an apartment, and their ad for apartments had a little box in the corner that said the company was hiring. I came in and asked for an application, and he interviewed me while I was filling it out. His name was Dave. He was a big, heavy guy about fifty. You know how with some people when you look at them you know exactly what they looked like when they were babies?"

"Sure. He was one of them?"

"Yes. He had that look, as though one day he was in his crib, and the next he was in the office going over a rental agreement."

"What I'm wondering was why, at the age of sixteen, you needed a grown-up job and an apartment."

"It's just another thing that happened to make me feel like a fairy-tale princess," she said. "I got evicted by my wicked step-mother."

"Tell me about her."

"The Divine Delia and I didn't really get along when I was growing up. I was the oldest, a leftover from an earlier marriage, and my father and I spent a lot of time together. He would take me places sometimes and leave my brother and sister home. It was because they were too young for where we were going, but what Delia said was, 'So change where you're going and bring all the kids, or go someplace that's really for adults, and take me.' It makes a certain amount of sense, doesn't it?"

"On a first hearing."

"We liked to be alone now and then. I was a preteen and then a teenager, and needed to talk to somebody, and the Divine Delia was a genuine bitch, so my father was the only candidate. And when their marriage started to turn sour, I was the only one my father could talk to. So when she started in on us, we were more drawn to each other, and also to the door. And that pissed her off even more, and probably accelerated things."

"I take it the marriage ended."

"Not in the simple way. First it kind of built up to one of those big moments, a blaze of clarity. She kept wanting more and more expensive things — cars, a boat, a lot of vacations, lots of walking-around money. We ate in restaurants so often that my friends stopped calling me before ten because they knew I'd be out. My father was miserable. He was getting more and more desperate."

"Desperate?"

"He had already blown two marriages — the one that didn't produce anything but me, and another one to a woman named Roz who would drive me to school in her nightgown and bathrobe and then go to some boyfriend's apartment and hop back in bed. My dad was already getting fat and worn-out looking and he knew it. I think he was afraid nobody else would ever love him. So he gave Delia everything, and he ran out of money earlier each month and charged the rest of the expenses to credit cards. I noticed at one point that whenever he got an offer for another credit card in the mail, he put it in his briefcase. Afterward I learned he filled them all out. How could he not end up borrowing some money from his company? Later, at his trial, the prosecutor went down a big long list of all the things he had bought and charged to his credit cards. It all sounded just awful, and he seemed to be this pig who stole money from his company because he wanted trips and dinners and luxuries. He didn't want all that stuff. He never wanted any of it. He wanted love."

"There was a trial? So the company caught him and called the police?"

"Not right away. The bookkeepers noticed that he had made out a transfer, and the account the money went to didn't seem to belong to the company. They found more, and found my father had requested all of them. The head bookkeeper told the president. He was a friend. He had known my father for twenty-five years, and he knew this wasn't what it looked like. He told my dad that he would postpone the regular outside audit for a month so my dad could get the money and pay the company back."

"That was quite a generous offer."

"It was a gamble," said Christine. "It meant the president was doing something just as illegal as what my father did, just because he trusted my father and wanted to save him. He also thought he would be saving the company from a scandal, but there wasn't much in it for him personally."

"Since you said there was a trial, I assume the plan didn't work."

"My father collected everything he could

and tried to sell it or get his money back. He took pictures of the cars, the boat, the house, and put them on the Internet. He tried to take back a lot of the things he or Delia had just bought. He cashed in his insurance and his retirement and went to the banks for loans. For the first time in years I was proud of him, because he was doing something to pull himself together. What he hadn't planned on was the Delightful Delia."

"What did she do?"

"Nothing. She wouldn't sign off on anything. The house was in both their names, and she wouldn't sell it. One of the cars was in her name and another in both their names, and she wouldn't sign the pink slips. She got a safe-deposit box by herself and put all the jewelry in it, and probably all the cash she had been skimming off and hiding from him. She wouldn't cosign a loan, get a job, or even stop charging things."

"How well did he do without her?"

"At the end of the month he had sold one of the cars — his car, with her name forged on the pink slip — for about twenty thousand, which was half what he had paid for it a year earlier. He sold his watch, a TAG Heuer my mother had bought him as a present about fifteen years earlier. He sold my laptop and my iPod and my DVD player for about six hundred. There were a lot of other odds and ends, mostly things he'd had before the marriage. The final count of what he had taken from the company was about a hundred and twenty thousand, and he came up with about seventy."

"Not enough."

"No," said Christine. "It was a horrible thing to watch. He was defeated from the moment he told Delia and saw the cold, ugly look on her face. He knew it, but he kept trying. He was wounded, bleeding inside, but he kept scrambling as hard as he could to get himself and us out of this mess. He had to keep working full-time, of course, or people would notice and start wondering what was up. He would sleep a couple of hours a night, then go to his computer again to check on the bids and put up more stuff for sale. It was all impossible, one of those situations where you know you can't get there from here. At the end of the month he brought the seventy thousand he had raised and begged for more time. But the president didn't have any more to give him."

"He couldn't do anything?"

"It was a public company — you know, with stockholders and directors and every-thing — and there were federal rules about how often they had to have the outside auditors in. He couldn't hold up any longer, or he might be fired, too. Or worse. The president was a friend, as I said. He took the other fifty thousand out of his own pocket — cashed in some of his retirement money — and added it to my father's seventy."

"That's a real friend."

"It didn't work. The money was paid back, but it was too late. The bookkeepers had ratted him out to the auditors, or thought putting the money back was dishonest, or something. It came out, and my father was arrested."

"I'm sorry."

"Well, it wasn't as though he didn't take the money. And the reason he did it was that he didn't want his wife to realize he was running out of money before the end of every month. I mean, I'm sure she knew what his salary was. So what was he protecting her from? Arithmetic? God. But in the process, he got his giant flash of clarity. The Delectable Delia wouldn't help him save himself, even by signing a paper to give him back a little of the money he'd spent on her."

"She never relented?"

"Even I was surprised, and I didn't expect

much from her. She said, 'I just can't throw away everything I've built and leave my children destitute' — meaning the children other than me. I was *his* child. She was right, in a way. All the money he got by selling his things he had to give to the company. It did him no good. All the things he or she had bought on credit that he returned to stores just went to lower the amount he still owed the credit card companies. That did nothing for him, either."

"Did she pay for his defense lawyer?"

"No. What she did was hire a lawyer to separate her assets from his, and she did that right away, so it would be a done deal before he was charged. That way, his creditors could come after her all they wanted, but get zero. This, you see, is a neat trick, because she'd never had a job. Her assets were all money he had earned, and probably even some of the money he stole. From her, Dad couldn't even get bail money."

"I'm sorry."

"The reason she could even hold on to the money was that he went along with all of it. He never contested anything. He signed every piece of paper her lawyer sent him, including things that were outright lies — that she had brought money with her when they were married. Actually, when she moved into our house, I remember she had one small suitcase, and what was in it was an outfit to wear to go on her first shopping trip."

"He probably thought if she had some money she'd take care of you and your brother and sister while he was away."

"I suppose. What actually happened was that the minute we got home from seeing him off to Lompoc, Delia sat me down at the kitchen table and had a long talk with me. Or, at least she wanted it to be long. Have you ever noticed that the worst people in the world always want you to feel sorry for them?"

"Yes," said Jane, "I have."

"Well, that was Delia. While she was working up to throwing me out of the house, she was telling me how much she'd been suffering with my dad, and how hard it was on her. She even wanted me to feel sorry for her for the pain it gave her to refuse to give him the money to save himself. It had ruined her forever, she said. Her health was shot, and she was too old now to get a good enough job to support us all. She was crying, so I could barely understand her half the time. But what she was expecting was that I would throw my arms around her and tell her I was sorry for living, and would make it up to her by leaving."

"You didn't?"

"No, so she gave me a month to get out. And that was why I ended up getting a full-time job and an apartment and lying to say I was eighteen when I was sixteen."

"Didn't you need papers to get the job?"

"I used Delia's computer at home. An eight with a little white on the upper right side turns into a six. I did that to my birth certificate and made a copy of it on the printer. A Social Security card doesn't carry a birth date, but I made a copy of that, too. In California a sixteen-year-old's driver's license has a birth date and a red stripe and a blue stripe saying when you'll turn eighteen and when you'll turn twenty-one. I scanned mine and Photoshopped it to change the years to make me eighteen. The day I started work I brought in the copies. There was no secretary — that was the job I was taking — so I put the copies in the file I made for myself. If my boss ever noticed anything odd, he must have realized I had given him proof that he wasn't the one at fault."

"Pretty effective. You'll do well to get some sleep while you can. We'll have to make a stop in a couple of hours, and I'll wake you up then."

"Okay." Christine's voice sounded small and distant now, and she fell asleep within a few minutes.

As Jane drove on along the rural road, she thought about what she had heard. What Christine had said about Sharon was true. The voice on the recorded telephone message had been Sharon's. And Christine seemed to be telling the truth about the way she'd changed dates on papers. She might have been exaggerating the story about her childhood, but probably not much if she had been on her own young enough to have to obliterate dates. There still seemed to be no lies, but there was much more she was leaving out.

4

Jane drove into the small town of Blackwater as the summer night took on its deepest silence. She slowed to twenty at the town limit, opened her window, and drove even more slowly, listening. Above the steady, gentle sound of the air going past, there was nothing. It was after two, and the town was asleep. She reached the center of town where the streets were lined with old houses that had been renovated by the latest generation of a long succession of owners. The house on her right looked about the way it must have in 1880, except that the white paint on the ornate cookie-cutter trim had been brushed on this spring. The house across from it still had the original brown sandstone foundation, but it looked to Jane as though it had just been professionally cleaned.

She decided that this set of owners must be rich, probably a wave of lawyers and brokers and executives who had retired early from jobs in New York City and come here to reproduce a vision of village life they imagined existed a hundred years ago. On Jane's previous visits, there had been an impression of gray peeled paint, overgrowth of vines, and patches of weeds. Now everything was neat and fresh and orderly. The lawns were rolled and cut, and recent plantings of bleeding hearts and currant bushes had appeared near the houses. Separate beds of heirloom roses had been cut into the side yards.

The biggest houses were all ranged around the small park in the center of town, each facing an ancient bandstand. As the road led off toward either edge of town, the houses got smaller, until they were simple, neat cottages that had been converted to stores, small restaurants, the offices of doctors, opticians, and realtors. Jane turned beyond the park, and kept going until she reached the barn-sized building that used to be the town's feed and hardware store. She pulled off the road to the gravel parking lot, and backed her car up to the rear of the building. As she got out of the car, Jane saw Christine open her eyes, blink, and focus on her. Jane whispered, "It's okay. Go back to sleep."

Jane walked across the dark, quiet street, and listened. She headed back to the center of town to the park and into the shadows of the two-hundred-year-old maples and oaks. In small upstate New York towns like Blackwater, people often left their dogs out in their yards on summer nights, and Jane knew if she came too close to the houses, she would set off a proprietary bark or two, so she stayed on the path to the bandstand. When she came under the tallest of the trees she saw the broad wings of a gliding owl carry it to a high limb and flap soundlessly once to pause in midair while the talons took hold, but then she lost sight of the owl in the foliage.

She passed the bandstand and crossed the street on the other side. She walked straight to the front of the big Civil War–era red-brick house, climbed the steps, and watched the door open in front of her. The person standing inside the dim doorway was shorter than Jane and slender, but Jane could see that there was a handgun in the right hand.

"Put it away," said a voice from somewhere deeper inside the house. "I know her. Evening, Jane."

"Hello, Stewart," said Jane. Now she could just make out the distinctive shape of

Stewart Shattuck, short and wide-shouldered, standing by the staircase.

"Come on to the office."

In the dim light that leaked from beneath a closed door at the end of the hallway she followed him to the door to the left of the staircase. The office was a room that must have been, at some early date, some kind of interior storage space. It was in the center of the first floor of the house, opposite the stairwell, and it had no windows. Shattuck was nocturnal, and during his business hours no ray of light escaped his workroom to raise suspicion outside.

When he had closed the door behind them, he moved the switch on a rheostat to bring up the lights. He said, "Will you sit down, please?" He settled himself on a straight-backed chair beside the eight-foot table he used as a desk, and made a few tiny marks on a piece of paper in front of him, bending so his face was within six inches of it.

Jane chose the straight-backed chair across from the table. It felt warm to her, and when she looked straight ahead she had a clear view of an array of video monitors from closed-circuit cameras mounted on the front, back, and sides of the house. She had taken the chair that belonged to Shattuck's guard. The images on the screens were now motionless, no living creature moving out there.

After a full minute in which he seemed to have forgotten Jane was there, Shattuck said, "It's been several years. I had assumed that you had been killed."

"Not yet."

He raised his eyes to look at her. "You're wise to think of it that way. I always thought that wisdom was the direction where you were heading, even when you were very young. Now that you've reached middle age, you've arrived."

"If I agree I'm wise, do I have to accept that I'm middle-aged? Or is accepting it more wisdom?"

Shattuck smiled so his glasses sent a flash of reflected light, then lowered his head to his paper again. "Of course you would see the way out of the trap. I've missed your visits."

"I only come when I've got trouble, so I don't share the feeling."

"There is that, isn't there? But most of the customers for a forger aren't pretty or wise." He sat up straight, took a look at the document he had been working on, and put it aside reluctantly, keeping his eyes on it all the way to the pile at the corner of his table.

"All right. Let's hear what you need this time." He lifted a pad and changed pens.

"It's a young girl, nineteen or twenty. First she needs ID to travel. It has to be good enough to pass, but only the essentials — driver's license, Social Security card, maybe a few simple things to fill a wallet, a library card, and so on."

"What next?"

"The hard stuff — a second good, solid set of papers that will last her forever, if necessary."

He squinted and stared past Jane's shoulder, then wrote as he spoke. "Driver's license, Social Security, birth certificate. MasterCard, Visa, American Express. Passport, too?"

"If you can get all that safely."

"Of course. But passports are taking at least six weeks these days."

"I'll give you a mail-drop address to forward it to."

Shattuck said, "Is it all right if we give her an address in Syracuse to start? That way I don't have to go far to pick it up."

"Sure. She can fill out change-of-address forms when she's settled somewhere. Until then, just forward everything to the mail drop." She pointed at his pad. "May I?"

He handed her the pad and pen, and she

wrote out an address and handed them back.

"Telephone?"

"Make one up."

He held out his hand. "Let's see her photograph."

"I have her with me."

"Even better. We'll take different shots for each form of ID. Anything else for you tonight?"

"Yes," she said. "When you have the first set of documents, I'd like you to put together a set of papers for a baby with the same surname. A birth certificate and a Social Security card. That ought to do it if she has to run."

"How old is the baby?"

"Make it two to five months from now."

Shattuck's head turned only a half-inch. "She's pregnant?"

"Yes." She watched him closely. "I guess the real birth date will be September or October." She could see he had stopped writing.

Shattuck said, "It's been a while since you've been here. I should warn you that the prices of all of these items have gone up. Increased security and new electronics."

"I had assumed something like that would have happened."

"Everything has to survive electronic scanners. It's got to be real."

"I'm not surprised."

"In order to get a driver's license, I have to send somebody with a birth certificate to some other city, and have her apply for the license and take the tests. The credit has to be grown over time."

"That was always the best way to do things," said Jane. "I expected it."

"Well, the good news is that once an identity is planted, it grows more quickly. That's much better than it used to be. Once anything is verified by anyone anywhere, it proliferates — moves from one data bank to another. That's one of the methods I've been refining since the last time I saw you. I plant articles about imaginary people on Web sites and blogs so that Google will pick them up when anybody searches. I'm constantly updating and expanding. That's all cheap and easy. But the planting of first-rate identities still works best if you can get someone on the inside to create a real record. People who get caught selling things like birth certificates and driver's licenses go away for a long, long time."

"Oh, one more thing," Jane said. "I'd like a simple set, maybe just a California driver's license, with my picture, in the name Delia

Monahan."

"Delia Monahan. I take it we're talking about a real, living person?"

"Yes."

"Then I can get a duplicate and doctor it."

"Good. How much are we talking about for everything I want?"

"I'd say we're probably in the vicinity of . . ." He put a dot beside each item he had written, mouthing "Ten, fifteen, eighteen, twenty-four," then said aloud, "Forty thousand. Could go as high as sixty."

"Can I pay you ten right now, and send the rest later?"

He looked regretful. "Janie, your word is the word of the saints. But the saints are dead. You could die, too."

"Someone has already been looking for this girl, haven't they, Stewart?"

Shattuck pursed his lips and stared at her for a second. "There could be other pregnant twenty-year-olds. I'll let you see if it's the same one." He walked across the room to a second table, woke up a laptop computer that was attached to a printer, and brought up an e-mail message. "Read."

Jane stepped to the computer. The screen read, "Christine Monahan, Female, age twenty, is worth one hundred thousand.

Open attachment to see photo gallery." Then it gave an 800 telephone number, but no name or address. Jane said, "Did you open the attachment?"

"No. If I took money for turning in people on the run, how long would I live?"

"May I?"

"Go ahead."

Jane downloaded the attachment and opened it. There were a dozen small pictures on the page. In a couple of them Christine was sitting at a desk that was set on a shiny slate floor in a room that seemed to be all glass with tropical plants behind it, like an atrium. In a few, Christine's hair was long and blond, and in others dark and shorter, pinned behind her head. They seemed to have been taken over a period of years. Jane said, "This isn't good news."

"I expect not."

"But it doesn't change our deal. I still need the ID for her. Can you charge a credit card for the price?"

"How much?"

"All of it — forty thousand."

He looked at the pictures on the screen, then back at Jane. "You barely know her. Are you sure you want to spend that much?"

"Think of the air miles I'll earn."

"That kind of charge usually triggers a

phone call. Will you be available to take it and tell the Visa people that it's really you?"

"No, but I'll call them before I drop out of sight, and authorize it."

"That works for me. You can bring her in."

When Jane opened the door, the thin, silent figure was standing on the other side, as she had expected. In the light, she saw it was a pretty woman about thirty, not a teenager. She was wearing a pair of tight black satin pants and an indigo pullover that made her look very slender.

Jane said, "I've got to go outside for a few minutes, and bring someone back."

"I know. You can park closer to the house if you want." The woman opened the front door, and Jane stepped outside.

The night air felt even warmer now that Jane was out of the air-conditioned house. She could see that the streets around the park were still deserted, but she stopped after she was away from the house and listened for engines. There was still the same silence. As she made her way across the park and she could see the Volvo, she strained her eyes to see Christine, but she couldn't. She must have gotten into the back seat to sleep.

Jane kept her eyes moving, but they returned to the Volvo. She had driven the car for a couple of years, so she had a practiced intuitive feel for the shape, the weight, the steering, and the way the car looked when it was parked. Something felt wrong. She stopped beside the nearest tree trunk, stayed in its shadow for a moment, and looked at the car. It was sitting too high. That's what it was. When Jane had gotten out of the car, she had looked back. The car had rested very slightly lower on its springs than it did now. It was empty. Jane trotted along the side of the park, crossed the street, and came back around the big old feed store slowly, listening for the sounds of movement. On her second turn she came up beside the Dumpster, and she could see Christine crouching behind it.

Jane said quietly, "Christine, it's me."

Christine's body jerked and she spun to see Jane. "Oh, you scared me so much. I didn't hear you."

Jane crouched, too. "Why are you out here?"

"I woke up and you were gone."

"I told you I was going."

"You did?"

"Yes."

"I must have been asleep. I woke up and I got worried. Where were you?"

"Come on. I'll tell you while we drive over there." They got back into the car and she pulled forward. "I was at that big brick house across the park. See it?"

"Yeah."

"It belongs to a man I know who sells identification, and that's something you're likely to need."

"Tonight?"

"Tonight is the time when we're here. Later we might be near other people who do this kind of work, but most of them aren't as good at it, and some of the others might sell us out if somebody waves enough money around. This man probably won't."

"Probably?"

"He hasn't in the past. That's all you really know about what anyone will do." Jane drove slowly around the park toward the house. "When he talks to you, listen carefully and answer him honestly and politely."

"I'm not a child."

"I'm sorry. I don't know you well, so I can't guess what you know. These transactions are tricky. We're all taking risks. He can sell us out, but we can sell him out, too. We're forming a temporary alliance. He and I are still alive because so far, in all of our temporary alliances, we've been selective about the people we trust, and we've been trustworthy. We've chosen the right ones and sent the wrong ones away."

"You're saying he's going to judge me."

"Exactly. He's got a soft spot for runners, but don't make it hard for him to believe in you." She pulled the car to the curb.

They got out and walked up the steps. The door opened again, and Jane nodded to the woman in the doorway, studying her without seeming to. She had a very pretty face, but her only expression was watchfulness. Now that the woman was comfortable with Jane she stared once into Christine's eyes, then devoted all of her attention to scanning the street, the park, and the other houses before she locked and bolted the door. "Go in."

Jane took Christine into Shattuck's office. He was working on another piece of paper like the one Jane had seen before. This time, because she was standing, she could see that the type in the center of its filigreed pattern said CERTIFICATE OF LIVE BIRTH.

Shattuck looked up. "You're Christine Monahan."

"Yes, sir." The sir was a surprise to Jane, but said in Christine's small voice it seemed not to be ironic.

"Is that your given name?"

"Yes, it is. Christine Ellen Monahan."

"And your actual birth date is . . . ?"

87

"August 24."

"How old?"

"I'm twenty."

He wrote down the information, and said, "It's good to make these things a little bit off, so nobody notices you have the same birthday as the missing Christine Monahan, or takes your picture and shows it to someone in the right high school class. Can you live with being twenty-one?"

"Yes, sir. Being older might help get people over the fact that I'm pregnant."

"And when would you like your birthday?"

"Uh, I don't care. How about April first?"

"April Fool's Day. Is that a joke?"

"No, sir. I just thought I'd be sure to remember it if it was the first of the month, and my baby should be born in September, so I wanted to save that part of the year for him or her."

He nodded. "Good thinking. Kids like to feel special, and people are born every day of the year." He gave her a half-smile that Jane interpreted as reassuring. "You'd be surprised at how many of them are born right here."

"Yes, sir."

"All right," he said. "Now I'm going to take your picture. There will have to be several shots that look like they were taken at different times. They'll look like you, but don't expect them to be flattering. Try to look attractive — no deer in the headlights or anything — but don't try too hard. No real photograph on a driver's license is pretty. There are a few that are all right on passports, because people get to pick, so we'll take more time with those."

He took her across the room to a plain wall that looked a bit whiter than the others. "Put your toes on the yellow tape." He moved a lamp on a stand to a spot where there was a blue tape strip, then took a digital camera out of a drawer and began to take pictures. He would snap one, then look at the display on the camera, and do it again. Finally he said, "That's good. Okay. New outfit. Francine?"

The woman opened the door and leaned in. "What?"

"Have you got anything different that she can wear as a top?"

"How about a sweater, like it's winter?"

"Great. Maybe after that a jacket, like for a suit."

"I'll be right back." She disappeared.

Shattuck sat at his table and began to make marks on a certificate, as though his drawing were automatic. "You might want to fool around with your hair, too. Anything that doesn't look like all the pictures were taken on the same day."

Jane opened her purse, took out a brush, and brushed out Christine's hair, then pulled it into a ponytail and held it with an elastic band. She produced a pair of earrings, and handed them to her. "Put on these earrings, and some eyeliner."

When they were finished with the photographs, Shattuck set his camera beside his computer and said, "Okay, ladies. Give me three hours, and I'll have the first set ready. The other set will be in your mailbox within six or seven weeks."

Francine said, "Come this way." She led them out of the room into the hallway and then to a large red sitting room with overstuffed Victorian furniture and a grand piano. She said, "I'm sure you're exhausted. I remember what this was like. Those two couches on that side of the room are the most comfortable for sleeping."

But Christine had stopped near the door. She was staring at the wall, where the paintings were hung five high. They were all nudes — standing in a bath, sitting in a garden, reclining on a couch. Christine said, "That's you on this couch," and pointed. She looked at Francine again. "They're all you." Then she looked flustered, as though she had no idea of the appropriate thing to say. "You're beautiful."

"Thanks."

"He painted them?"

Francine nodded. "Of course."

"He's so good. He should . . ." She had hit the barrier. There was no way to finish the sentence, so she didn't.

"He does," said Francine. "Get some sleep. Before daylight comes, you have to be gone." She turned off the lamp near the door, walked out, and closed the door, so the room was nearly dark.

Christine said, "I'm sorry. I should have kept my mouth shut."

"It's all right," said Jane. "This time, anyway. She seems to be benevolent. But Stewart is an artist. He couldn't do what he does without talent, but he also has training. It's what got him in trouble."

"Trouble? You mean he's already in trouble?"

"He was studying in Europe. He was nearly broke, and got desperate. He got involved with a gallery owner who sold things to collectors — mostly visiting Americans — who thought they knew more than they did. He hired Stewart to paint copies."

"Of paintings?"

"Yes. He told me he started with a few

small Dutch paintings that weren't terribly well known. The owner presented them as seventeenth-century copies by apprentices in the studios of the masters. They did so well that the owner started thinking bigger. In those days there was still a lot of talk about art that the Nazis had taken to Germany during the war and the Russians had taken to Russia afterward. The Russians had some in the Hermitage Museum — mostly French Impressionists — but they never would release a list of what they had. What that did was help create a market for paintings that looked exactly like Renoirs or Cézannes but didn't have any provenance. The gallery owner sold them to specially selected customers as what they would have had to be — stolen paintings that had probably belonged to murder victims. That way no buyer would hang them in public or have them appraised. It worked until one of the buyers died, and his granddaughter found a Monet hanging in a closet. After a quick look at the buyer's canceled checks, the police visited the gallery. Stewart had to leave the country quickly."

"It makes me sad," said Christine.

"Take a closer look at Francine, and at those paintings you found on the wall. Life is good to Stewart." She lay down on one of the couches. "And I'm tired." She arranged herself so she would be comfortable and closed her eyes. After a few minutes she pretended to sleep. Soon she heard Christine's breathing slow and deepen. While Christine slept, Jane lay with her eyes closed, thinking about a few men she had met at other times who might be looking at their computer screens tonight and learning that they could make a hundred thousand dollars just for finding a pregnant twenty-year-old.

5

"Wake up."

Jane sat up, and saw Francine standing in the doorway of the Victorian sitting room. When she moved, Jane followed her down the hallway.

Francine said, "I wanted to talk for a minute before you go."

"All right."

"I was on the run once," she said.

"How did you find your way to Stewart?"

"Luck," said Francine. "I got lucky and met somebody who had the same kind of problem I had, and she showed me her identification. She told me where she got it." She stared at Jane for a moment. "Stewart tells me that you're somebody we don't ever have to worry about. He said you were reliable. Is it true?"

Jane stared back at her. "I try to be. I've been out of this life for a long time. Before I quit taking on runners, I had found a few people I believed were safe to do business with, and Stewart was one of them. For all I know, all the others are dead or in jail now. So he's pretty important to me right now."

Francine kept her large, dark eyes on Jane. "I want you to know that I'm not jealous of you or paranoid or something. The reason I was running is that I killed somebody who deserved it. If the police take me in and fingerprint me, it's not going to make a bit of difference why, then I'm gone."

"I'm sorry," said Jane. "For my sake and yours, I hope they never find you or Stewart. You seem to care about him."

"When I got here, I didn't have any money left. I didn't have anything much to trade. I told him that I would pay him by being his personal whore."

"You don't have to tell me this."

"Yes, I do, because I want us to understand each other. When I was running I got to the point where I knew I would do anything to be safe again, and I figured that was something he'd want. It was going to be pure business, but I discovered that the idea, the badness of it or something, excited me. What happened since then is that we fell in love. If I had to open somebody's artery again to hold on to the life we have here, I'd do it in an eyeblink."

"Not mine. I'll keep your secret."

Francine glanced toward the door to the sitting room. "Will she? She's a kid."

"I'm betting my life on her."

"You are," said Francine. "There are people looking really hard for her and for you. Things have changed since the last time you were running. There are more people in the chasing business these days. I want you to be careful, because if you fuck this up, I'm probably dead."

"I'll do my best." Jane put her arms around Francine and held her for a moment, then released her.

Jane heard a door open behind her. "Jane?" It was Christine. Francine opened the door beside her and disappeared into Shattuck's workshop.

"What was that about?" Christine asked.

"We were wishing each other good luck."

"Good luck?"

"Yes. You'd be amazed at how much depends on luck."

"Now you're scaring me."

"Good."

The door opened and Francine said, "He's done. Your traveling documents are ready."

Jane went inside and examined the driver's license, the Social Security card, and the birth certificate. They were superb forgeries, all in the name Linda Welles. "Who's Linda Welles?"

Stewart said, "I like to give an old customer like you a bargain now and then. Linda Welles is an identity I grew. The Visa card is real, the birth certificate is a duplicate of a real one. The license has a counterpart in the North Carolina Department of Motor Vehicles. All I changed was the photo."

"Thank you." Jane took her cell phone and a credit card out of her purse. She looked at the phone number on the back of the card and dialed, listened to a recording, punched in the numbers on the front of the card, and then handed the card to Stewart. "Hello. Yes. My name is Cecilia Randazzo. The reason I'm calling is that I'm about to make a kind of big charge on my card, and I wanted you to know it's real. Forty thousand dollars." She answered a series of questions from the woman on the other end of the line, then disconnected. She said to Stewart, "All done. Charge away."

He scanned the card in his scanner, then returned it. Jane gathered up the false identification and said, "Thanks, Stewart. Take care of Francine and keep her safe." She turned to go.

"See you, Janie."

Jane stepped out the door, swept Christine to the front entrance, and stopped while Francine scanned the neighborhood. Jane said, "Persuade him that he's got enough money to retire, and get him out of here."

In a minute Jane was driving, and they were already out of town. It was after four A.M. now. They didn't speak much, just let the dark landscape float past the windows and the headlights reveal new stretches of road that weren't different from the last ones. Route 20 intersected with a big county road a couple of miles past the next town, and Jane felt an urge to take it, but she decided it would be better to keep going on the highway for a bit longer. They were making good time, and she wanted to do most of their traveling before the sun came up.

She began to consider where she would go when the road reached the Hudson. Years ago, when a runner showed up at her door with chasers close behind, she had simply started the car and begun to drive. When she was sure she had built up enough distance, she had gotten them both on an airplane. Even in those days, when she could walk into an airport, dream up a new name, and buy a ticket, flying had been a risk. Once a person stepped onto a plane there wasn't much mystery about where and when she would step off.

As Jane crested a rolling hill and began to coast down, she saw two big unmarked black American cars pulled across the center of the road in a V shape, with a third in the right lane about ten yards beyond. That would be the chase car, in case someone ran the roadblock. She said, "Roadblock up there. Sit up and look innocent."

Christine sat up and looked. "Is it the police?"

"It looks that way. I don't see how it could be the people who are searching for you."

"I don't either," said Christine. "They'd have to be psychics. But I'm scared. Can we turn around and go back the other way?"

"I don't think so. That's the best way I know to get stopped and have the car searched."

"So what? We don't have anything illegal in the car, do we?"

"Nothing but a few thousand dollars in cash and a few driver's licenses in different names."

"But what if it isn't the police? What about those people — Stewart and Francine? Did you tell them Richard's name? They could have called him while we were sleeping."

"That didn't happen." Jane slowed her Volvo and watched two men get out of one of the cars and step toward them. There was one walking toward each side of the car, and each held a large flashlight in his hand. That wasn't reassuring to Jane. It looked like what police did when they were checking cars looking for a fugitive.

She rolled down her window so she would be able to hear them. She could see that the two wore sport coats. There was a badge pinned to the belt of the man who was walking toward her. She said, "See? That one has a badge."

"No!" said Christine. "That's —"

"It's them!" the man shouted. He sidestepped quickly as he reached across his chest and under his coat.

"Get down." Jane wrenched the wheel toward the man and pressed the gas pedal. He sprinted for the side of the road. When his feet hit the gravel shoulder, he spun around to face the Volvo with the gun in his hand. His instant of understanding was visible in the headlights as he realized that he had not run far enough. There was a loud thump as the Volvo hit him, and a series of bumps as he rolled up and over the hood toward the windshield. Jane held the wheel to the left to keep the car spinning, and the centrifugal force threw him off onto the pavement. Jane saw him bounce, roll, and then lie still.

Jane turned off the headlights and accelerated up and over the hill. She realized she had heard shots behind them, first one gun firing a round, then three rapid shots, and then a second shooter firing steadily.

Christine yelled, "You hit him!"

"We each had a weapon, and mine's bigger," said Jane. "Sometimes I wish it were faster." She stepped harder on the gas pedal, steering with both hands and straining her eyes to keep the car on the pavement.

"My God," said Christine. "How can you see anything? It's completely dark."

"I don't have to see much — just where the road is." Jane steered for a few more seconds, still accelerating, but then let the car's speed stay constant. "We're out of sight and out of range for the moment. Did you hear any bullets hit the car?"

"I don't think so. What does that sound like?"

"You'll know when you hear it. We're alive and the engine still runs, and I think we're going to have to get rid of this car anyway. It'll just be easier with no holes in it." Jane looked in the rearview mirror every few seconds. "They're not following us. I wonder what's keeping them." She looked again. "I get it."

"Get what?"

"There weren't five of them back there, only three. They must have gone ahead to set up the roadblock, and the others have been coming along behind us. Now they'll be waiting for us somewhere along this road."

"What can we do?"

"There was a turnoff for a county highway back there. We'll head for that as fast as we can. Most likely the two who were following us will have heard we're coming back this way, and they'll be trying to block the road so we'll have one roadblock ahead and one behind. If we're faster than they expect, then maybe we can make the turn and never meet them."

Christine felt the car accelerating again, and pushed her body back into the seat. "Don't you think we could turn on the headlights?"

"I can make out the broken white line. As long as I keep it a foot to my left, we'll be okay. Just check your lap belt so it rides around your hips, tighten the chest belt so it's comfortable and holds you still, and let this happen."

Christine was silent, just did as Jane had

said. Jane watched the dark road, concentrating on keeping her speed as high as she dared, and steering partly by the memory of the road she had from driving it in the opposite direction and partly by staring down at the blur of lines coming at her from the darkness like projectiles, then slipping past her left tire. After a couple of minutes she caught herself letting the moonlight on a stretch of bare ground ahead fool her into interpreting it as part of the pavement, but she managed to correct the car's course and stay on the road. She looked into the rearview mirror for a second, but saw no sign of the cars from the roadblock, not even a glow of headlights approaching the top of the rise. Jane returned her eyes to the road ahead, and after the next turn, the rise was out of sight.

A set of headlights appeared far ahead of them, then another set. "Two cars," said Christine. "Do you think it's the others?"

Jane squinted at the two sets of headlights coming toward them. One car pulled to the left as though to pass, but it was the front car. Now there was one car coming at them in each lane. Jane switched on her headlights.

The car approaching in Jane's lane blinked its high beams on, then off.

Jane switched on her brights and left them on. She kept her foot on the gas pedal, maintaining her speed toward the car in her lane.

"Don't play chicken with them!"

"I'm not playing," said Jane.

The pair of cars stayed together, streaking toward them. In one of the cars, the driver punched the horn three times, then stiff-armed it, holding it down so the sound started high and seemed to go down the scale as the cars approached.

The row of four headlights kept growing bigger and brighter. The two cars seemed to be linked, impossible to separate, impossible to avoid. Christine put her hands in front of her face. "Oh God oh God," she said.

The car in Jane's lane wavered a little, then altered its course slightly and moved to the shoulder of the road to allow Jane to pass between the two cars, but Jane muttered, "It's not that easy." She pulled onto the shoulder, too, so she was once again on a course to collide with the car.

"Stop! You're crazy!" Christine shouted.

The driver of the car that was approaching them had no choice except to veer farther to the left and sail off the shoulder in the only direction that was open, into the sloping field below the road.

Jane and the remaining car passed each other at high speed, and she looked into the rearview mirror as she moved along the highway. The car in the field was stopped, enveloped in a cloud of dust. Jane couldn't tell how badly it was damaged. The car on the road pulled over. Its white backup lights came on, and it backed up until it was close to the spot where the other car had stopped. Jane saw the dome light go on and off, and someone ran from the car across the road, and then she lost sight of them.

Jane drove faster now, searching for the junction she had remembered, and then took the turn. She glanced at Christine. "You okay?"

Christine was breathing heavily, as though she had run a race. There were tears running from her widened eyes. "I can't believe you did that."

"I didn't chase them. They chased us."

"You know what I mean."

"They're hired hands. That means they're willing to kill us for money. It doesn't mean they're willing to die for money."

"You bet our lives on that? And my baby's life, too. You weren't just trying to get past. You wanted to force that car off the road."

Jane turned to look at her in curiosity. "Of

course." Then she returned her eyes to the road and kept driving.

Carl McGinnis lay on his back, exactly where the white car had thrown him, on the damp, weedy slope beside the shoulder of the road. He could smell the sweet aroma of crushed plants near his head. He knew he was hurt badly. He suspected he might be in some kind of shock, and he suspected that if he moved what was waiting for him was pain, so he had not tried to move yet. Breathing was difficult, so he supposed he must have broken some ribs. He lay there staring up at the sky with an expression like a man listening.

Steve Demming's head and torso appeared above him, a deeper darkness bending to block the night sky. "Carl, I know it hurts. But can you tell me how bad it is?"

Carl was unable to make out Demming's face well enough to read his expression in the dark. He was too frightened to complete the inventory of his injuries. He knew there must be a reservoir of pain waiting, and it would burst and overwhelm him if he moved in the wrong way. He had heard impatience and frustration in Demming's voice. What Demming wanted was to hear Carl say, "I'm all right," and then watch him get up and walk it off. Carl could tell that he wasn't going to be able to stand up. He stared up at Demming's dark shape against the sky, but was unable to gather enough air into his lungs to calm his impatience.

Carl heard a cell telephone buzz, then Demming's voice again. "Yeah?" There was a long pause. "I hear you. Jesus, what a night. You might as well keep coming and meet us. We're still set up here. Carl got hit by her car. Yeah. It looks that way. Okay. Bye." Carl heard Demming's heavy footsteps receding, and then some low conversation with Pete Tilton.

Carl heard one of the car doors open and shut, and the sound of the car engine as one of the two men moved the car off the road and parked it on the shoulder, then the same thing repeated as they moved the other car. Then there was silence again. He couldn't move his head enough to see, but he supposed they were sitting together talking inside one of the cars, while he was out here in the open, alone and helpless. After a while Carl heard more cars approaching from a distance.

Steve Demming got out of the car and leaned against the hood while he watched the headlights of the two women's vehicles coming toward him. The hot, humid air outside the car reminded him of how alien this place was to him. San Diego air was dry and flowing, either fresh from the ocean or fresh from the desert. This air was thick with moisture, and it seemed heavy, like something draped on him. As he waited, it seemed to him that the chirping of crickets was growing even louder. He sighed. This should have been a simple, easy errand, like going to pick up a stray dog at a pound. It occurred to him that he was as miserable at this moment as he had been in his life.

The two cars dipped forward a bit as the two women applied their brakes, and then they rolled off onto the shoulder. When they stopped, their headlights illuminated big clouds of dust in the air. One set of lights went out, and Demming saw the tall, slender shape of Sybil Landreau silhouetted for a moment in the headlights of the other car before the second set of headlights went out. A moment later he saw Claudia's shorter form trotting toward him. The two women joined Demming at the front of his car. "How bad is he?" asked Claudia.

"Bad," Demming said. "He can barely breathe. If you listen, you can probably hear it from here. When I talked to him, I think he was trying to move, but he didn't seem to be able to."

Sybil said, "Think it's his spine?"

"It could be."

Claudia walked to the spot where Carl McGinnis lay. She knelt in the weeds beside him, put a small, soft hand on his forehead, and then gently stroked his hair. "Carl," she murmured. "Carlos, Carlito. I heard you got clipped. How ya doin', baby?"

"I . . . I don't know," Carl said. "Maybe the four of you should start getting me into one of the cars. I think I need to get to a hospital."

"Can you walk?" she asked.

"I'm not sure, but I don't want to try and make things worse. I think my left hip might be broken. That whole side hurts like hell." He tried to move his head to see her clearly. "Claudia, honey. It's really late. Before too long, the sun is going to start coming up. I can't be lying here when that happens."

"I'll go talk to the others and see how we're going to do it," she said. "Just close your eyes and try to rest for a minute. Getting you into the car might be a bitch, so try to prepare yourself and save your strength."

Claudia got up and went back to join the others. Pete Tilton was out of the car now, too. He and Demming and Sybil looked at Claudia expectantly.

"He's really fucked-up," she said. "He winced when I touched his hair. His hair hurts, for Christ's sake. He thinks his left hip might be broken, but if the car caught him in the midsection, he could easily be bleeding to death inside."

Sybil shrugged. "I've got a bad feeling about this. We can't drop him off at a local hospital. They'll fill him up with painkillers while the cops ask him questions."

"I've been thinking about that, too," Demming said. "There's no way we can go in and talk for him. If he can't walk, we can't drop him off at the door."

"No way," Sybil said.

Demming said, "And every minute we stand here, Christine Monahan gets another mile away." He and Sybil and Pete Tilton looked at Claudia.

"I'll do it," she said. "I was the one who invited him to work with us, and he's still closer to me than he is to anyone else."

Sybil's body slouched and her head cocked, and the others knew she was giving her familiar smirk. "Something's closer than fucking? What did you do?"

Claudia felt her jaw clench. "He trusts me."

"I'm sorry," Sybil said. "I'll help you with it."

"I don't want him to know. Hold his hand, be nice to him, and I'll do the work."

"Okay."

When Carl McGinnis heard the small, light footsteps coming toward him, he knew it must be both women. Claudia sat above him on the slope and cradled his head in her lap, while Sybil held his hand. "Hey," he said. "Did you get her?"

"Sure," Claudia said. "We ran her off the road. She's not in great shape, but it's over. She's in the trunk of my car."

"Good. How about the other one?"

"She's dead," said Sybil.

"Good," said Carl. He was trying to hide the fact that he was getting more worried. He had felt intervals of cold, and then repeated waves of light-headedness, and he assumed that must mean he was getting weaker. "I really think . . . ," he said, then felt the pain find him. Getting past it was like climbing a hill, struggling as it got worse until he reached the crest and it went down again. "We've got to go. The guys. Tell Pete and Steve not to worry. I won't tell anybody anything. I was driving down this country road, got out to take a piss, and a car whacked me."

"Must happen all the time out here," said Sybil.

111

"They know you're going to be okay," Claudia said.

Sybil said, "They're just trying to put together a stretcher." She looked at Claudia. "I guess it's time for me to pull the car up." She relinquished his hand and kissed his cheek, then got up and moved off in the dark.

Claudia said, "Hold on a minute, Carl. The dumb bastards need me." She gently moved back, disengaging herself. Carl heard her take a few steps up the slope to the shoulder. He lost sight of her, and then the bullet passed through his brain. Claudia came back a few feet, just far enough from his body so the blowback wouldn't spatter blood on her clothes, and shot him again.

Christine twisted in her seat to look out the back window. Watching the empty road behind them for a few minutes seemed to calm her. She faced forward again and adjusted her seat belt. "I'm sorry. I'm scared to death. I've been scared for weeks. I've been moving around, and the most sleep I've had was in that crazy house back there. I sort of lost it."

"It's all right. All of this is scary, for both of us. But we're okay, at least for now."

Christine sat quietly for a time, and then

said, "You ran down Carl McGinnis."

"Is that who that was?"

"I saw his face in the headlights. Afterward it looked to me as though he was hurt really bad."

"It was all I could do once he took out the gun."

"Believe me, I'm not blaming you. I hate him. He gives me the creeps. He has a way of looking at you that makes you want to back away from him. Once I was leaving work when he was walking across the parking lot, and honestly, I got in the car as fast as I could, locked the doors, and started the engine in case he tried to get in." She looked at Jane. "Maybe the one who drove the car into the ditch is hurt, too."

"I couldn't tell, but I wouldn't count on it. More likely the air bag went off, and he couldn't drive after us right away."

"She, I think."

"She?"

"I'm pretty sure the other man I saw at the roadblock with Carl McGinnis was Pete Tilton. There was a third car, and the person in it probably was Steve Demming. That means the two coming up behind us would have to be Sybil Landreau and Claudia Marshall." She looked at Jane again, and noticed her preoccupied expression.

"What's wrong?"

"Just thinking," said Jane. "How could they possibly have known where to ambush us?"

"I don't know."

"Let me make sure I've got everything straight," said Jane. "You knew these six people because they worked for Richard Beale in San Diego when you did."

"That's right. They didn't exactly work for the Beale Company, because they weren't on the payroll. But I never heard of them working for anybody else but Richard."

"When you ran away, how did they know where you went? Buffalo is a long way from San Diego."

"I don't know," said Christine. "I figured they must have found out about the plane reservation. I didn't think they could. I didn't make it on my computer. I called on Sharon's phone, and then she drove me right to the airport a couple of hours later. If they were following me, I never saw them, and I was looking."

"And what about Buffalo General? How did they know you were in a hospital?"

"I haven't had time to figure that out. I'm pretty sure I would have seen them if they were on the same plane. And I waited

114

outside your house in Deganawida all night, and I know I would have seen them there. I was so scared that if anything had moved, I would have run. You know, when I went to the hospital, I had to show my ID and health insurance card. Maybe they called Richard's office to ask if I was covered or something."

"No. Hospitals don't call your employer. If they need to call anybody, it would be the insurance company. Since you were only there for observation, I can't imagine why they would do more than verify your coverage." Jane was silent for a moment. "Do you have a cell phone?"

"Sure. Doesn't everybody?"

"I mean with you — in your purse."

Christine reached into her purse, took out a phone, and held it up. "I haven't called anybody since I left — not even Sharon, because the bill would come to Richard's house at the end of the month."

"Did he give it to you — Richard?"

"Yes. When I was working for him, he wanted to be able to be in touch every minute. Then when we were —"

"I think the phone might be the way they keep finding you."

"Oh, my God. Of course. That's just like him. I'll bet he got me a phone with a satellite tracking program, the kind parents give their kids. All this time he's probably been tracking me on his computer."

Jane said, "I didn't say I was positive. I just think it might be."

"I'm sure. You just have to know Richard. When I worked for him he would call me at all hours and talk about something I had to do the next day, or ask me about some piece of property, just because he happened to be thinking about it, or even call to tell me to remind him of something he wanted to remember. Instead of just writing it down, he would call me. But once in a while he would say something like 'I'll bet you're on your way to the mall.' "

"And he was right?"

"Yes. It got to be a kind of joke between us. And then other times, he would call when it was really inconvenient. I would look at the phone and see it was his number and turn it off. Then he would be mad at me the next day. After he and I started dating, I stopped thinking about the phone calls. I kind of liked it. Stupid me. He was just checking up on me." She began to roll down the car window.

"Wait!" Jane said. "Don't throw it away. Just give it to me." Jane took it and put it into her purse.

The sky began to take on the purple-gray quality that indicated night was nearly over. A few miles ahead they reached the entrance to the New York State Thruway at Liverpool. Jane accepted a toll ticket and headed east. She kept going until she came to a Thruway rest stop with a franchise restaurant and a gas station, coasted off onto the approach, then parked at the far side of the lot where the big tractor-trailer rigs sat idling. She took two elastic hair bands from her purse and slipped them over her right wrist, then said, "Let's get some breakfast and use the restroom." She walked close to a big truck that had license plates for four states, none of them nearby. She didn't move her head, but scanned the immediate area. When she saw nobody looking her way, she quickly knelt under the trailer, slid Christine's cell phone on top of a big nut screwed to the steel frame, and slipped the two hair bands over the phone to keep it there. Within a few seconds she was out from under the truck and had caught up with Christine.

They stepped through the glass doors into the restaurant, and found a small table near the window overlooking the parking lot. They ordered food, and the waitress brought it quickly without much chatter or insincere

117

smiling. Just as the waitress came back with extra coffee, Jane watched a man in blue jeans and a baseball cap cross the parking lot with long-legged strides, climb into the tractor-trailer truck, and pull the truck ahead onto the entrance ramp to return to the Thruway. She watched him use the long entrance strip to crank his transmission up through its forward gears to bring his speed up high enough to merge the big rig into the fast traffic heading east.

Christine said, "Where do you suppose my phone is going?"

Jane shrugged. "New York, probably. Maybe Boston or Montreal."

"Do you think they'll follow it all the way?"

"Sometimes playing hide-and-seek isn't about who is faster, it's about who makes the fewest mistakes. We've got to give them a lot of chances to choose wrong."

"I guess we won't know for a while if we won."

Jane became silent, and sipped her coffee as she gazed out the window.

"What? Did I say something wrong?"

"No," said Jane. "A lot has happened to you very quickly. When I was doing this kind of work regularly, sometimes my runner would be a woman who was trying to get away from a man who lived with her. I would try to go to meet with her while she was still in her old life. I would spend time getting to know what — and who — she was afraid of. I would work out the best ways for her to slip away with a long head start. We would plan the time when nobody would be watching her. Sometimes I would arrange a distraction. Once or twice I even made sure the person she was worried about ate something that put him out of commission for a couple of days. When the runner went, she would have her new identification and a place to live in a new town. Obviously I couldn't arrange any of that for you. But maybe the worst part is that I couldn't talk to you ahead of time."

"Talk to me? What would you have said?"

"One thing I would have told you about was winning. They're dogs, we're rabbits. If the dog wins once, he gets to eat the rabbit. If the rabbit wins, all he gets is the chance to go on being a rabbit."

"Are you saying you think Richard wants to kill me?"

"I don't know what he wants. His people have missed some chances, but when we drove away from them I heard gunshots."

"I don't really understand what's going on with Richard. I don't know what he thinks he's accomplishing. He always said he loved me."

"Do you believe it was true?"

"I believe he wanted me. Maybe he wants to make me stay with him and be his girl-friend forever. I know there are men who do that — or try to, anyway."

"Yes," said Jane. "There are."

"But the six — Demming and the others — are doing things that could kill us . . ."

"They don't seem to have made up their minds. If the six had wanted to kill you — the five, by then — they could have fired on us as soon as they recognized you at the roadblock."

"I just don't know. Maybe Richard doesn't even know what they're doing. It's possible he just wants another chance. Maybe all he wants is to be sure he can see the baby when it's born."

Jane studied her for a few seconds. "The moment that bomb went off in the hospital, those six people were finished. Eventually the police will find them, and they'll be in jail until they're ninety if they're lucky. I don't have any proof that Richard knew about that, or that he knows about it now. Maybe if he knew, he'd be smart enough to turn them in."

"Maybe he would," said Christine.

"Maybe I should try to talk to him."

"If you want to talk to Richard, I think you should. The safe way is to use a pay phone, because it won't show up on caller ID. There are three booths over there outside the ladies' room, and they're the old-fashioned kind with a door you can close."

"Do you really think I should?"

"I think if you want to, this may be the last good time. Just don't tell him about your cell phone, where we are, where we're going, or anything about me."

"Of course not."

"I'll wait here," said Jane. "Don't stay on the line more than ten minutes."

Jane watched her go into the phone booth, close the door, and dial. Then she returned her attention to her surroundings. It was not unlikely that the six — now four — would make their way north to the Thruway, too. There were only about three big highways that ran all the way across the state, and they had blocked one of them. Jane had never seen the faces of the two women or the two remaining men who were hunting Christine, so she scrutinized every adult who walked into the restaurant. She also studied every car that coasted off the Thruway into the huge parking lot. She was still looking for a black sedan like the ones that they had been driving an hour or two ago, but by now they could be driving anything. Jane suspected that they would come off the Thruway and then drive up and down the aisles searching for her car, so she watched for any vehicle that seemed to be taking an indirect route to a parking space.

The tactics of the hunters reminded her of the police. There had been five of them in five cars, all apparently communicating by telephone or radio. Nobody caught more fugitives than the police, and the police did things in certain ways for practical reasons.

She kept her eyes up and scanning, but let her mind wander. It was still before dawn, but she could already see a subtle change in the quality of the darkness. At this time yesterday she had been in bed upstairs in the big old house. She remembered touching the button on the alarm and rolling over to wake up Carey by pressing her body against his big, warm back and kissing the nape of his neck. He had turned around and held her for only a minute because there had not been time.

Carey was always up early because his first surgery was scheduled for seven. She put on a bathrobe and went downstairs to make his breakfast, but she was already thinking about her day. She would have to get to the hospital to help prepare for the benefit that night. She remembered listening for Carey's heavy footsteps coming down the stairs. She'd had absolutely no premonition that in twenty-four hours things would be this different.

She saw a man standing in the entrance of the building, just inside the glass doors. He seemed to be browsing in the display rack for brochures for tourist attractions, but his eyes would flick upward to focus on Christine for a second or two, then return to the rack. Jane bent her legs to pull her feet back from under the table and shifted some of her weight onto the balls of her feet. She glanced at Christine, and saw her notice the man, but her face gave no sign of recognition. She simply turned away from him and continued her phone call.

Jane added the man to the array of sights that she was holding in her consciousness. He obviously wasn't one of the six, but he could be someone who represented some other danger. She would know him if she saw him again.

Her sense of how long things should take made her turn her attention to Christine in the phone booth. Jane saw her turn to the side, her head down. She was saying something emphatically, and she was crying.

Jane turned her eyes away to watch the road. She had been waiting for something, and now she saw it. Two identical black cars flashed past, and Jane waited, still looking out the window. After a minute or two another pair of black cars went by. Jane stood up, took the check to the cash register, and paid for their breakfast. Then she walked to the phone booth.

Christine saw her and hung up. Jane opened the door and handed her a napkin to dry her eyes. "They just went by, heading east. Let's use the restroom and get back on the road."

In a few minutes they were in the car again. As they buckled themselves in, Jane said, "Did you learn anything I need to know?"

"Not exactly," said Christine. "Nothing is different. It's all awful."

"In what way?" Jane drove out of the lot and accelerated along the entrance ramp.

"At first he sounded the way he used to when I was with him. He said he missed me and had been so worried about me, and where was I and what could he do to help me. He said he knew I must need money and a place to stay. He tried to get me to check into a hotel somewhere and let him know where, so he could come and pick me up. He sounded so sweet, so sincere."

"Did you ask him about the six people he sent after you?"

"He said he didn't know anything about that. At first he said it couldn't be the same ones who worked for him. Then he said they only used to work for him once in a while, doing security on buildings. He said they don't anymore, and maybe they're trying to kidnap me to make him pay a ransom."

"Is there any chance that any of that is true?"

"I know they didn't just work for him once in a while. They were in and out of the office all the time. They made a lot of money. He seemed to have forgotten that I paid them. And we never hired anybody for security on the buildings. They were all rented out, and if tenants wanted guards for their stores or offices, they hired them. When I was talking to Richard, I really wanted to believe what he was saying. I even said to myself that I would make myself believe him. Maybe he wasn't telling the exact truth, but that didn't mean that the lies were important. Maybe he was just telling little lies to keep me from worrying or being afraid. He said he loved me and wanted me back, so maybe he was just lying to smooth things over. But he blew it."

"How?"

"He said something about you. He said you must have turned me against him. He wanted to know who you were and how I knew you. Don't you see? How could he know you existed if the six didn't tell him?"

"I can't imagine."

"I told him it proved he was lying, and then he changed. He started trying to scare me. He said that I was carrying around his child and endangering it, and that if something happens to the baby, he'll consider me a murderer. And if nothing does, then after the baby is born, Richard will make sure it's taken away. It was so horrible."

"You've had your conversation. Is there anything he didn't tell you that you'll need to know?"

"There are a thousand things I want to know. If he wants me, why did he treat me so badly? If he didn't want me, why did he make such an effort to keep me around? What will he do if I don't get caught in a month? A year? What will he do to me if I do get caught?"

"He didn't tell you?"

"Not the truth."

"Then is there any reason to talk to him again?"

"No."

"Then don't. From now on, any time you talk to him, you'll be putting yourself in danger of having him find you and give you the answers." Jane reached the first exit after the rest stop, took it, and paid the toll, then drove back to the Thruway on the west-bound side and took another toll ticket.

"What are you doing?"

"It took us a long night and some luck. But right now, I think we have all four of them driving east following that long-haul truck with your cell phone attached to it. We have Richard thinking that they're about to catch up with us before we reach New York City. We have a good identification for you and a better set being made. It's time to drive as hard as we can in the opposite direction." Jane paused. "You might want to get some sleep."

"Can I turn on the radio?"

"Sure. But won't it keep you awake?"

"I go to sleep with the radio on," said Christine. "I know it's weird, but it's a habit." She turned it on and pushed buttons until she found a station that she seemed to approve of, and settled back in her seat.

An hour later when the music was re-placed for the fifth time by a commercial for a mattress store in Rochester, a news bulletin came on. "Late-breaking story," said the newswoman. "Seneca County Sheriff's deputies have found a man's body beside a road in a rural area south of Waterloo this morning. The man was carrying no identification, but he was driving a rental car, so the Sheriff's office expects that they'll have positive ID soon. Our information is that he was shot to death execution style some time during the night. His body also showed signs of having been hit by a car, but the spokesperson refused to speculate on how that related to his murder."

Christine was sitting up again. "They killed him because he was hurt?"

"Because they didn't want to leave him there to answer questions." She drove on for a few seconds before she acknowledged Christine's stare. "It helps to learn to think the way your enemies do. You spend less time being surprised."

6

Jane drove west as far as Exit 50 on the edge of Amherst with a growing feeling of tension. She took the exit onto the Youngmann Expressway, got off at Millersport Highway, and drove to the big old stone McKinnon house. She pulled into the driveway and around the house and stopped in front of the garage, where her car was hidden from the street.

Christine awoke as soon as the car stopped moving. "What?" she said, her eyes blinking. She sat up. "Where — What are we doing?"

"This is my house — the one where I live with my husband. We've got to do this quickly." Jane got out and stood still, studying the house.

She had already seen that there was nothing obvious like a broken windowpane or scratches around the door lock, but she was looking for signs that were subtler. The hose attached to the spigot at the corner of the house was still in exactly the same position, snaking along the back to the row of rosebushes she had watered before leaving for the hospital. There was dust along the outer windowsills on the first floor. She had noticed it yesterday, but not had time to clean them. The dust had not been disturbed. Christine was out of the car now, at Jane's side. Jane said, "They haven't found their way here yet."

"Why are we here?"

"Slight change of plan."

"We're going to stay here?"

"No, we're going to the airport to rent a car."

"Is something wrong with yours?"

"Yes. They saw it. I don't think they could have gotten the plate number — I certainly didn't have time to read theirs — but a white Volvo is a recognizable car. I'd rather be driving something else while they're looking for us. But we've got to be out of here before they realize we must have come back this way. Ready?"

"I guess so."

As they backed out of the driveway, Jane said, "Here's what's going to happen. I'll drive us to the airport. Watch closely how I get there from here. I'll get out, and you

130

drive straight back here and wait for me."

When they reached the departure level of the Buffalo Niagara International Airport, Jane got out carrying her shoulder bag, and watched Christine drive off. Then she hurried to the arrival level near the baggage claim and crossed the street to the car rental building. She took quick strides past the counters for Hertz, Enterprise, National, and Avis, and stopped at Daycars. She handed the woman behind the counter her Daycars card, American Express card, and North Carolina driver's license in the name Valerie Collins and said, "Hi. I'd like to rent a car."

"What sort of car would you like?" said the woman. "Compact?"

"A luxury sedan. Something big and comfortable."

"We've got a Lincoln Town Car and a Chrysler 300."

"What colors?"

"The Chrysler is white, and the Lincoln is dark gray."

"I'll take the Lincoln."

The woman put the key to the Chrysler away. She copied the driver's license number, ran Valerie Collins's American Express card through the reader, and handed them back to Jane. "You know where the lot is?"

"No," Jane lied.

"Through that door and downstairs." She handed Jane the key. "It's in space nineteen."

"Thanks." Jane stepped away from the counter. She'd had a brief moment during the transaction when she stopped breathing, waiting for something to go wrong, even though she was sure it wouldn't. She knew the Valerie Collins cards wouldn't make any alarms go off, because she had grown the Valerie Collins identity during the days when she was still regularly taking fugitives out of the world. She had gone to North Carolina to buy the birth certificate, taken the tests for the driver's license, and opened a bank account to pay the credit card bills. From time to time she had added to the cover by buying things as Valerie Collins, giving to charities, joining organizations.

The only part that could trip her up was a mistake in her manner that raised suspicion. She had been tempted to use a fake North Carolina accent until she heard the first words of the woman at the counter, who had a real southern accent. Then Jane had been too brusque, as though she were angry. In the old days her actions were quick and sure. She was going to have to get back in practice before something went wrong. Her manner had to be flawless.

Jane took the glass elevator down to the lower level, found the car in its numbered parking space, and drove to her house thinking over everything she had done so far to keep Christine safe, searching for errors. After she was on the expressway for a mile, she caught herself driving too fast, and forced herself to lift her foot from the gas pedal a bit, but it was difficult. The sun was well up now, and the second day had begun, and incredibly, they were still within ten miles of the place where they had started running.

Christine was waiting for her around the back of the house when Jane pulled in. The Volvo was already in the garage. Jane got out of the rental car, took the keys and the garage door opener from Christine, and put them in the house. Christine stood by the driver's side of the Lincoln, but Jane said, "I'll drive a bit longer. I know the area, so I can make better time."

As Jane backed the big gray car out of the driveway and turned toward the Thruway entrance, Christine said, "This doesn't look like your kind of car."

"That's just what I wanted to hear. But it's big and comfortable and has a powerful engine, which are all good qualities for what we're doing. And it doesn't look at all like my Volvo." Jane drove off, rapidly gaining speed. She checked her mirrors every few seconds.

"What's the rest of your new plan?"

"To drive far and fast," said Jane. "We're only a few miles from where we started, and by now it's possible they know we came back this way. Buffalo couldn't be more dangerous for you if it were on fire. We'll start on the south branch of the Thruway and head along the lake toward Erie, Pennsylvania, then either turn east toward Pittsburgh or west toward Cleveland. Is there anything about either place that makes it more dangerous for you?"

"No. In fact, I have an aunt and some cousins in Pittsburgh. It's my father's younger sister. Her husband was an incredible jerk — big drinker, big cheater — but he died of a heart attack a few years ago. She's great, and so are the kids. We could probably stay with them."

"I'm afraid that wouldn't be a good idea. In fact they're what I meant by something that makes the city more dangerous for you — somebody who knows your name isn't Linda Welles."

"They'd never betray me."

Jane sighed. "I guess it's time for another

lesson." Her eyes flicked to the mirrors, studying the cars behind her as she pulled onto the Thruway. She passed a truck and returned to the right lane, then watched for a few seconds to see if any other car came around the truck.

"You sound sad. What's wrong?"

Jane glanced at her, then moved her eyes back to the road and kept them there. "When you came to me just after the bomb went off, I was hoping you were just a hysterical patient. When you told me Sharon had sent you, I knew you had to be more than that. Then I saw what was after you. You're going to have to learn everything at seventy miles an hour."

"What don't I know?"

"That I'm the last resort. A person comes to me only when the possibility of living as the person he's always been is gone. I can show you the way to sink out of sight, and come up again somewhere else as a new person. I can do it. But that doesn't mean you can. It isn't easy, and there are terrible sacrifices."

"Sacrifice? You're saying I have to sacrifice *people*? The few relatives I have left?"

"Yes. And your friends, and your enemies. For quite a few runners I've taken out, the enemies are the hardest ones to give up. But if you go with me, there's no revenge — not even in small ways. No matter how wonderful you make your new life, no matter what you accomplish, you can never go back and show the people you hated. You can never say to your father's ex-wife, 'You treated me horribly, but now take a look at me. I've beaten you.' "

"Okay. I guess I can understand that. You think that if I do, she just might find a way to get me found or something. But honestly, I know who I can trust, and exactly how far. My aunt Mary and my cousins in Pittsburgh are just the best people. They wouldn't tell anyone where I was, and they certainly don't know anybody who knows Richard Beale."

"You're not getting this. It's not that they'd do anything to hurt you. It's about hurting them. If we succeed completely in losing the people who are chasing you, the next thing they'll do is start working the most promising ways of picking up your trail again. If Richard Beale knows who your favorite relatives are, his people will find them and see if you're there. For a time they'll watch the house. They'll probably examine the mail every day for a letter that might be from you. Maybe they'll plant microphones inside, tap the phone. If they believe that your aunt knows where you are, then your aunt will get a visit."

"You're trying to scare me again."

"Yes," said Jane. "I am."

"I know I'm a lot of trouble, but I'll try to be less. I know I'm not good at any of this, but I'm trying to learn as fast as I can. Scaring the shit out of me is just mean."

"I'm sorry it seems that way. But the last thing you want to do is put the people you care about in the position of being the only ones who can tell a man like Richard Beale where you are."

Christine sat in silence for a long time, staring out the car window across the fields at the trees gliding by as Jane drove hard toward the south. When Jane looked at her again she was expecting to see tears, but Christine was dry-eyed and motionless.

"It's your father who's bothering you, isn't it?"

She nodded. "He's going to be in jail for about six more years. If he doesn't hear from me, I don't know what he'll think, what he'll feel. Nothing good."

"As soon as you're settled in a safe place, I'll go and see him. If I can't get in I'll write a letter to him that will tell him what he needs to know, but won't reveal anything else. I'll mail it someplace far from your city and far from my city. Then he'll feel glad that you're not in danger anymore."

"Thanks. I'm not even sure how I feel about trying to see him anymore. I want him to know that I love him. But it's not just me anymore. I've got to do what I can to get my baby born."

"I'm sure he'll understand that, and he'll agree that you're making the right decision."

"He's got no choice. This is the only grandchild he's going to have."

Jane didn't remind her that the two half siblings she had left with her former step-mother might have children. Christine could hardly have forgotten them. Jane supposed that Christine had already banished them from her mind the day she walked out of the house at the age of sixteen. She said, "For now, the best thing to do is stop think-ing about the past, and turn your attention to the decisions you have to make next."

"What do I have left to decide?"

"We have a direction, but we still need a destination. Do you know where you'd like to live?"

"I guess Pittsburgh is out. And San Diego certainly is. I don't know. Someplace where it's not cold in the winter. I can do heat, but I hate snow and ice. I don't know how to dress, or drive, or even walk without falling."

"Maybe Florida, then, or the Atlantic coast as far up as South Carolina. Or the southern part of Texas, Arizona, or Nevada."

"I'll have to think about it. I've never been to any of those places so I don't really know. They all sound okay to me."

"Let's try another way, then. You're going to want to find a job of some kind. Is there anything new you'd like to try?"

"Even if there were, I don't have the experience or the education for anything but what I was doing for Richard."

"What was that?"

"I was Richard's secretary. I was supposed to help with what he was doing."

"Fine. He was selling real estate, right?"

"It wasn't just sales. We did property management, and built some new housing. We did some land speculation, too, buying, holding for a while, and reselling. And we found underpriced houses, remodeled and flipped them."

"Did you enjoy it?"

"I like to work. What I was doing was okay. I think if I had my choice I'd like to be a teacher. But I never went to college."

"You're going to be twenty-one years old, according to your ID. You've got plenty of time to get a degree part-time after the baby is born."

"I can't get into a college. I'll be living under a false name with no high school diploma, transcripts, letters of recommendation, or anything."

"I can help you with all that. I'll have some college transcripts cooked up to make you look as though you should be admitted as a transfer student."

"What is this, magic?"

"No. It's lying. I know where I can get transcripts made. It's a four-year college that existed for about fifty years in Tennessee, then went out of business in the late eighties. A man I know took over the name, changed the mailing address of the registrar's office to a P.O. box in the same city, and has everything forwarded. If someone calls or writes for verification of a degree or something, he's the one who answers. For a small fee he supplies anything that's needed. He's still at it. I looked online recently and saw that Hillcliff College has a Web page."

"How can I possibly get away with that?"

"Any manufactured identity can be penetrated, but most aren't. All you have to do is behave in a way that makes everyone around you want you to succeed. You work hard, you're nice to people. The secret is to be the sort of person nobody wants to harm. Another part of that is to go slowly. You claim to be a twenty-one-year-old girl who wants to be a student. Claim to be what you so obviously are, and nothing more."

"That's it?"

"It's the start. You don't set off any suspicions, so nobody double-checks what you say. Then, day by day, you get to know people in a natural way — people in classes, at jobs, in your neighborhood. You're just a nice girl with a cute little baby, who's trying to qualify as a teacher. Your story doesn't threaten anybody, and it's not the kind of thing that confidence women make up. They're always the daughters of billionaires, or runaway rock stars that nobody ever heard of because they're from Brazil."

"I'm pregnant and I'm not married."

"Is that a big deal to you?"

"Yes. It makes me feel like people think I'm a slut."

"It's been a long time since anybody actually thought that way — at least a generation. But if it makes you uncomfortable, let's fix that, too."

"Fix it?"

"You're in the process of getting a divorce. That way, you can wear a wedding ring during the rest of your pregnancy. You won't feel as though anybody thinks of you as an unwed mother. Later, when you're ready to date, you take the ring off, and the divorce is final. If you tell people the divorce story during those months, they'll not only believe it, but later on they'll be under the impression that they saw it happen."

"You've done all of this before?"

"Many times."

"And it works?"

"It always has." Jane checked the mirrors again, then nudged her speed up a little. Her manner had conveyed a confidence she didn't feel. It had been more than five years since she had taught a person to run. Since then a thousand obstacles must have been invented to keep people from changing identities, and she knew about only a few of them. Right now, the things she was doing to make Christine safe might be killing them both.

7

At ten in the morning, when they were a few miles south of Buffalo in Hamburg, Jane pulled off the highway and stopped in the big parking lot of the McKinley Mall across from the Wegmans grocery store. "Are you ready to drive?"

"Sure," said Christine. "I slept really well on that last stretch."

"I know." They got out of the car and traded seats. When Christine sat behind the wheel, she adjusted the mirrors and the seat to her shorter stature, started the engine, and looked around her twice before she put the car in gear and let it glide forward up an aisle toward the exit from the lot.

To Jane her behavior was a promising sign. Jane had stayed alive this long by observing people minutely — how they carried themselves, where they looked when they walked into unfamiliar buildings, where they chose to sit in movie theaters. The way they drove a car was a huge indicator. It warned her if they were stupid, crazy, careless, or selfish.

She pretended to relax and adjusted the passenger seat so it leaned back, turned her face slightly away from Christine, and closed her left eye. She was asleep as a napping cat is asleep, eyes barely closed and muscles ready to react in an instant.

Christine drove with a tentative quality at first, holding the wheel tightly with both hands and readjusting the mirrors once more. Jane waited and watched the window to her right, judged the speed of acceleration, and felt the deceleration when Christine applied the brakes. Jane opened her eyes while Christine got out on the main highway, and watched her test the car's power on the Thruway, take a space in the right lane and stay there for a time until she needed to get around a slow truck, then pull back in. She performed those operations with competence and assurance. She was not an aggressive driver or a timid one.

When the car crossed over into the Cattaraugus Reservation, Jane watched the familiar landmarks pass — Mile Strip Road, then Irving-Gowanda Road, and then Cattaraugus Creek and the ponds just past it. Jane closed both eyes. Christine was all right. She might not turn out to be a hero or a genius, but she was a good driver. A person who could be trusted to maneuver a metal and glass box containing one's fragile bones and tender flesh down a highway at a mile a minute was a valuable ally. In a moment, Jane began to dream.

It was night, but she was not feeling safe enough to sleep. She was in her compartment in a longhouse that belonged to the women of the Wolf clan, but her husband was somewhere else — out in the forest with a party of warriors, going south along the crests of the mountains to fight. There were always men out in the endless woods. So many men were killed in the fighting that more men had to be sent out to find captives to bring home and adopt to take the places of the dead.

There was shouting. She wanted to find out what it was, but couldn't get her muscles to respond. Someone threw back the hide that covered the doorway, and she could see bright orange flames outside. There were dark silhouettes crossing the doorway, footsteps thudding on the packed earth outside the longhouse.

There were sounds of fighting. Then she saw fire fifty paces down the longhouse wall, licking up the elm bark wall on the inner side, beginning to reach the support laths. She rolled off the platform to the pounded earth floor and stood.

She looked around her, and saw the shapes of two children in the compartment across the hearth from hers — her cousin's children, a boy and a girl. "Where's your mother?" They said nothing, so she said, "Come on. Come with me."

They both came to her and clung to her legs, but she took their hands and said, "There are men out there who want to kill us. We're going out, and we're going to run for the forest and go as hard and as far as we can. If one of us gets caught, keep running. There won't be any reason to look back."

She moved to the western doorway, opened the flap only slightly, so the light from inside would not show, and peered out. There were many people running — women and children. The men all seemed to be enemies, all dashing from one long-house to the next with torches, or chasing fleeing people and bludgeoning them to the ground with swings of their war clubs.

Jane couldn't tell by looking at the dark silhouettes who the attackers were. There was only a shine of reflected firelight on glistening skin, a flash of red or yellow or black paint across a face, scalp locks, and feathers. She watched them for a few moments, then whispered, "It's time." She pulled the two children out with her, timed her run to pass one of the raiders from behind before the next one could appear.

She was a very fast runner, her long, strong legs dashing for the dark ring of palisades that surrounded the village. Right away she saw that the children weren't going to be fast enough. The flames from burning longhouses were rising higher now, and they would be seen. She knelt and said to the boy, "On my back." When he had climbed up and clung to her neck, she scooped up the girl and said, "Hold tight." The vertical logs were set in place so they formed a spiral, leaving a narrow corridor as a portal. She stood and ran toward the gap in the stockade.

As she ran she heard terrible shrieks, some of them cries of final agony and others of wild exhilaration and joy. She could see the gap in the row of tall, sharpened tree trunks now. It was the opening she had used each day to go out into the fields. She ran hard for it. She knew that by now there must be enemy warriors who had seen her in the light of the fires, and as though her thought drew it, she heard an arrow flit past her ear.

She tried bending lower, and almost stumbled under the weight of the children, then regained her footing and ran harder. She sensed that enough time had passed now for a bowman to nock an arrow and draw the bow, so she abruptly dodged to the left. The arrow flew past her right arm into the ground ahead of her. As she passed it, she tugged it out of the earth and clutched it as she ran.

The gap was close. She ran into the space made by the overlapping palisades and saw the man blocking the passage. His face was painted red below the mouth and black above, so he seemed in the dim light to be headless. He lunged toward her in the narrow space, his arms out to reach around her and the two children, but Jane thrust the head of the arrow toward his abdomen just below the sternum.

As she pushed the arrow upward with all her strength, she felt her right arm jerk forward against nothing, and she was awake. She was in a car, the rented car. She could feel the mild vibration of the car over the road, feel the artificial unchanging breath of the air-conditioning on her face. She sat up.

"Good afternoon."

Jane looked and remembered Christine. "Hi," she said.

"You were having a nightmare, weren't you?"

"I don't think of them as nightmares."

"Your legs started twitching. We had a dog who used to do that in his sleep, like he was running."

Jane sat up straight, looked at the road, then flipped down the sun visor and opened the flap in the back to reveal the makeup mirror. Her eyes looked a bit puffy, but her hair hung straight, as usual. "I guess the dog and I must have the same dreams." She looked out to her right, searching for landmarks. "What was the last town you passed?"

"Erie, Pennsylvania."

"Good," said Jane. "You've made good progress. Want me to drive?"

"To tell you the truth, I was just beginning to think about waking you up. I'd like to stop someplace soon."

Jane looked at her watch. It was still the fancy dress watch with the tiny face and the diamonds. "I forgot to take this thing off after the benefit, and now I'm stuck with it. I guess it says one-thirty." She stared out the window again. "I think the next place that's right for your purposes is a little restaurant called Dill's. It's on the lakeshore right around here. I recognize where we are.

Take the next exit."

"You know this route that well?"

"I've driven it plenty of times. Even before the security at airports got serious, it wasn't always a good idea to take a plane. There were always too many people who got a chance to see your face, too many times when you had to give a false name. And when you get on an airplane, there's not much you can do about who gets on with you. So I've always tried to use the highways when there was time. Turn right up here. Now keep going straight. There will be a big sign on the left that says DILL'S. The parking lot is next to it."

Christine said, "This is going to be the best place around here?"

"Best for us."

"For us?"

"Two women driving west, one of whom is being hunted. Picking where you're willing to stop is a good skill to learn. Find places that cater to people who look just like you, if you can. You don't want to stand out any more than you have to. Dill's is a place where local people go, which means the food is dull but safe. It's too far from the main highways to get much of the passing traffic. The restrooms are very clean. That's a big sign. It means that there's

150

somebody in charge who cares about the business. If something seems to be threatening to one of his customers — meaning you — he's going to try to help."

Christine found the restaurant, and drove into the parking lot. Jane said, "Park between those two big SUVs. They hide the car from the road."

She maneuvered the car into the space Jane had indicated, and Jane said, "Now before you turn off the engine, look around. Is there somebody visible who seems to be watching every car that arrives, or has a particular interest in us?"

"Not that I can see."

"Good. Anything else that feels odd?"

"I don't think so. Does what I feel matter?"

"Absolutely. Your fear is the best thing you have right now. Use it. Listen to it. Always give yourself a few seconds to let those feelings come to you. If you feel things aren't right, then they aren't. How does it feel here?"

"Comfortable. Easy," said Christine. "It reminds me of the places my dad used to take my mother and me when I was little."

"The reasons your father picked a place like this are complicated, but they're essentially the same. He wasn't going to take a woman and a child into a place that wasn't safe or where they'd feel conspicuous. Now, what if you and I are both wrong about this place? Or what if things change quickly? If you know in advance what you plan to do, then you'll be able to do it efficiently. If the four come, can they block the exit?"

"Not really. If they tried, I can drive over the lawn to the street in a second."

"Heading where?"

"I'd take any direction that was clear, but I think I'd try to go that way if I had a choice." She pointed to the right.

"What's there?"

"If you make a right turn, you're hardly ever held up waiting to do it. And I think that's the way to the center of town. There will be people, maybe a police station."

"That is the way downtown. Very good." They got out of the car and walked to the front entrance of the restaurant. "When we get inside, read the place and the people for me."

They went in and a plump middle-aged waitress with red hair and smile lines around her eyes and mouth stepped up to them, taking long strides in rubber-soled shoes. She pulled two menus out of a rack near the door, and said, "This way, ladies." She stopped at a table near the side windows of the restaurant and said, "Is this okay?"

Jane looked at Christine.

"Sure," said Christine.

They sat down and watched the waitress disappear, and then Jane said, "Tell me. What do I need to know about this place?"

"I don't see any scary people. They all look like my aunts and uncles. The exits are through the back of the room by the rest-rooms, and the front."

"Where else?"

"That's it."

"No, it isn't. If you go through the kitchen you'll see a back door. They have to have a back way for deliveries and to take out the garbage. Even if you don't see it, you know there is one."

Christine looked at her closely. "You did have a nightmare, didn't you?"

"It was a reminder. I've got to give you everything I can, as quickly as possible. From now on, you've got to be careful every second. There aren't any decisions that don't matter. One choice makes you safer, and the other makes you less safe. If you can tell which is which, your chances go way up. You have to get out of certain habits. Pretty young girls are taught to enjoy being noticed, and, if possible, remembered. Beginning now you want to be overlooked

153

and forgotten."

"It's going to get harder as I get bigger and bigger."

"When the baby comes, the attention will end. Babies are all adorable and interesting. People's eyes are drawn to them, and they can't stare at both of you easily. Men in particular will stop looking at you. Their motives are pretty predictable, and when they see a baby, it will trip a switch that says you're not available for what they have in mind, so their eyes will move on. At this stage, all you need to think about are three things: Is this place safe? How do I keep from being noticed? How do I keep from leaving tracks?"

"Leaving tracks?"

"Everywhere a person goes, he leaves a trail. People see him. He has to pay for food, clothing, and shelter. At the moment I don't think the four know where you are, because we put a break in the trail. The longer you can stay invisible, the harder it will be to pick you up again. If you do everything right, it will be nearly impossible. You don't use any name if you can help it, travel at night, pay cash for everything you can."

A few other customers came in and sat nearby, so Jane and Christine ordered lunch and ate in near silence, talking only occasionally in quiet tones about the weather, the traffic, and the restaurant. Then Jane paid in cash for their food, and in moments she had steered the car back onto the road again. "Tell me about your dream," said Christine.

Jane kept her eyes on the road. "When I'm doing this — taking a runner out — I suppose I'm agitated. I have lots of dreams."

"Sharon told me that dreams are part of your religion."

Jane glanced at her. "Yours, too."

"I suppose so," said Christine. "But Sharon told me you took them seriously."

"I do."

"Are you religious?"

"No," Jane said. "I'd say that I'm a pretty staunch atheist until it gets dark. Then I'm not so sure. How about you?"

"My mother raised me to be a devout person, but she died when I was seven, and that was the end of it. I sort of forgot about the whole thing. Maybe I'll go back to church when the baby is born. What do your dreams tell you?"

"If you're a religious Seneca, you believe a dream is either advice from a spirit guide — a supernatural being who cares about you — or your soul's way of expressing a wish or a need."

"Have you had any that might be messages?"

"I think that mine tend to be a guide telling me something I need to know, only the guide is my own brain."

"Huh?"

"When important things are happening, events sometimes move too fast for us to evaluate everything we see or hear. Later on, when we dream, our minds seem to point out to us things we didn't pay enough attention to while we were awake, or maybe didn't interpret right. Something can be tickling the backs of our minds, and the dream is our chance to look at it in a different way."

"So what did your last dream tell you?"

"That I need to pay attention."

"Where are we going?"

"West."

"Because of your dream?"

"Because the last time I saw the four, they were going east."

8

Jane drove for three hours and then let Christine drive again. They moved in the afternoon across the flat plain left by the receding prehistoric Great Lakes. They passed signs for Youngstown and Cleveland, Akron and Toledo. Soon the signs advised them of the distances to Detroit and Chicago. Christine said, "Are we headed for Chicago?"

"No. We're going to keep moving west a bit longer, and stopping in big cities is a lot of time and work. You have to fight traffic all the way in, then find a room in a place you think might be safe but don't really know. Even expensive hotels can fool you, because they're in the center of things, and certain criminals like that. The room will cost twice as much as it should. Then you have to find your way out in the morning rush hour."

"So where do we stop?"

"Suburbs, or smaller towns along the way. The chain hotels near airports can be good because they're generally on big highways and they're cheap, quick, and anonymous. They're full of business travelers who check in late one day and head out early the next. They have restaurants, so you don't have to show yourself outside."

Christine looked apprehensive. "Are you trying to tell me that big cities are out? That from now on I'll never be able to live in a real city?"

"Not at all. Probably you'll end up in one, or near one. That's where the jobs are, and most of the universities that will offer what you want to learn. It's where the big hospitals are — which for the next few months, you'll need. And big cities are easy places to hide."

"But which one?"

"Right now we need to find a place to simply put you for about four months. You'll live under the name Linda Welles."

"Four months? But what am I doing?"

"As little as possible."

"I don't understand you."

"You're pregnant. You'll take care of yourself — eat right, get the sort of moderate exercise your doctor should have told you about, get a full eight hours of sleep at night. We'll buy you a few of the better child-care books, and you'll read them. You'll make lists of the things you'll need to buy for the baby — clothes, diapers, crib, changing table, toys, blankets. The more of that you do ahead of time, the less you'll have to do later."

"That's it?"

Jane looked at her thoughtfully, and kept driving. "You've been out of their sight for less than twenty-four hours, but we've created a break in your trail. Remember, the bigger we can make the break — the longer you haven't been seen or heard from — the harder you'll be to find. While you're spending your time taking care of your health and your baby's, what are the four hunters doing?"

"How should I know?"

"They're searching for you. They won't have any idea where you are, so they'll be working very hard, trying everything at once to pick up any hint of your location, or even your direction. That's one of the ways that we'll slowly manipulate the odds in your favor."

"Against those people? It doesn't sound as though the odds ever go in my favor."

"It depends on how you think about it. Every day that you're free and healthy, we're wasting their time, tiring them out. We'll get you into a comfortable, safe place. Then, every time it rains, I want you to think of them standing outside in the cold and wet, watching some hotel entrance a thousand miles from you. While you're sleeping, they're sitting in a car in an airport parking lot watching for you to step off a shuttle bus. Every day will make them more tired and frustrated. And eventually Richard will run out of money or patience and stop paying them. Then your odds go way up."

Christine thought about it for a few seconds. "I guess I'd like that to be true. I'll try to think of it that way." She paused. "Most of the time I've felt the opposite way. Every day I'm getting bigger and heavier and slower. A lot of the time I don't feel so great."

"That's just for now. We'll use the time keeping you invisible, and preparing for the next stage. After the baby is born, you'll be ready to be a new person."

"Two people."

"Right," Jane said. "The main thing is not to allow yourself to feel defeated. You're already having a lot of hormonal changes, and there will be others later that might make your head spin. So we'll give you specific practical things to work on that will help."

"You seem to know a lot about this — pregnancy and everything."

"I've thought about it a lot."

"But you don't have kids."

"No. You don't always get what you want."

"Maybe you will."

"Maybe," said Jane. "But you're the one we've got to get through it right now." Jane had been feeling more and more deprived as they talked about babies, but now the feeling had grown into a painful emptiness, and she wanted it to end. She had admitted she wanted a baby, and it was obvious that she didn't have one. What else was going to be required of her?

Christine was quiet for a time. Then she said, "Jane?"

"What?"

"When it happens, do you think you could be there?"

"Be there? At the hospital?"

"In the delivery room. At least at the hospital, though. It's just that being there, doing this alone, with nobody around who even knows who I am or cares about me, it just scares me so much. No, I'm sorry. I guess it's too much. I'm sorry."

"I understand. I'll try to be there when it

happens. There are all sorts of practical reasons for me to be with you then, and for at least a few weeks afterward. I'm a pro at dealing with doctors, and I'm pretty good with babies, too."

"How did you learn?"

Jane hid her emotions and spoke about it as though she were speaking about someone else, some future Jane who could look back on this and feel no sadness. "When I was a teenager, I used to babysit a lot. I was an only child, so babies were great fun to me. Then when I grew up I married a surgeon. I wanted to be the best wife the world has ever known, so I had to find volunteer work I could do at the hospital. There are hierarchies to volunteer organizations. You can't just pop in one afternoon and announce you're going to be chair of some important committee. You have to find things to do, help out where you can until people get to know you. Since I knew babies, I started out volunteering to hold the babies who needed it — preemies and drug babies, mostly. I would come in and read to the toddlers and watch them in the playroom. I also spent a lot of time doing fund-raising mailings. It made me a world-class envelope stuffer, but I'm still better with babies."

"Will you teach me?"

Jane hesitated. "Sure. I'll tell you everything I can in advance, and then show you when the time comes. And, as I said, the books can be useful. If you do your homework ahead of time, you probably won't find yourself at three A.M. holding a screaming baby in one hand, trying to find the page about colic with the other."

"It's intimidating, but it sounds so — I don't know — normal. Colic is a regular problem that other people have to think about, too. It's just as though everything is okay."

"Things are going to be okay. We're going to make them okay."

"When I used to think about this, I always thought I'd be a little older, and that Richard would be there with me. We would figure everything out together."

"Of course."

" 'I always thought.' That's stupid, isn't it?"

"No. It isn't. The most common mistake that women make is sleeping with the wrong man. And most of the time, the men aren't even trying to hide what they're really like."

"Have you?"

Jane hesitated, then relented. "Yes. But I'll leave it at that. No details."

Early in the evening Jane said, "We'll be

near Madison, Wisconsin, in about an hour. That ought to be a good place to spend the night."

"I'm ready," said Christine. "I feel as though we've been driving forever."

"It's been over six hundred miles since we left Buffalo." They watched for signs, then came off Interstate 90 and took smaller roads toward Madison, but stopped outside the city at a tall, monolithic white building that Jane judged to be the right kind of hotel. Christine said, "I hope they have a room for us."

"They will. It's already evening, and the parking lot is just over half-full. We're not near the airport, and there isn't any congestion here, so people probably don't take taxis."

"You're so conscious of everything. You think about everything ahead of time."

"You will, too. You're already learning. Remember what I told you. Look for signs that the place is safe before you even turn off your engine. Most people leave their cars with the valet, or at least near the main entrance while they check in. We'll leave the car around the side where it's less conspicuous." They got out and walked toward the front of the hotel.

Christine glanced over her shoulder at the

car. "It doesn't look conspicuous. It's just a big dark gray car."

"With New York plates."

"Oh. Yeah," Christine said. "I suppose if they were right behind us, they'd start looking for a car with New York plates, wouldn't they? But I'm supposed to be looking for exits. The big one in front. One along the side of the building. That's probably at the end of a hallway with rooms. One in the back, at least."

"Good. There could be half a dozen. The good thing about hotels is that there are always lots of exits. The bad thing is that they're also entrances. If the four were right behind us, they would want to enter the hotel unobtrusively and take you out by one of the side exits."

" 'If they were right behind us.' You keep saying that. Do you really think they could be?"

Jane shook her head. "I doubt it. I've been watching the road behind us since we left Buffalo, and I've seen nothing that worried me. I don't know where they are, so I don't stop looking. All the time, no matter what we're doing or where we are, I try to ask myself all the what-if questions. I want you to do that, too. Make it a habit. Look at everything the way you would if you thought they might be here in five minutes. What would you look for?"

"Hiding places. Ways out of the building that they won't notice right away. People who might help us."

"Good. Now let me add a couple of things. They seem to be trying to take you rather than kill you. That means they have to trap you. Look for anything you might use to break out of a trap. Sometimes there are valet-parking attendants who take your car when you arrive and bring it back when you leave. As you go by them, watch to see where they put the keys. A lot of the time it's just a box with hooks in it. During slow times there's often one guy on duty, and when he runs to get a car, there's nobody."

"You're telling me to steal a car?"

"You'd take it just long enough to get out of here, and ditch it before anybody really knows enough to call the cops. The other thing to look for is a weapon. Obviously the car is the best one."

"I remember."

"There are always others. They're often better than a weapon concealed on you, because once you notice them, they're in plain sight where you can simply pick them up and use them without carrying them around."

"What kind?"

"Suppose you're in the dining room at the buffet. There are steak knives and big, sharp forks. There are coffeepots and soup kettles and servers full of hot liquids. A gallon of coffee won't kill anybody, but it could send him to the hospital. Around the building there will be gardeners with pruning shears, shovels, and rakes. Inside there are often handymen with hammers, linoleum knives, heavy wrenches. In the bar you can break off a bottle and kill somebody with it. The point isn't to make a list. It's to walk through the world with your eyes open. You'll see danger ahead of time, and you'll see ways to escape."

They entered the lobby, and Christine waited while Jane went to the desk and registered with a credit card in the name of Carol Stevens. The transaction was uneventful, as Jane had known it would be. The five years since she had used any of her home-grown identities for anything risky had added depth to them. She met Christine at the elevator and punched the three button.

"Why the third floor? Did you pick it?"

"Yes. Normally I like to be a bit higher up if I'm trying to be invisible. But the people we're worried about wouldn't hesitate to set something off to smoke us out or cause a distraction. Hotels are a nasty place to be if there's a fire, and no fire department in the world has a ladder that reaches above the fifth floor."

"But they don't know where we are."

"In the town where I live, there hasn't been anyone who came to find me in five years, and there hasn't been a murder in at least seven. Every night I lock all the doors and set the alarm. Then I make sure the shotgun is where I left it — loaded, with the safety on."

"Am I going to have to do all that?"

"Not the same things. You'll take other precautions that fit your situation. The point is to take every one that's available."

The elevator doors opened, and Christine noticed that Jane was holding her suitcase differently, resting it comfortably on her hip and gripping it in both hands. Christine could see it protected her torso, and she could throw it if she wanted to. She leaned forward to look to the left and right in the hall before she stepped out, carrying the suitcase by its handle.

The room was a suite at the far end of the hall. Jane unlocked the door and looked around before she moved inward to admit Christine.

Christine went to the farther double bed,

near the window. "What a nice room. I'm so glad to be here. I feel like we've been traveling for weeks."

Jane stood at the side of the window and opened the curtain a couple of inches. "I see a better place to put the car. Lock everything, and I'll be back in a couple of minutes." She walked out, and Christine closed the door, bolted it, and put the chain in its slot.

She went to the window and looked out. After another minute she saw Jane drive the dark gray Town Car around the building. There was only a single line of spaces, most of which were filled. Christine could see there were signs in front of the first six spaces. She guessed that they were reserved for people who worked at the hotel, but the rest of the spaces were unmarked. Jane pulled into one of them, got out, and went to a door in the side of the building.

Christine let the curtain swing closed again, went to the door, and looked out through the peephole at the empty hallway. From this room she could see all the way up the hall to the elevators. She watched for Jane, but she was startled when Jane suddenly slid into view right in front of the peephole and reached up to knock. Christine opened the door, then closed it behind

Jane and engaged the locks again. "Where did you come from?"

"Just now? The stairs. This is just like any other place we've stopped. You look for entrances and exits, and then if you can, you try a couple."

"Is that the best way out?"

"Probably, if we have to leave in a hurry. Parking there will also give us the chance to check on the car once in a while. If someone is watching it, or getting in position to block it in, we'll be able to see." She paused. "Would you like a nap before dinner?"

"I think so, if it's okay."

"Sure. I'm going to go take a look around the hotel. Lock up again, okay?"

"Okay."

"When you lock everything from inside, my key won't work, so you'll have to let me in again. But don't open the door unless you can look through the peephole and see me."

Christine locked the door behind her, and then lay on the bed by the window and fell into a deep, dreamless sleep. She awoke to the sound of Jane's knock. It was sharp and insistent, and Christine had an indistinct memory of a quieter, more tentative knock that had not seemed quite real. When she opened the door, Jane came in carrying a rubberized canvas tote bag.

"Sorry to wake you," said Jane.

"Your hair is wet. Did you go swimming?"

"Yes." She opened her bag, held up a black nylon swimming suit, and hung it on the towel rack in the bathroom. "I bought the suit and goggles and some shorts at the gift shop. I went to the gym, and after that I got into the pool. They're always overchlorinated, so my new black suit will probably be gray, but a swim always feels good."

"I admire you. Even before I was pregnant I wouldn't have done that."

"Later on, after the baby, you should try to get into the habit. Do it while you're young. It gives you energy, fights off depression, keeps you healthy. Part of beating these people is making a life that works."

"I don't find it easy to think that far ahead right now."

"Then don't," said Jane. "Keep your mind on today, and we'll do just fine. Let's go have dinner."

The next morning they checked out of the hotel at nine, drove out on Interstate 90 and switched to 94. They were in St. Paul in the middle of the afternoon, and then crossed over into Minneapolis.

After a few minutes Christine said, "Wow. This is so beautiful, so green. I love all the

171

little lakes right in town."

"I was thinking of this as a place to stop. What would you think of spending the next three or four months here?"

"I don't know. Doesn't it get awfully cold?"

"Colder than you can imagine. But from now until September you're more likely to complain because it's hot and humid. The idea is to be someplace where nobody expects you to be and there are good doctors and hospitals during your pregnancy. Your due date is in September, right? We could leave here a few weeks after that, before winter sets in."

"Do you know the city?"

"Pretty well. I would sometimes stop here because a man who lived here used to sell me things."

"Like the one in New York?"

"This one was different. He was a fixer, a go-between. He knew people who would supply forged papers, but also cars with several sets of plates, or guns, or whatever else someone would pay for. You would come to him, and he would go to them."

"Is he still here?"

"No. He wasn't selective about the people he would deal with. Some of the people who came to him were pretty scary, so he lived

172

in a big old house on a hill overlooking a nice little park with a lake on it, and had bodyguards living with him who were even scarier than the customers. One of them killed him."

"That's awful."

"I can't say I was surprised. If you pay people to be willing to kill, then you're surrounded by people who are willing to kill for money. You have money. It's a built-in problem. But don't worry. He and his bodyguards have been gone for years."

"Are there a lot of people like that here?"

"There aren't a lot like that anywhere. One reason he set up his business here was that there wasn't a lot of crime. It kept him safe, it made his customers — some of whom were carrying a lot of cash — safe, and drew very little attention. And, as I said, they're all long gone."

"Is this where you would stay if it were you?"

"The right place for you depends on lots of things. Settling in an apartment in a quiet neighborhood anywhere is better than being on the run. Minneapolis is a place you've never been to before, right?"

"Yes."

"And it's not the sort of place a San Diego girl usually would pick, because it sounds

173

alien to people from Southern California."

"But is it the place you'd pick for yourself?"

"Probably not. I've been here too often. And it's not as much of a stretch of the imagination to see me living happily in a cold place. I've lived in this latitude, and I've seen winters. I can't say what city is the best for you, but I know this won't be the first place they'd look."

"I'll stay here."

Jane found them a hotel in Minneapolis. It wasn't as luxurious as the one in Madison, but it was a big hotel that was part of a chain, and it was comfortable. When the desk clerk asked how long they'd be staying, Jane said, "Five days." He said, "Tonight through . . ." and Jane answered, "Monday the first. We'll check out on the second." She bought a newspaper on the way to their hotel room.

When they were in the new room, Jane took out the classified section and began circling the ads for apartments. Christine stood behind her for a few seconds, looking over her shoulder.

"Uh . . . Jane?"

"Hmmm?"

"Those are all expensive. I never had very much money, and I spent a lot of what I

174

had just finding my way to you in Buffalo. I have to get a cheap one I can pay for when I find a job."

Jane didn't look up. "Don't think about that."

"But I have to."

"Surely you must realize that when people come to me, most of them haven't had time to plan ahead and save up for the trip. Some don't have time to pack, and some don't even have time to dress."

"Like me."

"Like you. I'll get you what you need."

"How do I pay you back? And what about your fee?"

Jane closed the section of newspaper and looked into Christine's eyes. "I don't charge a fee for helping someone who's in mortal danger, or for anything else. I'm doing this for the reasons I've always done it — because it's what you need, and because I can. When I think you're safe, I'll go home. I won't communicate with you again, and you should forget about me unless you think you've been found."

"Can't I send you something later? I want to."

"No. Sending me anything would only give your enemies one extra chance to trace you, and endanger me, too. When I started doing this, sometimes people I had helped sent me presents — birth certificates, guns, money — mostly money. In a few cases it was a lot of money. I never used much of it, so it grew. So now the fund I've always kept for travel has grown big enough to make me uncomfortable. You're my last runner. I won't be needing it for somebody who shows up at my door next week."

"Then what can I do for you?"

Jane shrugged. "You've come along too late for that. There's not much that you can do that will help me. I would like you to concentrate for the moment on being safe and having a nice life. That would mean my effort didn't go to waste. Then someday, do something for somebody else."

"You mean some innocent victim. That's who you've helped, right?"

"Not everyone who wants to disappear is a victim, and very few are innocent. All I can say is none of them deserved to die." She opened the classified ads again to signify that the topic was closed.

She didn't have enough patience to try to explain to Christine the proper way to think about money. Among the old people, a person's status had never been determined by how much wealth he could accumulate, but how much he brought back to give away. The way that the first white visitors learned to identify the most powerful Seneca leaders was to look for the men who seemed to be poorest.

Christine whispered, "Damn." She got up and began to walk toward the bathroom.

"What's wrong?"

Before she closed the door she said, "Morning sickness. And this time it's not even morning."

9

Linda Welles moved into one of the two front apartments on the second floor of a nearly new building that had eight units. Christine was now getting used to calling herself Linda Welles, because she'd had to use the name so many times. Jane had needed to take her to a bank to open an account before she could write a check for the security deposit and two months' rent. Jane presented herself as Linda's sister, who was helping her get settled. The bank gave Linda a debit card and a pile of brochures about mortgages, car loans, and other services.

They bought a few pieces of furniture and a television set and arranged to have them delivered on the first of the month. Jane was very patient as Linda chose pictures, rugs, sheets and blankets, and other furnishings because she knew that those things would help make the apartment feel good to her. Jane had done all of this many times before, and she allocated days for each of the tasks they had to complete.

There was one day to find a car for Linda. Jane picked out a four-year-old Volkswagen Passat station wagon. "This is just about right. You don't want a new car. The people who are looking for you will expect a rental, and they're all new. This has the look of something you've been driving a while, which is good. We'll take it to a glass shop and have the side windows tinted a bit so you're hard to see from outside."

There was another day to shop at the Mall of America for clothes and incidentals for Linda and the baby. That was harder for Jane, but she was careful to keep it from Linda. Jane made sure that the pregnancy clothes would be big enough for the final months. She also made sure that Linda picked out fashionable clothes that would fit after the baby was born. If Linda could keep herself optimistic and cheerful, she would have a better chance.

They spent another morning finding baby furniture and accessories, and an afternoon assembling the crib and the changing table in the spare bedroom of the new apartment. In the evening Jane came out of the spare room with a bag.

"What's in the bag?"

"Women's magazines."

"That's nice."

"It's another chore. I want you to look at the pictures of models in these. You want a hairstyle that's different from the one you have now. Pick one out. When you've found one, we're going to take the magazines with us to a good stylist, and get your hair done."

"Do you really think that's necessary?"

"Any change is helpful. I know they got photographs of you from Richard Beale. We don't want them to be able to show the pictures to people, say, 'Have you seen this girl?' and find you. Anything you can do that will make you different from the girl you were could save you. Normally, I would want you to dye your hair, too, but I'm not sure the chemicals are a good idea for a pregnant woman. Pick a style you like, or you won't be able to stand it for long."

"Okay." Linda took the magazines and began to look through them. After a few minutes of browsing, she said, "This is actually sort of fun. What will Linda Welles look like? A hippo, of course, but maybe a stunning hippo."

"Not stunning, please. Elegant, stylish, cute, or fetching. The hippo thing only lasts a couple of months, and then it's back to gazelle. And one more thing. Do you have perfect vision?"

"It's my one perfect feature."

"Then while we're out tomorrow, we'll get you some nice glasses. You'll want a pair of sunglasses that are big and dark to change the shape of your face when you're out. We'll need a second pair with a lighter shade, probably brownish. You'll also want some that are clear, so you can wear them in places like movie theaters and grocery stores."

"Ugh."

"I'm giving you the means to be safe. When I'm gone, you'll decide which ones you can tolerate in which situations."

"Are you getting sick of me?"

"Not yet," said Jane. "You're actually growing on me."

"Very funny."

"That's another thing. We've got to start shopping for an ob-gyn for you. We need one who works out of a hospital in this part of town."

"I could call the office of my doctor in San Diego and ask him for a referral."

Jane looked at her, shocked. She was so young. "Bad idea. Before we do this, we'd better do some preparing. First we have to get you some new health insurance as Linda Welles. You're young enough so we can probably say you haven't had a job with health benefits yet, and that this is your first policy. Then we'll go for your first checkup."

"Why can't I call my doctor in San Diego? I'd just ask for a name."

"Any time you get in touch with anybody from your past life, you give the hunters another way to find you. You can't ask for doctors in Minneapolis without someone making a note on your file that you moved to Minneapolis. Nothing that happens in a doctor's office is supposed to be public information, but there are a million ways to get it. No place where there are physical files or computer records is safe from people who are willing to break in."

"They don't know the name of my doctor in San Diego. While I was there I never told anybody but Sharon I was pregnant."

"But Richard knows. Even if some doctor's bills haven't come to your house by now, Richard is your employer. I'm sure he can get the insurance company to list the payments they've made to doctors and figure out which ones are yours. It's likely that his people have already begun to check your medical records. They'll be waiting for you to go to another doctor somewhere. Let me handle this part. I'll get started on it today, with the insurance."

That afternoon Jane made a telephone call and arranged to add an employee named Linda Welles to a group health insurance contract for one of the imaginary companies she had incorporated years before. When she had first started giving runners new identities, she had found it useful to create corporations that could produce work histories and references for them. After that she had found more and more uses for the shadow companies. She could make purchases with a certain amount of anonymity just by reciting account numbers over a telephone. After the insurance was arranged, she began the search for a doctor to oversee Linda Welles's pregnancy and deliver the baby.

While Jane concentrated on getting Linda Welles settled, she instituted new routines. Every morning Jane got up early, put on a sweatshirt, shorts, and running shoes, and went for a run before the sun came up. She would begin by running the streets and parking lots of the apartment complex. During the first two mornings she memorized the cars that belonged to the tenants along the nearby streets, and each morning after that, as she ran, she watched for ones that didn't belong. When she had been through the complex she ran along the street beyond the entrance, and then returned to Linda Welles's apartment. She stood barefoot on the carpet in the spare room and went through the ordered poses of tai chi.

One morning Linda was up early enough to watch her. "That's tai chi, right? They're all animals, aren't they?"

"They're stances that each animal uses when it fights."

"Why do you do it?"

"It makes me feel good. It keeps me flexible, improves my balance and coordination." Jane smiled. "It makes me easier to get along with. I can start teaching you a little, if you want."

"Not today," Linda said. "Where did you learn to fight?"

"By fighting."

"Before that. You've had training."

"I learned tai chi in a class about twenty years ago. I've been running since I was a kid. I was on the track team. But I wanted something different that kept me flexible and strengthened my upper body. Later on, I took a man out of the world who happened to be a black belt in aikido. He was being hunted hard, so I had to stay with him for several months to make him safe and teach him how to be the person he was going to be. You're a young girl, so you don't have to account for much time. Most people you meet will just assume you've been in school from the time you were five until now. It's much harder for a middle-aged man. He has to account for twenty or thirty years of history beyond that — jobs, wives, hobbies, friends and relatives, education, experiences. That's tricky. He has to account for what he knows, but also pretend he doesn't know certain things, or people will figure out where he must have come from. We used to have long talks. I would ask him to tell me stories about his imaginary life, and I'd try to pick holes in them. When we got tired of that, he would teach me aikido for five or six hours a day."

"You must have done more than that. I saw you fight."

"Not exactly. You saw me not-fight. This is fighting." She pretended to deliver a series of punches and kicks that were so fast that Linda could barely follow the movements. "That's karate, of course. That's called a kata, and it's a set routine you can go into in a certain situation. You work on a kata until you can do it correctly. Then you practice it in exactly the same way a few thousand times. After two thousand you can usually perform the movements well enough. Another two thousand times and

185

you have it ingrained deeply enough so you might think to use it if you were attacked. After you've done it many more times, you can do it very fast. It takes two-tenths of a second for the eye to receive and transmit an image to the brain and the brain to interpret it. If you can deliver a punch or a kick faster than two-tenths of a second, then you can hit an opponent before he sees the blow coming."

"That's what you did that night. Why do you call it not-fighting?"

"I broke his knee before a fight could start, and then I ran away."

"But you could fight."

"Only because he didn't think I could. He thought I couldn't hurt him, so he didn't pay enough attention to me, or protect himself. There was a huge difference between us. No matter how much work I do, or how much I learn, I'm never going to be as strong as even the average out-of-shape man. He has at least seventy or eighty pounds on me, a lot of it muscle. I have to attack very fast, fight very dirty, and get back where he can't reach me. I can't stand around hitting him and letting him hit me. If he lands one good punch he'll break bones."

"But you beat him."

"No, I tricked him. That man saw the two of us, and what he was seeing was like a pair of little pussycats. You can go up to a hundred cats, one after the other, and they're all perfectly docile. Then you meet that one that looks the same, but suddenly it has its claws digging into your arm to hold on while it sinks its teeth all the way into your hand. That's me. I'm the one that bites."

"That's what I want to be," said Linda. "I want to be able to fight back."

"You don't want to fight," said Jane. "You want what I want, which is to get away."

"I guess that's true."

"I was planning on helping you with that. We'll start tomorrow after the appointment at the doctor's office."

The next day was cooler but bright and clear, with a breeze that seemed to Jane to be an early summer treat before the humidity set in. Jane drove Linda along East River Parkway to the edge of the University of Minnesota campus. When she reached Harvard Street she turned left and pointed at the big building that dominated the area. "That's it."

"That's what?"

"The hospital. The Fairview-University Medical Center."

"It's big. And impersonal."

"Two wonderful qualities that we really want right now."

"I was thinking of maybe a small, private kind of place where everybody knows me and stuff."

"I know this seems as though it ought to be about your preferences, but it isn't. When you're having a baby, you've got to prepare for the possibility that things are not going to go smoothly. If they don't, the place you want to be is a big urban hospital with lots of really good surgeons and pediatricians and specialists and fancy equipment and superbly trained staff. We'll go in and interview Dr. Molinari. If you don't love him, we'll keep looking."

Jane drove up Harvard Street until she came to the parking structure for the hospital. They parked and walked to the main building, then rode the elevator up with a pretty woman about thirty years old who looked about six months pregnant. The woman said to Linda, "When are you due?"

Linda shrugged. "Early fall. Late September, early October."

The woman said, "Are you with Dr. Kwan?"

"Molinari."

Jane stood with a fixed smile on her face.

The woman craned her neck to look across her at Linda as though she were some obstacle like a piece of furniture. Even the way the woman held herself when she spoke, leaning close to Linda, made it clear she was speaking only to Linda. The elevator door opened, and Jane led the way down the hall to Dr. Molinari's office.

Inside the waiting room, Jane saw that there were five women in various stages of pregnancy waiting for Dr. Molinari or one of his partners. While Jane waited, she found herself studying them, wondering what made it so easy for them to conceive, when it didn't seem to be possible for her. Had she simply waited too long? That didn't seem to be it. Two of them were about Linda's age, but the other three looked older than Jane. As the nurse came to the doorway and called them, one by one, to go back to the examining rooms with her, Jane watched them and compared her body to theirs. Maybe it was all the exercise she had done for the past twenty years, the running and martial arts. Maybe the stress on her body had stimulated some receptor, released some unnoticed chemical, that told the body not to reproduce. There were all of those teenaged gymnasts who never got their periods. Maybe —

"Linda Welles?"

After they had met with Dr. Molinari, Linda Welles decided he was the one. She officially selected him as her doctor, and made her first set of appointments.

When they got to the car, Linda said, "Now we're done with doctors for today. Can you show me some self-defense moves?"

Jane nodded. "I'll show you something that will work for you." Jane drove them out of the city into the nearly flat, empty land to the north. When they had driven for about an hour, she slowed down, looking for a particular spot. Finally, she turned off the road and guided the car along a barely visible unpaved road consisting of a pair of tire tracks winding through a forest of second-growth trees. She stopped in a place that looked as though it had been used as a turnaround. "This ought to be the right sort of place."

"For what?"

Jane pulled the car around so it was facing out again, then turned off the engine. She picked up her purse, opened it, and took out a small snub-nosed revolver.

Linda gasped, "Oh, my God. A gun?"

Jane swung out the cylinder, showed Linda that it was empty, and closed it again.

"Where did it come from?"

"When we stopped at the house in Amherst, this is one of the things I picked up. When I go, I'll leave it with you. It's a tricky thing to have a gun in the house at the best of times. When you expect to have a curious baby crawling around, it definitely has to be both locked up and well hidden. I have mixed feelings about doing this, but I don't see any other way for you to be safe."

"You don't? I thought you would teach me something from martial arts."

"You're pregnant. Even if you weren't, it takes years of practice to learn enough to do you any good at all. Ninety-nine percent of the time, all the practice does for a woman is to make her think she can stand her ground against some male attacker who takes her apart in a second. This works."

"But I've never even fired a gun. And I heard experts on TV say having one is more dangerous than not having one."

"The only experts whose opinions mean much are cops. Every cop in the country has one strapped to him right this minute."

Christine looked at the gun warily. "What do I do with it?"

"We'll buy you a purse that has a center compartment, and you'll keep it there, where you can reach it instantly, but you can also open the other parts of your purse without showing it."

"But how do I use it?"

"That's why we drove way out here. Come on." Jane got out of the car and set off into the woods. "This used to be a farm once. Now it's part of a huge piece of land that's been put together. The Manitou Paper Company owns all of it. Nobody lives around here anymore."

When they had walked far into the woods, they came to a clearing. It looked like a meadow, but the ground was too soft and swampy to walk on. "Stay here." Jane skirted the meadow, walking among the exposed roots of trees. She picked a tree twenty-five feet from Linda, took a white handkerchief from her purse, and hung it on a pair of thorny twigs. Then she made her way back.

Jane stood beside Linda, and opened the cylinder of the gun. "Notice how I open the cylinder. The barrel is away from us, pointed down at the dirt. I don't have a finger inside the trigger guard."

She took a box of bullets out of her purse. "Here. Hold this. It's .38 caliber ammunition. It's what police used to use in most towns until nine millimeter automatics became popular. This load is a little hotter than I would have chosen for you, but people send things to me with the idea that I'll be the one to use them. If you ever fire at anybody, you'll wish it were more powerful." Jane began to load the gun.

"If I lose it or something, will the police trace it to you?"

"No. This one was part of the inventory of a gun dealer who died. Before his death was reported, his suppliers were all paid in full, and a lot of guns and the records that came with them disappeared mysteriously. If somebody asks you, this one was in a trunk you bought at a garage sale in Oregon."

Jane closed the cylinder, stepped to the side, and aimed the gun with a two-hand stance. "This is probably the easiest for you. Shooting a pistol is like pointing a finger. Holding it with two hands doesn't change that. You point, line up the sights on the target. You don't close one eye. Then you squeeze the trigger so the barrel doesn't get dragged off target. This is a double action, so pulling the trigger cocks and fires." She handed Linda the gun. "Do what I did, but don't pull the trigger."

Linda assumed a stance, and Jane adjusted her limbs to make it right. "Your arms should be out ahead a bit more, and your knees flexed, not locked. If you're aiming that at somebody, he's going to want to be moving, so you may have to move, too. Open your other eye, Linda."

"Sorry."

"You're fighting for your life. You can't afford to lose depth perception or peripheral vision. You're not going to be firing at something a hundred feet away. You'll be fifteen at the outside."

"It feels weird to me."

"It won't if you get used to doing it right. Now, some preparation. It's going to be much louder than you expect. There will be a bit of a kick that will make the gun jump back a little, and the natural tendency is for the barrel to jerk upward. Be ready for it by keeping a good, firm grip on it so you don't drop it. Instead, you want to bring it back down to aim again. Can you remember all that?"

"I think so."

"Then hand me the gun, but keep it aimed downrange." Jane took the gun. Then she handed Linda a set of earplugs. "I picked these up for us at the drugstore. The best would have been to get real ear protectors that look like earphones, but these will do." She put hers into her ears and waited for Linda. "Now I'm going to fire one round, so you can see what I mean."

She aimed and there was a sharp bang,

and the handkerchief jumped.

"You were right. That was loud."

"It's worse in an enclosed space. Your turn."

Linda took the gun and assumed the stance. Jane stood beside her and watched to be sure she was doing it right. "Any time you're ready."

Linda fired. The gun jumped up and she winced, then leveled it.

"Again."

She fired once more.

"Again."

This time the handkerchief puffed backward as another hole appeared in the thin white linen. She aimed again.

"How many rounds are left?" Jane asked.

"Two."

"Good. Fire again."

The handkerchief jumped and fluttered downward toward the foot of the tree, but caught on a small branch jutting from the trunk. "There's one left."

"Then fire it."

Linda fired. She was controlling the recoil better, not flinching at the sound, and she appeared to be holding the gun with more comfort and confidence. She lowered the gun and held it out to Jane, the barrel pointed away from them.

"Want some more practice?"

"Yes."

"Then you load it this time."

Jane held the box while Linda opened the cylinder, poured out the brass casings, pushed in another six rounds, and closed it. Jane said, "Hold your fire. I'm going to walk to the tree and put my poor handkerchief up again."

"Okay."

While she went to the tree and returned, Jane watched the way Linda handled the gun. She was careful, she was alert, and she was getting more comfortable. Jane said, "All right. Fire when you're ready."

Linda fired the next six rounds, hitting the handkerchief each time.

Jane said, "You seem to be getting the idea. Do you think you can do that if you have to?"

"I can fire the gun. I don't know about shooting a person."

"That means we're done, I think. I don't have another handkerchief." She scooped up the empty casings at their feet, counted them, and then retrieved the shredded handkerchief. "This wasn't much of an introduction. I just wanted you to be able to load and fire in an emergency. People practice for a lifetime and still keep learning things. What I want you to do when we get back is go through your apartment with the lights on and again with the lights off, figuring out exactly what you would do in an emergency — where you would take a firing position, what you would be able to see from there, what you wouldn't be able to see. Where you would retreat from there. Everything you know and don't have to spend time deciding will help."

As they walked back to the car, Jane suddenly bent down in a clearing, and began picking leaves from a vine with red berries on it that ran along the ground.

"What are you doing?"

"This is partridgeberry. I didn't know it grew this far west. But of course it would."

"But what are you going to do with it?"

"The berries are full of seeds, and they don't taste like much. But you boil the leaves in a little water and make a tea out of it. It's a cure for morning sickness. The old people say it even helps make childbirth easier later on."

"Are you sure it's safe?"

"If you're worried, I'll drink it first. You can watch me for a day and then try it." Jane picked a pound or more of the leaves, then put them in the trunk of the car. "You'll thank me for this."

They drove back to the city. On the way they stopped at a grocery store and replenished the supply of staples and picked up lots of extra food that Linda particularly liked. Jane used a plastic bag from the store to hold the partridgeberry leaves, then loaded the car trunk with groceries. While they were driving back toward the apartment, Linda said, "You're getting ready to leave, aren't you?"

"Yes."

"When?"

"When everything I can do here is done."

The next morning Linda had her first dose of partridgeberry tea, and her last day of morning sickness. Over the next few days they filled the cupboards with canned and preserved food. They went to bookstores and bought pregnancy and child-care books, magazines and novels. The health insurance card in the name Linda Welles arrived, and they went to the doctor for Linda's next checkup.

One morning, when Linda woke, Jane was sitting in the living room with her suitcase packed. "It's today?"

"I think it's time," Jane said. "You're Linda Welles now. Your identity has held up, and you've been out of sight for a couple of weeks. You're in a safe place with just about everything you'll need, and you've got a car with Minnesota plates. Your neighbors are used to you already. It's up to you now."

"I'm scared to do this without you."

"Don't be. All you have to do is live quietly, take care of yourself, and let the time go by. Do exactly what your doctor says. And don't worry. I'll be back near the end of the summer to help you get everything ready for the baby."

Linda looked relieved. She put her arms around Jane and hugged her, holding on for a few seconds before she let go. She wiped her tears with the back of her hand. "Thank you, Jane. I'll see you then."

Jane went out, and looked carefully at everything she could see, trying to sense anything that might be out of order. She got into the rental car, then drove around the apartment complex once before she went up the long drive to the main street and turned right to find the entrance to the long highway.

10

Richard Beale had lived in San Diego all his life, but he didn't like the Pacific Ocean. His father had been wasting money on boats since before Richard was born, and this was just the latest boat, maybe the fifth one named after his mother. This one was fifty-eight feet long, all gleaming white hull and deck. The steps and rails and benches and roofs were all outlandish molded fiberglass in soft streamlined shapes, so it looked as though they had melted in the sun and begun to smear. The sun was another thing. Where the hell was the June gloom — the cloud cover that was supposed to make this time of the year dark? The sunlight this morning was the cruel, sharp kind that usually came during full summer. It seemed to always be at the worst angle for the whole day, so no matter where you looked it was in your eyes or bouncing back into them from something like the glass and steel on this big white boat. Even the surface chop of the ocean was full of mirror surfaces that popped up and were swallowed again in their millions, throwing a dancing glare into his eyes.

The monotonous thrum of the two enormous engines below the deck made him feel tired and irritated, and the repeated rise and fall of the boat on the long Pacific swells brought back dozens of episodes of motion sickness. Each time was exacerbated by his expert nonseaman's knowledge of every aspect of seasickness — exactly how bad it was so far, how long it would take to get worse under these specific conditions, at what point he would begin to fear the nausea would lead to vomiting, and how long after that he would accept his fate, surrender to it, and finally welcome it. He stood near the stern and stared back at the harbor.

"Richie."

Ruby Beale's voice was still high and a little screechy when she was straining it, but it had a gravelly unevenness that a lot of old smokers got. Richard turned and looked up the steps toward the flying bridge. That was what they called it: flying. When the ocean was choppy it felt up there as though the boat were trying to fling everyone off it. She was holding on to both railings at the top, her cigarette hanging at the corner of her lip. She was wearing a brightly flowered orange one-piece bathing suit with a voluminous pair of shorts over it, leaving the flabby white flesh of her arms and calves a feast for the sun.

"What, Ma?"

"Come up here."

"Why don't you come down? I like it down here." It wasn't true. He hated it down here, but at least he didn't feel as though he was about to be catapulted into the sea.

"Your father wants to talk to you."

He muttered, "Oh, shit." That was what he had been dreading. When he had arrived at the marina this morning, he had seen that flinty look in his father's blue-gray eyes. He had hoped the expression was just because it was a bit after six in the morning and the old man was still gruff from being up so early, but even then he had known it wasn't. The old man had told Richard to be there by five-thirty. It had always struck Richard as insane that people always went fishing at that hour. He could understand if they had been on their way to a tiny trout stream in the mountains, but how could anybody think the sort of fish that swam in the

Pacific Ocean — half of them a mile below the surface and as big as a truck — would be so picky they cared what time it was?

But Andrew Beale was the sort of man who attached moral values to his own preferences. Men who were worth anything were on deck before the sun's rays touched it, their goddamned gear stowed and ready to cast off the lines. When Richard had roared into the marina parking lot in his Porsche Carrera at six-twenty-five, he had known his father would be less than cordial. As he was stepping cautiously along the little gangplank, he had heard his father saying something to his mother about leaving him on the dock.

Richard tested the lowest step to the bridge, and felt slightly relieved. The darker strip on each step was a substance like sandpaper that kept his foot from slipping, and the double railings on this boat were thicker and more substantial than they'd been on the last one. He fought the rocking of the boat by gripping the rails hard as he climbed, so by the time he was aloft and taking his first step onto the bridge, he felt as though he'd been lifting weights.

His father was at the wheel, staring through the huge windshield at the feature-less, changeless ocean as though he could see something ahead that was invisible to Richard. At least the sound of the engines was quieter up here. Andy Beale was a man who looked as though he were made of blocks — big head with a neck invisible from behind, square shoulders in his starched white shirt with epaulets, short khaki pants. He was wearing his old navy blue USS *Constance Kerr* cap. He glared over his shoulder at Richard to see that he had arrived, but he let him wait.

After a couple of long minutes, Richard said, "What's up, Dad?"

"Want to take the helm?"

"No, thanks."

"Suit yourself." The old man throttled back a bit, so the big yacht slowed, and the side-to-side motion became more pronounced. "I've been thinking of talking to you for some time now."

"What about?"

"I'm sure you're smart enough to know that your mother and I keep an eye on you. Just because we might not be actively in your business at any given time doesn't mean we don't know what it is."

"What is it?"

"For months we've been wondering why you haven't seen fit to mention to us that your girlfriend was pregnant."

"What girlfriend?"

"All right. Your secretary, then. Whatever the hell she is to you. Christine. She's sort of a cute little thing, and people tell me she isn't stupid. A bit on the young side for a thirty-eight-year-old man, but that could pay off later. When you're my age, you'd have a woman who was still on the young side for you. Your mother has been trying to think of a way to do a party for you, complete with presents and so on. But she couldn't get very far with that, because you haven't told us. So I'm forced to ask."

Richard Beale felt even sicker. He could see that his father had reverted to his military personality again. His father was still a marvel to him. At various points in Richard's life he had been prompted to ask himself what the hell the navy did to people in four short years to change them so much. His father had been an Oklahoma farm boy until he went in the navy, and he had come out like this, and stayed this way for forty years. Richard knew he had to say something. "Oh, I don't know. I guess I didn't feel ready to start all of that in motion. I don't want any parties or fuss, at least until I know if this is going to work out."

"Seems a little late for that kind of wondering, doesn't it? If you weren't prepared to make a decision about her, maybe you should have kept it in your pants."

"I don't mean that."

"Not that we weren't pleased. Your mother has been running around with a pen and a special notebook writing down things for the wedding. She hasn't even finished figuring out the lists for the engagement party yet, but she has to make some moves to streamline this whole process so the bride won't be too obviously far along at the wedding. I haven't seen her this happy in twenty years."

Was the boat just drifting and rolling with the swells? Richard kept feeling worse. "Look, Dad. I've been trying to protect Mother from getting all excited and then being disappointed later, and you, too. I don't know how you found out Christine was pregnant. She didn't actually come out and tell even me."

"That's not good," said Andy Beale.

"How *did* you find out?"

"If I had wanted you to know that, I'd have told you. And for weeks, the mistake I thought you were making was trying to keep this to yourself and then springing it on your mother too late. But I guess you were making a different kind of mistake. With you, it's always some kind of mistake."

"That's not fair."

"Pah!" Andy Beale spat out something that was almost a laugh, but carried no happiness. "What I told you four years ago hasn't changed, Richard. I was the one who started this life with nothing but a pair of calloused hands and a reasonably serviceable brain. When the navy sent me here, they sent a million other guys here, too. I was one of the ones who had his eyes and ears open. I could see that lots of those guys were from cold, hard, barren places. Once they'd been here, they were going to come back. Hell, that's been going on since World War Two. That's why there is a San Diego. Some of us were willing to take risks and work hard. I bought my first duplex apartment by working two jobs before your mother and I were even married. I saved the rent on that one to put a down payment on another, and used your mother's savings from her nurse job to buy the third. I never looked back. We both worked for other people until we were over fifty while we were doing real estate deals at night and showing rentals to prospective tenants on our lunch hours. You get to be a big shot and tool around in a Porsche at twice the speed limit and live in a house like a palace and make million-dollar deals all day. But you'd do well to remember that none of it is yours. I let you get used to all of it because I'm not going to live forever, and I need somebody who knows how to run it after I can't. I didn't want you to inherit it at the age of fifty or sixty and know so little that you let somebody take it away from you."

"I know, Dad, and I'm grateful. I've always been grateful. I don't say it often, because I know you wouldn't think much of me if I followed you around all day saying how grateful I am."

"No, I wouldn't. But there are certain things that you are required to do, and you've known that from the beginning. Your mother wants grandchildren. Sometimes I think that's all that keeps her interested in staying alive. She's waiting to see them and spoil them. I want grandchildren, too. All the work and sacrifice and agony I went through to make something of this family is going to be thrown away and wasted if there are no more Beales to make use of it. I didn't do all that — work eighteen or nineteen hours a day, leveraging everything I had on each new deal over and over again — just so you can live this bachelor existence, screwing around until you're eighty, and then die and have everything I built confiscated by the fucking State of California. I want heirs, and I want the first one this year."

"Dad, if you know about Christine, you must realize that I'm trying to do what you expect of me."

"It's about time. I was pretty much convinced that you were gay, and she was just around to type and pick up your clothes at the cleaner's."

"So now you know I'm not gay."

"Yeah, yeah. You like girls. It's an enormous accomplishment. Now I want you to see something." He reached into the rack where the nautical maps were stowed, and pulled out a long white envelope with a string-tie closing at one end.

"If that's your will, you showed it to me when we talked about this four years ago. If I don't have a child before you die, then the money goes to the cousins. How could I forget?"

"I changed it again. This is a new one, and there are copies with people I trust all over the country, so don't even think about waiting until I die and tearing it up. It can't happen." He held out the white envelope.

Richard Beale had been up on the bridge too long. He was in a bad state of seasickness brought on by the slower speed, which had permitted some of the diesel exhaust to find its way up here. He waved the envelope away. "Why don't you just tell me what it says?"

His father shook his head in a gesture of disdain for people who had no sea legs. "All right. It says that when your first child is born, you get a one-tenth share of every-thing — the business, the property hold-ings, the bank balances." He lifted his eyes from the will and glared at Richard. "That was going to be the first of your presents that we had intended to reveal at the engage-ment party. I can see you know there's more coming. You're waiting for that. You're right. We waited and waited for you to share your news with us, until I got a bad feeling about it, so I added something. You've got until the end of this year."

"What do you mean?"

"We figure this baby, our grandchild, is going to be born around September or October. Is that right?"

"I don't know. Yeah, I guess so. The fall, anyway."

"Then you'd better make it work. If I don't have a grandchild by the end of this year, I give up on you."

"What?"

"You heard me."

"What does it mean? That if I don't hand

you this baby by New Year's Day, I don't inherit anything when you die?"

"That's part of it. You'll also be out of the company on January 2. I'll pick somebody else to run it for me. You can go off on your own and work with what you've got, and maybe grow up and make something of yourself, or maybe not. Either way, you will have blown the opportunity you got by being born."

"You didn't say this before. It's June. If Christine doesn't work out, I don't have time to father another baby by the end of December. This is completely unfair."

"You think I got what I have by being fair to the guy on the other side of the table?"

"But this is one twenty-year-old girl. Sometimes relationships don't last. Maybe she doesn't want to marry me. Maybe she'll abort the baby."

"If she was going to, she would have. She's almost six months."

Richard was feeling worse. He couldn't meet the old man's eyes, but when he looked out the window to the side of the bridge, all he saw was the sea, then the sky, then the sea again. How did the old man know the exact moment of conception? "Then she might give it up for adoption. She always said she wants to go to college."

"Have her give the baby to you then — to us. I'll settle for a second chance to raise an heir with some sense of duty. I'll give the girl the cost of four-years' tuition and living expenses in exchange for the baby. More, even. You can keep screwing around and playing with cars, and keep being caretaker of the business until the kid is ready to take over."

"Why are you suddenly in such a rush? This doesn't have to be the only chance for a grandchild. There are millions of other girls out there who might work out."

"This is the only one you knocked up."

Richard, in his nauseated state, almost protested that it wasn't, but caught the words before he ruined himself. "What I'm trying to tell you is that I want to do what's expected, but this isn't a situation where I have absolute control."

"Then take control, for Christ's sake. Be a man. As you just said, she's a twenty-year-old kid who's pregnant. She liked you well enough to let you get her that way. She's young, she's alone, she's probably broke. How hard can it be to persuade her to marry you?"

"Hard."

"Christ. You want me to talk to her? Or your mother? She's another woman, and if she tells the girl how welcome she would be, that ought to do it."

"In this case it wouldn't. Let me handle this myself."

Andy Beale's sharp eyes stayed on Richard's for a moment. "All right. Do it."

"Are we done?"

"Yeah. You can go down and puke now. I'll head back to the harbor and let you off so your mother and I can get back out here in time to fish a little."

Richard Beale walked off the dock, stood in the parking lot, and watched as the *Ruby B.* slowly turned its fat stern toward him and began chugging back out of the harbor. He could see his father was feathering the throttle, trying to bring it up beyond the speed limit of the harbor without getting caught by the patrol. The boat sent waves spreading from its wake to rock the rows of boats tied in their berths, and make them buck and strain against their lines and shoulder into the bumpers, trying to break loose.

He stood on solid, unmoving asphalt and watched for ten minutes, long after the *Ruby B.* was out of his sight. He took deep, regular breaths to settle his stomach and get rid of the smothered, choking feeling. When he felt like less of an emergency case, he took out his phone and punched in Steve Demming's number, then changed his mind and deleted it.

Richard dialed Sybil Landreau instead. He knew that calling one of the women instead of Steve Demming and Pete Tilton wasn't terribly subtle, but he didn't want to be subtle. He hoped the bastards were shocked enough to begin worrying about their reputations. That was what people like them lived on. They couldn't put an ad on Channel 10.

"Yes?" said Sybil's voice.

"It's me," he said. "I'm calling to find out what's going on."

"Hold on. I'll give you to Steve."

"No!" He realized too late that he was shouting. He looked around to see if anyone in the parking lot was near enough to have noticed. "Don't hand me to anybody. I want to talk to you. Are you still there?"

She said, "Yes."

"Then you tell me. Do you have her?"

"Not yet."

"That means no."

"It means we're working on it, and that we will have her, but it takes more time than this. We're doing all the right things. It just hasn't happened yet."

214

"Wow," he said. "Wow. You're a bigger bullshit artist than Demming."

"I'm a woman. I'm verbal. You want to talk to him now, or do you want to flirt some more?"

"Talk to him. But I want all four of you individually to know that I'm not a happy client. This should have been done the first night, when she was in Buffalo, which is — what? — three weeks ago?"

"I'll give you to Steve."

He heard Steve Demming's voice, and he could detect the irritation in it. "Yes?"

"It's me. I'm calling to find out what's the matter. I expected to see her back here three weeks ago."

"Richard. You know we're on this, and we're doing the best job possible. This isn't a time to start losing faith and insulting each other."

"There were six of you to one of her. I gave you her phone's Global Positioning locator so you knew exactly where she was at every second."

"It's not six to one. You know this. She met up with a pro the very first night we were on this. They managed to slip her phone into the back of a truck on the New York State Thruway. We caught up with the truck when it was almost to New Jersey. If

215

you want her phone back, I can give it to you. I just don't have the girl yet."

"Tell me about this pro. Who is she?"

"We don't know a lot about her yet. She's probably a private detective working as a bodyguard. A lot of women don't want a man protecting them. They want somebody who can go into the ladies' room with them. We think that Christine flew all the way to New York just to hook up with her. She took over that night at the hospital, and we haven't been able to catch up with them yet. We will."

"Come on. I don't believe this. How could Christine know anybody like that?"

"You wouldn't be the first one to think he's the only guy some chick knows, and be wrong. Somebody sent this woman to pick Christine up at the hospital. When we tried to keep her from driving her off in a car, she broke Ronnie Sebrot's knee. We had to drive him to a hospital seventy miles away in case the police knew somebody got hurt that way. He was in such pain he was screaming half the time."

"Jesus, that's awful."

"But we didn't give up. All the time we were still tracking her cell phone's signal. Late that night we blocked a road ahead of them, had two cars coming up behind them.

What does this woman do? She clips Carl McGinnis with her car and takes off. We couldn't leave him lying out there by the road waiting for the state troopers to find him, could we?"

"I guess not. But did you have to shoot him?"

"That again? Yes. We had to shoot him."

"Why?"

"The woman ran him down. He was hurt bad. We couldn't leave him there to suffer, and we couldn't take him in. He was in and out of consciousness and might have said just about anything on painkillers."

"It's unbelievable."

"We're not animals, Richard. The girls held his hand and talked to him, and never let on that we were even thinking about doing it. Claudia just waited until he lost consciousness for a second and shot him in the head. He never knew."

"I still can't believe this," said Richard. "It's awful." He was breathing hard through his open mouth. There didn't seem to be enough air. He felt as though he were falling — dizzy and faint.

"You're the one who wanted us to do this. Sometimes this is what it takes."

Richard lowered his voice to a raspy whisper, so he wouldn't be overheard. "But you killed somebody. It doesn't matter if it was your friend or not. If they connect us with this, we'll all go to jail for the rest of our lives."

"Richard. You hired us to kidnap a pregnant girl and bring her back to you, remember? What do you think the penalty is for that? Or for setting off a bomb in a hospital so she'd be evacuated and left in the open? Whatever we've done since then is just extra stuff they add on beyond your life sentence to make themselves look like hard-asses for the next election. The point is to not let them catch you and give you *any* sentence."

Richard Beale didn't answer. He was light-headed, but his stomach felt as though it contained a rock that was somehow expanding. He looked out across the parking lot at the boats bobbing beside their docks in the marina, but they only made him feel that the ground under him was moving, so he stared far past them at the line of the horizon.

"Are you still there?"

"I'm here."

"You have any other questions?"

"Not a question," Richard said. "I called you because this is getting critical. I need to have Christine back. She needs to be alive and not too beat up. Do you hear that?"

"Yes. Alive. That's what we've been doing. If we hadn't been trying to take her alive, we wouldn't have lost Ronnie and Carl. We're doing it."

"It matters a hell of a lot more than I thought. I need that baby. Christine has to be alive and healthy long enough to deliver that baby. You don't know the kind of pressure I'm under. It's got to happen as soon as possible."

"We're doing our best, but if I've got to be on the phone all day, well, what can I say?"

"Nothing. Go do it." Richard Beale slipped the phone into his pocket and took his eyes off the ocean, but it didn't help. His fate had been settled on his father's boat. Staring and heavy breathing had only made him dizzy. He walked with purposeful determination to a trash barrel at the side of the parking lot, grasped its rim where the plastic bag was fitted over it, bent at the waist, and succumbed.

11

Jane drove from Minneapolis to O'Hare International Airport to return the rental car. There was little chance the four hunters could know that the car existed, let alone trace it from the Buffalo airport to O'Hare. If they managed to trace it, they would only conclude that she and Christine had driven to Chicago and gotten on a plane.

She was at the airport before dawn, took the car rental agency shuttle to the terminal, and arrived at five-thirty A.M. when the crowds were thin for her flight to Austin, Texas. She had not been to Austin in several years, but she remembered it as the right kind of place for a few months from now, the time when Christine had the baby and stopped being Linda Welles. Austin was warm most of the time, and it had a lively atmosphere. Austin was the state capital and the home of the University of Texas. Big universities created whole communities around them like ripples spreading outward from a splash. There were large groups of unattached, interesting people, lots of night-life, music. There was no better place for providing cover for a woman of college age, particularly one who would arrive in the early fall, like thousands of others.

The airport required caution. O'Hare held dangers for Jane that had nothing to do with Christine Monahan. It was one of the big-gest airline hubs in the country, placed right in the center, and so it had always attracted lots of hunters — cops and bounty hunters watching for fugitives, criminals watching for victims, an array of professional search-ers trying to spot particular travelers. There might be men in the terminal who would remember her face if they saw it. As Jane moved through the lines waiting to get through security, she kept scanning the places where people could stand and watch the passengers. When Jane was through the security checks, she walked past her gate, sat in the waiting area two gates farther down the concourse with her back to the big window overlooking the flight line so the morning glare would be behind her, and studied the faces that came near enough to see. She saw nobody who struck her as a threat, so when her flight began boarding she walked slowly to her gate and stepped through the door into the short tunnel to the plane.

When the plane landed in Austin, she rented a car, checked into a hotel near the airport, and went out apartment hunting. This was a good time for doing it, when much of the campus population had left for the summer, and not all of the apartments had been rented for the fall. Jane's story was that she was planning to enter a graduate program at the university in the fall, but would be in Europe for most of the summer. She wanted to rent an apartment right away for herself and a roommate with a baby. She was willing to pay the rent for the rest of June, July, August, and September in advance so she could store her books and furniture until university classes began. The simplest arrangement, she said, was to put the apartment only in the name Cecilia Randazzo — her name — and she would sign the lease and be responsible for the cost.

Cecilia Randazzo didn't want to live in the sort of building that housed a lot of undergraduate students. They would be too noisy, stay up too late, have too many parties. She wanted an apartment in a complex that catered to married students in their late twenties and thirties, or families, if they were quiet and well behaved.

She found a very desirable three-bedroom apartment not far from the university. The manager was a native-born Texan in her fifties with perfect silver hair named Mrs. McGowan. She said, "Of course we'll try to be sure you're happy, dear. But every single one of our tenants is an imperfect, living human being, so once in a while they do make a peep or two." But Jane's feigned fussiness made her appear to be the ideal tenant, so Mrs. McGowan was eager to get her to sign a lease. The building was occupied, Mrs. McGowan assured her, almost entirely by junior faculty members, joined by a few very quiet graduate students. As Mrs. McGowan showed her the crown molding along the ceilings and the tiles in the bathrooms, Jane was looking at other features that mattered more — the thickness and solidity of the doors, the quality of the locks, the view of the front door from above, the line of sight that would allow a tenant to see who was in a car parked on the street in front of the building. There was a garage under the building with a steel grate that closed after a tenant's car entered, so nobody ever had to walk from a lot to the door in the dark. Jane was pleased, so she said she would consider the apartment.

She walked around the complex, then drove back once in the evening, once late at night, and once in the morning to see what the neighborhood was like. The area had none of the signs that would have worried her. There were no groups of young men on the street with nothing to do. There were no loud parties in the nearby buildings, no abandoned cars or unoccupied houses on the surrounding streets. The nearest stores were big supermarkets — there was a Winn-Dixie just a few blocks away — banks, or the sort of stores that attracted students — Gap, Abercrombie & Fitch, Banana Republic, Urban Outfitters. Another half mile on and there were a Target and a couple of office supply stores. And there were lots of women in evidence from early morning until fairly late in the evening. That was always an important sign. If a neighborhood wasn't safe, women were always the first ones to disappear.

Jane signed a lease as Cecilia Randazzo, and stayed a few more days in Austin. She had a fairly clear idea of the styles and colors that Christine liked, based on their shopping trips in Minneapolis, so she bought a few necessities. She hung curtains that would ensure Christine's privacy and make the apartment look occupied, then bought many of the same items she'd bought for the apartment in Minneapolis: a bed, a dresser, a crib and changing table, a dining table with four chairs, pots, pans, and silverware. She spent a day buying small appliances and a television set. Another day she went out and bought a couch, a couple of matching chairs, some bookcases and lamps. She didn't want Christine to arrive exhausted with a baby in her arms and find a place that was empty and inhospitable, but she didn't want to deny Christine the chance to personalize her apartment, so as soon as the place seemed comfortable, she stopped shopping.

She slept in the apartment for the next three nights to be sure she had not missed something, and ran in the early mornings to become familiar with the neighborhood, as she had in Minneapolis. She spent the rest of each day learning about the city — where Christine might find a job, places to take the baby, ways of getting around, and places to avoid. At the university she picked up brochures about admission and university employment. At the Chamber of Commerce she picked up more leaflets on local businesses and attractions. She stored everything in a box for Christine.

On each of the three evenings, Jane went out looking for trouble. She walked alone to restaurants and bars, movie theaters and clubs, trying to find the places where bad things happened to people. And at the end of each excursion she made a point of walking back to the apartment late at night, using herself as bait to bring out any danger she had not detected. When Jane had satisfied herself that she had done everything she could, she confirmed her return ticket from Austin to Chicago, and bought a new ticket for the trip from Chicago to New York City. It was time to make her way home.

Jane traveled carefully. She arrived at the Austin airport an hour before the flight with only a carry-on shoulder bag, went through the security checkpoint, found her gate, and waited in the nearest ladies' room until she heard an announcement that her flight to Chicago was boarding. Then she stepped across the concourse diagonally and onto the plane. She had chosen the identity of Rebecca Silverman for flying home, because it was one of the solid old identities she had grown herself, and she had not used it during her travels this year. The driver's license had been renewed twice, and the credit cards were nearly as old. She had been submerged and invisible for a month, but she was rising close to the surface again, where being noticed was dangerous.

She got off her plane in Chicago, then waited for her flight to New York. She studied faces without seeming to, picked out the places where she could wait without attracting attention. She never left the areas where only ticketed passengers were allowed, and where everyone had been through the metal detectors and sniffers. She knew that security systems weren't unbeatable, but they made it much more difficult for anyone who was watching for her to harm her when they met. As she made each step closer to Buffalo, she knew the likelihood increased that someone would be waiting. She had arranged to fly into New York City on a different airline, so if someone ever found out what flight she had taken, the record would only show that she'd boarded in Chicago. It wouldn't show that she had begun her trip in Austin, Texas.

When the plane had almost reached New York it was directed to go back and complete a big circle that took it as far as Syracuse before it was allowed to land at Kennedy. Jane was tired of being locked in an airplane, and when the seat belt sign went off, she was glad to stand up in the crowded aisle while she waited to step out into the accordion tunnel that had been joined to the plane.

When her turn came she walked along the tunnel in quick strides, feeling better as the crowd thinned out. She stepped into the terminal and time seemed to stop. The tall, bony man with dirty blond hair and skin that was roughened by a long-gone case of acne looked like Brent Ketter. Jane focused on the eyes, and saw that they were already focused on her, because he was recognizing her, too.

It was a nightmare she'd had so many times that it didn't seem quite real now. She looked away and kept walking at the same brisk pace with the other passengers who had been freed from the Chicago flight. She knew there was no chance he had missed her. He had been standing just to the side of the gate staring at each face as the passengers moved past him. The only advantage Jane might be able to salvage was to make him think she had not seen him. If he tried to stay far back out of her sight, it might buy her enough time to lose him.

She tried to remember what she knew about him from twelve years ago. For Ketter hunting people was a business, so he had never worked alone. Before he moved in on anyone, he would be sure he had the quarry outnumbered and at a disadvantage so he could make a safe capture. Tonight he would probably follow her at a distance while he used his cell phone to call the friend or two he had waiting outside. Ketter couldn't have a weapon in an airport, but whoever was waiting outside could.

Jane veered to her right toward the shops and paused near the bookstore, using its big windows as a mirror. He was there, fifty feet behind her, talking on the telephone. He closed the phone and started walking, and so did Jane.

After a moment she half-heard, half-felt his presence at her shoulder. She could feel his huffing breaths move her hair near her ear. "Hi, there." His voice was choked with glee, the muscles in his throat tight.

Jane was shocked. She had expected him to follow her, not take the risk of approaching her. She didn't look at him. "What do you want?"

"I knew it. I knew you were out again. I read that e-mail that was getting bounced around, and I asked myself, 'How the hell does a young girl like that stay invisible all this time?' and the answer came to me. She's got some professional help. And then the next e-mail said she was traveling with a dark-haired woman, and that clinched it."

Jane repeated, "What do you want?"

"Don't you even remember me? I'm Brent Ketter. I've got eighteen inches of knife scar on my chest and belly to remember you by."

"You should be more careful. If you're smart you'll get away from me."

"Not this time," he said. "I know you're not going to scream for the cops. If you're out here flying somewhere, then you're carrying fake ID. These days they'll put you away for a hundred years and give me a medal. I'll tell you what's going to happen. I'll start by having you just keep walking to the baggage claim with everybody else, and out the door where we can have a talk."

"I'm not going outside with you."

"All I want to know is two things. First off, where is the girl you're traveling with right now? Is she in the airport, or are you meeting her someplace? I need the money they're offering. And second is, you're going to tell me where I can find David Tyler."

"I'm traveling alone, and I haven't seen David Tyler since the last time I saw you."

"But you know where he is. And when you tell me, I'll let you go."

Jane's mind was racing. If he was watching for somebody at the departure and arrival gates, he must have bought a ticket —

probably to somewhere cheap and close, to save money. It was late now, and his flight had probably left hours ago. Jane made an abrupt right turn into the ladies' room, then pivoted just inside the doorway, waiting for him to be foolish enough to step inside.

He didn't come, so she moved to the far end of the room, stood by the sinks, and took out her boarding pass and cell phone. She dialed the number of the airline printed on the ticket envelope. A woman's voice answered, and Jane said, "Hello. My name is Rebecca Silverman, and I'm in Kennedy Airport. I've had to hide in the ladies' room near gate forty-two, because there's a man outside who's been following me, raving and threatening me. Can you call the airport police or give me their number?"

The woman on the line said, "I'm calling them right now." There was a pause, while the woman put Jane on hold. Then she came back. "Can you tell me your name again?"

"Rebecca Silverman."

"What does the man look like?"

"He's about forty-five, six feet one. He has light hair, almost blond. He's wearing a gray sport coat and dark pants, and a light blue shirt with the collar open."

"Hold on, please."

Jane held the line for at least fifteen

seconds before the woman returned. "Okay. The police are on the way. Don't go out of the ladies' room until they get there. You should lock yourself in a stall and wait."

"Thanks so much. I just didn't know how —" and Jane turned off her telephone.

She prepared herself, then stepped just outside the ladies' room, where Ketter was waiting.

His face was red, and his jaw was clenched. "Don't you ever pull that on me." He reached to grab her arm.

Jane was ready. She struck his arm aside, delivered a quick jab to his face, and dodged backward. Her knuckles had hit him just at the upper lip where it covered his front teeth.

Ketter was enraged, not only at the pain, but at the memory of the terrible thing she had done twelve years ago. That night he had rushed in the back door of the apartment building where David Tyler was hiding. He had seen the distinctive shape of a woman — this woman — standing alone in the dark, narrow hallway. He could see Tyler slipping out the front door toward his car. Ketter had to keep from letting this woman slow him down. He ran toward her preparing to slap her aside, saw her right hand come down, and then saw his own shirt had opened. He didn't feel the cut at first, because the razor had made such a clean slice. After a second, when the cold air reached his wound, the stinging came. He looked down and saw his blood soaking the shirt.

That night was so long ago that she had probably forgotten it until now, but he hadn't. And here she was again, defying him, goading him with a sucker punch. Ketter lunged toward Jane, but she dodged him and threw a sharp elbow into his side as he passed her. Now, in his anger and hatred, he ignored appearances. He spread his arms and ducked toward her, trying to gather her into an embrace so he could wrestle her to the floor.

"Hold it!" The shout was sharp and authoritative. Jane resisted the temptation to turn her head and look in the direction of the cop. She couldn't look away from Ketter while he was still so close to her.

A different cop's voice said, "Don't move. Hands up, and lie down on your belly."

Ketter looked at the three cops moving to surround him. He was outraged, but he had been arrested enough times to know that if he didn't make it very obvious he was complying, he was going to be in danger. "All right, all right, yes sir," he called out, holding his hands up in the air as the men rushed in on him, threw him down, dragged his arms behind him, and handcuffed his wrists.

The three cops kept him on the ground. "Wait, wait," he yelled. "Take a look at her identification. Make her show it to you."

Two of the cops were busy patting him down. One of them said, "Are you armed? Do you have anything on you that I need to know about?"

Ketter said, "I'm not moving. Somebody make her stay."

One of the two reached into Ketter's pocket and brought out a flat object about eight inches long. "Hey, look at this!" he called to his colleagues. "It's a ceramic knife."

The third cop, who seemed to be slightly older, said, "Sir, you're under arrest. You have the right to remain silent. Anything you say may be used against you in a court of law. You have a right to have an attorney present during questioning . . ."

There were more police officers around them now, and two of them lifted Ketter to his feet and backed him to the wall while the warning continued. "If you can't afford an attorney . . ."

One of the first three cops stood close to

Jane. "Do you know this man, miss?"

"No. I don't. He must be crazy."

She could hear the cops talking to Ketter a few feet away. "If she's got false identification, then who is she really? Can you tell me her name?"

"I don't know. If I knew that —" He stopped himself.

"You'd what?"

"I want a lawyer."

The officer with Jane said, "Can I see your ticket and a picture ID, please?"

She handed him her plane ticket stub for the flight from Chicago and her Rebecca Silverman license. He examined them and nodded wearily to his colleagues — genuine, of course. They immediately lost interest in her. He took out a notebook, copied Rebecca Silverman's name, address, and phone number from her license, then handed the license and ticket stub to her. "Miss Silverman, you're free to go. We'll handle this."

"You don't need me?"

"Not right now. Those are cameras." He pointed at the dark glass globes at intervals along the ceiling. "And he was carrying a weapon in an airport. That's more than enough to hold him. We'll call if we need anything."

Behind him, Jane could see the other cops escorting Ketter away. Beyond the shops, there was an unmarked steel door on the left wall, with a keypad. One of the cops punched the keys and they opened the door and pulled him inside. "Thank you so much," said Jane. "You were so quick. You probably saved my life."

The officer shrugged, and Jane hurried off down the concourse. Jane knew she still had a problem. Ketter had called someone, and she had no idea who it was or what they looked like. But Ketter would certainly have described her to them.

Jane kept going along the concourse, then came to another row of shops. The first was a newsstand, the next a place that sold nothing but baseball caps. The next store sold golf clothes and accessories. She bought a white sweater, a blue nylon windbreaker, a pair of khaki golf pants with a sharp crease in them, and a straw hat shaped like a man's panama hat. She moved on until she found the next ladies' room, changed her clothes, and stuffed the jeans and sweater she had been wearing into her shopping bag, and then spent a few minutes getting her long hair hidden under the hat. She looked as unlike herself as she could on short notice. From a distance, outside in the dim light, she hoped she might even look ambiguous enough to be mistaken for a man.

As she went toward the escalator that would take her down to street level, she put together the little she knew. Ketter had said he wanted to walk her out through the baggage claim, so he had probably told his people to wait there. Being there would be of no use without having a car waiting at the curb to take her away. Jane went down the escalator, turned to her left away from the baggage claim, and walked to the lobby, where there were ticket counters. She could see the traffic outside in the circular drive was moving from left to right across the windows, so she kept going to the left. If any watcher saw her, they couldn't back the car two hundred yards to push her into it. She went out the last door of the terminal and walked to the next one before she got on the shuttle for the rental car lots. She sat on the bench seat on the right side of the shuttle near the driver, so her back would be to the terminal. When the shuttle made its first stop, Jane stepped down and went into the rental agency without caring which one it was.

She rented a car and drove from Long Island to New Jersey, crossed into Pennsylvania and took the Pennsylvania Turnpike to Harrisburg before she turned north into New York State and made her way north toward Rochester. Along a rural road she spotted a thicket of sumac bushes, so she stopped, broke off a few twigs, and took them with her. Late in the morning she stopped at a tobacco store on a plaza on West Henrietta Road and went inside to look around. There were lots of cigars behind the glass wall along the back, a supply of the usual kinds of cigarettes and pipe tobaccos, and a glass case that held lighters, pipes, cigar cutters, and cigarette cases, but Jane knew what she was looking for. She went to the rack where packs of exotic cigarettes were sold, and picked out two packs. The brand name was Seneca. The cigarettes were made by Grand River Enterprises, a company based on the Six Nations Reserve in Ontario, of tobacco that was grown, cut, and hung to dry in sheds on the Cattaraugus Reservation in New York. She brought the cigarettes to the cash register, and the tall, bald man who owned the store took her money and put the cigarettes into a small brown bag. She wondered if he remembered her from other times, but she preserved their impersonal relationship by not asking.

In the drugstore across the small plaza she

bought a set of fingernail clippers and a newspaper. When she returned to her rental car she spread the front section of the newspaper on her lap, trimmed her fingernails, and poured the clippings along the crease in the paper into her bag with the cigarettes. Then she drove on up Henrietta.

It was nearly noon when Jane drove into the middle of the city and turned off onto a quiet, narrow street called Maplewood Avenue. At this time of day the sun was high enough so the spreading canopies of the tall trees on both sides threw the pavement into shadow. She left the rental car at the curb and walked down the street past the two rows of big old houses, all of them three stories, with steep peaked roofs. They were all edged right up to the sidewalk, built in the days when lawns were not of much interest. In those days people liked to have a carriage pull right up to the front of the house so a lady would not get mud on her thin shoes or the hem of her dress.

The houses had been built big to hold lots of children and a few servants, but as the world changed, many of them had been partitioned into apartment buildings, with extra kitchens and bathrooms where the original builders never intended them to be.

Jane walked to the end of the street to the

long, narrow, quiet park that began at the white Romanesque Christian Science church and ran beside the street for a few hundred feet. Along the far edge of the park was a steel railing to keep people from falling off the cliff into the Genesee River below. The Genesee River was like an artery that ran down the center of Nundawaonoga, and if she stopped walking she could hear it running just beyond the edge of the park, past the railing.

This was one of the places where Jane sometimes stopped after she had been on the road. Until the 1770s there had been a big Seneca village here. There were dozens of Seneca village sites in the land between Sodus Bay on Lake Ontario and the Niagara River, but this was one of her favorites because it was so quiet and empty during the day, even though it was in the center of a busy city. There was only Jane walking toward the edge of the park beneath the tall shade trees, listening to the wind moving through their leaves. She reached it, looked back over her shoulder to be sure she was alone, and climbed over the railing.

The bank was high, at least thirty feet above the Genesee River, but she had been here a number of times, and she could see that the way she had found to get down to the river was still passable. It didn't deserve the name of path. It was just a slight protuberance, a stony shelf in the gray shale along the side of the cliff set at a gradual angle to lead her down. She had to use a series of thin saplings that grew out of the cliffside as handholds, but in a minute she was at the bottom of the gorge walking on the dry pebbly ground along the river. The water was deep enough at midstream to move in lazy silence to the north where it would flow into Lake Ontario, so she could hear small birds chirping in the trees far above.

Along the riverbed the river was wider and shallower and there were some flat stones big enough to sit on. She could hear a faint sound of the water moving over pebbles here. She opened her shoulder bag, took out the bag of cigarettes she had bought, opened the two packs, and sniffed the strong, fragrant aroma. She tore the paper on each cigarette and emptied the shreds of tobacco onto the rock, then took out her broken sumac twigs. She peeled them, crumbled the bark, dropped it into the tobacco and used a twig to mix it. Then she shook the fingernail clippings out of the paper bag onto the rock beside the tobacco.

She said aloud, "Jo-Ge-Oh." That was the name of the little people. "Jo-Ge-Oh.

Grandfathers." The little people were only a few inches tall, but they were a very ancient race. They had already lived in the gorge of the Genesee when the Nundawaono had come into being on the big hill at the foot of Canandaigua Lake near Naples, New York, so they were properly called grandfathers and grandmothers.

Jane had always felt close to them, because they were compassionate and performed a particular service to human beings who came to them in trouble. The Jo-Ge-Oh would reveal themselves to people who were hunted, and spirit them away from the human world to live with them for a time. When they felt that the moment was right, they would return the person to the place where he had met them. To the fugitive it would seem that he had been with the Jo-Ge-Oh for only a few hours or a day, but when he walked home, he would find that so much time had passed that his enemies were dead.

"Jo-Ge-Oh," she said. "Come on, little guys. I know you're around." The Jo-Ge-Oh were very shy, and they seldom appeared to people who weren't in danger. But they always lived in places like this, very near to the settlements where full-sized Nundawaono lived. If they had been here in the

1700s, they were still here. The intervening centuries would not strike them as an especially long time. They might even still be harboring refugees from wars before then, planning to return them here in due time.

"Here you go, little guys. I've brought you the usual presents. Here's some of the only tobacco." She took half of the tobacco shreds and placed them on several other flat rocks. The Jo-Ge-Oh were known to be addicted to tobacco, and they liked it the traditional way, raised in this part of the continent and cut with a bit of sumac bark. It was commonly referred to in the Seneca language as "the only tobacco."

She took her collection of fingernail clippings and scattered them over the rocks. "I brought you some of my fingernails. I hope they work for you." The tallest Jo-Ge-Oh were only a few inches high, and so the small scavengers and predators that lived along the Genesee could be a source of real annoyance to them. The scent of full-sized people on the clippings helped to keep the raccoons, skunks, and possums at a distance.

She placed the rest of the tobacco into another pile on another flat stone. "I hope you enjoy your presents. Thank you for

Christine's life and for my life." When Senecas spoke to the supernatural beings that inhabited their country they never asked for favors or future services of any kind. They only gave thanks.

She folded the empty cigarette packs into the small paper bag and put it into her jeans pocket, then stood still for a few seconds, listening to the quiet murmur of water through the stones at the edge of the river. Then she made her way back to the long, narrow incline up the side of the gorge. When she reached the top, she climbed back over the rail, put the tobacco bag into the nearly empty trash can, and went back to the rental car. She drove to the Outer Loop and made her way onto Buffalo Road.

The New York State Thruway felt too dangerous, so she drove the last seventy miles west along the straight rural highway. The closer Jane came to her home, the more careful she became. She had not forgotten that the only time the hunters had seen Jane she had been in western and central New York.

When she arrived in Deganawida, she passed her house three times before she was satisfied that she had not been followed and that there was nobody waiting at the house for her. She turned into the driveway and closed the garage, then opened the back door of the house. At each stage she kept all of her senses alert, searching for signs that someone had been here. She checked the telephone upstairs, but there were no messages. Then she went down to the cellar. She moved the ladder and climbed up to the old heating duct, then removed the steel box and opened it. She put the remaining stack of hundred-dollar bills into the box, then restored the driver's licenses and credit cards in different names she had been carrying. The only identity she kept out was Rebecca Silverman. She hid the box and went upstairs.

In the kitchen she took the Rebecca Silverman license and credit cards, and cut them up with a pair of scissors. As she took the tiny shreds, put them into an envelope, and returned them to her purse, she felt regret at losing such a solid identity. But she knew that there was no salvaging Rebecca Silverman after an incident in an airport. Even being a victim of a crime made the name too dangerous to use again.

When she was ready to leave, she checked the windows and the locks again, adjusted the timers on the lamps to be sure the house looked occupied, and then drove out of the garage and up the street. She took the direct route to Amherst on surface streets, driving down Delaware Avenue toward Buffalo, then turning left onto Brighton Road and following the long, straight highway until it became Maple Road and passed the University at Buffalo campus. All the way she watched for cars that might be following her. She stopped at the Boulevard Mall for a few minutes and used the opportunity to disperse the bits of Rebecca Silverman in two trash cans. Twice she turned off on small residential streets to see if anyone made the same turn, then returned to the main road and went on.

Jane turned into the driveway of the McKinnon house at four-thirty, and kept going all the way up the drive around the house so the car would not be visible from the street. She studied the doors and windows of the house from outside to be sure the glass was intact and that there were no suspicious marks on the windowsills, no gouges in any doors near the locks. When she was satisfied that nobody had broken into the house, she unlocked it and went inside.

When she stepped into the kitchen, she was reminded that Carey was, in some ways, a disturbing sort of husband. He had been a bachelor through medical school and internship and residency, so he knew perfectly well how to cook for himself. His life as a surgeon had given him little tolerance for microbes, so the sink and counters were as clean as they ever were when she cleaned them. She opened the dishwasher and saw that it had already been emptied and the dishes put away. There was a kind of military precision to everything he did when she was away.

She went to the telephone mounted on the wall and called Carey's office. After one ring the receptionist answered, "Dr. McKinnon's office."

"Hi, Julie. It's Jane. Is he in?"

"Hi, Jane. He just got off a call, and he's getting ready to go back to the hospital for rounds. I'm sure I can catch him, if you'll hold."

"Sure."

A few seconds later there was a click. "Jane? Are you home?"

"Yes. I just got home a minute ago."

"Was there any trouble?"

"No trouble," she said. "None at all."

12

Jane lay in the bed in the darkened room and listened to the regular, deep breaths that indicated her husband had fallen asleep. She looked beside her at his big, familiar shape. When Carey slept, his face acquired a lineless, peaceful emptiness that made him look like a teenager. She liked to see him, but the moon had moved so it was no longer shining in the bedroom window. She looked at the glowing display of the alarm clock on Carey's nightstand. It was two-thirty A.M. already. She felt happy, but she wasn't ready to sleep yet. She got out of bed, put on her bathrobe, and walked out of the bedroom. She walked along the hallway a few yards to the spare room that faced the front of the house. This was the room she had begun two years ago to prepare as a nursery. She stood at the edge of the curtains to look out the window without being seen.

She looked out at the long, open road, now lined by large houses that had been built in the past forty years since Amherst had gone from farm country to suburb. There was nobody out there, not even a car parked where she could see it. During the winter a car left on the road was liable to be hit by a snowplow, and even now that summer had come, people stuck to the habit of putting cars away in their garages. There was nobody out there. Her house, her husband, her identity were all safe.

Brent Ketter was on her mind. Even in the old days, she had known there was no question that if she kept being a guide, then one day she was going to walk down the wrong street in some distant city, or go into the wrong building. A face would be waiting for her, and it would acquire a sudden look of recognition, and then hatred. He would be someone she hadn't been thinking about, maybe hadn't thought about in years, but he would have no trouble remembering her. He would open fire before she could move. It had almost happened last night. If Ketter had seen her anywhere but in an airport, she would be dead.

She had taken many people out of terrible lives, and for each of them there was at least one person like this — a professional killer who had not collected, an abuser robbed of his victim, a rival who had been cheated out of his little victory. Each time Jane had gone out with a runner, she had made another chaser aware that she had beaten him. She had gotten through last night, but someday, one of them might be more alert, faster, luckier.

But she was home now. She had made a very brief, necessary return to the old life. Now Jane had returned to the life she had half-chosen and half-invented, the life with Carey. As she stared out the window at the familiar configuration of trees and rooftops arranged on the broad, flat country where she had always lived, everything looked the same as it had been before Christine. But nothing was the same as it had been. The world had a tension to it, an expectation like an indrawn breath.

Carey had told his colleagues that Jane had been referred to the ear clinic at UCLA for treatment of minor hearing damage she had sustained in the bombing. She supposed that Carey was a better judge than she was about what would satisfy the curiosity of other doctors. She also supposed the nature of the imaginary injury would help. The problem had to be something that a doctor would shrug off as dull, and that didn't require Jane to look or behave differently. Carey had been at work every day since the bombing, telling the necessary lies. It made her feel peculiar — sad, grateful, regretful, guilty — that she had forced her husband, the man she had admired since she'd met him in college, to become a liar.

But the lies were over, at least for now. She would be home with Carey for the summer. She had put the pursuers far behind, and she was almost sure she had left them no way of tracing Christine. At first Jane had maintained a small hope that at least one of the six would be arrested, but after a couple of weeks passed with no news of arrests, she had given that up. People who made a living doing armed kidnappings seldom used their original names. Earlier tonight Carey had said, "I'm really sorry they weren't caught."

Jane said, "That's okay. They're not important anymore."

"They're not?"

"No. I would have loved it if they were caught, or if something bad had happened to them to make them give up. But time will do the same thing. I'm not trying to get revenge on these people for the bombing, or bring justice for the ones who got hurt, or make sure someone gets punished. I don't really know how to accomplish any of those things. All I took on was a pregnant girl who came to me for help. I did what I could, and if she does what I taught her, she'll be safe."

"Was that what it was — the fact that she was pregnant?"

Jane studied him. "You mean is that why I helped her?"

"Well, yes. It wouldn't be so strange. For years now you've thought about having a baby. And one night, here's a young woman who's pregnant. After five years of staying out of sight, she's the one you decide to risk your life to help. I wondered if that had anything to do with your decision. Just now you said, 'All I took on was a pregnant girl —' "

" '. . . who came to me for help.' That's what I said."

"Right," said Carey. "But the pregnancy was the only quality you mentioned."

"I helped her because she's the first person to find her way to me needing my help. The pregnancy made it harder for her to run and harder for her to hide. It was only one of the reasons why she needed help."

Carey shrugged, and Jane could see he had noticed she was getting angry. "Fair enough," he said. "I didn't mean to accuse you of anything. I was just trying to under-stand you because I love you."

Jane closed her eyes for a few seconds, then said carefully, "You're right that what I want most right now is to have a baby. It bothers me a lot that it hasn't happened. We both know that. But what made me take Christine away wasn't a sudden wave of female hormones at the sight of a pregnant woman, or some kind of sentimental crazi-ness brought on by infertility. What I did — putting her out of the way of the people who were after her — was the only thing I could do. I didn't look for her, or tell anyone I was available or anything. I'm not going back to making people disappear."

"Why not? You just did."

"Because I've changed. The world has changed. When I started I was twenty, and running was easy. Whether you get caught or not depends on who's searching for you. In the old days, it was always just creeps, or once in a while somebody who was willing to kill someone for money. Now the whole government is looking for people with false identities, even for people who have blanks in their histories. Everybody's financial information is passed from one computer to another all day and all night. This country is a harder place to move people around."

"So you're not going to do it again?"

"I can't say that, Carey. I can say it's not practical anymore. There used to be holes in the system, and I was keeping people alive by sneaking through them. Now there are fewer holes. But if Christine Monahan came to me tomorrow, I would have to try."

Jane had said it, and the conversation had ended, and within a few minutes, the tension between them began to fade. What they had been talking about was painful to her, but after all, it was simply that she loved him and wanted to have his baby. He loved her, and wanted her to be safe and happy and understood.

Jane walked back to the bedroom in the dark, then lay on the bed beside him and watched his chest rising and falling peacefully. This was the place where she had always wanted to be. Maybe the growing sense that something was changing, that something was coming near, was just her frayed nerves from the trip home.

13

Richard Beale was in his office with the door open, staring out over his empty desk, across the lobby. This had been his father's office originally, and Andy Beale considered windows a distraction and a threat to privacy. But with the office door open Richard could look across the lobby with its glass walls opening onto the sunny courtyard. In the courtyard was a captive garden full of green tropical plants — sago palms, huge bromeliads, a few large ficus trees and one exotic eucalyptus with bark that looked like human skin. The receptionist's desk was right in front of the glass wall, so the sunlight always came in above and behind her and made her glow like an angel. Richard thought the view probably had been partly responsible for his troubles with Christine Monahan, and with a few of her predecessors.

Receptionists were beautiful. They simply

were, just as bouncers at clubs were big and muscular. The physical attributes were part of the job. No skill or training, no other quality would do. The job of a bouncer wasn't to escort the unruly out of the bar and kick the shit out of them. The job was to scare the potentially unruly out of that train of thought by looking big and fierce. An adequate receptionist was at least pretty. The better she looked, the more substantial and respectable she made the company seem, because beauty was a commodity like anything else on the planet. Straight white teeth, delicate features, shining hair, a thin waist cost extra money, just as comfortable, well-designed waiting room furniture cost more than bad furniture.

Richard's father, Andy Beale, had often hired women who had been in beauty pageants. They had all learned to dress conservatively, walk gracefully in high heels, speak pleasantly, and produce convincing smiles. He had only been interested in those young women who had risen to become either queen of something or runners-up — what he referred to as "win, place, or show" — because they were the ones who had learned the most and tried the hardest. He was quite open about it, too, because the pageants all claimed loudly that they were about character, leadership, and scholarly ability.

The only time he'd had the threat of a lawsuit was an incident when he had been taken by surprise early in the morning. He had come into the building right at opening time and found that the receptionist he had hired only a week before had gotten her hair cut short. Andy Beale had let his disappointment slip out. "I hired you for your hair, damn it. That long, shiny black hair was the one thing that put you ahead of three other applicants."

Andy Beale had made himself into a multimillionaire because he was able to observe human behavior accurately. He had spent forty years noticing that when women cut their hair short, other women would say it was "cute" or "smart" or some such thing, but he had never, in any of the thousand times when he'd seen it, heard anything approaching approval by any male. He also had developed a clear-eyed view of the competitive nature of women. He knew that when one woman said to another that her hairstyle was "smart," she meant the opposite. The pleasure that could be heard in the woman's voice was delight over the temporary downfall of a rival.

He had stepped inside Richard's office

and explained the true dimensions of the girl's mistake. Not only had she diminished her attraction for the Beale family's real estate customers, lenders, clients, and tenants, most of whom were male, she had also persuaded Andy Beale that she did not have the practical, commonsense variety of intelligence that he knew was necessary for success in business. He told Richard, "I had hopes for her, but no more. She was a contest winner, too. Most of these pageant winners are street fighters. We've got eight of them selling condos in that Phoenix development right now. They would never handicap themselves like that. I can't get rid of her, but I want her moved. Have her answer the general company phone number from a cubicle in the big office down the hall. That's all she'll see of this company."

A few weeks later, while the former receptionist was sitting near the back of the building answering phone calls in her cubicle, her lawyer paid Andy Beale a visit. Andy had not threatened to fire the girl, and she had accurately reported that to her lawyer, much to the lawyer's disappointment. But the lawyer felt that she deserved some sort of compensation in exchange for not filing a complaint. Andy Beale declined to pay off, and within a month, the woman resigned.

The reception area became a problem for Richard as soon as his father began to relinquish the daily operation of the business to him. The green plants and the light beyond the glass walls of the lobby made the reception area more inviting than the windowless office his father had insisted he take. As soon as he stepped out there for relief, the sight of the receptionist would distract him. His father never knew it, but by now Richard had caused half a dozen receptionists to quit. Richard had dated three of them, including a married woman whose husband caught her coming out of a hotel with Richard on the fifth date, one who broke up with Richard and quit on the second date, and one who threatened to charge him with sexual assault on the morning after their first date. A couple of them had refused to go out with Richard at all, and he had bothered them so often that they had begun circulating their résumés within days after accepting the job.

There had also been the case of Tracy Williamson. She had given Richard a slow case of surprise. He had not been careful. She had told him on the second date that she was on the pill, and so he had left birth control to her. But after only a few more weeks, he had realized that his firm belief in her efficiency and dependability had been induced by the way she looked in her glasses. She wore very flattering business suits to work — little tight skirts with matching jackets — and she had glasses with designer frames in about five colors to match the suits. She always looked put-together and organized. The idea that a girl like her would forget to refill her prescription for birth control pills and then forget that she had forgotten simply never occurred to Richard until he began to notice the work she had been doing at the office. There were messages she had forgotten to write down, or written down and given to the wrong rental agent or realtor. There were appointments written in Richard's calendar on the right day of the wrong month. There were letters and bills she had completed so late she'd had to take them out to mail instead of leaving them for the regular pickup, only to find them in her purse or her car a week later. She had gone out with the letters and forgotten why she was out, so she would salvage the trip by going to lunch or shopping.

When he realized how forgetful and disorganized she was, Richard sat her down in his office, locked the door, and tried to have a serious conversation with her about whether or not she had actually been taking the pills. His first attempt was unsuccessful, because when they had gone in and locked the door the other times, it had been so they could have sex in the windowless office during the day, something that they both relished. Richard allowed the click of the bolt in the doorjamb to trigger the impulse again. But the second time, she initiated the conversation. She walked into his office, locked the door, and told him she was pregnant.

Richard offered to pay for her abortion, but she had no interest in that. She wanted Richard to marry her. He refused, she insisted. She threatened to file a paternity suit. Richard knew that he couldn't stand a lawsuit the way his father could. Tracy would demand, and probably win, full support for her and the baby for eighteen years. It was a sum that would be impossible to conceal from his parents. Richard didn't have any serious money of his own. What he had amounted to a house and car that belonged to his parents' company and a pocket full of spending money, essentially a continuation of the allowance he had received as a child.

He offered to keep Tracy on the payroll long after she had the baby and stopped working, so the company would be paying for her support. But since he had turned down her proposals, she wanted a lump-sum payment, and told him she intended to have their brief affair declared a common-law marriage. It was absurd, illegal, and unfair. But she was showing herself to be very stubborn and surprisingly efficient.

As the weeks passed and he knew that the time was coming for her condition to become visible, Richard became desperate. What Tracy didn't know was that Richard Beale would do anything to keep his parents from finding out he had made her pregnant. Richard was an only child who had been born to a difficult mother and an impossible father. He knew that their reaction to the news would be unpleasant. They had already been ordering him to marry soon and give them grandchildren. If they knew Tracy was pregnant they were likely to take her side and give her what she had wanted in the first place — Richard as a husband. He would be tied for life to a woman who was essentially an enemy. The plan he had been pursuing of embezzling a few dollars at a time until he had enough to be independent would be effectively blocked. But leaving things as they were wouldn't prevent trouble either. If his father learned that he had proposed paying Tracy off by making her a phantom employee of the company, he would fire him and throw him out on the street. The business belonged to his parents. There was no way Richard could let the pregnancy proceed long enough so his parents could see it for themselves.

Richard called Steve Demming and asked him to have lunch at a restaurant in Del Mar. He had met Demming through Jerry McGern, a lawyer he had worked with on a development five years ago. Richard had told McGern about the trouble he was having with a roofing company. They were holding the whole project for ransom by delaying and asking for extra money. McGern had said, "Let me send a guy I know to see you." The guy had turned out to be Steve Demming. The roofing company had abruptly changed its position, and the roofs began going on the houses two days later.

He had hired Demming and his crew a number of times after that, but it was always on company matters. The real estate business in coastal California was tough and competitive, and the Beale family's interests were complicated. There were employees, suppliers, and subcontractors who needed to be watched without their knowing it.

There were competing developers and speculators who needed to be persuaded not to bid on certain projects. There were buyers and tenants who signed agreements they didn't think they needed to keep, and had to be taught to keep their word. There were payoffs to be delivered to inspectors, commissioners, and politicians. It was important that the people who performed these services not be employees of the Beale Company. Whenever Demming's crew did any work for Richard, he would pay them by placing one of them in the separate budgeted account of a current building project.

Richard and Demming sat on the patio of the restaurant in Del Mar looking out at the horizon, where the blue-gray sea met the blue-gray overcast sky. Richard explained his problem with Tracy and asked for Demming's help. Steve's understanding and discretion had surprised him. Steve told him that one of the women on his crew, Sybil Landreau, had too much to drink now and then, and had managed to get pregnant a couple of times. She had a cordial relationship with a doctor just over the border in Tijuana who was a favorite with the local hookers. Steve and Sybil and Pete Tilton would simply drive Tracy to the doctor and return her to the United States in a day or two. When Richard said, "Tracy won't go to Mexico with you," Demming said, "This doctor won't mind if a patient arrives anesthetized."

Richard knew that the problem had been solved, because he never heard from Tracy again. It gave him a warm feeling about Demming and his people — not just gratitude, but a kind of camaraderie. Like Richard, they were reliable. And they weren't the sort of people to look down on him for being human. They were people who sometimes had done foolish things themselves, and knew they probably would again.

The crew had solved Richard's trouble with Tracy, but that had not cured him of his receptionist problem. There was another occasion a couple of years later. The receptionist's name was Heather, and Richard had to ask Demming to handle the problem again. Heather had seemed to welcome his attentions until they had sex, but then she had begun to make snide remarks. They had sounded like jokes at first — that she was just teasing him about the fact that the way they had gotten together was, technically, sexual harassment. But the jokes came more and more often, and then she asked him for a raise. She wanted her salary doubled, and she wanted to move into one of the new condominiums the company had built and live there for free. A couple of days after Heather vanished from San Diego, Richard's cell phone rang.

"Richard? It's me — Heather."

His breath caught in his throat, but he recovered. "What's up?"

"You know damned well what's up."

"I don't."

"Your friends, your scum, drugged me and kidnapped me. I woke up in Mexico."

"Aw. That's too bad."

"Too bad? *Too bad,* Richard?"

"Yeah. It sure sounds that way."

"When I woke up I was in some crummy hotel with a couple of your friends. The woman said if I ever told anybody anything about you or them, they'd sell me to a Mexican whorehouse where the pimps would kill me if I tried to run away."

"Jesus, Heather. If that's true, maybe you shouldn't have told me."

"You knew, you bastard."

"No way."

"You paid them to do this to me. All I'm asking is that you admit it. Tell the truth once."

"I don't know anything about this."

"I don't believe you."

266

"What do you want from me? Do you want to come in and talk?"

"I can't come in and talk. I'm in Ciudad Juarez, where your friends dumped me. I don't have any money to get home. I don't want to go talk to you. I hate you. You'll never see me again, you pig." She hung up.

Richard stared at his cell phone. *What could be better?* he asked himself. It was perfection. They had made sure all she had was a crazy story that she would be too scared to tell, and she had just given him a guarantee that she would leave him alone forever. This was science. It was art. Richard began to cherish Demming and his crew. They never seemed to be surprised at what he asked of them, and they were never at a loss about how to accomplish it.

Of course, having Demming solve a problem was expensive, and as this Christine Monahan problem dragged on, it was becoming more so. Keeping four people traveling around searching for somebody was like keeping four people on a perpetual vacation, running up bills at hotels, restaurants, airlines, car rentals. And having Ronnie Sebrot dealing with hospitals and doctors for his knee was worse. Richard wasn't sure what it was going to cost him for Carl McGinnis's death. He was hoping that Carl was a bachelor, without a widow to pay off. He remembered hearing some remark that Carl had something going with Claudia Marshall, but that proved nothing. The crew had spent a lot of time together — lots of it nights away from San Diego — for years, and he supposed that they must have routinely taken care of each other in that way.

The phone on Richard's desk rang, and he waited while Marlene, the new receptionist, answered it. In a few seconds, his phone buzzed, and he snatched up the receiver. "Yes?"

"It's a Mr. Demming for you, Richard." The voice was musical and efficient and cheerful. He knew that what he had been thinking should have made him immune to any thoughts about the new receptionist, but it hadn't. He modulated his voice carefully so it was businesslike, yet friendly.

"Thanks, Marlene." He hit the button that was blinking. "Hi, Steve."

"Richard, I wanted to give you an update on what we're doing."

"I was hoping you were calling to say you had her."

"Not yet."

Richard hated *Not yet,* but he was sure Demming must remember that he hated that answer, and be saying it anyway. He couldn't afford to alienate Demming now, so he ignored his irritation. "Okay. So what's happening?"

"We've been circulating the pictures of Christine online to people around the country we think will look for her if there's money in it. We've set the payoff at a hundred thousand."

Richard swallowed, but his throat was so dry he swallowed air. "I guess that's okay. I don't actually have to pay anybody, right?"

"Actually, Richard, if they find her for us, you do. If somebody can find her, he can find you. Some of these people aren't anybody you want to fuck around with."

"Look, Steve. I'm not sure if I made this entirely clear. She's not in the same situation as the other girls I asked you to help me with. I really need Christine back here healthy and in a receptive mood."

"A receptive mood?"

"If possible, I'd like her to be happy to see me."

"It's kind of late to worry about her mood. But I'll think about it, and see what we can do."

"Thanks," said Richard. "And I appreciate your keeping me up on everything. I really need to have this work out."

"Good-bye, Richard."

Richard sat there, staring at the phone for a moment. Maybe this extra aggravation was the price for letting Demming and his crew handle personal problems for him. There was a kind of unwelcome familiarity to the way Demming had been talking to him for the past couple of weeks. He seemed at times to think he was indulging Richard's whims. Maybe that was Richard's imagination, but Demming didn't sound like an employee talking to his boss.

Richard decided that he needed to get out of the office. Maybe he would take an early lunch. Maybe he would ask Marlene the new receptionist to go with him.

"There you are." The voice was his father's.

Richard looked up. "Of course I'm here. This is my office, where I work."

"That's why I'm surprised." He came in and sat on the couch. He always sat in the center of a couch and rested both arms on the back, taking up as much space as one human being could. If anybody else wanted to sit, they would have to endure a terrible proximity to him, and only after they actually sat would he move slightly. He looked at the door as though he hadn't seen it before. "Close that door, will you, Richard?"

Richard kept himself from expressing what he felt. He got up from his desk, walked around it to the door and closed it. "What's the occasion?"

"Maybe I'm here to take a close look at what you're doing to my business. Maybe I brought fifteen CPA's and four computer experts to snoop around and see if there's anything being hidden from me. Would that bother you?"

Richard fixed a smile on his face, but he knew it was the sort of smile a man put on when he didn't want to fight an opponent he knew would crush him. "Not unless they wasted a lot of time doing it."

Andy Beale smiled, too, but his smile was more convincing, and to Richard it was chilling. Why would he say that if he didn't think Richard had something to hide? "Well, I'm just here to talk to you about Christine. Have you talked to her since the day we were out on the boat?"

"No."

"Have you even tried?"

"Of course. She left her apartment a month ago and hasn't been back. No one has heard from her."

"That's it? You knocked on her door and talked to her friends?"

Richard took a moment to decide. There

were a hundred reasons not to tell him any more than he had to, but there was no way to get rid of him without meeting each of his insinuations with an answer. "I've done a lot more than that. I hired some professionals to develop their own leads and find her for me."

Andy Beale cocked his head as though he had heard a sound in the distance that he couldn't quite identify. "Well, that's interesting. Who?"

"They've done some work for us before, and they've done it well, so I trust them. They're security specialists."

"I didn't ask what they were. I said, 'Who?'"

"The head man is named Steve Demming. He has a crew of three other men and two women."

"Women? That sounds sensible. It ought to reassure her if they find her."

"That's what I think. And they will find her."

"But they don't have her."

"Not yet."

Andy Beale looked at his son with new interest. "So how are they going about it?"

"I just got off the phone with Steve. He's offering a reward and distributing photographs of her. He's also using the Internet

272

to get people to e-mail him if they see her. He has his own sources." He saw the un-changed look of curiosity on Andy Beale's face, and knew what his father was going to say before he said it.

"That's pretty convenient for you, having somebody else do it all?"

"I've been running credit checks on her every day to see if she uses a credit card or anything. So far, she hasn't. There's a skip-tracing company that I've occasionally used to find tenants who skip owing rent. I've got them searching the big commercial databases for any sign of her."

"She's been gone for over a month. How much cash could a girl like that have — a week's worth? After that she couldn't buy a meal or fill up at a gas station without the credit bureaus noticing. She's got to be with somebody."

The conversation had moved from the uncomfortable to the excruciating for Rich-ard, but he could not think of a way to change the subject. He tried retreating behind a haze of vagueness. "Well, we'll see."

"Yeah. You damned well ought to see. Somebody's helping that girl, probably put-ting her up and paying her bills and signing for things so she doesn't leave a trail.

Everything you're doing only works if she's alone, and she isn't. You must have some idea of who the guys are she might know well enough. You were fucking her for six months or so. Who else was?"

Richard felt his cheeks heating up. "Nobody. She was a virgin when she came to work here. And after that I was with her all the time."

"A secretary, about half your age, who had never been with anybody else. She wasn't exactly a difficult girl to impress, was she? Wasn't that a little too easy even for you?"

"She was a pretty, young girl, good-natured and unmarried. I work very long, hard hours, in case your spies hadn't mentioned it. I'm not out very often where I might meet a lot of women."

"Yeah, I know. You're a regular monk. One way or another, you found her and got her to sleep with you. But somebody besides you is taking care of her right now. Don't you think you ought to be curious about who the guy is?"

"It's not a man. It's a woman."

"What woman? Her mother? A sister? Just trace her the way you would Christine."

"My man Steve says it's a pro — a detective or a bodyguard or something. The night they found Christine in Buffalo this woman

274

broke one guy's knee and ran into another one with her car. I don't know much more than that, but we're assuming she's keeping Christine out of sight for now."

"This isn't normal," said Andy. "Are you sure your man Steve isn't just full of shit?"

"He's not. Why would you say that?"

"Where the hell would a girl like Christine get to know somebody like that?"

"We don't know that yet, either."

"What do you know about her relatives? Her parents?"

"Her mother died when she was a kid. Her father's in jail. He's serving a ten-year sentence for embezzling money from the company where he worked. She also has a stepmother and a half sister and brother she hates. The stepmother ended up with all the father's money and threw Christine out of the house when she was sixteen."

"It's the father, then. You've got to go see the father."

"In jail?"

"If that's where he is, that's where you see him."

"Why would I do that? He's not hiding her."

Andy Beale's expression showed his frustration and hopelessness. He didn't seem to see any point in raising his voice, or to have enough energy to do it. He blew out a breath and said carefully, "Christine is a kid. Somebody found this woman professional for her and hired her. The wicked stepmother didn't do it. The father is the most likely one. He's also sitting twenty-four hours a day in the best place there is for making contacts who know women who break legs and run over people. Maybe he talked to somebody in prison who could get in touch with the woman on the outside. From what you just said, of all the people Christine knows, the only one she's going to talk to again for sure is her father."

"And?"

"If you want to get a message to her, he's the one you have to leave it with."

"What am I supposed to say to him — that I knocked up his sweet little daughter, but he should be my buddy and help me out?"

"I said to get a message to the girl. You tell him you're in love with her. There was a spat, just a misunderstanding, and she got hurt feelings and ran out on you."

"Do I tell him I was her boss?"

"You tell him everything that will make him think you're a reasonable prospect for his daughter. You're not only her boss, but also the future owner of the company, a rich, successful guy. You're worried about her, you miss her, and you want to marry her." He glared at Richard with irritation. "Sometimes I think you're not a regular person, Richard. You're like some kind of lizard or fish or something, and you don't feel what other people feel. You have to make some kind of leap of imagination so you can figure out what to tell them to make them feel the way you want."

"What am I trying to get from him?"

"Maybe he hired this woman pro, and you can get him to let something slip about her. The least you want him to do is pass your message on to Christine. You want him to help you get her back. A twenty-year-old girl who was sleeping with you might think hearing from you is good news. But the father first. You need him on your side. If he's showing signs that he might think you're good news, too, then ask him for permission to marry his daughter."

"Why would I ask some jailbird for permission to do anything?"

"There. That's what I'm talking about. You've got to put yourself in this man's place. Yes, he's in jail. He's feeling guilty because being there made him unable to protect his daughter, so she got chucked out on the street. He wants to believe you, because it would mean everything worked out all right. She found a nice, steady, prosperous guy who loves her. So you help him believe in you. If he does, he'll try to get her to give you a chance."

"Why should she listen to him?"

Andy Beale studied him for a moment. "The more I think about this, the more I think you're not right for this. Forget I said to see him. I'll do it for you."

"I didn't say I wouldn't do it."

"No," said Andy Beale. "But you probably shouldn't. We get one chance with this guy, and you'd probably fuck it up. I'll just let you know what happened."

"Whatever." Richard shrugged and leaned back in his chair.

"What I want you to do is try some other angles on your own. Think. She's pregnant. She's going to be seeing an obstetrician. She's not going to wait and walk into an emergency room when the baby comes. You're her employer, so try to work with the health insurance company. We're the real customer, because we pay the premiums."

"They're not going to tell us anything about her medical file. It's private."

"Try. All you need is the name of a doctor. Hell, even a city would do. Another thing she'll need is an apartment. We're in the rental business. Send a picture of her to a thousand other large owners and say she's somebody who stole from us and we want to find her. Think about her. What does she need to get by? Who does she know to ask for help? Work on it."

"I will."

"Be sure you do," said Andy Beale. "If you screw around until after she's had the baby, it will be a whole lot harder to persuade her that she needs you." He stood and walked to the door, opened it, and looked out at the receptionist thoughtfully. "What's her father's name?"

"Monahan. I think it's Robert Monahan."

"And where is he?"

"Lompoc."

"All right. I'll talk to you soon." He spared Richard only a glance. "What's the new girl's name?" He returned his eyes to the receptionist.

"Marlene."

"Don't complicate things by fucking her, too."

14

The nightmare that woke Jane slipped away before she could hold on to enough of it to remember. Panting and sweating, she sat up and looked around her. Carey was still asleep beside her, the sheet only partly over his leg now. She must have thrown it off when she had jerked awake, so she gently pulled it back over him to the shoulder and looked at the red numbers on the alarm clock. Four already. He would have to be up at five-thirty so he could drive to the hospital. Ahead of him was another morning of surgery.

Again she tried to remember her dream, but it was gone. There was still enough time to go back to sleep, but she knew she couldn't do that while she could still feel her heart pounding. There was a very faint breeze coming through the screen of the open window across the room, pushing the thin white curtains inward an inch or two and making the sweat on her back feel cold.

After a minute she stood, stepped out of her nightgown, walked down the hall to the farthest of the guest rooms, shut the door, and went into the bathroom. She ran the shower until it wasn't cold, and then stepped into the spray. There was no uncertainty about what had caused her dream. She had been home for a few days, and she had been getting used to being Mrs. Carey McKinnon again, the doctor's wife who lived behind the thick, solid door of the big old stone house. But Jane had promised that she would go and see Christine's father. As she stood in the shower she wondered whether she regretted not having kept her promise more than she regretted having promised at all.

Visiting the prison where Christine's father was serving his sentence would be incredibly dangerous. Jane supposed she must have been thinking about it for days without acknowledging it consciously. She knew she would have to do what she had promised. If she didn't, the man would probably be so devastated by the loss of his daughter that he would find a way to kill himself. He was a middle-aged convict who apparently didn't have much left except his daughter.

Even years from now when he was out of jail he would never have a job as good as the ones he'd had, might never find a woman to love him, probably never even have friends who completely trusted him. Jane had promised Christine that at least this man would know that his daughter had not erased him from her life.

When the shower had soothed her and made her feel fully awake, she put on a bathrobe, and went downstairs to the kitchen. She made coffee, set the table for breakfast, took out eggs and butter and bread for toast, then went to the computer in the small office off the den and made flight reservations in the name Donna Ruggiero, then printed out the tickets and confirmations.

At five-fifteen she climbed the stairs to the bedroom and stood for a moment watching Carey sleep, then touched his shoulder to wake him. He opened his eyes, then gave a sigh and looked up at her, smiling. "I had a dream that we . . . Oh, yeah. I guess that wasn't a dream."

"No, it wasn't," she said. "Good for us."

He sat up, looked at the clock, and then stood and put his arms around her. "I'd better brush my teeth before I kiss you." He went into the bathroom, and as she straightened the bed she heard the hum of his electric toothbrush, then the buzz of his razor.

As she had each morning since her return, she looked out the upstairs window at the road outside, trying to detect any change since the night before. Then she went downstairs and walked out toward the end of the driveway to pick up the morning newspaper. She could hear faraway sounds — robins on the lawns today and crows in the big trees of the McKinnon yard, and others calling to one another along the road. Jane pretended to look at nothing, but she used the walk down the long driveway to scan the neighborhood for unfamiliar vehicles and people who were out of place. There was nothing to disturb her. She stepped back in through the kitchen entrance and locked the door.

Carey was standing beside the kitchen table, and she could see the papers in his hand were the airline tickets she had printed. He looked troubled, but when he saw her he erased the expression and turned to hand them to her. "You're leaving today?"

"I was going to talk to you about it after you were awake, but you were a lot faster coming down than I thought you'd be. What I have to do will take one day, but it'll take me a day to fly there and at least two to make it back home. I'll be back here on Saturday, probably."

"Why do you have to go at all?"

"I don't want to. It's just something I have to do."

"You won't tell me more than that?"

"It wouldn't make anybody safer — you, me, the girl."

"Look, I don't want to start a fight with you, especially just before you go away. But maybe you ought to spend some time asking yourself why you don't trust me."

She put her arms around him and kept them there, rocking slightly. "You know I trust you. We went through this years ago, and I thought you understood. I've made promises. One was that I wouldn't tell anyone where this person is or what I'm doing for her. Not that I'd only tell my husband."

"Getting married is a promise, too," he said. "There's not supposed to be anybody who knows more than you tell me."

"There isn't," she said. "I'm sorry, Carey. Right now just isn't a good time for this conversation. When this trip is over, we can talk. Please, just don't make this harder."

Carey studied her for a second, then relented. "Just make it back here safe, and get this whole thing finished."

"I will." She released him, then stepped back to look at him. "What do you want for breakfast?"

"Nothing."

"Nothing?"

"I'm not hungry right now. I'll get something at the hospital later."

"I love you," she said, and kissed him on the cheek, then picked up the carton of eggs and put it back in the refrigerator. "I love you" had always struck her as a foolish, inadequate thing to say, but it was exactly what she meant in exactly the way she had said it. She remembered times, years ago, when she had called him from various places around the country, only daring to talk on a pay phone for a minute or two. In her memory it was always night, and always raining. She wouldn't be able to tell him where she was because she was afraid his phone would be tapped or he would forget and mention the name of the place to someone else. He would be impatient for her to come home, and she would say, "I love you," and what it meant was "I'm sorry." And then when it was time to hang up she would say "I love you" again, and wait, holding her breath and listening, because it meant "Do you still love me?" In the past five years, since she had quit going away, the meaning had always been happy and sure. Maybe five years of that was as good as a life. It was more of a life than many people had, and she felt lucky to have had it. By this time tomorrow she could be dead.

15

After Carey had left for work she completed the rest of her preparations for her flight. Seeing Ketter in Kennedy Airport had reminded Jane that for her, airports were dangerous places. All she could do was alter her appearance enough so that if she was not face-to-face with an enemy, he might not recognize her immediately. This time she wore tinted glasses to hide her eyes, a cashmere sweater that softened and rounded the thin, sinewy quality of her arms and shoulders, an understated pendant with a single diamond, and a skirt. As soon as she had gone through security in the Buffalo airport and shown her driver's license for the last time, she hid her black hair under a blond wig. She flew to the US Airways hub in Pittsburgh and then boarded her plane to Santa Barbara without ever taking her eyes off the people around her.

Her plane turned and lowered above the

ocean off Santa Barbara while the sun still hung well above the blue horizon line. The plane hit the runway and rolled to the terminal, and the sky had a late-afternoon golden glow. Jane stepped off the plane quickly with her sunglasses on and her carry-on bag over her shoulder, scanning the faces of the people in the airport, then went to the car rental to claim the car she had reserved.

She had asked for a luxury car, and when she got to the rental area she found a Cadillac waiting for her. She had decided she wanted something big and overpowered for the drive up the coast. Lompoc was about an hour north of Santa Barbara, and if something went wrong she didn't want to be easy to outrun or bump off the road. She got into the car and drove out Sandspit Road to Ward Memorial Boulevard, a straight strip of concrete over the protected wetland at Goleta Beach, then turned onto Interstate 101 heading north away from Santa Barbara. After a few minutes, when the traffic thinned and cars were far apart, she pulled off the blond wig and shook out her hair.

She looked in the rearview mirror at the mountains that rose abruptly like a wall above Santa Barbara. She had always liked

Santa Barbara in the old days because it was beautiful and warm, a city of white buildings with red tile roofs built between a mountain range and a white sand beach. Now it had become a city of ghosts.

Jane could remember the night when she had broken into the apartment on Ocean View Avenue where Harry Kemple had been living for years as Harry Shaw, the name she had given him. Before she got there, the police had already spent hours in Harry's place, and they had left greasy black fingerprint dust all over the windows, the doorknobs, the smooth surface of the table in the kitchen. Harry's body had been taken away, but there was a huge reddish brown stain in the dirty shag carpet where Harry had bled out after his throat was cut. His heart must have taken a long time to stop, to pump out that much blood.

Harry was the only runner Jane had ever had who had been caught, and he had died because of her. His killer had fooled her into believing he was a friend of Harry's who needed help, so she had brought him to Vancouver to the shop of Lewis Feng, the man who had made Harry's identification papers. Days later, when Jane had learned Lewis Feng was dead, she had rushed to reach Harry, but she arrived too late. Since then, Harry Kemple had sometimes visited Jane in her dreams.

Santa Barbara wasn't the best place for Jane to stay the night, anyway. It was too close to Los Angeles, and it had become crowded over the past few years. There were too many people from other places on the street, and any of them might be one of the people who hated her, and might see her face before she saw theirs. The best place to stop would be one of the smaller towns to the north — Buellton, or Solvang, or even Lompoc — but when Jane reached them she kept driving.

She chose Santa Maria. Since she had last been there Santa Maria had begun to evolve from a largely blue-collar ranch area to an overflow community for Santa Barbara. The open spaces looked like vanity ranches where rich people rode expensive horses. She selected a motel off the interstate and checked in for the night. The room was small and thin-walled, and there was a sliding pocket door to the bathroom that kept going off its track, but it was adequate and she was tired.

Jane prepared her clothes and belongings for the next day, checking them off against the sheet of prison regulations she had printed out from her computer at home.

Visiting hours were eight-thirty to three on Friday, Saturday, and federal holidays. Processing of visitors stopped at two P.M. A visitor could carry only a clear plastic change purse, eight inches or smaller, forty dollars, and a comb. Jane would be permitted to wear "a reasonable amount" of jewelry. If she brought a baby she could have a clear plastic diaper bag with "a reasonable amount" of baby food, clothes, bottles, powder, and lotion. Shorts, halter tops, sheer clothing, skirts more than three inches above the knee, or khaki clothing were prohibited. Khaki clothes were what inmates wore.

She examined the picture ID she had asked Stewart Shattuck to make her the night she had brought Christine to see him. It was a duplicate of a California driver's license with Jane's picture in place of the original. Jane had known from the moment when Christine had told her the story of her family that she might need it one day. Jane put the license on the dresser and then went to bed and let the fatigue of the long day overtake her. In a few minutes she was asleep.

In her dream she was driving into Santa Barbara. She took the Salinas Street exit from the freeway, and then went by the corner of Ocean View Avenue, but didn't dare to take the turn. She couldn't avoid recognizing the tall hedge at the corner — at least twelve feet high and so thick it was opaque. The hedge was one of the first things she had seen when she had gone to Harry's apartment. She kept going and drove through the city, trying to get away from the memory of Harry's death. And then she made a turn and saw the old main building of Mission Santa Barbara ahead.

The sight of the Mission made Jane feel sick. It was an old adobe church with a tower and a long, low wing continuing to the left of it, the whole complex situated at the top of a vast sloping green lawn set off by big rose gardens. There was a small parking lot and a fountain, and to the right of the church was a high wall. It was what was behind the wall that was important. That was where the truth was hidden.

When the Jesuit missionaries came to the Senecas, they were promptly sent to their heaven. But the people who once inhabited this part of California coast weren't like the people of the eastern forests. They hadn't been fighting for a thousand years like the Iroquois. It took only a few Spanish soldiers on horseback to round them up and make them live in captivity. They died in such numbers that the cemetery filled up and the bodies had to be dug up and reburied elsewhere over and over to make room for the new deaths. Jane couldn't help walking out through the side door of the church into the cemetery. There were old stone markers here, with names and dates worn away. And there were green plants and flowers growing with the vigor of Santa Barbara's perpetual May. There was a melancholy silence here, interrupted about once every two minutes by the whispery sound of a car passing beyond the wall.

"So you're back."

Jane shut her eyes tightly, but she knew she had to turn around, so she did. She opened her eyes, knowing. There he was, the way he always was in her dreams. "Hello, Harry," she said. He was wearing the moss green sport coat that had always seemed slightly too big for him. It made her wonder if he'd bought it that way to hide cards in poker games, or if he had begun to age and get smaller before she had even met him. Harry was leaning on the high stone cemetery wall, his sad brown eyes fixed on her. She added, "I was thinking of you when I flew into the Santa Barbara airport today. I can't come here without thinking of you."

"I'm hard to forget even after all this time."

"You are. I'm so sorry, Harry." She could feel the tears beginning to well in her eyes.

"I know, I know. It doesn't matter to me anymore. Dying was one nasty surprise on one night of my life, the big hand in my hair jerking my head back, and then the knife going right across my throat, as quick as that. The experience was really all over before I even figured out what had happened. The result was determined, I mean. He let go of me, and I was already dead, while I was standing up." Harry tilted his head back, and she could see the mortician's crude stitching across his throat. "Looks like a baseball, doesn't it?"

"A little."

"It doesn't matter. By now I could be dead from a bad piece of meat. Don't waste time blaming yourself. This was just the twins, the grandsons of Sky Woman. Hawenneyu the right-handed twin creates, and Hanegoategeh the left-handed twin destroys. We're all just part of the battle they've always fought with each other, and we don't even know what part we're playing. Hawenneyu creates a bright little boy who grows up to be an anesthesiologist, but Hanegoategeh has already given him a blind spot in his peripheral vision so he won't notice that the dial on the meter is too high and so he'll kill a patient. But maybe Hawenneyu has made sure the patient is the one who would have grown up to kill whole countries. Each move has a countermove, and only the twins know which is which."

"That example is pretty far-fetched."

"Is it?" he said.

"Why are you here?"

Harry looked around at the old cemetery with exaggerated interest. "Somebody belongs here more than me? Somebody deader than I am?"

"You know what I mean. Why tonight?"

"I'm here to warn you, Janie," he said. "You've been living a quiet life for a long time. You don't get to know why you were allowed to do that. Hawenneyu raises his right hand to strike, but Hanegoategeh raises his left to grasp his wrist, just like a mirror image. Maybe he blocked the blow, but maybe Hawenneyu was just keeping him from moving."

"Meaning what?"

"It's over. They're moving. You're out again."

"I know that."

"But do you know which twin is doing it — day or night? Creator or Destroyer? The good twin or the bad one?"

"You just reminded me that I don't get to know."

"There are always results. Somebody lives. Or dies. Think about the woman."

"What about her? She's just a kid."

"Woman. There are a lot of questions you never asked. You accepted her because she said Sharon sent her, but you never talked to Sharon."

"There were men with guns waiting in the parking lot. They persuaded me."

"What were they going to do with the guns — kill her? Kill you?"

"It doesn't much matter. I couldn't let them do either. I couldn't let them take her. I couldn't ignore the fact that they set off a bomb to get to her."

"You couldn't. You couldn't. Somebody put you in a position where you couldn't make any choices. Or maybe they were just making the right choices unthinkable. Who was it?"

"I don't know."

"Make sure you're doing what you think you're doing."

"I think I'm doing what I'm supposed to. I'm keeping my word."

Harry shrugged. "I can't hang around here all night. You hid the woman. Now you're going to see her only living connection, the only person who seems to give a shit if she lives or dies. The boyfriend must know about him, right? Would you send somebody else there?" He gave her a compassionate look, then reached out and touched her cheek.

The hand was cold, with a texture like wax. She shuddered and jerked her head back involuntarily, and awoke. She lay in the bed staring up at the cottage-cheese ceiling above her. There seemed to be light behind the curtain, so she sat up. The clock said it was five A.M., but she didn't want to go back to sleep. She was afraid that she would see Harry in her dreams again. She showered and dressed, then packed, checked out of the hotel, and drove to Lompoc for an early breakfast.

Jane hated jails. Twice she had gone in because that was the only way to get to a woman and talk to her privately before she was released into danger again. Two other times she had allowed herself to be arrested because the alternative would have been to injure a police officer. Every surface in a jail seemed to her to have its own special cruelty — the bars, which were mostly symbolic in women's jails, but also the beds, the toilets, the showers, all of them rough, cheap, nasty versions of things that existed on the outside, as though someone wanted every instant of life to be a reminder that the prisoner was in a different world where everything was bad.

She drove around the perimeter of the parking lot as though she were undecided about where she was supposed to park, and looked at the cars, trying to detect a watcher. The cars all appeared to be empty. As she parked the car and began to walk toward the main building of the complex, she felt an instinctive urge to run, but she steadied herself and walked on.

About half the prisoners at Lompoc were assigned to the federal prison, the United States Penitentiary, a high-security section that had all the usual architectural reminders that the government had no intention of letting any of these men decide to leave — fences, towers, bars. The other half were in the Federal Correction Institution, the low-security section. She had checked in advance on her computer, and learned that Robert Monahan was one of these inmates.

She went to the front lobby and saw that things were less ugly than she had expected. The place reminded her of a military base. But she knew what she was seeing was a gloved fist. It might seem smooth and not terribly threatening, but inside was still a fist. Jane told the first person in a uniform, a young man, that she had an appointment, and he told her to show her ID to a woman called the Front Entrance Officer, who checked her off the visitor list.

The man held a metal detector and moved it up and down her body, and the woman patted her down. Jane had brought only the plastic see-through change purse to hold her driver's license and sunglasses and money, but the male officer opened it and searched it anyway. Then she was directed to a waiting room consisting of bare painted walls and rows of chairs, where another officer handed her a copy of the rules that she had already read. One rule was that a violation of the rules could result in a sentence of twenty years for the visitor.

Jane sat on a chair in the nearly bare waiting room for an hour and a half, watching the other visitors. Most of them were women, some with babies or toddlers, others apparently mothers whose babies had grown up and gotten convicted of federal crimes. At nine, and then at ten, a man announced that he was the Visitation Duty Officer, then called names from a list on a clipboard and let the visitors into the visiting room. When the man called the name Jane was listening for, she stood up and followed the Duty Officer into the room, where the Visiting Room Officer showed her to a seat at a long counter.

Across from Jane was a man in his fifties with graying hair cut short and a khaki uniform. On his feet were a pair of white socks and plastic sandals. When he saw Jane he stared at her in shock and disappointment. His mouth gaped open.

Jane stepped quickly to him, her arms extended. "Bobby, give me a hug." She glared at him. "I've missed you so much."

"You're —"

"Really glad to see you. Christine wishes she could come, but today it has to be just me."

The man allowed her to throw her arms around him. She held him tightly in that awkward position with the counter between them and whispered, "Christine asked me to do this." She sensed that the guard was moving in their direction, so she released him and sat down across from him. The guard moved off.

Jane said, "I'm sorry to be so insensitive to your feelings. I pretended to be Delia because it was the only name besides Christine's I knew you would have put on your list of visitors at intake."

"And you knew that nobody here would ever have seen her," said Monahan.

"I guessed, after what Christine told me about her," she said. "I'm sorry."

"Where is she?"

"Christine is in a situation now that won't allow her to be here and visit you. We both felt that we had to get word to you somehow that she still loves you very much. She isn't dropping you or forgetting about you or feeling any different about you. She simply can't be near here, or come to visit."

"How long will that be?"

Jane hesitated. "I don't know. It might be for a few months, or it might be years."

"Why?"

"I'm not sure how much you know already. She was in love with her boss, Richard Beale."

"She's talked about him. You said 'was in love.' What happened?"

"I'm not sure of everything. She got pregnant. She decided not to tell him, just to leave."

"What do you mean? Why wouldn't she tell him?"

"She hasn't told me every detail. But I get the impression he wasn't treating her well. She was afraid of him, and she was beginning to admit to herself that a lot of his business deals had a suspicious side to them. He was also paying some creeps to handle unpleasant problems for him, and that scared her. She could see the relationship wasn't going to end well if she stayed, so she didn't."

Robert Monahan had put his head in his hands right after he had heard the word "pregnant." He looked up. "Where is she now?"

"She's safe."

"Where?"

"She's far away from here, and she's well and safe. I can't say where right now."

"Why did she want to be hidden? Is he stalking her or something?"

"It's more than that. He sent his six creeps to find her and drag her back to San Diego. They're very —" She saw the Visiting Room Officer was about to pass close to them. "— and then I said to her, 'If you don't like the neighborhood, don't buy the house. You can't remodel the neighborhood.' " Then the officer was out of earshot. "These are not people you want to have find your daughter."

"But what does Richard want? Why send people like that after her?"

Jane looked at him in silence for a few

seconds. "That part isn't what I do. I haven't got any smart theories to tell you. Maybe he's afraid she'll tell the police about something she saw at work or at his house. Maybe anything. I don't try to psychoanalyze men like him. I teach people how to run away from them."

"My God," he said. "What can we do?"

"What I did was take her from a place where people were trying to harm her to a different place where nobody knows her. I promised her I would find a way to tell you so you wouldn't think she suddenly didn't love you or that she had dropped off the face of the earth. Now I have." Jane stood up.

"Wait," said Monahan. "Don't go yet. What happens when I get out? How do I find her?"

"When you're out you can write me a letter. They won't let me hand you any paper. It's Post Office box 96919, Chicago, Illinois 60637. Can you remember it?"

"96919. 60637. Yes."

"When you write, just give me a phone number, and I'll let you know how she is. If it's safe by then, we'll arrange something."

"Is she going to have the baby?"

"Yes. And she's planning to keep it. I don't know the sex, but he or she is healthy. Christine has medical care and money and a safe place to live. After it's born, I'll move them again and give them new names, so there won't be any chance of tracing her through birth records or anything like that."

"Will you tell her I love her?"

"Sure. But she already knows it. I'll tell her you're okay."

"That's accurate enough. Mostly tell her I love her, and whatever she does, I'm on her side."

Jane looked around her again, then into his eyes. "I'm going to have to tell her again that getting in touch with you would be stupid."

"I know you'll have to say that."

"I just had to be sure."

A few minutes later the Visiting Room Officer began calling names. After each, he would say, "Your time is up. Please leave by the door at the back of the room." When he called "Monahan," Jane and Robert Monahan stood. She held out her arms to him, and they shared another awkward embrace. "Sorry it was only me," she whispered.

"If I forgot to say anything, will you tell her I said it?"

"Of course I will. Take care, Robert."

They had to end the embrace, and Monahan stood and watched the tall, dark-haired woman follow the Visiting Room Officer to the door on the other side. He never blinked, just took every moment of the sight of her into his memory. As the door closed he sent her a silent benediction, really only a fervent hope that the strength he sensed in her would be great enough to keep Chris safe from harm. Then he turned around to face the other door, where the corridor took him back into his prison.

16

Jane stepped out the front door of the prison and walked toward her rental car. It was just before eleven, and the day was beginning to heat up as the haze that had drifted in from the ocean during the night burned off, and the sun reasserted its intensity. Jane took the sunglasses out of her plastic purse and put them on. She liked the morning fog that settled over central California during June and July. She acknowledged that it was probably because every time she had been here, she had been trying to keep from being noticed, and the glaring sun that prevailed most of the time had always made her feel vulnerable.

She got into her rented Cadillac and drove out to Klein Boulevard, the road she had used to reach the prison. She glanced in the rearview mirror and saw other cars pulling out of the lot, but she was preoccupied, thinking about Robert Monahan. She knew she should have been more definite with him. If the four people who were still looking for Christine were any good at all, they would know her father was in Lompoc. He was the only person that Christine was almost certain to try to reach. It might never be safe for Robert Monahan to see his daughter, and Jane should have been clear about that. She had been intending to tell him that his greatest comfort was going to be knowing that his daughter was safe and wasn't doing anything foolish. But when Jane had thought about the fact that he had six more years, she had decided to say something less harsh and less certain. In six years things could change all by themselves. Richard Beale could be run over by a bus, and his four hunters could all be in jail.

The visit was over. Whatever she had accomplished would have to do. When the day came for Robert Monahan's release, there would be no doubt whether or not she had said the right things. And there was no doubt that Monahan had understood the message. Jane glanced in the rearview mirror again to check on the cars behind her. She didn't like the fact that the visitors were all let in and out on the hour. The little road away from the prison seemed unnecessarily well traveled. Jane didn't have to accept that. She watched for a safe place to pull her car over to let the other cars pass. Some of them probably had a long way to go, and it was better to let them head for the interstate than to have them tailgate and make risky moves to pass her. Jane wasn't in a hurry. She had already accomplished everything she had come to do, and all that was left was to make it home safe and un-noticed.

She found a turnout, a wider stretch of shoulder where she could let the others pass. As each car went by her, she looked at the driver. Each of the first four cars was driven by someone she had seen in the visiting room. Two of them were young women driving alone, and both of them looked as though they were crying. The third car held a mother and three young children. The mother drove with stony-faced resolution. In the next car was an elderly couple who were the parents of an inmate. She had noticed them in the visiting room walking in slowly, in that stiff, careful way that indicated they were afraid of falling. They sat across from a handsome dark-haired man about thirty years old. The mother and the son had been talkers, sometimes inter-rupting each other or talking at the same time, as though they shared the gift of talking and listening simultaneously. The father had sat back a bit so his wife could be closer, and said nothing. He simply listened.

The next car to appear in Jane's rearview mirror was a full-sized dark blue model. It had pulled over, too, at least two hundred yards back. As she watched it for a few seconds and it showed no sign of pulling out again, small alarms began to sound in her mind. There was a white van coming, still far off. She returned to the road and accelerated to thirty-five, and then checked the mirror again. The blue car let the big white van pass, and then drove after it. She wasn't sure about the blue car yet, but if she had been trying to follow someone, she would have done the same thing — let the van pass so it would be between them.

Curious about the driver of the blue car, she let her car drift out a bit to the left edge of her lane, and tried to use her side mirror to see him. The car was too far back. She knew that no matter who was in the car, it would be best if she didn't let him spend too much time behind her, but she wanted to see him. Waiting outside the prison until someone came to see Robert Monahan and then following her was exactly what the four would do. Jane tried repeatedly but she couldn't quite see the driver. She sped up and watched the mirror. Nothing happened, so she put more distance between her car and the van.

As she accelerated, she tried to picture each stretch of road ahead, waiting for the place where she could make a sudden turn and force the follower to either drive past the turn and lose her, or commit himself to a pursuit. She couldn't let anyone follow her back to the Santa Barbara Airport and learn what flight she was taking. The farther she went with him behind her, the greater the possibility that he would learn something about her that she didn't want him to know.

There was only one traffic light on this route before the road took them into the city of Lompoc. She would drive fast around the bend, across the bridge to the traffic light. If it was red she would go through it, and if he was guilty he would, too. If it was green she would wait for it to turn red. If he was guilty he would wait with her.

Jane pressed harder on the gas pedal and increased her speed. She was going over sixty before she reached the end of Klein Boulevard. She slowed only enough to make the turn without spinning off into a field. Her tires squealed a little, but she kept the car in control, and accelerated again. This time she built her speed to sixty-five and held it as she drove on, checking her mirror. The other car peeked out from behind the van, then veered around it into the left lane to pass. The car kept accelerating, trying to keep Jane's Cadillac in sight.

The time was coming for Jane to make her move. She could see the start of the curve ahead, just a place where the road seemed to dissolve. She took the bend in the road and then knew what she wanted. Jane hit her brakes, pulled off onto the right shoulder, and stopped. The dark blue car had been accelerating to catch up with her, and as it came around the bend, it could barely hold the road. Jane saw the front dip down, then dip again as the driver applied the brakes, but it was moving far too fast to stop in time. The car slowed only to about thirty as it went past her, the driver fighting to slow it down.

The driver was a woman. She appeared to be in her thirties, with long hair that appeared slightly unnatural as though it had been straightened and dyed coal black. She glared at Jane, and the expression on her face was a mixture of anger and fear. It was clear that she knew she had failed to keep Jane from noticing her and by slamming on her brakes she had convicted herself of trying to follow her. The woman was no longer anonymous.

Jane could see that the woman had a Bluetooth mic on her ear, and was talking to somebody on the telephone as she skidded past.

Jane pulled out onto the road after her. The woman saw Jane's car in the mirror and began to accelerate. Jane accelerated, too, coming up behind the woman fast, as though she meant to come up on her left and force her off the road. The traffic signal at the intersection was visible now and turning yellow, then red. The woman added more speed as she approached the bridge. Her car bounced when the tires hit the metal seam between pavement and bridge, and Jane could see that she was going to run the light.

Jane stayed behind her, but before they reached the red light, Jane took her foot off the gas pedal and fell back. The woman was watching Jane, and she didn't see until the last moment that there was a truck coming into the intersection on the cross street from the left. She made a panicky attempt to avoid it by standing on her brakes, but the driver of the truck had seen her coming and begun to stop, too. They were entering the intersection at the same time.

The woman wrenched her wheel to the right and hit the gas pedal to swing into a right turn around the corner. The truck driver saw what she was doing and swerved to the left to avoid her, so both the woman's car and the truck moved off down the road side by side, the truck in the left lane and the car in the right.

Jane accelerated past them both and through the intersection. Even though the light was still red, there was no other vehicle coming. She kept going into the business district of the city of Lompoc, made a few quick turns to be sure the woman couldn't find her easily if she tried to catch her, and then drove on residential streets until she reached the next intersection with a busy street, turned and followed it to the entrance to Interstate 101. There was no question in Jane's mind that the woman would know she had come to Lompoc from somewhere nearby, almost certainly Santa Barbara, an hour to the south. Jane drove to the right onto the northbound entrance and drove hard toward San Francisco.

She reached San Francisco in the late afternoon, and stopped at the Bank of America branch on Market Street where she kept an account in the name of Valerie Collins. The teller seemed only mildly surprised when she withdrew four thousand dollars in cash. The teller in the Wells Fargo branch up the street behaved the same when Carol Stevens withdrew thirty-five hundred in cash from her account just before closing time. As long as the amount wasn't large enough so they had to fill out extra forms, everybody seemed to be unconcerned. It was clear now that Christine was going to have to keep a low profile and pay for everything in cash for a longer time than Jane had anticipated. She would have to visit a few more banks in the months before she returned to Minneapolis to pick her up.

In the early evening she stood at the car rental at the Oakland airport. She turned in the car she had rented in Santa Barbara, then took the shuttle to the terminal. The first flight to the east that had an empty seat to sell her was headed for Atlanta, but she took it. She knew that when she got there she would have to get on a flight to Philadelphia or Newark in order to catch another one for Buffalo. The trip would probably take her the rest of the night and most of the next day, but if she got home by midnight it would still be Saturday, technically.

Jane went through the security checkpoint, watching the crowds, searching for familiar faces. As soon as she was beyond the checkpoint she went into a ladies' room and put on the blond wig and the outfit she had worn when she had flown to Santa Barbara. On her way to the gate where her flight to Atlanta would be boarding, Jane stopped at a pay telephone and dialed the number of the apartment in Minneapolis.

There was no answer, but the voice mail kicked in. Jane was pleased to hear the generic female voice the phone company had chosen to personify it. "We're sorry, but the customer at this number is not able to answer right now. If you would like to leave a message, begin speaking after the tone." After a few seconds, the tone sounded, and Jane said, "Hi. It's me. I wanted to let you know that I visited your father today. He's fine, and he said to tell you he loves you very much. He understands exactly why you couldn't be there, and that you won't be able to visit in person. He said he wanted to be absolutely sure you knew he didn't blame you for anything that's happened, and he's very glad about his grandchild. I told him how to get in touch with me when he's out. So don't worry about him. I should tell you that there was a woman waiting in the parking lot of the prison when I came out, and she tried to follow me to you. She had long hair —

dyed an unnatural black. I suppose it could be a wig. I'll see you in a couple of months. Stay safe." She hung up, moved off, and walked past her gate, scanning the waiting areas near it for familiar, unwelcome faces.

17

Andy Beale sat in his study and listened to what Grace Kandinsky, his private detective, had to tell him about her day of watching Richard's hired woman at the prison. After a time he realized that he was sitting with the phone pressed against his ear and wincing. The whole situation had turned into a disaster, in spite of all his advice. It wasn't that difficult, either. Richard's people had known the woman would be coming, and probably bringing Christine with her. All they really had to do was wait outside the prison for her to walk right into their trap. Instead, they had sent one woman to sit in the parking lot to watch for her. Their attempt had been stupid, inadequate, and halfhearted. When she sounded as though she had finished her report, he said, "Is that it?"

"That's it," she said.

"Then you can come home now. Send

me a bill."

"You bet I will."

Andy Beale hung up, put on his sport coat, walked out to the car and began to drive. When he reached the freeway and turned south toward La Jolla, Beale only got angrier. Richard had been a disappointment when he was in nursery school, and he had never improved. He had been a mama's boy without being particularly nice to his mother. That probably should have been a sign and a warning. The kid had wanted every bit of Ruby's attention twenty-four hours a day, but when he had her attention, he used it to make her miserable — whining, crying, and complaining.

Throughout childhood, Richard was always too hot or too cold. He was hungry but he hated whatever food she gave him, cranky and sleepy but never willing to go to bed and give everybody a rest. In school he was a bully, but he got beaten up more often than the school's weakest kids because he was so cowardly about only picking on them that he attracted bigger bullies. The reason why Andy and Ruby Beale had started spying on him after he was in high school was that he was so damned sneaky.

Richard was always hiding things he had but wasn't supposed to have, lying about things he did, and pretending he had done things he hadn't. By Richard's junior year in high school, Andy Beale had seen exactly as many fake report cards as real ones. The fakes always arrived early. When the fakes came, Andy would wait a week and call the school to ask that a set of duplicates be sent to his office. He never explained to anyone at the school why it was necessary. Was he supposed to tell them his only son was a liar and a fraud? The purpose of the exercise wasn't to expose Richard's crimes and get him kicked out of school. It was only to allow Ruby and Andy to know what their son was really doing. It always amazed Andy that the false report cards didn't hide anything very serious: All Richard had been concealing was laziness and mediocrity.

In certain dark moods, Andy Beale had even considered the discrepancies between the real and the fake cards amusing. Richard always found it necessary to make himself into a phenomenon, a straight-A student who inspired flattering comments from teachers, even though there was no space on the card for them. In this Richard apparently had only been imitating his teachers' actual practice. Now and then an exasperated teacher would scrawl in a margin, "Seldom came to class!" or "Failed

319

midterm for violation of honor code!"

Upon reflection, what Andy Beale objected to most wasn't Richard's sneakiness. It was his stupidity, his lack of foresight. If Richard gave himself straight As, didn't he realize his mother would expect him to be valedictorian? Didn't he realize that she expected him to be admitted by every college he applied to? No, Richard didn't think that far ahead. Everything he did was for temporary advantage, or even a brief reprieve from work.

Being Richard's father was heartrending for Andy Beale. He felt that Richard deserved to get caught, but he couldn't bring himself to rat on his own son. Telling school administrators what a little shit Richard was would cause Ruby terrible pain and, if she found out who had told, make her angry at Andy in a way he would never overcome. He was afraid her resentment would eventually lead to the end of the marriage. As the offenses Andy knew about accumulated, he became paralyzed. If the school ever found out, then Richard would lose the most precious possession of all, the opportunity to change. He would always remain a bully, a sneak, a loafer, a coward. So Andy had let him go on, hoping that as Richard matured, he would improve. It had, in the end, been the worst thing he could have done. Richard had only grown from a little snake to a big one.

The one change during Richard's time in college was that Ruby had gradually given up. One day when Richard was in college at San Diego State, she had gone to visit him at his off-campus apartment. She knew the way and had a key because it was a unit in an apartment complex that belonged to the Beale Company. She had called ahead and told him she was going to take him out for a nice dinner. When she got there, he was gone. He had stood her up. She had called and come back the next day. He had stood her up again. He had treated her that way on her birthday. Richard had kept doing things like that over and over. He was always too busy to see his mother, but he compiled an academic record so dismal that it astounded Andy that Richard didn't flunk out. He would stop answering his phone, and then Andy would find that someone had charged a vacation for two in Hawaii to Ruby's credit card number. There were bills for an incredible number of dinners, trips, even charges at jewelry stores, but no steady girlfriend that Andy ever saw.

Richard had always had trouble with women. What man hadn't? But his trouble was always peculiar. Richard had inherited Ruby's eyes and facial structure, so he was a very good-looking man. He had inherited Andy's physique. He looked the way Andy had forty years ago — flat stomach, broad shoulders — and he was reasonably light on his feet. He was very good at attracting women, but terrible at keeping them once he had them. After a short time with Richard they always left. Andy wondered if women were taking advantage of Richard.

Andy had called a woman private detective named Grace Kandinsky, just like the painter, to get in touch with a few of Richard's old girlfriends and a few women who had dated him, and see what they had to say about him. Andy had even listed a half dozen who had merely worked in the office. The project had taken Miss Kandinsky months, and when it was over, Andy asked her to give him the short version.

She was a difficult young woman to shock. She had begun as a police woman working vice, and later, narcotics. She said, "Summary?"

"Yes."

"He's not a nice man."

"I'm paying you thousands of dollars for that?"

"No, for wasting countless hours of my

time asking questions. If you'd like to listen to all the recordings I made, you're welcome to them. I spent so much time talking to women in bars, my boyfriend asked me if I was a lesbian. What I found out is what you'll find out — he's not nice to women."

"Tell me something specific. One thing."

"He tells them he'll love them forever, but forever means until he gets tired of them. In the meantime he controls everything they do. He checks up on them and spies on them — runs in your family, huh?"

"I'm not paying extra for comedy."

"I'm sorry." She looked at him sympathetically. "I really am."

"You're sorry for me because what you're telling me is that my son is a creep."

She cocked her head. "I think that's true. I'm also sorry for making jokes. It's just because I'm nervous. It's a serious situation for you, and for him, but he doesn't know it, or care, or something. I guess that's the common theme of what I found out. He just doesn't care about other people."

Andy had paid Grace Kandinsky and gone on with his life as though he had never met her. He had never said anything to Ruby about the detective when he had hired her, and he didn't say anything afterward.

Ruby still cared very much about Richard. But she cared for Richard the way she would have cared for a mangled toe. She had no high expectations for what it could do, but it still hurt like crazy, so there was no question that it belonged to her.

Ruby had begun to yearn for grandchildren at that time. She had said, "Andy, I want Richard to find a wife as soon as possible, and get started making grandchildren. That's the best we can do now — get as many of them as possible and start teaching and training and guiding. I'd hate to think that the culmination of our two family bloodlines was nothing but Richard. We can't let that happen. We'll spend a lot of time with his children, pick out a couple of the best ones after a few years, and see if we can do it right this time."

He had thought about it. Ruby had worked a lifetime beside him and hadn't asked for much in return. While he was building the real estate business she was working, too, first as a waitress and then as a nurse, keeping each of her paychecks only long enough to verify the amount and the deductions and then signing it over for deposit to their company, so Andy could use the money to buy more property. She had spent her evenings and weekends during most of those years working beside him on the company bookkeeping and paper-work. The rest of her time had been devoted to Richard.

Andy Beale was willing to do a great variety of things that people didn't anticipate. The only thing he couldn't do was turn down a serious request from Ruby. Their only child, Richard, had been a disappointment to her, so if she wanted another chance with the next generation, he would try to give it to her.

When he reached the office, he almost drove into the reserved space at the end that belonged to Richard, but thought better of it. There was no point in irritating him just for the sake of irritating him. Andy pulled his Lexus around the building and parked in the back on the far side of the Dumpster, where it wasn't easy to see.

He went into the office, sat at Richard's desk, and began examining the files that contained the notes and reports on current operations. He happily occupied a half hour that way, and then Richard came in, looking harried.

When he saw his father at his desk, he froze, trying to hold his temper. "What are you doing here? Is this going to be a habit?"

"I doubt it," said Andy. "I've got better things to do than sit in an office."

"Oh, that's right," said Richard. He took his coat off and hung it on a hanger in a high, narrow space in one of the teak cabinets that covered the far wall of the office.

"I've noticed you've been doing a lot of work." Andy closed the file he'd been reading and tossed it on the desk with a flop. "Cut it out."

"What?"

"I said cut it out. Stop it."

"I thought you were always worried that I wasn't running the business properly. Not enough profit to fill the gas tank of your flagship."

Andy Beale pursed his lips, and congratulated himself on having the presence of mind to recognize that his irritation proved he really was too defensive about the boat. He said cheerfully, "I've built a good business, and over the past five years or so you've done pretty well with it. The rents are coming in, and the last developments are built and selling very well. But it's time to turn all your attention to what I asked you about last time."

"Christine?"

"Yes, Christine. It's important to your mother, and that makes it important to me."

"I thought you were going to solve the

whole thing for me. Didn't you say that? I'm not sensitive enough to handle it, so you were going to."

"Not sensible enough is more to the point. It's a situation that calls for some understanding of women. If a girl will move in with you and let you get her pregnant, then you were the one she wanted. They all walk around looking at each man they meet and asking themselves, 'Could this be the one?' and she decided you probably were. Whatever else happened afterward that made her leave can be gotten over. Women have an infinite capacity for fooling themselves about men."

"Apparently."

Andy kept himself from blustering, "What the hell does that mean?" and said, "Speaking of women, I just heard that the woman who helped Christine leave you has been to visit Christine's father in Lompoc."

"How do you know that?"

"I knew your Mr. Demming and company were watching for her, so I hired somebody to watch your people watch."

"Jesus Christ," said Richard. "You paid Demming to report to you before me, didn't you?"

Andy Beale shook his head sadly. "Richard, we're on the same side. We're a father and son. And since I'm assuming the pay for Demming and his people isn't coming out of your personal salary, I'm their real employer. But I didn't do what you think. I hired a detective. Period."

"You're interfering and getting in the way of what I'm trying to do."

Andy stared at Richard for a second, and couldn't help thinking what a fine-looking man he had grown into — and what a fool. He shrugged. "I didn't interfere with your people. What they were going to do, they did. They were watching the prison parking lot. When the woman came out, who did your Mr. Demming have there to see her and take advantage of the opportunity? One lone woman, who proceeded to follow her a few miles and then lose her in Lompoc, which was not, last time I looked, a huge and complicated metropolis."

"What you're saying is they made a mistake. If they didn't get her, then you're right. It happens. There are only four of them at the moment, and all four can't be in one place waiting for a woman who isn't even Christine."

"Exactly," said Andy. "So I'm changing the way we go about this, as of now. I want you to put business aside. Most of the money is invested in undeveloped land that

328

will keep passively growing in value as long as we don't set off a nuclear weapon on it. The rental properties are pretty much the same, and we have people for maintenance and bill collection. The real estate sales people work on commission. So let it go."

"I think you're underestimating what it takes to run this business now. It's grown a lot since you retired."

"I'm not as out of touch as you wish I was. If we both died today, the property would still keep making money for years. I want you to concentrate on getting your girlfriend back."

"You know I've been doing that."

"Your girlfriend is at least six months pregnant, and she's been gone at least a month. It's time to stop waiting for spontaneous changes of heart or your half-assed crew of security people to come through. It's pretty damned clear that your people have had chances and blown them all. It's time to make an emotional appeal, which is what you should have done in the first place."

"How do you suggest I do that — put a note in a bottle? Hire skywriters?"

"This is a twenty-year-old girl. Kids don't read newspapers anymore, so you put what you want to say into your computer and find a way to be sure she'll find it. You could start a Web site and type your appeal into it. You tell her you love her and want to marry her and raise your baby together. Find other ways to get into her computer. See if she has a Web site under another name, or a MySpace page or YouTube or whatever else they do. Do it today. I'll want to see what you've done tomorrow night when I get back."

"Get back from where?"

"Lompoc. I told you I was going to see her father. You may have to see him, too, after I've made my visit. We'll see. I needed to write and get the man to agree to see me, and then get special permission from the prison authorities. I'm going tomorrow morning."

"All right," said Richard. "I hope it's not a waste of time."

"But you think it will be?" said Andy. "Just get your stuff done, and you won't need me."

The old man left, and Richard walked out of his office to the lobby window to see the Lexus pull out of the driveway and down the street. The last time he had come, Richard had devoted six hours to searching his office for cameras and microphones, but had found nothing. His father had been in here reading over the files on Richard's desk, and might have had time to do just about anything.

It was hard to know what the purpose of his visit had been. Maybe he had hidden cameras and microphones in here before, but had known that when he'd started bragging about how much he knew, then Richard would search for hidden devices. He might have come in during the night and removed them. Today's visit might have been to read what he could no longer see on a monitor. Or it could have been to reinstall the cameras and microphones now that Richard had completed his search. In spite of his crudeness and bullying, the old man was very cunning. He had always been particularly good at predicting what Richard would think and feel, and making pitiless use of it against him in these battles. If he hurt Richard's feelings it seemed to be a bonus for him. He was capable of putting bugging equipment in just for that purpose.

Richard took a quick look around the office, paying particular attention to electrical outlets, where some permanent bug could be planted. He examined the telephones and the computer to see if their shells had been opened. Then he looked under the furniture and stood on his desk to lift a ceiling tile and look around in the empty space above the frame. He heard a noise coming from outside the door, so he hastily climbed down and waited, but nobody entered. He leaned against the door. Nothing happened. He walked out into the lobby past Marlene, the pretty receptionist he had hired to take Christine's place. Or had he hired her? He had selected her, but who was to say why she had applied? She could easily be working for his father. Richard felt sick. Having his receptionist spying on him would be a thousand times worse than being bugged.

The thought made Richard feel panicky about Christine again. She knew too much about him, had been present for too many transactions, whether she had enough experience to know how to sort out what she knew or not. She was like a bomb, hidden somewhere and getting ready to go off in less than three months and obliterate him. Richard went outside to the parking lot behind the building and used his cell phone to call Demming.

"It's me," he said. "I hear one of your girls saw the woman who's been hiding Christine."

"How the hell did you hear that?" Demming said. Demming's surprise and annoyance made Richard feel in control. He was almost grateful to his father for a second.

"My father told me. He had somebody watching your person at Lompoc. I hear the woman got away."

"What do you want me to say?"

"Then it's true."

"Yes."

"Well, my father is going to visit Robert Monahan tomorrow."

"How is he going to do that? When you're sent there you have to give the warden's office a list of the people who might visit you — family and no more than three friends. He sure as hell couldn't have put down your father."

"My father says he wrote letters to Monahan and the prison people, and got permission."

The silence told Richard that Demming felt humiliated and angry. After a few seconds Demming said, "Does he know what to say?"

"I think he does. He's going to try to get Monahan to tell his daughter to come and see me. You know — that I can't wait to marry her and all that."

"Look, Richard. The woman got there first. If she said anything to him, it will be that he should tell his daughter to stay out of sight. She will have told him everything we did to try to grab Christine and bring her back. Maybe it's not such a good idea to have your father do this."

"I can't stop him."

"Do you think he'll accomplish anything?"

"I don't know anything about this woman who's helping Christine. I know my father has sold a few hundred houses and dozens of square miles of land over the years. He's a good salesman."

"Well, then, let's hope he's having a great day tomorrow."

"Maybe," said Richard. "I was wondering. Who was it that was watching the prison today?"

"That doesn't make any difference. If she lost this woman, then anybody would have."

"Who? Claudia?"

"No. It happened to be Sybil. You would have lost the woman. I would have. This is a person who played chicken with us on a dark highway in upstate New York at like ninety miles an hour, and she never swerved or touched the brake pedal. She's shown us a couple of times that she's ready to die to keep us away from Christine. She's a fucking crazy person and I think we've got to recognize that and work around her. It's not a wonderful situation, but it's the one we're in. Now, if we can trust your father to do this right, maybe he'll get Christine's father to tell him something, or pass his daughter a message."

"Uh, Steve?"

"What?"

"Can you have whoever is watching the prison tomorrow pay special attention to my father?"

"Of course. We were going to put Claudia there. She's already on her way to Lompoc. That woman might have come just to see if it would be safe for Christine. If she doesn't see Sybil she may think it's safe. But we can make sure she doesn't harm your father."

"No, I meant something slightly different. I'd like you and the others to get a look at him, get used to his clothes, his movements, the car he drives. And try to spot the person he's hired to watch the prison."

"Just what are you planning, Richard?"

"I'm not planning anything."

"Of course you are."

"I'm asking you to keep an eye on my father for a couple of hours, and you have someone there anyway."

"You're putting him under surveillance like somebody who might become an enemy."

"All right, all right. I'm in trouble here. I'm under terrible pressure. What I want most is that you find Christine before she has the baby and bring her back here to see me. That's all I really want, and it's what I hired you to do. If I had her now, there wouldn't be any problem. Since I don't have her, I have to start worrying about what happens if I don't get her."

"What happens?"

"My mother wants that grandchild. If I don't get Christine by the time that baby is born, my father is going to give up on me. It's what he's wanted to do for years. He'll take control of the company away from me, fire me, and evict me from my house. I'll be out on the street with no job and no place to live. I'm thirty-eight years old. I've never worked anywhere but the family business, so I wouldn't even have anything to put on a résumé. Meanwhile, Christine will be out there somewhere. She's twenty, but she won't be twenty forever. At some point she's going to understand everything she saw while she worked and lived with me. She'll either hold it over my head for money or just flat out turn me in. Are you starting to get the picture?"

Steve Demming's tone changed. "If I were you, I'd be setting aside a lot of cash, pulling it out of the businesses as fast as I could, and hiding it."

"What do you think I've been doing? But I don't know how much my father knows. I don't know who works for me, and who works for him."

"So you've decided to prepare for the chance that things don't go right."

"Yes," said Richard. "For all I know, everything is going the right way, and he'll get what we need from Christine's father. But if he doesn't, and Christine doesn't turn up where you're looking, then I've got to have a way to save myself."

"Of course," said Demming. "And what about your mother? If he's gone, will she be on your side and keep from asking questions?"

"No," said Richard. "We'll have to think about her, too, I suppose. But not yet. Give my father some time."

18

The next morning, as Andy Beale drove into the parking lot outside the prison, he saw his detective Grace Kandinsky getting out of her car so he would see her. She turned her head at an odd angle to her left as she lit a cigarette, so he couldn't help following her eyes to see a woman in a black sedan across the lot. She seemed to be young, and had a sweet-faced attractiveness, with long blond hair. That had to be the replacement for the woman Grace had told him about, the one Demming had assigned to watch the prison. The blond woman took out her telephone while Andy parked his car a distance away from hers. He supposed she was going to report to Demming that he was here, but when he got out of his car and walked toward the prison entrance, he realized that she was taking his picture over and over with her cell phone as he walked. He looked the other way and pretended he hadn't seen her do it. It was always best to keep to himself how much he knew and how much he didn't.

He went inside the prison entrance and separated himself from the proceedings emotionally. The prison officials cleared him and briefed him and made him wait. He reminded himself that the guards didn't have anything against him and no reason to be impressed by him. They just needed to be sure he wasn't going to hand one of their prisoners something dangerous or forbidden. Andy Beale had learned in the navy that a man who tried to resist authority was wasting his time. He could see that prisons were the same. Getting by was really just a matter of going where they pointed you and waiting quietly until they were ready to point you somewhere else. In due time he found himself in a visiting room, being ushered to a counter across from a man about fifty in khaki clothes. "Mr. Monahan?" he said. "I'm Andy Beale."

Monahan sat down. "Hello, Mr. Beale."

There was no handshake, no smile. Andy Beale sat down, trying to use the seconds before he talked to read Monahan's face. There was a lot of wrinkling around the forehead and eyes, where he saw a look of anxiety that he was sure predated the prison term by many years. Monahan had the look of a man who had gotten used to losing. "Mr. Monahan," he said, "the reason I drove up here today is to meet you in person and see whether you and I can help our children. I'm the father of a strong, healthy, successful son who's had his heart broken."

Monahan was impassive. "Is that something I'm supposed to worry about? When you drove into this place did you happen to notice it was a federal prison?"

"Maybe I'm just teasing myself with false hopes. I know from Richard that Christine loves you very much, so I thought she might have confided in you a little, and you would know what I'm talking about."

"She does confide in me. I know who Richard is."

"I'm glad," he said, in spite of the fact that Monahan's expression didn't indicate that he'd heard anything good. "Then what I have to tell you is that since Christine left, he's been absolutely devastated. He's always been a cheerful, optimistic young man. Now he's moping around all the time. For a few days he'll throw himself back into business and be in the office working from dawn until dark the way he always did, but it's not the same. I can see he's just desperate to take his mind off her for a few hours. I can see he hasn't slept much. His eyes are hollow and he never smiles. Then he'll exhaust himself and one day he won't even get out of bed. I'm telling you, I'd turn him over to the psychiatrists, except that I know what's wrong. All they could do for him is load him up with antidepressants, and that won't solve anything."

"I'll be honest with you, Mr. Beale. When I first heard Chris was dating your son, I didn't encourage it. She was eighteen years old, and that's too young to be getting serious with anyone, let alone an employer, a man who is twice her age. He had no business putting her in that position."

"I understand what you're saying," said Andy Beale. "I get the sense that you've spent most of your life the way I have — working in business. And we've both seen a lot of times when executives have fooled around with young secretaries, and been real users, and haven't cared about those young women at all. That's why the laws have changed and become very punitive about sexual harassment. But if you've talked with Christine about Richard, you know that isn't what was going on between them. I respect your worries, and I respect you for having them, but your daughter and my son are in love."

"The reason I didn't try to interfere was that I was in here," said Robert Monahan. "I wasn't in any moral position to tell anyone that what they were doing was wrong. And Christine has had to be independent, making all of her own decisions and working to support herself, since she was sixteen. All I could do for her was just to help her feel good about herself."

"You're a sensible man," said Andy. "I admire you for that. If I'd known, I would have discouraged it, too, but Richard is the same — self-motivated, self-reliant, and not someone to come to his father for permission. You and I couldn't stop it, but maybe we can salvage it. Do you know what went wrong for Christine? What made her decide to leave him like this?"

"Not specifically. Until recently I didn't know that she had moved in with him, and I don't know exactly what made her decide this was the time to leave. I do know she isn't planning to go back."

Andy Beale looked down at his feet and shook his head. "Kids. They do these things on impulse, without thinking." He looked at Robert Monahan again. "You know she's going to have a baby?"

"It doesn't make me happy, but I know. She'll be a good mother."

"She's a girl you can be sure will be responsible. My son has told me a lot about her, and I saw a lot of her when she worked in our family business. But I use the word 'girl' intentionally. She's not entirely grown up."

"And your son didn't give her much time to finish growing up, did he?"

"You have my profound apology for that. He's always been a fine young man, and no fool either, until he fell in love. I was deeply surprised that he would ever take such a chance, put the girl he loved in that kind of jeopardy. He's not the first to do that, but it wasn't like him. I talked to him about it in pretty harsh terms, I can tell you. He said that at the time they were taking all the precautions, but maybe they got careless once because they both knew they'd be married before long and it wouldn't matter."

"He asked her to marry him?"

Andy Beale sensed the first bit of surprise, the first real interest in the conversation. It was like a spark on tinder, and he had to keep fanning it, trying to coax a flame into life. "He said they talked about marriage often, and she told him she wanted to. He told me he thought the only reason she was putting it off was that she wanted to wait to make it official until after you had been in here long enough to qualify for some kind of furlough to give her away at the wedding." He looked at Monahan in curiosity. "Was she being straight with him? Does the prison work that way?"

"I asked if he actually proposed to her."

Andy Beale sensed that this might be a trap. She might have told her father that Richard hadn't asked her. "They discussed it. I don't think he went through the whole production of getting down on one knee yet. I know he bought the engagement ring and a matching wedding band, and was keeping them as a surprise. I've seen them. The engagement ring has a three-carat diamond that cost him about fifteen thousand dollars. He said he was waiting for her to be ready to accept a proposal before he officially asked, or he would just make her feel bad." He kept his eyes on Monahan's, wondering if he had gone too far. He wished he could have brought a ring in here to show him, but that was against the rules.

Monahan said, "What do you want from me?"

"I want you to help me make my son happy. The reason you should do it is that it will make your daughter happy, too."

"How do I do that?"

"When you next talk to Christine, tell her what I've told you — that Richard's heart-broken because she left. He wants to marry her and bring her home with him in time to have the baby. He loves her and misses her every hour of every day. He thinks she must have misunderstood something he said or did, and if she would just talk to him, he's sure he could clear it up."

"You want me to say all that?"

"Yes. I know that being in here, you worry about her all the time. Hell, I'm a father, too. But Richard will take care of her. He'll treat her like a queen for the rest of her life."

Monahan folded his arms across his chest, and Andy Beale knew that this did not signal anything good. Monahan said, "Her story isn't quite the same as your son's. She's not going to take anybody's word fourth hand over her own memory."

"I'm not asking her to, only to listen to what he has to say. Please. Things sometimes happen between a man and a woman that their fathers don't know, and probably shouldn't know. I don't know what made her mad. I just know he's sincere, and never meant for this to happen. If she won't listen to Richard, is there somebody she knows who will?"

"What do you mean?"

"Somebody she trusts. Maybe somebody a little older, who can talk it over with Richard and then report back to her."

"No."

"Come on," Andy pleaded. "Give my son a chance, at least."

"I haven't seen Christine in over a month. I don't expect her any time soon. I don't even know what city she's in."

"I accept that. But isn't there anybody who can give my son a phone number or an e-mail address? Anything?"

"Not that I know of."

Andy Beale knew nothing about Christine. He was reduced to a bluff. "What about that friend of hers, that Sandy or Sarah or Susan or whatever it was?"

"Sharon?"

"Yeah. What about her? Do you think she could set something up so Richard could get a message to Christine? Even if they're thousands of miles apart, I think Richard could make her know how much he cares."

"You'd have to ask Sharon."

"Do you have her address?"

"No," said Monahan. "I don't have addresses. If anybody wants to reach me, they know where I am." He stood up and nodded to the guard across the room.

Andy Beale tried to cover his disappointment by standing up, too. "Just think about what I said. The day they marry I'll give them each a wedding present of a million dollars. And I'll throw in a nice house on the beach."

"I don't think this is about money."

"Of course not," said Andy. "It's about love. I'm just trying to treat her like one of the family."

"Good-bye." The guard had arrived, and he took Robert Monahan beyond the steel door.

As Andy Beale walked out of the building he reflected that Monahan had surprised him. There was a part of Andy Beale that thought there might have been a time when the two fathers could sit down for a beer together — maybe out on Andy's boat — and learn to get along fine. But he had a bad feeling it wasn't going to work out that way this time. Whatever Richard had done, Monahan wasn't ever going to forgive him.

Richard Beale was upstairs in his bedroom watching the Padres playing the Braves on the big-screen television when his cell phone rang. He got up off the bed and hurried to the desk where he had left the phone, and snatched it up. "Hello?" He waited to hear whether it was his father's voice or Christine's.

"Hi, Richard."

"Sybil?"

"Yes, it's me. I'm in my car outside."

Richard walked across the hallway to one of the spare bedrooms on the street side and looked out the window. He could see her sitting in his driveway in her red Corvette. "Is something happening?"

"I was going by on my way out for a drink, and I thought I'd see if you were thirsty, too."

"Did you just drive in all the way from Lompoc?" He began to walk to the stairs.

"I flew, grandpa. These days we have flying machines."

"You know, I'll bet I have everything here that they have in most bars. There's no loud noise, and you don't have to wait in a line to use the ladies' room." As Richard walked toward the front door, he glanced around the living room to be sure it was still neat and no clutter had accumulated on the white furniture.

"I know," she said. "I've been to some of your parties. It might be a good idea to have a drink here even if we do go out. That way we can talk about business a little without feeling as though everybody's listening."

"That's right," he said. He studied his reflection in the big mirror above the credenza by the door. His shirt was still looking unwrinkled and the suit pants had held their crease. He looked good.

He opened the door to beckon to her, and saw she was swinging her long legs out the car door. She was wearing a very short skirt, and her tanned thighs looked shiny in the dim light from the open door. She closed her phone and dropped it in her purse. "Sold."

She walked to the door. She was as tall as he was, and as she passed him she brushed his cheek with her lips. There was an instant of perfume and soft breath, and then she stepped inside a few paces and turned around in a circle to look at the living room.

"You've had this room redone recently."

"About six months ago. You'd be amazed at how quickly things like furniture and floors wear when you live at the beach."

"I could learn to live with the amazement. So where's the drink you promised me?"

"What would you like?" He walked toward the bar at the end of the room.

"Vodka on the rocks."

"Grey Goose, Belvedere, Stolichnaya, Absolut, what?"

"Belvedere."

He went behind the bar, filled two glasses with ice, then set a tall frosted-glass Belvedere bottle beside them. "I'll put it here, where you'll be able to find it if you want another one."

Sybil splashed vodka into the glasses as Richard walked around to her side of the bar. She clinked her glass against his, then sipped. Then she walked toward the back of the house to the sunken sunroom with large windows that looked out on the swimming pool, the beach, and the boiling white surf far down the sand. "It's so beautiful out there. I love the ocean."

"Me, too," he lied. "This house is a great place to come after a stressful day. The sound of the ocean is probably the most restful sound there is."

Her eyes moved to the pool with its artistic arrangement of fake boulders and its waterfall and the bubbling spa at the end of it. "Can we go outside?"

He opened the French door and followed her out to the lighted pool. He pulled a deck chair close to the spa, then another, and sat down. She strolled around the edge of the pool to the spa, then kicked off one sandal and touched her toe to the water. "Warm." She looked around. On one side was the house, and the walls on the other three sides sheltered the pool from view.

She stepped out of her other sandal. "I guess the main reason I stopped by was that I wanted to apologize for screwing up yesterday. I was in the Lompoc prison parking lot watching for your girlfriend, and then I spotted the woman I'd seen with her in New York. Naturally, I followed her. She pulled over and waited for me on the road away from the prison, and I thought she must be trying to lead me away so Christine could go in. That made me too hesitant. After that I overcompensated and chased her, and almost got smeared by a truck in an intersection. And then, well, let's just say I could have handled it better. I'm sorry."

"Steve said it would have happened to anybody."

"I don't like it when things like that happen to me." She stared at him over her glass as she took a drink. "We'll still get your girlfriend back for you."

"She's been gone for a month and a half."

Sybil shrugged with mock concern. "Poor thing. I'll bet you're really horny."

He laughed, partly out of surprise, and partly because no other response came to him in time. "That wasn't what I thought you were going to say."

She sat at the edge of the spa and put her feet in.

Richard said, "If you'd like to go in the spa, you're welcome."

Sybil cocked her head and looked at him.

He added, "There are lots of bathing suits upstairs. Christine left all of her clothes and things here. With a two-piece suit the difference in height wouldn't matter, right?"

"You'd better get rid of all of her things, Richard. If, by some remote chance, anything goes seriously wrong, those clothes could hang you." She looked away, and took a sip of her vodka. The ice clicked against her teeth to signal the glass was empty. "Maybe I will go in the water."

"I'll get you some suits to choose from."

"Just bring towels and that bottle of vodka." Sybil stood, pulled her tank top over her head and off, then pulled her bra down and turned it so the hooks were in front, took it off, stepped up onto the deck and out of her short skirt and her panties, and tossed her clothes onto the deck chair. She pretended not to notice Richard standing there staring at her, then raised her arms and turned all the way around to show off her thin, graceful body. "Feel free to look. You might as well get your money's worth for yesterday's mistake."

"Thank you," he said. "I feel a little better already."

She stepped down into the spa and sank low in the water. "This is great. Come join me."

Richard turned and went inside, then returned with the Belvedere bottle and two long yellow beach towels. He undressed and left his clothes on the other deck chair, stepped into the spa and sat beside Sybil. He refilled her drink, sipped his own, and then put his arms around her and gave her a kiss that in a slow, leisurely way became more and more passionate and greedy.

After another minute or two they both pulled back in a mutual, silent agreement, and sipped their drinks. Sybil looked at Richard with amusement for a few seconds, then took another sip of her drink. "Okay. I guess you're right. I do owe you the whole deal. Kiss me like that once more, and then we'll go inside to wherever it is you like to fuck."

They moved together in the warm water and shared a long, silent kiss. When they parted again, Sybil sighed, then opened her eyes. She stood and got out of the spa, quickly wrapped herself in one of the thick towels, and moved toward the French door. Over her shoulder she called to him, "Bring

the bottle with you and I'll throw in a blow
job."

19

It was another hot, humid evening in Minneapolis, and Christine was getting tired of the constant hum of the air conditioner, but she was still sweating. She turned off the television set, dropped the remote control on the coffee table, and lay back on the couch. She was tired. It actually took energy to conform to strict rules. Self-discipline was an effort. She was lonely and big. That was the feeling, really, the sheer unpleasantness of having lost control of her body. Even if she could have ignored her growing belly, her face felt puffy, her legs, even her fingers.

She had been extremely careful in the three months since she had come to Minneapolis. She hadn't gone out much except to buy groceries and paperback books. She wished she had a computer. Jane had left more than enough money to buy one, but there was a certain amount of red tape and verifying of credit to get an online account, and Christine sensed that was a bad process to begin. She would wait until after the baby was born and she moved to a new city using a permanent name and all her credit cards were real.

She didn't want to start taking chances now. The reason she was safe was that she had been smart from the beginning. She had gone to see Sharon Curtis, and Sharon had sent her right to Jane. Jane had taken only three days to bring her all the way to Minnesota and hide her in a place where nobody would ever think to look for her. And Jane had hurt two of Richard's people so badly that they would probably never want to come after her again. Seeing it happen would probably affect the other four, too. How could the others keep from becoming hesitant and tentative now that they'd seen the first two hurt? Could they imagine that what Richard paid them was worth getting hit by a car?

When Christine remembered the four people who were after her, it didn't seem so hard to be Linda Welles of Minneapolis. She felt as though she and her baby were in a different world from San Diego, and perfectly safe. Even so, she kept the revolver Jane had given her in her purse. When she drove anywhere in her car, the purse was there beside her on the passenger seat where she could reach it. When she was at home like this, the purse was never more than a few feet away. She had promised herself that she would never let herself be captured by Richard's friends.

When she and Richard had been together, she had given him more than enough chances, but he had never taken her seriously. And Richard had hurt her. The first time he had hit her she considered leaving, but she had not been sure he'd meant it. There had been too much ambiguity. They had been in their house in San Diego. It was really just Richard's house, but she had been living with him for at least six months by then, and so she thought of it as their house. They had just come home from work to get ready for dinner with some clients, so she was in the shower. She came out of the bathroom with a big bath towel around her, and when she passed Richard, he was standing in front of the full-length mirror on the door of the closet, buttoning a shirt.

His arm shot out like a whip and wrapped around her waist. He spun her around as he pulled her close, and the towel came off. She tried to get away, and they wrestled around a little. She struggled and she ended up on the bed bent across his lap. He gave her a light slap across the bottom. She shrieked, but not too loudly because there were neighbors, and she was laughing, too. She squirmed and wriggled, pretending to try to escape, but really just doing it because she knew it would excite him. The truth was that she liked the fact that he was strong and aggressive, and that he was paying this kind of attention to her. She knew he found it erotic, and she found his arousal erotic.

Then he hit her again, another slap. It was harder this time, and it stung. She could feel her eyes watering, not quite producing tears yet, just a reaction to the pain. "Richard! Don't. It really hurt that time! Stop!" But he hit her again and again, and the playful spanking wasn't fun anymore. It was painful. She tightened the muscles of her buttocks and put her hands behind her to fend off the slaps. "Stop!" She was crying, but he didn't seem to notice. After a few more blows she became silent and stiff like a dead person, and he finally stopped. She ran into the bathroom, locked the door, then put on the clothes she had taken off before the shower, still weeping.

He knocked on the door, he called to her, he even made a halfhearted attempt to push the door open with his shoulder, but she knew he wasn't going to break it down. She could hear him move off, and a few minutes later he came back, knocked quietly, and said it was time to leave. She called out that she wasn't going anywhere with him. She stood behind the bathroom door holding her cell phone, ready to dial 911 if he came inside. He didn't. She heard him walk off down the hall, and then thought she heard the front door slam.

She waited a half hour before she was sure he was gone. She cautiously left the bathroom and then hurried out to her car. She drove to an inexpensive motel off Interstate 8. He called her cell phone a couple of times before she decided to answer.

He said, "I thought you were just kidding. You were laughing."

But by then she'd had time to stand in front of the mirror and see the red marks starting to darken into blue and purple bruises, and the pain was not going away. She waited another day to make him sweat and give the bruises time to ripen and darken, and then drove to the company building, went into his office, locked the door, and showed him.

He seemed sincerely shocked, and he apologized. She went back to the motel and spent the next three days thinking about what to do. There were many reasons to go back, and one reason not to, and that was fading with the bruises. She wanted to be sure he really deserved another chance, that he'd misunderstood what she had wanted, and not meant to do her harm. Christine wanted to believe that her own motives were simple and pure, too — that if she went back it would be because she loved him, and not because if she left him she would lose her job and her only place to live. There was also the nagging, uncomfortable question of whether she had misled him by giggling and being playful at first. In the end she decided she could not be sure about anything. She decided to start over again with Richard as though nothing had happened, and wait to see if anything important had.

The next time he hit her was during an argument. She would have hesitated to even call it a fight. They were at a party and she was tired and wanted to go home. He wanted to stay, and he wanted her to stay with him. It was after two A.M., and they were at a house all the way up in Capistrano. He had been drinking, and it was a long drive home. She asked him not to have another drink. She whispered discreetly, her face close to his ear and her arms around him so nobody else knew what she was saying. He didn't argue with her, but he took another drink. She sat down beside him and waited.

When it was three, he was ready to go. As they walked out toward the car, she held out her hand. "Can I have the key, please? I'll drive." He clutched her shoulders and shook her, then held her face close to his. "Listen," he rasped. "Don't you ever tell me what to do again." He slapped her face, pulled her around the car, and shoved her into the passenger seat, then got in and drove.

Before they even reached home, he apologized. He said it was the alcohol that was to blame, and swore he would never drink and drive again. It was four days before she would speak to him. She stayed home from work and wore sleeveless tops so he would have to look at the thumbprints on her upper arms.

The next time, she began to complain to him about the way he left his clothes on the floor of the bedroom and expected her to pick them up. Suddenly he gripped her hair and gave her face three or four slaps. Each time he was angry at her, the violence got a bit more sudden and harsh, and each time, he would apologize longer and more extravagantly. But then, after a week or two, he would speak to her with boredom and contempt in his voice, as though her forgiving him made her stupid and weak.

After that she tried to avoid doing anything that might provoke him. She managed to find ways to live with him without getting hurt, and her success made her believe he was improving.

But by then, the other things had begun to bother her. As she came to understand the business, she admitted to herself that he wasn't always honest. There were discrepancies between what he told customers they were signing and what she knew was on the paper because he'd told her to put it there. The extra, unexpected construction costs he charged to customers were inflated tremendously. Still later she noticed that he was lying about the costs of things in his own company's books. She could tell he was doing it so nobody would notice he was moving money out of the business.

Richard rented out some apartments in big complexes, and listed them on the Beale Company books as vacant or under remodeling, and then collected the rents under the name Richard Beale Rentals. There were even times when she saw him take cash home in a briefcase and lock it in the safe built into the floor of his closet.

During the next few months she tried not to notice what he was doing at work, and pretended at home that their relationship was getting better. It was only after she missed a period, and then another, then a third, that Christine awoke from the trance. She bought the pregnancy test, and the little X turned bright blue, and she was pregnant. She didn't need to spend much time thinking about the implications, because they were already in the back of her mind waiting. She couldn't stay with Richard. She couldn't give birth to a baby as Richard's girlfriend. She couldn't live in Richard's house where he could use the baby as a hostage to control her. She had to get out. But she wasted more time trying to think of a way to do it. Soon she was desperate, because she couldn't hide the pregnancy much longer, and she had to leave before he found out.

One day Christine pretended to be sick and waited until Richard went to the office. She packed a small overnight bag. Then she left her keys on the kitchen counter and her car in the driveway, walked to a pay phone at a nearby restaurant, and called a cab to take her to Sharon Curtis's house. Christine had a natural sneakiness that must have been developed when she was young, trying to outwit the Divine Delia. She knew from intense observation how the minds of tyrants worked. Neither Delia nor Richard would ever walk off and leave a car. For Richard, seeing her car still at his house would be the same as seeing Christine there. It would never occur to him that Christine would leave most of her possessions and a car behind. He would spend days in complete confidence that she was just in a snit and that she would return.

Christine knew that she should have called Sharon in advance, but she was already afraid of leaving that telephone call as the last one on the bill that Richard received. Sharon had been her favorite teacher at Poway High School. She had been younger and more glamorous than any of the others. She taught science — all kinds of science, from first-year biology to advanced placement physics. Science was messy, so she was invulnerable to the formal dress requirements for teachers. She wore the same brands of jeans that students wore, white lab coats so clean they glowed, and had an array of bright-colored sneakers. She had a set of safety goggles around her neck most of the time. She was bright and tough, and kept her students alert by keeping up an ongoing conversation in which she addressed first one, then another. Christine loved her. Watching her was like seeing herself in ten years and being really pleased at how she was going to turn out.

When Christine's family troubles finally caused the household to collapse, she had confided in Sharon Curtis, and Sharon listened to each stage of the disaster and to each of the revelations about Christine's father, but she never made a comment until she was asked. After Christine left school and went to work, she and Sharon met for lunch about once a month. Each time, Sharon would find a way to remind Christine that she should go back to school and then go to college.

The day Christine ran away, she told Sharon all the things about the relationship with Richard that she had been withholding — the growing violence, the dishonesty, the dangerous people working for him — and Sharon changed. She said, "I'm going to tell you something that nobody knows, and when you hear it, you'll understand why you can't tell anyone. I wasn't always called Sharon Curtis. I lived somewhere far away from here. There was a boyfriend, and some of the things that have been happening to you happened to me, too. I always found a way to fool myself into thinking I should stay with him. Things got worse. They can get a whole lot worse than I ever imagined in about a second."

"What's your real name? Who are you?"

"Sharon Curtis is my real name. It's the one I agreed to, and it's the name of the person I am now. We don't really have time for questions about the person I used to be. Not if Richard is in the habit of hurting you and knows you could reveal things that will get him arrested."

"I don't know what to do. He has those people I told you about. They sometimes hunt people down for him, ones who don't pay what they owe or something. I know he'll send them after me."

"Then you've got to be gone before that happens." Sharon looked at Christine with a sad expression. "You've got to disappear."

"But I don't know how."

"There's a woman. About ten years ago, somebody sent me to her. If they hadn't, I'd be dead."

"Who is she?"

"Her name is Jane. You have to go to her. The first thing you do is tell her that I sent you. Then you tell her about yourself, and about Richard and his people." Sharon tore a piece of scrap paper from a pad beside her telephone and wrote the name Jane

Whitefield and an address on it in her neat schoolteacher handwriting, then handed it to Christine. "Memorize this and then give it back and I'll destroy the paper."

"Like in the movies."

"Not like the movies. This is real. Don't be careless. The address on that paper has been more precious to some people than anything in any bank. If anything happens to her, a door will close, and nobody will ever be able to go through again."

"I'll be careful. I promise."

"I'm going to drive you to the L.A. airport, just in case he's noticed you're gone and he's watching the San Diego airport. Fly to Buffalo, New York, tonight, and take a cab. If she's not there, wait for her."

"What if she doesn't come?"

"Then try going to Buffalo General Hospital and asking for her. There are people there who know her."

"What does she look like?"

"Tall and thin, with black hair. She wore it long when I last saw her. She has dark skin, and eyes that look as though she can see through you. They're the part that might help. They're blue — bright, clear blue, like water is supposed to look but doesn't. And that reminds me. Don't ever lie to her, not even an innocent little lie."

As Christine thought about that night, she missed Sharon even more than before. Now that she'd had the experience that Sharon had prepared her for, she wanted to tell her about it. She wanted to thank Sharon for taking the risk of telling her she was living under a name she'd only had for ten years. Now that Christine had become Linda Welles, she knew what an extravagant gift that information was. But there was one extra question that hadn't existed for Christine before. She wanted to know why Sharon, the person in her life who always seemed to be in complete control, had ever needed the kind of help that Jane Whitefield offered.

There had been hints that night, but Christine wanted the whole story. Now it was important to Christine to know. Maybe Sharon Curtis was somebody Jane had invented because she wasn't much like the young girl whose life was in danger, and the young girl had worked and studied until she had grown into being Sharon. Christine hoped so. Sharon had a stronger sense of who she was and how that person was supposed to behave than anyone else Christine had met. Was that something Sharon started with, or something she had been able to earn? After ten years, was her identity a disguise, or was it the person she had grown to be?

Christine was up off the couch and pacing, ranging the room the way Sharon did when she was running a science lab. Without really thinking about it, Christine went to the telephone and picked it up. The loud dial tone startled her. She had half-expected the phone to be dead, because nobody had ever called her. The message from Jane about her father was the only call she'd had since she'd bought the phone, and she had missed even that one. All she had heard was the voice mail Jane had recorded.

As Christine stared at the telephone, the dial tone seemed to get even louder and more insistent. She dialed Sharon's number and waited. It was ten here in Minnesota, so it was only eight in San Diego, a perfect time to call on a weeknight, when Sharon probably hadn't gone out.

"Hello?" It was Sharon's voice, sounding a bit tired from a day of teaching, and yet, there was something else. It was something Christine had never been sensitive enough to hear before. The tone was guarded, as though some small part of Sharon was prepared for a voice from the distant past.

"Hi, Sharon. It's me, Christine."

"Are you all right?"

"Yes," she said. "I found the woman you told me about, and she moved me to —"

"Don't!" she interrupted. Then she said more gently, "Don't say where."

"To a safe place. I was just going to say it was a safe place. Don't worry," said Christine. "I'm not stupid."

"You're okay, though?" Sharon asked. "You're healthy? You're getting enough to eat and everything?"

"I'm fine and the baby's fine. The doctor says everything's fine. That's one of the reasons why I called. I was sure you would be worried about me since I left, and I wanted you to know that things worked out. She set me up in a safe, dull place and told me how to get by without drawing much attention to myself. She says she'll be back in time for the baby, and then help me move again."

"I'm so glad," Sharon said. "Tell me something without saying anything specific that we'll regret. How is she? I haven't seen her in over ten years."

"She's just the way you said she was — like nobody I ever met before. To tell you the truth, while I was with her, I was a little bit afraid of her."

"Don't be. But take her seriously and do everything she says, to the letter. I'm really happy to know that you made it. You were right that I was afraid something would happen to you on the way. But —"

"A lot did happen, and if she hadn't been with me, I'd have been caught. Let me tell you —"

"Honey," said Sharon. "I'm sorry to interrupt you, but don't tell me what happened. In fact, this is a problem."

"What's a problem?"

"This call. Making phone calls to people you knew before you left. Didn't she say anything about that?"

"Well, sure. But she called me once, and I thought you'd want to know what happened to me."

"I did, and I do. But this is one of the small things that can get you into trouble. If someone is watching me, they'll now have your number and can get your location. If they've got the right equipment they're recording the call, and may be able to trace it. When you run, you have to give up some important, valuable things. One of them is talking to relatives and friends."

"You're telling me never to call you again?"

"I'm telling you not to do things she tells you are dangerous. She's taken you out of your old life and into a new one. That life will be hard to get used to, but sooner than you think, you'll be comfortable. Pretty soon you'll be too busy and preoccupied with being a mother to waste much time on anything else. I want you to know that I'll be thinking about you often, and I'll feel happy because I know you'll be happy — if not tonight, then in a few months. We'll still be just as close, even if we can't talk to each other. We're on the same side, and want the same things for each other. You've always been one of my favorite people, and that will never change. But look ahead now, not back."

"Oh, my God," said Christine, and she realized she was crying. "I'll miss you."

"And I'll miss you."

"We'd better get off now, huh?"

"Yes. If we don't talk very long it's harder for them. Good luck."

"Good luck to you."

They both hung up, and Christine lay back down on the couch. She cried for a long time, but then she awoke, still on the couch, and it was four A.M. For a few seconds, as she was making her way to her bed, undressing as she went, she wondered if the telephone call might have been a dream.

20

Christine drove past the FedEx Kinko's store a half dozen times every week on her way to buy groceries or rent movies or go to the pharmacy. She had not noticed it the first few times she passed it, but then one day she parked nearby and walked past. She saw the glass-enclosed room with its two rows of glowing computer screens. After that day, the computers lived in her memory, the nonsensical images of screen savers bouncing across their lighted screens.

A few weeks after she had spoken to Sharon she happened to be in the pharmacy waiting for her prescription prenatal vitamins. She shopped for things she didn't really need, like makeup and a new hairbrush, but she was thinking about the computers again. She missed the Internet. She had liked to start her day by going online. She would check the San Diego weather and traffic, read her e-mail, find out which movies had been released, soothe herself with some dumb celebrity gossip, and, if she had time and nobody was looking, read her horoscope.

When she had everything at the counter she paid in cash and went out the front entrance and walked along the sidewalk staring in the windows of the stores. She had often window-shopped when she had still lived in San Diego, but now she looked in windows for other reasons. She was fascinated with her own reflection in the big plate-glass surfaces. Since she had been in Minneapolis she had begun to look really, unambiguously pregnant, and if she stayed a few feet away from the glass she could see herself from head to foot from the side, walking along.

The reflections also gave her a way to keep her face turned away from the people driving along the street or walking nearby and still see them. Today as she walked she thought about the computers again. Sharon Curtis had been really critical of her for calling her on the telephone, but a few weeks had passed, and nothing had happened. If somebody had been able to trace calls to Sharon or had a list of phone numbers for people who had called her, then Steve Demming and his friends would have been here long ago. And the Internet was even safer. It was almost completely anonymous.

She walked into the FedEx Kinko's store, past the rows of copying machines, and up to the counter. There was a boy there about her own age, and his name tag said he was Mark, a "coworker," which she guessed was probably about as low in the hierarchy as he could get. She said, "I'd like to use a computer. How do I do that? Do you rent them by the minute or something?"

Soon she was in a quiet, private corner staring at a screen, just as she had been doing since she was a little girl. It made her happy to feel the click of the mouse and hear the clatter of keys again as she typed in her screen name and password. She waited for her mailbox to open, then drew in a breath. There were 287 new messages for her. She glanced at the hour and minute on the lower-right side of her screen. This was going to take some time. Christine went down the list deleting the notifications of sales, the ads, the offers for things she might have wanted a few months ago. Then she began to count the ones that had been sent from Richard's e-mail address.

There were two or three for each day since she'd left San Diego, and they all had subjects like "I miss you," or "Please write," or "Where did you go?" They all seemed to be different, and most of them had attachments.

Christine considered whether it was wise to open any e-mails from Richard. If he had been standing in front of her, she would never have listened to anything he wanted to say to her. But there was something safe and familiar about e-mail. He couldn't reach out and grab her through the screen. If she read his e-mails, he wouldn't know where she was. All he could ever know was that they had been received by a server at some building that belonged to the Internet provider's company, and that could be anywhere in the world.

Her hand shook a little as she clicked on the first of the e-mails from Richard. The screen said, "Do you know who sent you this e-mail?" Then there was the usual lengthy warning that began, "You are about to display an e-mail containing a picture or file attachment. If you don't know who sent you this e-mail . . ." At the bottom it said, "Do you wish to view this e-mail? Yes/No." She chose *Yes* and watched the blue line fill up the download box.

There was a picture of Richard, and when he moved she gave a little gasp. It was a video. He was standing in his office at work, in front of his computer. He must have plugged in a Webcam. He said, "Hi, Chris. It's me all right. I know this isn't something you would think I'd do. I just figured that maybe if you could see me face-to-face again and hear my voice whenever you wanted, you might remember how happy we were when we were together. I know things must have gotten too intense for you, and you just have to get away for a while. I can understand that, and I don't blame you. But while you're away, I hope you know that I'll be thinking about you every day and every night." She moved the cursor to the red box in the upper-right corner and clicked the white X to close the e-mail. Then she opened the next one.

This time he had put the Webcam on the computer in the bedroom at home, and he was sitting at the desk in one of the T-shirts she had bought him to sleep in a month before she left. It was the blue one, and she tried to remember whether she had ever told him that was the color that looked best on him. Part of her hoped that she had, and he had been listening to her and remembered, then chose it to please her. But why did she hope that? She detested him.

He said, "Hi, Chris. I hope it's you who's watching this, but of course I have no way of knowing. I'm sorry if that sounds kind of gloomy. I'm just tired and depressed to-night, I guess. Since you've been gone I've tried to keep myself busy working as much as I can." He gave a sad smile. "Because of that I've been making a hell of a lot of money, but that's not much of a consola-tion, because I don't have anybody to spend it on. The time when it really gets to me is always at night like this. I suppose it's partly because I'm tired at the end of these frantic, crazy days. Night is the first time when I can't keep moving and talking to people and staying occupied. I'm alone here in the empty house, and I can't avoid thinking about you and about every stupid thing I ever did or said in front of you. I keep go-ing over and over everything and telling myself what I should have done instead." He stared at the camera with the dark, injured gaze he had often used on her. "I apologize, Chris. No excuses. I'm sorry for all of it. I'm not sure what day it was when you decided I couldn't be salvaged, but I know you must have been thinking about leaving for a long time before you did. I just wish that during that period when you were planning and arranging to leave, I had said or done something good that made you change your mind. Well, I've probably said more than you want to hear already. I love you, and I still will tomorrow. Close your eyes." It was what he used to say just before they went to sleep when they were together and he wasn't angry at her. He reached toward the camera and the video ended.

She looked at her reflection in the dark screen, and she could see her puffy, sad face with tears glistening on her cheeks. She told herself it was just the familiarity that she was missing so badly. That was all. She was alone in a strange city where the trees looked big and leafy and threw shadows that made everything seem dark. The houses were tall and close together and old, and the streets were too narrow. The people looked and sounded different, and the air always seemed thick with moisture so it was almost hard to breathe. Anything that was familiar seemed inviting to her now.

Christine felt sorry for Richard, especially now that he seemed to know that he had lost something he couldn't replace. He seemed surprised at everything that had happened, and unsure about what to do. He couldn't admit that he wasn't going to have her anymore. And he was such a man. He never talked about anything just to get it out, to have it said. He never talked about any problem at all unless he was working on a way to solve it. Even if every solution he thought of was stupid and unworkable, there he was, working away on it. He was so sad to watch.

Richard's mind was operating the way it always had in business. No deal? What can I offer you to make the deal more attractive to you? Do you want me to suffer? Here's how much I've suffered so far. Is it enough? Okay, then how about if I learn from my mistakes? Still no deal, huh? Well then, I'm at a loss. You tell me what it would cost me. I'm very interested in closing on this — I'd like to do it today if I can — and I'm not giving up unless it's just impossible. Not even then, in fact. I'm giving you all my attention. Here, see how many e-mails I've sent.

Christine moved up the list to recent e-mails and selected one sent this week. Richard had apparently bought a digital video camera, because there never had been a computer in the spare bedroom, and the quality of the picture was much better this time. The room was easily recognizable because she could see the window that overlooked the deep end of the pool beside the waterfall with the big fake boulders.

The room had been repainted a pale yellow. The regular bed and dresser and chair were gone. Everything had been replaced. She could see the crib was a Bellini that she had admired in the Mall of America, but considered too expensive for her. There was a big, low dresser with a padded changing area and railings on top. He had bought a rocking chair. There were built-in shelves now that held receiving blankets, stuffed animals, books, and a baby monitor.

Richard said, "Hi. I was keeping this room as a surprise, but it occurred to me that now that the baby isn't all that far off, I should probably show it to you. I realized that maybe you wanted to come home, but you would be afraid we wouldn't have a nice place all ready for the baby, so you might wait. I didn't know a whole lot about the subject, but I went to a couple of nice baby stores and started asking what we were likely to need." He stepped aside so she could see the furniture and supplies. Every piece was the most expensive, the best. She could see on the floor there were also a stroller and a car seat. He opened one of the drawers and lifted a stack of folded baby clothes, then held a couple of outfits up and made them dance for the camera. The clothes were perfect, and they seemed to be in a range of sizes. Since he didn't know if the baby was a boy or a girl, everything was in yellow, orange, green, or beige. She didn't wait for the rest of what he would say, just made the video go black and went on to the one he had posted yesterday.

This time he was in the bedroom again. He was looking a bit sad, but not so tired as he had in the earlier videos. It was daylight. She could see soft late-afternoon light coming in through the white curtains, and she missed the room. The master suite was placed on the northern side of the house so the light there was always a bit less sharp and unforgiving than it was on the south side. As she thought about the room she missed San Diego and the Pacific, and palm trees and the flowers that grew in the garden behind the house.

Richard said, "Hi, Chris. I love you. I hope your day is good. It's five-thirty and I came home earlier than usual. I'm wondering whether you're thinking of me this afternoon. Today is the seventeenth of August, and when we're together again I'll ask you if you had a feeling today that was different. I'll tell you why. Today I was thinking about you all the time, wondering about what you like and don't like, and picking something out for you." He looked into the camera, his face as close as it could be without distortion.

"I love you, Christine. I love you more than I really knew when I had you. I've thought about you most of the time. I realized that if this is what living without you is, I don't want it." It occurred to Christine that he had come very close to repeating a song lyric. "I want my life back," he said. "Christine, I want you to marry me." He reached into his coat pocket and took out a small velvet box. He held it up toward the camera and opened it. The large solitaire diamond sparkled and flashed in the light from above the desk as he took out the ring, held it between his thumb and forefinger, and turned it around for her to see. It was spectacular.

In spite of her determination to remain unmoved, she couldn't help looking, trying to imagine what the ring would have looked like on her finger.

Richard said, "I had it sized to fit your finger. Four and a half, right? I brought in the little peridot ring you left here in your jewelry box, because I knew that it fit you."

Christine felt a sharp stab of regret. How could she have left that ring with him? It was a birthstone her father had given her before he went to jail. She felt sick. She had a strong urge to find a way to have it again. Her father would be hurt if he knew. She hit the X in the red box again, and sat with her eyes closed for a time, trying to reconcile her confusing feelings.

When she was calmer, she went back to the list of e-mails. She read a couple of little notes from friends who wondered why she hadn't answered their earlier e-mails, or had not answered her cell phone. She wrote a reply to her friend Rhonda. "I'm out of town now, and I'm trying to spend some time alone sorting out my mess of a life. I dropped everything in San Diego, and decided it was time for me to start all over again in a new place. I've always valued your friendship more than you know. I just can't be there anymore. Please think of me as your good friend always. Love, Chris." She sent a slightly altered version to her friend Emma.

Then she saw one from Alexis Donaldson. Alexis was her closest friend since junior high school. She was the one who stuck with her when she had acne and baby fat, then stayed her friend in high school when her father's legal trouble was in the newspaper, and who even kept inviting her to school events and parties after she had quit school and gone to work. The address was a new one. It looked as though Alexis must have gotten a new job and written to her from the office. Christine wrote her virtually the same cryptic e-mail as the others. She added, "You've always been my very best friend." On an impulse, Christine typed, "If you need to reach me, you can call me." And then she typed in her telephone number and clicked on *Send.*

21

It was morning. Richard Beale parked his black Porsche in his reserved space behind the building, walked into the office, turned on his computer, and went out to the lobby to get a cup of coffee while the computer ran through its antivirus and antispyware scans. As he walked past Marlene, the new receptionist, he nodded and smiled, and she said, "Good morning, Mr. Beale," and smiled back. He had to play Marlene a bit differently from the earlier ones because of what had happened with Christine.

He knew that his father was having him watched, but he wasn't sure how. Richard had searched his office several times for bugs and cameras, but had found nothing. He still hadn't eliminated the possibility that Marlene was working for his father. He glanced at the small forest of tropical plants in the glassed-in atrium behind her. There could be a camera in every tree, for all he knew, and a microphone in each drawer of her desk. He wasn't prepared to have a discussion with his father about getting involved with another receptionist, so he took his coffee, returned to his office, and shut the door.

He sat at the desk, turned to his computer and looked at the list of screen names, and clicked on the first one, which was in his name. There was nothing from Christine, and there was nothing from Demming, and anything else barely mattered. He was devoting his full time to finding Christine. Then he patiently changed his screen name to each of the ones he had invented. He had sent e-mails to Christine from each of them about twice a week.

Richard opened Emma Peterson's mailbox, and saw that it had received its first piece of mail. He opened the e-mail and took in a quick breath. Christine had written to Emma Peterson. He could hardly believe it. He read the long paragraph eagerly, and felt the disappointment settle on his stomach. She wasn't writing to her old friend to reveal anything about what she'd been doing or where she was. She was giving her friend the final kiss-off. When Richard found virtually the same message in the e-mail for Alexis Donaldson, he was in despair. He almost closed it before he realized that this message had something more. There was a telephone number. He plucked a pen from the cup on his desk to copy it on paper. He pulled a sheet of white paper from the printer tray.

Richard knew that there was no need to do this, because all he had to do was save the e-mail or print it, and the information would be preserved. But he had an almost superstitious fear that the electrical impulses that had brought the e-mail would be cut off unexpectedly and the precious number would disappear forever. When he had written it down, he felt a heart-thumping moment of excitement. It was as though he had closed his hand to capture and hold a wild bird.

He clicked on *Print* to make the capture more secure, and when he saw the page slide out into the tray he felt a calm settle over him. He had done it. He had all but found Christine. He wanted to call his father on the phone. He wanted to say, "You old bastard, you self-righteous old sack of shit. You kept goading me and taunting me and saying you knew my girlfriend better than I did. Now I have her phone number, area code and all, and you've got nothing."

He knew he wouldn't do that. Even having the phone number wasn't good enough. The old man would say, "I was the one who had to tell you that the way to get to a twenty-year-old was the Internet." He would say that to his last breath, in the face of any evidence Richard put in front of his face to prove he had been using e-mails since the very beginning. He had put the fake e-mails out as bait in the first few days, and then had added more bait nearly every day to lure her in. That was why it was called *phishing.* And now he had hooked her.

Richard stepped out of the office, across the hall to the door that led to the parking lot. He went out, leaned on his car, and dialed Demming.

"Yeah?"

"It's me. I did it."

"Did what?"

"I set up some e-mail addresses that looked like they belonged to friends of hers. She just sent one of them her phone number."

"You didn't call it, did you?"

"No," he said. "You're the only call I've made."

"Then don't."

"I thought you'd congratulate me."

"I'm happy. It's good. I just don't know

how good yet. It could be her house, but it could also be a cell phone that she got somewhere along the way. If it's a cell, then the number won't tell us where she is, only where she got it. We need to check it out before I say anything more. Give me the number."

Richard read the phone number.

"Area code 612," said Demming. "Give me a minute." Richard could hear Demming clicking the keys of a computer. "Minneapolis. The phone is from Minneapolis, anyway. Let me look into this, and I'll get back to you within a couple of hours." There was a brief pause, and then Demming said, "And Richard?"

"What?"

"You're ready for her, right?"

"What do you mean?"

"The house and everything? If we show up with her in a few days, you've got the place ready? She isn't going to wait until you're asleep and then walk out the front door again?"

"Oh, no. Don't worry. It's hard to know everything that could happen, but I think it's all set."

"I'm glad to hear that. But maybe I'll have Sybil take a look around this morning and see if she has any suggestions."

"That would be good," said Richard. "I'd appreciate that."

22

Linda Welles felt reluctant to go out tonight, but she wasn't quite sure why. Nothing had happened. It was nine in the evening, the time when she had found it was best to go out shopping. After night had fallen she usually felt a bit safer than in daylight. People were out, but not in such crowds, and they couldn't see her as well. The ones who were out buying groceries were too tired to pay much attention to her. They had worked all day, then probably cooked and washed dishes, then had to drag themselves out to buy more food, a process that would leave little time before going to bed and starting over tomorrow. As long as Linda was back home before around ten-thirty, the ratio of good people to people who made her nervous was very high.

The thought of the timing made her want to get started before more minutes went by. She picked up her list from the kitchen counter, put it into her purse, and went to the door. Before she took her hand out of the purse, she touched the center section, so she could feel the reassuring hard, round shape of the gun inside. She locked her door, walked down the hall to the back stairs, opened the steel door a few inches, and looked before she entered the underground garage. Linda was glad that nobody else was there, even though she knew it was not a wise preference. The more neighbors who knew her and watched out for her the safer she would be, but she didn't feel much like cheerful conversation right now. She got into her gray Passat, locked the doors, started the engine, drove to the ramp, and pressed the remote control to open the steel grate.

She drove up to street level, stopped to see if anyone was coming, and then whether there was anyone parked nearby, and drove out to the traffic signal at the entrance to the apartment complex. She drove the half mile to the parking lot of the big grocery store, turned left into the lot, and looked for a parking space. She felt the urge to park very close to the entrance this time, but she knew that impulse was laziness. It wasn't smart to have her car sitting right out there under the bright lights. People would see her get out of the Passat, and know that was where to wait for her when she came out. Linda drove to the far edge of the lot, where there was less light, and parked at the end of the last row of cars. She got out, locked the car door, dropped her keys in her purse, and took a few steps toward the store.

The car seemed to appear behind her rather than to drive up. Suddenly it was there, over her left shoulder. Doors opened, and two men lurched out toward her. It was a second before she recognized Steve Demming and realized the other must be Pete Tilton. She thought of the gun in her purse, slung the strap off her shoulder, but wasn't fast enough. Demming snatched the purse away from her and tossed it to Sybil Landreau. Linda tried to scream, but the two men were so strong and fast that they had her in the back seat of their car between them before she could make a sound, and one of them slapped a length of duct tape across her mouth, so her scream became a muffled moan. The doors slammed, and she could see Sybil Landreau moving quickly toward the gray Passat, fumbling in Linda's purse.

She found the keys, held them up so Linda's captors could see them, then began to open Linda's car. In an instant the captors' car shot forward, and Linda's surprise made her notice the driver. She saw blond hair, and knew it was Claudia Marshall.

Linda tried to struggle to turn her body — didn't anybody see what was happening? But the two men on either side of Linda clutched her arms tightly, so she couldn't move.

"Don't," said Demming. "We can fight you all the way back to San Diego if you want, but you won't enjoy it."

It was the seventh breakfast. Ruby Beale walked out of the kitchen, along the back hallway that ran the length of the big house, carrying a loaded tray. She held it high, balanced in her left hand with surprisingly little effort, as though it weren't heavy. She was big and blond and in her fifties, with a face that was in the process of changing from a ripe beauty to a preview of how she was going to look as an old lady. The blue eyes that must have been striking even ten years ago were half-hidden by puffy cheeks and lids. The skin above her full, red upper lip had wrinkled, and the soft skin on her neck and under her chin had begun to loosen. Her body still had the same rounded hourglass proportions, but it had widened everywhere.

She stopped at a door near the back of the house, put her ear to the wood for a few seconds before she straightened and knocked with one plump pink hand. She nodded to herself, took a key on a ring from her apron pocket, unlocked the door, pushed it open with her hip, and pivoted inside holding her tray. "Hi, honey. It's me, and I've got your breakfast."

She set the tray on the table at the wall of the room away from the window and looked at the girl on the bed pretending to read a magazine. "How are we doing today, sweetie?"

"I don't know about you," said Christine. "I'm doing shitty."

Ruby lifted the pitcher of orange juice and poured it into a glass, then looked back at Christine. "I've got poached eggs, toast, some really nice blueberry jam, some honey — everything organic. What would you like on your toast?"

"A set of keys." Christine looked away from Ruby at the window.

"Don't let your eggs get cold."

"I'm not hungry."

Ruby followed Christine's eyes. The window was old-fashioned and pretty, vaguely French, consisting of two small doors with panes of glass that opened inward. The steel burglar-proofing bars on the outside were nicely spaced so they matched the laths between panes. They weren't at all obtrusive unless the window was open, and then the five acres of lawns and gardens were visible. "Don't worry," she said. "It won't always be like this."

"How can it not be?" said Christine. "You kidnapped me."

"I kidnapped you? *I?*"

"You know what I mean."

Ruby stepped closer and sat at the foot of the bed. "Things sometimes happen in life that at the time don't happen the way we'd like them to. Maybe the bride is pregnant, maybe somebody gets a speeding ticket on the way to the church, maybe there's rain on the reception. But these things pass, and after a while, you don't remember all the particulars. What you remember you forgive and forget. It's like that in every family."

"I'm not in your family."

"You're my only son's wife, and that's my grandchild in your belly."

"That wasn't a legal marriage. It's not real."

"Let's not waste our time arguing. You and I are a lot more alike than you can admit in your present mood. When you get to know me, you're going to like me a lot. I'm going to be your friend, somebody that in the end, you'll be glad you met. We're going to have fun and we're going to be happy."

"Sometimes I think you're actually crazy. I was minding my own business thousands of miles away, when your gang of thugs dragged me across about ten states to get me here. I'm a prisoner. I'm locked in here. You're all criminals."

Ruby slowly moved her head from side to side with a kind of empathy. "Think of it as an arranged marriage. The parents arrange to bring the girl home, that's all. Not everything in life is the way the feminists tell you it is. Most of the marriages in the world are arranged. And the vast majority of them end up happily — much happier than the regular kind."

"This isn't an arranged marriage, or any other kind of marriage."

"It's legal enough. The papers are all filled out and it's been witnessed and filed with the county clerk's office and everything. I know what you mean, of course. You didn't get to wear a white dress and walk down the aisle and all that. I don't blame you for being annoyed. I don't blame you for anything." She looked closely at Christine. "Richard didn't rape you, did he?"

"No."

"You actually fell in love with him, and voluntarily went to live with him and then got pregnant in the usual way, right?"

"Yes! Yes, I did. I'm stupid. But being stupid doesn't mean anybody who wants to can grab me and lock me up. That's kidnapping. You go to prison for that."

"Honey," Ruby said, "I really like you, and I'm happy you're in our family now. You're going to have my grandchild, and I'll always be very grateful for that. And it's really not going to be bad for you. You started out as a girl deprived of an education, with no family left to speak of, and no way to make money but answering a telephone. Just being married to Richard makes you worth a few million if you end up divorcing him. And Andy and I have much, much more."

"I don't care about your stupid money."

"You'll get the last laugh, and there's not a thing we can do about it. Your child is going to be the one who ends up with everything we have. We intend to raise him or her to be the one who runs the business and inherits everything. I can see your face, and I know what you're thinking, but you can forget it. I'm not going to interfere with your mothering him. That's all you. I wasn't interested in that when I was the right age for it, and I'm never going to get in your way. Jesus, if I ever again have to spin one more of those arrow things and move some game piece five spaces, I'll blow my brains out."

"Exactly what crazy thing do you want?"

"I want grandchildren. I'm perfectly happy to stay in my place and let you raise your kid. But I'm going to be the one — mostly behind the scenes — who makes sure the kid is growing up strong and smart. I'm going to be sure you never have to worry about anything practical, and I'm going to pay for the best schools, from preschool through graduate school."

"Yeah, you really did a great job with Richard, didn't you?"

"Richard is another story." Ruby stared at Christine for a second, then said, "Okay, I'll admit he's been a disappointment. He's healthy, good-looking, athletic. He's even smart. Having him was like taking a photograph. You know how sometimes you take a picture and you just know it's going to be beautiful, and then you get the stack of snapshots back from the developer, and you flip through all the rest just looking for that one, but it's not right? The picture has the same outline, and the right shapes, but it's not what you thought at all. It hasn't got any of the feeling it's supposed to have.

Something just didn't get reproduced that was supposed to be there. That's Richard."

"That's what you think of your own son?"

"For a long time, I thought Richard would change as he grew up. Andy wasn't so sure. Then he was grown up, and he wasn't much different. When Andy and I found out you had been living with Richard for months, we started to have some hope. His father said, 'Well, at least we know he's not queer, and he's not dating them once and strangling them.' That wasn't funny to me. I started to have hope that maybe you were what was missing."

"I'm not interested," said Christine. "Not for any reason, not ever, so you might as well let me go. He's always been a creep, an idiot, and now he's a gangster."

"Obviously I can't let you go at this point. It's sort of up to you what you do with Richard. If you manage to solve his problems you'll get every bit of the benefit out of him and deserve it. I'd like to see you get along and have more children and stay together. Maybe that's too much to hope for. But I can tell you, you're not going anywhere before the baby is born."

"I can't fix him, and I don't want anything to do with him, or you, or your husband."

Ruby shrugged. "I'll never be one to

blame you if you can't do what I couldn't do in thirty years of trying. You'll go on and live your life. You'll have all the money you ever wanted, because we need to keep you free to raise your kid. And God help anybody who tries to hurt your child or his mommy. That'll be true whether you stay with Richard or not." She reached out and grasped Christine's hand. "You're a Beale now, Chrissy. You're our beautiful daughter, and you're having our only grandchild."

Christine shook the hand off and held her hand up in a fist, ready to repel another touch. "You're out of your fucking mind. I'm not your daughter. I'm the person you kidnapped. Your jerk Steve Demming and his stupid friends set off a bomb in a hospital to get me out. People got hurt. When the cops get here they'll put you all in a cell forever, not me."

"This is hardly a cell, honey. This is a master suite in a twenty-million-dollar house. People would kill to have a vacation like the one you're having."

Christine sensed the menace in her voice, and reminded herself that making Ruby angry at her wasn't smart, so she modulated her answer. "They'd be wrong. It's not good being locked up."

Ruby smiled and said, "We love you, and

we'll take the best possible care of you. There will be plenty of time for you to come around. I think in the long run, when you throw into the balance all the good we're going to do for you, then you'll wonder what all the fuss was about. In the meantime we agree on the only important thing — having a healthy baby." She patted Christine's knee, stood, and said, "I've got to go. Try to eat your breakfast."

Christine watched her turn and step to the door. The key to the dead bolt was in her apron pocket. It looked like the key to the exterior door of a house, and the lock was heavy, like the lock on the storeroom in a business. The door was like the outer door of an apartment — thick, solid wood. Christine watched Ruby unlock it and pivot out so the door closed immediately. For a big woman Ruby was graceful, and she was surprisingly quick. But she did everything the same way every time. For the whole week that Christine had been here, it had always been the same, like a dance.

When Christine was about ten, her stepmother, Delia, moved in and brought her cat, Sue. Because Delia had brought it from Santa Barbara where she had last lived, she was afraid to let it out in San Diego, where it would get lost and probably killed. Sue the cat sat in the living room or in the kitchen whenever people were around, and patiently watched people opening and closing doors. Then one day, Delia's car pulled in the driveway, Delia unlocked the front door and pushed it inward, and the cat was already there, streaking out. Sue was so fast that she was off the steps and prowling through the brush beside the house before Delia had even begun to react. Delia let out a howl that was so late in coming that at first it seemed to Christine that a second, actual catastrophe must have happened.

Christine had also watched Sue, and knew the cat wasn't going to run off into traffic. She went out, found the cat walking on the grass and sniffing her surroundings, scooped her up, and delivered her to Delia. After that Sue was allowed to go out. Now, years later, Christine found herself envying the cat. If Christine hadn't been so pregnant, she was pretty sure she could have timed her move as Sue the cat had, bumped Ruby aside, and run for it.

But she was pregnant, and now was the time when she would have to make a move. The baby was due in two weeks. The whole prospect terrified Christine. Was she supposed to give birth here on her own? And it was very clear to Christine that Ruby and

Andy were absolutely fixated on her baby. Ruby had said a dozen times that they were placing all kinds of hopes on this tiny unborn child. The day Christine had learned she was pregnant she had been afraid that Richard would see the baby as leverage, a hostage to force Christine to stay with him. Now she was beginning to believe that Ruby was the one to worry about. Ruby wanted to control Christine and her baby for the rest of their lives.

Christine got up and examined the food tray. Ruby really was a good cook. Christine had been smelling the food since Ruby came in, and it had made her hungry. She sat at the table. No matter what happened she was going to need to be healthy. During the first few days, she had worried that Ruby would put sedatives or something in the food, but now she knew better. Ruby would never do anything that might affect the baby. Until the baby was born, the food would be fine and she would be safe.

As Christine picked up the knife to spread blueberry jam on her toast, she noticed that there was another knife this morning. It was a sharp, serrated steak knife, probably put there so she could cut the thick, old-fashioned chewy bacon more easily. She looked around the room, then thought of the bathroom. She stepped in, looked around, and decided that the best spot was inside the big green plastic shampoo bottle in the shower. She unscrewed the wide top, pushed the knife into the thick shampoo, and closed the bottle again. She examined it carefully to be sure the knife hadn't displaced enough shampoo to make it drip over the side, then closed the shower door. Christine could hardly contain her excitement at her acquisition.

She went back to the bedroom, ate her cold eggs, and resumed work on her project. She used the fork to dig away at the plaster that covered the wall beneath the window. She was sure that if she kept at it, she would soon expose the spots where the bolts that held the framework of bars across the window were anchored in the wall. Her plan was to gradually loosen them from the inside, and then on the day when she was ready to go, push the bars into the shrubbery and go out the window. She had been working on her project since the day she arrived a week ago and opened the window to see the bars. She had refused to eat each meal until Ruby left her alone. When she heard Ruby's footsteps retreating down the hall, she would eat quickly and then use her silverware to scrape away at the plaster.

Each mealtime, she worked as long as she dared, and then cleaned the silverware and returned it to the tray. She used wet toilet paper to clean up the plaster dust from the floor behind the bed and then flushed it down the toilet. This time she was careful to stop scraping before she heard footsteps coming. She had used some time to hide the steak knife, so she had to be careful.

When Ruby returned a few minutes later to take the tray, Christine pretended to be napping. She couldn't let Ruby look into her eyes and see that she had a secret. She was sure that Jane would be proud of her for hiding it so well.

23

Ruby didn't serve lunch at noon that day, as she always had every other day. Christine stared at the clock and waited, trying to prepare herself for Ruby's arrival, and the conversation that was sure to come with it. She had been persuaded that Ruby wasn't evil. Ruby wasn't cruel or spiteful like Christine's stepmother, Delia. She was just crazy, deluded into thinking that she had a right to things she couldn't have. Today Christine was determined to be less bitchy about things. She couldn't be completely nice about being held captive, or Ruby would know she was up to something.

Christine planned exactly what she would do as soon as Ruby brought the tray and left. Christine was becoming very efficient now, making her movements economically and without having to stop and think. Today her goal was to expose the first of the bolts that held the bars over the windows. It was the lower left one that was hidden by the bed. She was sure that if she bared one, the others would be much easier to expose and remove. She would know how to get directly to the others without unnecessary digging, and she would know what the next steps would have to be. Christine might need to fashion a wrench of some kind to remove a nut that held the bolt on this side of the wall. Or she might learn that the bolt was the pointed kind, just a big screw that bit into a two-by-four and held tight.

Her main goal was to use every second. She would only have about a half hour to work and ten minutes to clean up and hide what she accomplished. She had to exert all her strength and speed during that brief period. The three mealtimes constituted her whole workday. She thought about the sharp, serrated knife she had kept after breakfast. No, she couldn't use that to scrape plaster. The knife was too precious to use that way. She might need a sharp blade before this was over.

It was nearly one before Christine heard the sound of footsteps coming up the hall, and the sound was wrong. It was bigger, heavier than Ruby. Christine looked around her to see if there was anything to clean up, anything to hide, anything she needed to keep people from seeing. The key slid into the lock and the door swung open.

Richard. He stood in the doorway, smiling. "Hi, Chris," he said. There was an amused, ironic look in his eye, as though he were the one who had a secret, and not Christine.

"Why are you here?" she said. "What do you want?"

He stepped in and closed the door, but he didn't lock it. Christine kept her eyes on his, hoping he wasn't aware of the opportunity he was giving her. She thought about the loose maternity dress she was wearing, and the open-toed shoes. If only she'd worn something she could run in. He said, "It's really not necessary to use that nasty tone with me, Chris. It doesn't help you, it doesn't help me. Whether we like it or not, that baby means we're going to be involved with each other for life."

"I wouldn't count on that. The baby and I aren't likely to go to jail with you."

Richard shook his head. "I don't think that's going to happen. I brought you home, but I wasn't trying to hurt you. I just wanted you back."

"Richard," she said. "You hired Steve Demming and the others to kidnap me. They set off a bomb in a hospital. They did

410

all kinds of terrible things along the way, and finally got me. It was wrong. It was also big-time illegal. You're acting as though if I stop making a big deal out of it, then it will be like it never happened. It won't. People got hurt. There were dozens of cops. They don't just forget."

"There's nothing I can do about it now," Richard said. "I've got to concentrate on things I can change. I can make sure you're safe. I can try to make things more pleasant for you."

"How about getting me to a doctor? Have you thought about that?"

"Of course we have. Don't worry about any of that."

"Please," she said. "You're just so full of it."

"I'm here to tell you it's lunchtime. Come on," he said. "We're going to eat in the garden."

"Don't you know they won't let me leave? That I've been locked up in here for a week?"

"You need to get some air and sunshine. It'll put you in a better mood."

Christine was surprised, and she was suspicious. There didn't seem to her to be any reason for them to let her go outside. Everything about the idea was to her advantage, not theirs. It really would be better for her health and the baby's. She could try to figure out where this house was, where the cars were parked, and how to get out when the time came.

Richard repeated, "Come on."

"Now?"

"What? You got another date?"

"I wish." She followed him to the door. She was a bit disappointed to realize that leaving the door unlocked had not been inadvertent. Richard had been planning to take her outside all along.

They walked along the corridor, with Richard slightly ahead because the space was too narrow to walk comfortably together. Christine hung back more and more. They had brought her here at night, and the combination of the blindfold and the tape across her mouth made her worry more about her breathing than about trying to peek. She saw that the corridor had four more doors at regular intervals, so she assumed they were all bedroom suites, but the doors were closed.

The corridor spilled them into a huge open room that had a three-story ceiling with exposed beams and a second floor with a loft walkway running the length of the room and disappearing into halls on both ends. Facing Christine on the far end was an enormous stone fireplace and chimney, and on the near end a whole wall of shelves that looked as though they had been designed to hold books, but instead held the same arty junk that decorated the realty office lobby. There were rows of pots that looked Central American, a few small statues of stone, wood, or metal, a few hideous wooden masks from various countries. She wondered if she could hurl one of the statues through one of the glass windowpanes beside her to get out. As she walked she looked out the wall of windows to see high, impenetrable hedges and acres of lawn ending in a grove of trees. The vast, lake-shaped swimming pool and the bubbling spa dominated the paved areas near the house.

When Richard saw her looking at the water he said, "We've already got the crew set to put in fences and gates to keep the kid safe. They start work in a couple of weeks."

"Don't bother. The baby and I won't be visiting this place."

"Oh. Right," he said, and rolled his eyes.

Christine stopped, turned all the way around, and tried to memorize everything she could see. The view through the front windows was not what she had hoped. A paved area in front of the main entrance stretched all the way from the house to a high hedge. There was a break in the hedge for a tall iron gate. There was a six-car garage to her left, but all six doors were closed and, she presumed, impossible for her to open without a remote control unit. There was nothing she could see that she was able to associate with a particular street or use in an escape.

"What do you think of the place?"

Christine turned her head. It was Richard's father. She had always thought of him as Mr. Beale when she had worked at the company, but somehow his crimes against her made her feel it was wrong to call him Mister. "Oh. Hello, Andy. It's very big."

Andy Beale resumed his progress across the room toward the door. "And how are you feeling?"

"Like a prisoner. It's not a good feeling. You'll see."

"I'll pass it on to the complaint department. Just take good care of yourself." He pulled open the front door, stepped out, and closed it.

"Jesus," said Richard. "That was rude." He started walking again. At the end of the great room there was a corridor that led off to the left, and he took it.

Christine hesitated once more to examine the latches on the big windows, scan the room to see if there was anything she could use as a weapon, and look out the front window again. Andy Beale had one of the garage doors open and he was driving a black Mercedes out and through the gap in the hedge. There was no way she could see how the gate opened from here.

Richard's hand clamped her wrist. "Come on."

"What?"

"Pay attention. We're heading for the garden."

"Did you grow up here?"

"In this house?"

"Yes. Did you?"

"No. In fact, I was the one who found this place and arranged for the purchase a few years ago. It was built by a guy from the east who wanted to retire from his law firm and have a lot of parties. I think he forgot that he didn't know anybody here. But it was too much house for him anyway, and people in Rancho Santa Fe don't like the noise and traffic from big parties. If he hadn't sold, they probably would have kicked him out."

"I'll bet the big attraction for you was the land."

He looked at her in surprise. "It was."

"Must be at least five acres."

"Twenty," he said, and there was pride in his voice. "Eight in the back here, and twelve more beyond that fence. It's not just the fact that it's a single twenty-acre parcel that makes it valuable. It's that this is Rancho Santa Fe. Every parcel is big, a lot of them much bigger than this. This has both privacy and status. And because every landowner is a member of the covenant, you get control over zoning and public works, so you can protect your investment from politicians."

Christine had manipulated Richard into complacency with a couple of words. Talking about real estate, money, and control distracted him. The rest of the news wasn't so good. The night she had been brought here she could not even have guessed what state she was in. Rancho Santa Fe wasn't a good place to be locked up. It was rich — she had once heard it was the richest community in the whole country — and the properties were huge. She could scream until her jaw got tired, and nobody would hear her. The houses were hundreds of yards apart, most of them owned by people who also owned other houses in distant places and so were gone much of the time. The roads wound among gentle hills wooded with low California oaks, and there wasn't much traffic. If Christine made it to the road, she wouldn't necessarily meet any rescuers before she got caught.

Richard took her hand, this time less roughly, and led her out one of the glass doors into the garden. If he had called it "the secret garden" she would not have thought it was a joke. On one side was the wing of the house where her room was located. On another was what seemed to be a pool house, and the third was blocked by a windowless wall that must be the back of the garage.

There was a table set for two people on a small stone patio surrounded by rock gardens. There were summer flowers and native plants — agave, Mexican sage, and matilija poppies. It was a beautiful spot, and so isolated and private that she felt an impulse to look around for witnesses to be sure Richard wasn't about to kill her. He sat at the table and waited until she sat in the chair opposite him. She saw pitchers of water and fruit juice, a basket of bread, and a large wooden bowl of salad. She said, "Did you make this lunch?"

"No," he said. "My parents have a cook. I just wanted to be alone with you for a while and let you enjoy being outside without a lot of people around." He paused. "And I wanted to talk to you about our future."

She frowned. "Isn't this getting tiresome for you, too? We don't have a future. I spent a couple of years trying to make things work. They didn't, and I left. It's over."

"You didn't really think it was over, or that I'd let you do that."

"You're right. I thought you'd do something crazy, and you have. I tried to be very hard to find, but I blew it, and you found me. That doesn't mean we have a future."

"Step back about five paces in your mind and look at us," he said. "We're married. You may not like the way it happened, but if you go to the county clerk's office you'll see ours is the same as anybody else's marriage. We're going to have our baby in a couple of weeks. I know it's my baby, and a DNA test can prove it. We're sitting in a garden at a beautiful house my parents own in one of the most desirable places in the country."

"Richard —"

"No, let me finish. I made mistakes with you. I took you for granted, and I didn't make enough of an effort when we were

418

together. I apologize. I've apologized a hundred times. I'm planning to make it up to you. I know you're mad at me, but we've got to be able to deal with each other."

The way he had raised his voice and talked over her to force her to listen to his apology was like a recapitulation of the changes in their relationship. He had always been overbearing, but now his vehemence had become frightening. Christine tried to speak calmly, to choose her words with great care so he wouldn't lose his temper.

"Richard," she said. "I didn't leave because I was mad at you. I left because I was scared to death. You hit me a lot of times. I didn't know how you would react when you found out I was pregnant, but I knew I no longer had the right to take the chance and find out."

"If you're so scared of me, why are you trying to piss me off? If I hit you now, then you're right? Is that it?"

"I'm not trying to piss you off. I really don't want to make you mad. I'm just trying to get you to accept the situation as it is."

"That's just the situation as you think it is. You're young, practically a kid. You'll learn more about life as time goes by, and then you'll feel better about the one you have." He watched her for a second, then sighed and picked up his fork.

Christine stopped looking at him while he ate. She looked at the silverware on the table, but saw it was actually good silver, so it would be soft metal, useless as a tool or a weapon. She looked at the shadows on the lawn to figure out which way was west. When she slipped out of here, it was probably going to be night, and west was the best direction. Interstate 5 was just to the west of Rancho Santa Fe, and that would be where all the traffic was. If she made it to the freeway shoulder and started waving her arms, she wouldn't have to wait more than a minute or two before she got picked up, or maybe even arrested.

She studied the trees, the hedges, the buildings. What she would need was luck. If only one of the gardeners had been careless and left a trowel or a pair of clippers lying around, she might have a chance to conceal it under the big, loose top she was wearing. She studied the rock garden. Where was everybody? What if Richard really was alone? She had seen Andy Beale leave. The cook Richard had mentioned wasn't visible anywhere. The whole estate was silent except for the chirping of small brown birds with off-white breasts. Maybe this moment was her last opportunity. If she could get behind him and pick up one of those rocks, she could hit him on the head with it. Richard always had his car keys in his right front pocket. She could grab them, run around the far side of the garage away from the house, find the black Porsche, get in and drive. She would be free.

But she thought about how horrible it would be to crack somebody's skull with a rock. It could kill Richard, or leave him paralyzed or something. As she tried to visualize it, she raised her eyes to gaze across the table at him. He gave an insincere smile, and behind it, there was a smirk of self-satisfaction. He thought he had charmed her, fooled her into some relapse of bad judgment. She felt a tightening in her chest. He wasn't trying to get her back. He was trying to fool her, to destroy her life, and then laugh at her for it. Yes, she decided. Yes, she could hit him. She looked past him and chose a smooth oval rock about the size of an ostrich egg. If she were behind him she could probably lift it in one hand and bring it down hard.

How would she get behind him? She was nearly finished with her salad. Maybe she could get up, go pick a flower, and tell him she wanted a few of them to put in a glass of water for her room. She played the whole conversation in her mind, and decided she could be convincing. The only remaining problem was forcing herself to act.

His cell phone rang. He still had the same irritating little tune for a ring tone. She watched him snatch the phone out of his shirt pocket and flip it open. "Yes?"

The phone call was like a message to Christine that she should act. She had been reluctant, but the call took all of Richard's attention. He was scowling down at the table, not even looking at her. Christine stood up and slowly, casually walked a couple of steps away from the table with her hands clasped behind her. She saw him look up at her for a second, but somehow he satisfied himself and stared down again.

"Of course it's me. What's the problem?"

She looked at the house. It still seemed quiet and empty. She walked a few more steps, pretending to look at the flowers in the rock garden, until her course led her around behind Richard. She moved her eyes to his back as she dug the rock free of the soil and started to pry it up.

Richard suddenly stood and pivoted, and his hand jumped to her throat like a striking snake. He clutched the front of her top so it tightened on her neck. "What the fuck have you been doing?"

"Nothing," she said. "I just stood up to look at the flowers. I thought maybe —"

He shook her. "In your room!"

She understood. Her eyes flicked to the window of her room. Behind the bars she could see the heads of two people moving around in there, and after a second she recognized them. As one of them passed close to the window and the light fell on blond hair, she could tell it was Claudia Marshall, and then she saw the long black hair of Sybil Landreau. They were searching her room, and they must have found her secret.

Christine considered trying to reach for the rock, but Richard's grip on her blouse was too tight, the fabric almost choking her. She could barely move.

His face was close to hers, and she could feel the puffs of wet air on her face as he spoke. "I left you alone," he said. "I made them give you some space to yourself. I trusted you!"

He started to walk, dragging her along by the front of her blouse. She was bent over, unable to quite keep up with him and afraid she would trip and fall on the uneven flagstones of the patio. He jerked her inside, then sped up as he hauled her down the long hallway to her room.

Christine was bent forward, looking at the floor and trying to keep from tripping and hurting herself, trying to hold back a bit to slow their progress. Her resistance seemed to make him more angry and rough. When they reached the slightly open door to her room he gave it a kick so it swung open the rest of the way. Richard yelled, "Shit! I can't believe this!" The curtains had been taken down and tossed on the floor, the bed had been pulled away from the wall and the mattress flipped over. Every drawer and all the cupboard doors were open. She could see that the top was off the toilet tank in the bathroom, and Steve Demming was kneeling in front of the sink searching the cabinets.

Staring at Christine with distaste were the two women she had gotten used to thinking of as bad angels. They were tall and attractive and stylish like the mean girls at school, and they looked at her the way those girls used to — as though she were less than human.

Christine felt her strength draining from her as soon as Richard pushed her inside the room. The damage she had done to the plaster wall and the mess the two woman had made reduced her to shame and humiliation. She hated herself for being so vulnerable that these enemies could make her feel anything, but she couldn't seem to overcome her discomfort.

Sybil Landreau arched an eyebrow and said, "You're no housekeeper, honey."

Claudia Marshall gave a bark of a laugh, just a single harsh sound. Then her mouth returned to the familiar smirk as she watched Christine.

But Richard didn't see anything amusing. He seemed stung and outraged by the damage she had done to the plaster. She had seen little reaction to her angry words in the garden, but the gouged plaster of the wall had thrown him into a rage. "You little moron," he said, and pulled her closer to the wall. He changed his grip to the back of her neck. "Look at it." He thrust her face close to the damaged wall. "What the fuck did you think you were doing?"

Christine sensed that if she gave in now, in front of these smirking women, she would be lost. "I was doing what anybody would do — trying to get out."

Richard increased the pressure on her neck until he had pushed her face against the plaster. "There's no way you could get out. Didn't you pay any attention when you were working for me? Didn't you see how old houses were built? There are wooden laths and plaster, then two-by-fours and insulation, then sheets of plywood, then siding."

He didn't seem to see that she had been trying to reach the bolts that held the bars over the window, but she didn't want to use that to defend herself. She was beginning to fear he would break the bones in her face against the wall. "I guess I didn't pay that much attention."

"I guess you didn't." He jerked her backward and pushed her so she fell onto the bed. He said to the others, "Take her to the other room, will you? I don't trust myself with her anymore." He didn't stop on his way out the door.

The two women pulled Christine to her feet. They seemed to think she was resisting. Claudia bent her wrist and twisted her hand to make her walk beside her. Sybil Landreau held her other arm. They steered her out of the room, down the hall two doors to another bedroom. This one was smaller and plainer, with very little furniture. They released her in front of the bed, and she sat down, fighting back tears.

Sybil said, "You stupid cow. You don't know when you've got it good, do you?"

"Maybe not."

Sybil bent slightly so her black eyes held Christine's. "There's something you ought to think about. We're working for Richard. If we weren't, there wouldn't be anyone to tell us what to do and what not to do."

"What does that mean?"

Claudia Marshall was standing a few paces back with her arms folded. "You still don't get it? What's happening here is what Richard wants to happen. You think that without him you'd be free. The truth is, all you'd be is dead."

Christine said nothing.

"You haven't paid for what you've done, because our client wants that baby you're carrying to be born. That's all that's kept you alive. As long as he wants you here, you will be here."

The two women turned and went out the door. Christine heard the door lock. No one returned with food or to check on her. A few hours later, a bit after seven in the evening, her water broke and contractions began. At seven the next morning the contractions were making her strain to keep from screaming, so she was sure her labor must be nearly over. Ruby came into the room, saw what was going on, and ran out.

At nine a man that the women addressed

as "Doctor" arrived with a bag full of medical supplies and equipment. He spoke little, and when he did, it was in Spanish. He took Christine's temperature and blood pressure, listened to her heart and lungs, and then went away. The woman he brought with him as an assistant spoke no English either. She wore tight jeans, high heels, and a black top that was extremely low cut to show the gold chain with a heavy cross on it that rested between her breasts. The woman read Spanish-language magazines about movie stars, which she put down once every hour to examine Christine. Afterward she would go outside for a while and return smelling strongly of cigarette smoke.

After her fourth trip, in the late afternoon, she brought the doctor back with her, and together they pushed the television set from Christine's old room in on a cart. The woman watched shows on the Spanish-language stations in which people were invited down from the audience by young women in bikinis to participate in some kind of competition, while Christine's pain almost made her faint.

After midnight Christine went into the final stages of labor, and only then did the woman in high heels seem to wake up and become active. The baby was born, and as soon as the doctor cut the umbilical cord and got the baby to breathe, the woman washed it and wrapped it and took it away. Christine did get to see that it was a boy, and that it was big and seemed healthy. She cried for joy and relief. After a few minutes Sybil and Claudia and Ruby appeared and moved Christine to her old room, which had been restored and rearranged. There was a white crib pushed up close to the bed, and a changing table by one wall. The Mexican woman gave Christine an injection, and she lay in the bed, still crying, until she fell asleep.

When Christine awoke, Ruby Beale was in the room with her. "Good morning," she said. "How are you feeling?"

"Where's my baby?" Christine said. She was overcome with a feeling of panic. Was he dead? Had they already taken him away?

"Ready to see him?"

"What have you done with him?"

Ruby went out the door, and a moment later, the Mexican woman came in carrying the baby wrapped in a soft cotton blanket and wearing a small cap, so only his little reddish face peeked out, his puffy eyes like slits. The Mexican woman seemed to have softened since the baby was born, and as long as all of her attention was on the baby, she was cooing and making little sounds with her lips. When she looked at any adult, she seemed to bristle and glare. But she brought the baby and set him at Christine's breast, and kept rearranging him until he began to nurse. This was the strangest feeling of all for Christine.

"He's a little bit early," said Ruby, "but I wouldn't even call him a preemie. He's over five pounds — just about normal weight."

After a few minutes the two women left, and after that, the world was populated only by Christine and her baby.

When they had been together for an hour, the door opened again and Ruby and the Mexican woman returned. The woman lifted the baby off Christine and took him out of the room. "Let me hold him," said Christine, but the woman didn't seem to hear or understand.

"Don't worry," said Ruby. "He'll be back soon enough. He just needs to be changed, and you need breakfast. If you're going to nurse, you've also got to eat."

Christine said, "I want him. You have no right to take him away." She felt terrible fear and love for the baby. "Can't you hear me? I want him with me."

"Have you figured out what to name him yet?"

"I'm sure you have."

"No. The mother gets to do that. I have some suggestions, though. Andy might be a good name."

"His name is Robert."

"Robert," repeated Ruby. "Robert Andrew Beale."

"Robert Monahan. His name can't be Beale because it's not a legal marriage. And I'm not naming him after your husband."

Ruby patted her, but her expression was cool and distracted, and not nearly as gentle as she had been before the birth. "Please yourself."

Routines developed over the next few days. At first the Mexican woman brought Robert in only to be nursed. But then Christine began to spend more and more time with Robert, and to change and dress him and hold him.

It was when she was alone, without Robert, that Christine was forced to think. A big healthy boy was just what the Beales had wanted. Maybe if he had been a girl, the Beales would have been disappointed in Christine and decided she wasn't suitable, and would have let Christine take her baby and go. But Christine reminded herself that during the past two weeks she had spent many hours listening to Ruby and Andy

Beale talk about the baby, and neither of them had ever expressed any interest in whether it was a boy or a girl. They wanted a baby, period. The thought made Christine panicky, and sent her mind off again on its circular course. She kept remembering what Claudia and Sybil had said about Richard keeping her alive. Maybe they would be allowed to kill her now that Robert had been born. The thought made Christine's heart pound and her head ache, but she couldn't think of anything she could do to stop them. Whenever she heard a sound in the hallway, she jumped, then tensed her muscles and waited, listening intently.

After a week she said to Ruby, "Richard hasn't been to see me."

"Do you want him to?"

"No."

"Are you sure?"

"Has he asked if I was okay?"

"Sure. I told him you were fine."

Christine came to the part that worried her. "Has he been to see Robert?"

"That he did," said Ruby. "The first day. Or at least the second. He came in and looked him over."

"He hasn't been alone with him, has he?"

"No. He knows nothing at all about babies. He's not going to be the sort of father who changes a diaper. Get that out of your mind."

At around that time they began to grant Christine more freedom. She was allowed to sit with Ruby, Robert, and the Mexican woman in the gardens, and sometimes to walk with them on the grass or dip her feet in the pool. The one thing that nobody would ever allow Christine to do was be outside with the baby alone.

"Why don't you let me be alone outside with Robert?"

"Too much sun isn't good for him."

"Or for anybody else. We're never outside for long, and he's always shaded."

Ruby eyed Christine wearily. "Let's just say it helps the rest of us to feel at ease. If he's inside, you can wander around out here pretty much as you please. We know you won't go anywhere. The gate is locked anyway."

"Then what are you worried about?"

"Honey, this is for your own good. For everybody's good. You must know that I have some control over certain things around here, but not others."

"Then who does have control of them?"

"Mostly my husband, Andy. But there are complicated issues here. Everybody has his own set of concerns. Getting into trouble, for instance. Richard and his hired people have a say in those areas, whether I want them to or not. None of them wants to be vulnerable, and I don't think any of them will tolerate much risk."

"They didn't mind the risk of kidnapping me."

"If you were to take off and run to the police, then by the time you got back, Robert wouldn't be here anymore."

"You mean they'd kill him?"

"I mean exactly what I said. I didn't say dead. I said gone. His crib and his toys and his clothes would be gone. You would never, ever know what became of him." She stared at her with what looked a lot like compassion. "I think you and I have got to team up and be sure that never happens. Don't you?"

It was only a few days after that conversation that the rules changed again. Christine was still nursing Robert every couple of hours, and soon it felt like too much work for someone to hear the baby cry, pick him up, and carry him down the hall, unlock the room, and bring him to Christine. They let Robert stay with her. She liked it much better that way. At first she did what she was told and had Robert sleep in his crib until he woke up crying for milk, but then she brought him to bed with her and kept him there until daylight.

She got up one day and began to take stock of the world outside Robert. She needed to escape — now more than ever before. Now that he had been born, the Beales really didn't need her. She was a threat to them, a dangerous person who just might sneak out of her room sometime and get them arrested. The two women, Claudia and Sybil, were longing to be allowed to murder her. Richard certainly had no affection for her anymore, and he didn't even seem to have a sexual interest in her.

It occurred to her that there was a way, and a time, to escape. She realized now that she had been foolish to try so hard when she was nine months pregnant. There never had been a way out then. Everyone had been watching her, expecting her to try. Even if she had made it out of this room into the sunlight, there was no way a woman near the end of a pregnancy was going to outrun anybody who thought his life might depend on catching her.

But now Robert had arrived and changed everything around him. Ruby and Andy Beale were absolutely enthralled. Nothing mattered to them anymore except their grandson. Ruby never talked about Richard anymore, and barely noticed Christine. She would come into the room and head straight for Robert, not even looking directly at Christine even though she was nursing him.

Richard was still lurking around the premises part of the time. He went to work as usual, and Christine was under the impression that he still slept at the house where he and she had lived together. But he was sometimes visible through the window or down the hall in the late afternoon or evening. He would sit at the outdoor table smoking cigarettes with the Mexican woman. Other times he would be on the back lawn talking to Steve Demming, Pete Tilton, Claudia, and Sybil. The two men just came here to meet with him, but the two women were here all the time. Apparently they had moved in to guard Christine, but they seemed to spend more and more time with Richard. Once the three of them went swimming in the pool, and it occurred to Christine that it was the only time she had seen anyone go near it, although she had been here for two weeks.

She realized that people weren't very interested in her anymore. They were only watching Robert. And they were all so arrogant and sure of themselves. She needed to keep them that way.

During the night Christine got everything

ready — two receiving blankets, two one-piece outfits, two little knit caps. Andy and Ruby had begun bringing toys when Christine arrived, and Robert was still just "the baby," a theoretical person who might be male or might be female. One of the toys was a cute baby doll. When Christine had seen it, she had wondered if Ruby had lost whatever weak hold on reality she'd had. No child would be able to play with that for two years or more. The odd thing was that now that Robert was born, the doll seemed to bear a faint resemblance to him. It had the same light skin and the same cap of dark hair. Christine supposed that Ruby had looked at her and at Richard and made a fairly accurate guess at what the baby was going to look like. She hadn't done as well at guessing the sex.

At ten in the morning Christine opened the window of her room. She had dressed the doll and wrapped it in a blue receiving blanket, then put the little stocking cap on it. She opened the window, looked to be sure nobody was outside, pushed the doll between the bars, and let it drop to the ground behind the thick shrubs. Then she closed the window again.

She fed Robert, dressed him in a one-piece suit exactly like the suit she had put on the doll, and wrapped him in an identical blue receiving blanket. At ten-thirty Ruby came to her room just as she had been doing for the past few days.

Ruby said, "Our boy is looking pretty good, isn't he?"

"*Robert* is doing great," said Christine. Sometimes it had occurred to her that Ruby said things that appeared to test her acceptance of her life of captivity, but were really meant to test her sincerity. If Christine had suddenly acted as though she was getting used to this, then Ruby would have known she was about to try something. She had to be very careful with Ruby.

Ruby said, "Want to take him out for a while?"

"I don't know," said Christine. "Is it hot out there? I don't want him in the sun."

"So sit in the shade with him. A little fresh air and indirect sunlight will be good for both of you." Ruby held the door open. As Christine walked to the doorway past her, Ruby said just above a whisper, "And if you don't mind my saying it, honey, there's nothing wrong with a little exercise for you, either. The sooner you get rid of that weight, the better things will seem. Nobody feels her best with an ass like a tugboat."

Christine carried Robert down the hall.

Her jaw muscles were working, but she didn't realize it until the muscles suddenly felt tired. She artificially relaxed them and blew a breath out through her teeth. When she reached the first sliding glass door she opened it and stepped outside.

Christine walked toward the back of the yard, keeping Robert's face in the shade of her shoulder. When she got a few yards from the house she realized that Ruby had followed her.

Ruby said, "I hope I didn't hurt your feelings, Chris."

Christine gave her a look she hoped was withering. "What hurts me is being a prisoner. I don't really care what any of you think about my ass."

Ruby pursed her lips and moved closer. "I apologize. Sometimes I'm a little too quick to talk without thinking. But I'm just trying to be your friend. I've been watching Richard. It's possible he's gotten over the shock of everything that's happened, and he'd be receptive to some sort of reconciliation if you made the right move."

"I didn't do anything to him — before I was kidnapped or after. If he's unhappy, that's his fault."

"That's not the point. Robert deserves a father. Don't you want to know why I think he might be interested?"

Christine shrugged. "No, but if you want to tell me, I can't stop you."

"I saw him watching you with Robert yesterday. He was in the house while you were out here. He didn't come out to talk to you or anything, but I could see there was something going on in his mind. The two of you just looked so pretty — you with Robert in your arms around sunset. You and I talked about this before. I know that you cared about him once. Loved him, even."

"You mean I'm supposed to try to get Richard to take me back?"

"I know that isn't on your agenda right now," Ruby said. "But sometime you might feel less bitter. You've also got to realize that looking your best isn't giving in to anybody. It gives you the power." She patted Christine's shoulder and stepped back. "Well, I've got to get going. I've got shopping to do, and the cook wants some help picking out dinners for the next few days. We've got so many more people living here now."

Christine began to feel her heart beating faster and faster as Ruby crossed the lawn. Could she be forgetting that Christine was alone out here with the baby in her arms?

Ruby went inside and started to close the door, but before she could do it, Sybil and

Claudia both slithered outside and started across the yard toward her. As they came she could see their eyes were like the eyes of cops, full of suspicion and yet detached, confident that they would detect her hidden intentions and be able to block them. They turned their heads this way and that to scan the yard to be sure Christine was alone, then stared at her to be sure she wasn't up to something and wasn't planning to move.

The fact that they would be the ones to watch her this time made her frightened, but she also felt eager. Fooling them would make her revenge even better. Then she wondered if she had been unconsciously feeling reluctant to fool Ruby, or maybe afraid she'd have to hurt her to get away.

As Sybil and Claudia stepped in her direction, Christine pretended not to notice them. She held Robert and turned to walk along the grassy edge of the garden, being sure to turn only to the right so when they arrived she was innocently moving away from the gap in the hedges that led to the driveway.

Sybil stationed herself between Christine and the driveway, and Claudia stopped about twenty feet away, ready to move to the right or left if Christine changed course. Christine kept her face close to Robert's, and murmured to him musically about the green grass and the blue sky and what a beautiful boy he was. And she kept walking. But she could see from their dull expressions and their slouching posture that Claudia and Sybil were already finding this guard duty dull. Christine would pit her love of Robert and her determination to escape against the two women's ability to fight their boredom and laziness.

She knew that they would tire of this job in a few minutes. It had surprised her at first to see that Sybil and Claudia had absolutely no interest in Robert. Most women were fascinated with newborn babies, wanted to look at them and touch them and hold them, but these two didn't. The only attention they paid to Robert was the attention necessary to keep him and Christine imprisoned at this house.

Christine kept walking, looking at Robert's face and cooing to him, and that was something she already knew she could do for hours at a time. She never looked at the two women, never talked to them, but kept herself intensely aware of where each of them was.

Christine kept at it for an hour and a half before the two women decided it wasn't necessary to stand while she walked. They sat down, Claudia beside the gap in the hedge and Sybil near the spot where the grass gave way to the grove of trees. Christine waited, and gradually the two began to let their eyes stray and look elsewhere — at the house, the gardens, and each other. When she saw them step close together so they could talk, Christine slowly made the course of her movements take her closer to the house. She picked a poppy at the edge of the lawn and held it up so Robert could see the bright orange flower. She sat on an Adirondack chair overlooking the pool and concentrated on keeping the sun out of Robert's eyes and off his baby skin. She knew that thinking about him would make her able to outlast Sybil and Claudia. Robert was awake, and it seemed to Christine that he was looking with curiosity at the light and shadows as the wind made the trees sway back and forth near the buildings.

The two women were more comfortable now that Christine was away from the forbidden places — the gap in the hedge, which Christine could now see was an open wrought-iron gate, and the pathway around the garage to the cars. As long as the pair were between her and those places, they felt comfortable enough to sit talking. When

Robert cried for milk they looked up for a second, saw Christine lifting her shirt to nurse him, and looked away again.

After Robert was fed, Christine began to walk again, holding him upright to burp him with his face resting on a cloth diaper on her shoulder. This time she walked along the side of the house. Robert was happy and full, and after a few minutes he fell asleep. Christine continued walking along in the shade of the house looking in the windows at the deserted rooms, and then came to the barred window of her own room. She used the diaper from her shoulder to wipe a little milk off Robert's lip, but then dropped the diaper. She knelt down, and checked to be sure she was behind the Adirondack chairs and out of sight of the women.

Christine's heart began to speed up as she lay her beautiful, perfect son in his blue blanket on the bed of cedar chips under her window, picked up the diaper and the baby doll wrapped in the same kind of blue blanket, cradled it in her arms just the way she had cradled Robert, and walked along the side of the house in the direction of the sliding door.

She was confident that Claudia and Sybil would never offer to take Robert in to the nurse or to watch over him while he slept.

But she was not so sure they wouldn't move close enough to see what she was carrying. She had to dawdle just enough to let them notice that she was taking the baby into the house.

In the reflection in the glass wall she caught the glance that Sybil gave her, saw her say something to Claudia, and then the two got up off the lawn and began to move toward the house behind her. She resisted the temptation to hurry in order to stay far enough ahead of them. They were predatory creatures, unconsciously cruel like a pair of wide-eyed feral cats, and any tiny sign of fear or nervousness would be like the shriek of a wounded bird. They would be on her in a second.

Christine went inside and left the sliding door open, hoping it looked as though she simply didn't care enough to shut it. She forced herself to walk slowly down the hallway with the doll wrapped in the blanket, swaying gently from side to side to rock the lifeless piece of rubber to keep it asleep.

As she reached the open door of her bedroom, she turned back and let herself see first Sybil, then Claudia step in through the sliding door and then move beyond her sight into the great room. She slipped into the bedroom and quickly arranged the doll in Robert's crib. She placed it on its side and pushed a small, firm pillow behind its back to keep it on its side, facing away from the doorway, then covered it with another receiving blanket.

Every second that passed, Christine was listening for the sound of Robert's little voice to rise from outside the window a few feet away. She already knew him so well that she could hear in her imagination the first, tentative cooing sound that he would make if he woke up on the ground behind the shrubbery along the house. Then there would be an inquiring noise, a sound that was intended to call her. If he didn't see, hear, or feel her after that, there would be a loud cry. Someone would hear it, and they would know.

She felt afraid to delay by even a second, and afraid to go on with this. She wished she had done more to prepare, wished she had tried instead to find the Beales' bedroom in this huge place and sneak into it alone. There might be an actual telephone plugged in, and not just empty jacks as there were in the rest of the house. But Christine dismissed those thoughts. She was already moving, and she had to think about what she needed to do.

Christine snatched up the magazine she

had been reading the night before. The impression she wanted to make was that she had put Robert to sleep under the eye of the baby nurse, and was now taking a break by herself. She sauntered back down the hall, fixing a tired, bored expression on her face.

Where the hallway opened onto the great room, she walked along, aware of Sybil and Claudia. Each of them had arranged herself on one of the big white couches in feline repose. They paid little attention to Christine, but she knew they saw her, and had appraised how she walked and held herself, what she was carrying, how her face looked. If there was a tremor in her hand or a stiffness to her gait that she hadn't suppressed, she knew they had already detected it. She held her mind empty for a few seconds, waiting for one of them to spring up or yell or even shoot her. Nothing happened, so she walked on.

Christine wouldn't do anything but step outside through the same door they had just come in. It was the simplest, most direct route to the safe places, the ones where she was allowed to be. She went out and sat in one of the Adirondack chairs where they could see her without moving from their couches, and began to leaf through the makeup advertising at the front of her magazine.

All of her senses were raw, as though the skin had been peeled back and the nerves were exposed to the air, throbbing and waiting to be irritated. Robert wasn't making noises yet, and the women were lying still. Two cars went past on the road beyond the hedge, and Christine felt worried at first that they would pull into the driveway, and then devastated because they might have been the last cars to go by for an hour. She had missed them, and maybe they had been the ones that had been meant to find her and Robert by the roadside and save them.

Time was short and diminishing now, a lit fuse. She looked up, shaded her eyes from the sun petulantly, got up and moved to another chair, closer to Robert's place under the barred window, and invisible from the couches inside. She needed one of the two women to see her, so she waited. She counted to twenty, then counted fifty more, pretending to read her magazine but unable to concentrate on the sentences, which seemed to be lists of disconnected words.

She caught a movement in the corner of her eye, so she lazily lifted her gaze toward the grove of trees at the end of the yard like a person lost in thought, then half-turned her head and saw Claudia. She was standing on the inner side of the glass door, craning her neck slightly to look along the side of the house at Christine.

Christine sighed and half-turned her body to face away from Claudia, and turned more pages. She counted to seventy again, then glanced back at the door. Claudia was gone. Christine stood quickly, hurried around the Adirondack chairs to the shrubs under her window, and gently lifted Robert. He was still asleep, still peaceful and unharmed.

She followed the steps that she had been imagining in fragmentary form since she had been caught and brought here. She walked briskly along the edge of the vast green lawn toward the back. She had always known this would be part of her route, because she could see the grove of trees, the deep, cool shadows from her room. She had known she could make it all the way — or nearly all the way — to the grove before the angle of the path made her visible to the people behind the glass in the great room. But walking it in real life was an ordeal. It was much farther than she had imagined it to be, and the need to walk fast was a terrible temptation, because walking fast might wake Robert. She held him like a shallow bowl of water, keeping him level and never allowing him to tip or feel a bump. When at last she reached the shade of the trees, she was already breathing hard and sweating. She kept going farther from the house for another hundred feet, so the number of tree trunks between her and the house would make her harder to see.

Christine turned right when she got to the big brick wall at the back of the property. She could tell that she wasn't as hard to see from the house as she had hoped. If they missed her and began to look around, they would certainly be able to spot her within a minute or two. But she was far from the house now, and that would help. The grove was wide — at least as far as a football field — and she had to cross it quickly. The piled-up leaves were slippery and noisy, and once her toe hit a raised tree root, and she jolted Robert so hard that he gave a startle reflex. She hummed to him to make him aware she was there, and corrected the way she cradled him to make him more comfortable, and he sank back into sleep.

The sweat was pouring from Christine's scalp down her forehead now, and her breaths came in little huffs, as though she had been jogging. She could see the back of the long garage ahead through the trees. She kept moving as quickly as she could, corrected her course to go along the outer wall so close that she sometimes brushed it. And then she was there. She walked to the corner of the garage, slipped silently along the narrow passageway between the back wall of the property and the side wall of the garage toward the open brick pavement in front.

She approached the end of the passageway, and she knew there would be open garages and probably cars parked in the open. She stopped, leaned forward slowly and carefully, and looked. There was Richard's car. Her chest seemed to tighten and her eyes watered for joy. She knew the car, knew Richard's unbreakable habit of leaving a magnetic case with an extra key in it in the compartment that held the gas cap. She looked out farther, saw that the six garage doors were all open, and saw the front ends of cars, but saw no people. She stepped out.

Sybil Landreau stepped out of the garage beside her. "Where do you think you're going?"

She had failed. All of that effort had failed. Christine gave a wan smile. "For a little walk, that's all."

"Lying bitch."

She noticed for the first time that Sybil

had a gun stuck into the waistband of her jeans. Sybil took a couple of strides toward her, and Christine turned and took two steps to get back around the corner of the garage. When Christine looked the way she had come, she could see Claudia standing at the far end of the passageway, walking toward her.

Claudia called, "This time you don't get another chance. Take a last look at him."

Christine's heart froze. They were going to take Robert away from her. She heard Sybil's footsteps, knelt quickly, set him down, and then leaped toward the sound. She threw her fist into Sybil's face, but somehow the face wasn't there when her fist reached it. She felt Sybil's first blow as a revelation. She had never been hit in that way before, a strike so fast and hard that her head snapped to the side and she felt dizzy. The second blow was a quick punch to her chest. She was down on the hard brick pavement, wondering if the paralysis she felt was permanent. She heard a door slam some distance away. She looked up to see Ruby's overweight, middle-aged body coming from the house, a great deal of arm-pumping and bouncing, but steps that were too small to bring her here in time. Christine heard Ruby's voice: "No! Don't!" and suddenly she knew. Claudia hadn't meant that Robert was the one going away.

Christine saw Sybil Landreau tug the pistol out of her waistband, and hold it out toward her with a straight arm. Christine saw the muzzle flash, heard the bang, and felt something like fire spreading over her upper body.

24

When Carey came home from the hospital at precisely six-fifteen, Jane knew that the traffic had moved at its usual pace, with none of the sudden fits of highway repair that occurred in the Buffalo area during the late summer. Jane stood at the side window in the dining room and watched him drive his BMW up the long, sloping driveway, follow it around the corner of the house to the carriage house his great-grandfather had converted to a garage, and stop. He didn't pull in beside her Volvo, as she had expected. Even though Carey's car wasn't particularly small, when he got out he seemed to be unfolding, his long arms and legs straightening. She could feel the sense of freedom he was feeling to stand at his full height.

She had known him for so long now, listened to him and watched him so many times since she had met him in college, that it often seemed to her that she could feel what his nerves felt, and see what his eyes saw. She turned from the window, then heard him open the kitchen door and then close it.

As Jane walked through the dining room to the kitchen she saw his eyes focus on her and his smile appear, and she felt it again. She began to see herself in his expression. She touched her hair to sweep it back from her eyes.

"Wow," he said. "As I was driving here, I hoped a stunningly beautiful raven-haired woman would just show up. I need a date for dinner tonight."

"Raven-haired?" She laughed. "Do you actually *think* in words like that?"

"I don't think when I talk to you. I just start talking." He reached out, pulled her to his chest, and kissed her. "So how about that dinner? I made a reservation at Oliver's."

"I'm perfectly happy to cook. It's all easy stuff that could be ready in twenty minutes — a couple of steaks, fresh asparagus, corn on the cob."

"Keep them for another day. Tonight we're going to celebrate, not do dishes."

"What are we celebrating?"

"I guess we're celebrating a great August day."

"I can support that. But you know, I always feel a little sad when it's August. It's sunny and warm and the leaves are all as thick and green as they can get, and everything has grown all summer. It's so perfect, but that means it's going to end."

"Then it's even more crucial. We've got to get this in before the end. Pretty soon fall will descend on us — fall on us, in fact. Besides, maybe I'm just learning to appreciate you because I missed you so much while you were away this summer, and I want to show it."

"That gives me something to celebrate," she said. "But I hadn't been suffering from a lack of appreciation before. When is the reservation you made? I assume you've given me no time to get ready."

"Seven-thirty. You have an hour."

She stood on tiptoes and kissed him. "Then come on. Let's get started. We can share a shower and save water."

He followed her to the staircase. "I love saving water."

"I'll bet." And as she climbed the stairs, she felt the same sensation she had felt earlier — that she could see herself through his eyes, and what he was seeing made him feel not just a sense of warmth and contentment, but actual joy.

■ ■ ■ ■

At four in the morning Jane was asleep, but she was becoming more and more aware that she was cold. She snuggled closer to Carey's side, trying to get farther under the cover and be in the zone of heat his body radiated.

"Janie, you can't lie around like this."

"Harry?" She sat up. As always in her dreams, Harry wore his moss green sport coat. When he had picked it out, he'd undoubtedly had no idea that he would wear it forever.

He said, "You're cold, aren't you?"

"Yes." She rubbed her bare arms.

"The summer is over. Days are shorter already. Things are in motion."

"What things?"

He shrugged to make the coat sit properly on his narrow, rounded shoulders. "You know."

"She's safe, isn't she?"

His chest rose and fell in the characteristic sigh she remembered from when he was alive.

"What is it?"

"You're suddenly interested again? You take a little vacation and pretend the whole universe has stopped to wait. You took half the summer off, mostly to lie around in bed with your husband."

"That's not fair. I checked on her twice through her doctor. Communicating with a runner makes her weak and homesick, and sometimes it helps her enemies find her."

"Oh. Then I take it back."

"And I've tried to find out more about the people who were after her. I haven't gotten past the false names yet, but I will." She stopped. "Harry, what did you come to tell me?"

"Remind you."

"What don't I know?"

"The cold told you. It's already time. It's begun."

Jane awoke, and she was lying in the bed, the covers thrown off. The air had changed during the night. In the few hours while she was asleep, the smell and taste of it had changed. The hot, humid summer air had been replaced by a dry, still cold. Jane got up and went to the window, pushed aside the gauzy white curtains, and quietly slid down the sash to close it. She went back into the bed, lay close to Carey, but didn't close her eyes. Today would be the day.

She knew why she was having Harry dreams. Christine had seldom been out of her mind since the beginning of the summer, but Jane had resisted the strong temptation to keep calling her. Jane had waited, making plans. She still had over two weeks before Christine's due date, and first babies were usually late, but she wanted to be there in plenty of time. Jane got up and dressed in the dark.

She drove to Deganawida, went into the house where she'd grown up, and then up the stairs into the bedroom. She knew what she needed to bring, and packing didn't take long. There would be one suitcase that contained the minimum wardrobe and could be thrown away. She was going to carry a different purse this time. This one had two main compartments and between them a space for a handgun.

As always Jane's suitcase contained a lot of black — black jeans, black pullovers, black running shoes, black flats, a black dress. She had also gradually gathered a large collection of hundred-dollar bills. Once she had Christine set up in Austin, she would leave the excess with her to delay the day when Christine had to do anything that would make her visible — pay by credit card, get a job, put the baby in day care.

Jane had nagging feelings of uncertainty about this trip. Things had not seemed right from the beginning, but she had not been able to identify what she was missing. The cities and apartments Jane had selected were right for Christine. The name Linda Welles, the look, the backstory were all right for her. What hadn't Jane seen? What had she forgotten to do?

Jane went down to move the ladder in the basement, disconnected the old disused heating duct, and looked in her hiding place. She picked up the identification packet that Stewart Shattuck had sent her for Christine. He had done a thorough job of collecting the identification she would need. That was one of the things that had moved one generation further while she had been out of the profession. Now the business consisted of creating antecedent documents and using them to apply for real ones of another sort, then using the first real ones to apply for other real ones. For an artist like Stewart, the work was making birth certificates, marriage licenses, fake driver's licenses that a runner would use as identification in applying for a real license in a different state or a foreign country.

She looked over the documents in the kit. They were all genuine — driver's license, passport, birth certificate, Social Security card, all in the name Mary Watson. Jane smiled when her eyes passed across the name. Stewart always had favored names near the end of the alphabet, on the theory that some searchers gave up or got careless by the time they reached the ends of lists. He had gotten her Visa, MasterCard, and American Express cards, then thrown in a health-club membership, a library card, an auto-club membership. Jane put them all back in the wallet and took it with her.

She reached far back in the duct and pulled out a canvas bag. Inside were two nine millimeter Beretta M92 handguns, a box of ammunition, and two spare magazines. One she would carry in the purse and one in the suitcase. She carefully closed the heating duct, moved the ladder away from it, and went back upstairs.

Jane drove back to Amherst to the McKinnon house before Carey woke. She was making breakfast when she heard the sound of Carey's feet coming down the stairs. "I'm in here," she called.

Carey walked into the room, saw that Jane was dressed in the black clothes she favored for traveling, saw the suitcase near the back door, and stopped. "Oh."

She looked at him apologetically. "I'm afraid it's today."

"How long?"

461

"I don't know. I'm going for the birth of the baby, which could happen as soon as next week. But first babies tend to be on the late side."

"I've heard," he said. "I'm a doctor."

"I thought you just said that to get dates." She could see he wasn't amused. "And after the baby?"

"After the birth, I'll wait at least a couple of weeks letting the two of them get stronger so we can travel. I'll move them to their new home, spend a few more weeks helping her get settled, and making sure they're safe."

"That sounds like five to six weeks," he said.

"It will be if everything goes really well," she said. "Otherwise it could be longer — maybe much longer. I'm sorry. She's a tough person but she's very young, and she's alone."

"Will you call and tell me how it's going?"

"Of course not. If they've figured out who I am, they'll be listening."

"I didn't think so. Will you tell me where you're headed now?"

"I'll go, and when I'm done, I'll come home. You know how this works. Nobody knows anything about places, and it makes everybody safer."

"I'm not sure what to say. Drive carefully?" He sat at the table and watched her. The silence grew longer, until it was a barrier between them. "I'm wondering how much of the attraction is the girl, and how much is the baby. Can you tell me that, at least?"

"I'd say half and half," she said. "Two people." She turned toward him, her eyes narrowing.

He met her stare. "You're avoiding the question. You haven't done anything like this in years. Why this one? Because it was a pregnant girl. Other times, you took people away from their troubles, gave them new names, and that was the last they saw of you."

"I left when I thought they were safe," she said. "I don't think she's safe yet, and she asked me to come back. If I'm there to help her make the big transitions, she'll be more likely to survive them. You're right that I like babies, Carey. I love babies. But if you think it's going to make me happy to watch another woman having a new baby and then spend a couple of months teaching her how to take care of it, you're wrong. That's pure pain. She's going to have what I want most, and that's not pleasant. But I'm going to do it."

He looked down at the table, and she set

his plate of eggs in front of him carefully, as though she were keeping herself from throwing it. He looked down at the plate, and pushed it away. "I love you. I'm sorry."

"Me, too."

He put his arms around her and held her. "I know you believe you have to do this."

"I do have to."

"When are you leaving?"

"In a minute or two. I just wanted to wait until you were awake so I could say goodbye."

"Then there's no point in having the last thing we remember about today be an argument." He put his arms around her and held her.

She gave him a long, lingering kiss. "Thanks, Carey." She stepped back. "This is a good time to go."

They walked to the back door and he picked up her suitcase to carry it. If he noticed that it was much heavier than it looked because of the guns and ammunition, he didn't show it. They went down the steps by the back door and walked to the garage. He said, "Be careful."

Jane took her suitcase from him, kissed him once more, then turned away. During the summer she had bought a five-year-old Ford SUV under the name Willa Stahl.

She'd bought new tires, had the vehicle serviced, and made sure it would get her across the country. She took out the pair of thin goatskin gloves she had in her purse and put them on before she touched the door handle, got in, and looked back at the house, then at Carey. "I love you." Then she started the engine. Carey stepped away from the vehicle, and she backed out, waved once, and drove off.

As she steered along the quiet street under the big trees and turned onto the boulevard in the direction of the Thruway entrance, she couldn't force her thoughts away from Carey. It had occurred to her that if Carey had not been persistent, she would never have married. By the time she was twenty-two she had lost nearly everyone she loved. Her father had died in a construction accident on a bridge in Washington when she was twelve, and her mother had died of cancer shortly after she graduated from college. Her grandparents were long gone. She had retained relationships with the relatives on the Tonawanda reservation and a few in other places. She spoke frequently with Jake Reinert, the elderly next-door neighbor in Deganawida who had been her father's closest friend. But because of the work she did, she had become more and more adept at being elusive and difficult to corner. She was on the road most of the year, came and went quietly, and didn't cultivate any relationships that required her to answer questions.

Jane had met Carey at a party years before when they were students at Cornell. He was from Amherst, which was close enough so they could occasionally share rides home on holidays. She had lost touch with him for years after graduation, when he was in medical school and surgical residency, and then one day he had simply turned up at her front door in Deganawida. She opened the door and there he was. He said, "Hi. I was just updating my address book." He had come back to live in Amherst, just as she had come back to Deganawida. He had set up a practice doing surgery at Buffalo General.

They became better friends than they'd ever been at college. She asked him to the movies, he took her to dinner. She did not recognize for the first year that he was courting her. He dated other women constantly, complained to her about them and asked for her advice. He was a tall, handsome, funny young surgeon in a city where such men were as rare as whirling dervishes, so he got no sympathy from Jane Whitefield.

Jane had never wanted to fall in love with Carey McKinnon. She had resolutely remained his friend without encouraging anything more, until the evening when everything changed. She had been away with a client for a month, and came home physically exhausted and emotionally drained. He was at her house waiting for her with roses. She was simply too tired to care about her determination to keep him at a distance. He offered to rub her back, and while he was doing it, the barrier between them dissolved. Afterward, he had been so concerned about her feelings that she'd had no choice but to admit she liked him more than before. A few months later he asked her to marry him, and she refused. She explained that she was perfectly willing to keep having sex with him, but she couldn't have the sort of relationship that restricted her movements or required her to answer questions.

For the next year he stayed near her and waited. Eventually, as he had probably known it would, a day came when her reluctance stopped making sense to her. It was pointless. After she had spent a year going out with him most nights when she was in town and then sleeping with him, he asked her for the hundredth time why she wouldn't marry him and she gave in.

Today was one of the reasons why she had been reluctant. She had not wanted to feel this way over and over, to experience this sense of loss, the knowledge that she might never see him again. She supposed she resented him a little, too, at the moment. Letting someone get so close to her had been an act of faith that she had known was a risk. Intimacy — letting someone see her weaknesses and doubts — shouldn't have been a license to use them in an argument. He should never have talked about the baby.

It had been five years since she had taken to the road like this to meet a runner. What she was beginning to wonder was whether she had spent those five years trying to make herself into a different woman so she would be a good wife to Carey, or if she had been using her marriage to him as a disguise to hide herself from her enemies. If it was the first, she was cheating herself, and if it was the second, she was cheating Carey.

Her route was the same one she had driven with Christine three months ago, but now the world she moved through was different. The northern latitudes had changed from summer to fall, so the air that rushed by outside the car was cooler, and the sun seemed always to shine at a lower angle so it was in her eyes most of the day and went down just at dinnertime. She drove as much as possible in the dark. At night a car was just a pair of bright lights in a rearview mirror. She was harder to see, and when she was seen it would be harder to tell that she was a woman driving alone.

Jane knew the best places to stop late at night as she made her way west. After midnight the interstate highways outside cities were largely the domain of long-haul truckers, and the roads inside cities were mostly occupied by young men who would be better off doing their drinking at home. Jane stayed with the trucks, and kept her speed just a few miles above the limit. She didn't want to take the chance of being pulled over by a cop and having him find two M92 Berettas and thousands of dollars in hundred-dollar bills. She made one stop to sleep at a motel outside Chicago, and then pushed on to Minneapolis, heading into the city after dawn with the sun at her back.

25

It was a clear, warm morning in Minneapolis. Jane waited until she judged that most of the people in Christine's apartment complex were up and off to work. She performed a drive around Christine's neighborhood, searching for signs of watchers. There were no men sitting in vehicles parked where they could watch Christine's apartment, no windows in nearby apartments with curtains hung too low so an eye or a lens could peer out above them. Jane drove through a second time and looked in all directions, not trying to detect anything specific, just looking at everything and being open to the possibility that she would see something unusual. There were more cars parked in the complex than there had been in June, because the students had returned from summer break.

She found a parking space on the street, half-opened the tailgate of her SUV, then changed her mind and closed it again. She would leave the suitcase in the back until she had spoken with Christine. She walked to the front door of Christine's building, carrying only her purse. She pushed the buzzer for number 4, Christine's apartment, and waited, then pushed it again. It was nearly nine, and she had assumed Christine would be awake. Maybe she had gone out already.

Jane walked to the driveway that led to the garage beneath the building. There was an iron gate across the entrance. Beyond it she could see there were sixteen spaces, two for each apartment. Seven had cars in them. She looked for the small gray Volkswagen Passat she had bought for Christine, but didn't see it.

Jane took out her new phone and pressed Christine's telephone number. The phone gave its ringing signal a few times and Christine's voice came on. "This is Linda Welles. Please leave a message at the tone." The cheerful, girlish voice didn't reassure Jane. She heard the tone and said, "It's me. I said I'd be back, and here I am. Here's my number." She recited it and closed the phone.

Jane went back to her car, drove up the street, and stopped at a hotel she had seen on the way into town. She checked in and went to her room. She showered, changed her clothes, went down to the hotel restaurant, and had breakfast. Then she called Linda Welles's number again, and heard the same message.

She went out to her car and drove back to the apartment complex. She walked to the front door again and buzzed Christine's apartment several times, but there was still no answer. She saw a small car coming up the main road of the complex. Its turn signal began to blink as the car approached Christine's building. Jane pivoted and went back down the steps as the car stopped in the driveway. The woman in the car looked young, only a couple of years older than Christine, with wavy red hair. She appeared not to notice Jane as she pressed her remote control and the iron gate across the entrance swung upward. The woman drove in and turned to the right, and Jane cut across the flower bed and sidestepped into the garage just before the iron gate came down again.

Jane stopped beside the nearest car and sat down on the pavement between its grille and the cinder-block wall. She listened as the woman who had driven in turned off her engine. That was reassuring to Jane. If the woman had seen her slip inside, she

would have kept the car running, and probably driven out again. Jane waited and heard
the door slam and echo in the enclosed
space, then heard her high heels — pock,
pock, pock — go to the door and into the
building.

When Jane heard the door swing shut, she
got up and moved to it. The door was steel,
and it was locked. Jane reached into her
purse and took out a bookmark made of
thin, flexible plastic. She slid it into the
crack between the door and the jamb, then
moved it down to the metal guard beside
the door handle that kept people from slipping credit cards into the space to open the
door. She pushed the plastic a few times
until it slid the lock's plunger out of the
way. She tugged the door open, stepped into
the stairway, and climbed up to the corridor. When she was at Christine's apartment, Jane used the plastic bookmark again,
went inside, and closed the door.

Everything was wrong. The air smelled
old, as though no window had been opened
for a long time. Jane felt uneasy. She walked
into the bedroom. The bed was made. Jane
bent down and sniffed the pillowcase. There
was a very faint perfumy scent from Christine's hair, but there was also a thin layer of
dust.

Jane noticed a copy of *Vogue* by the lamp beside the bed. She stepped closer and glanced at the date: September. It was a month old, because Jane had noticed that the October magazines were already out. Under it was a copy of *American Baby*. There was no address sticker on the front of either magazine. Christine didn't subscribe, almost certainly because she was only here using the name Linda Welles for a few months. She had undoubtedly bought the magazines at a supermarket or drugstore, where the only issues for sale were the latest. Would she buy them and not get around to reading them for so long?

Jane went back through the living room and into the kitchen. She reached out to the refrigerator door. Before it was open an inch she knew. There was plenty of food — butter and eggs on the top shelf, squash, broccoli, asparagus, lettuce, tomatoes in the bottom drawer, a steak in its market package. Jane looked at the date on the open milk carton. The milk was about two weeks past its "sell-by" date. She looked at the steak. It was gray. The label's "sell-by" date was three weeks ago.

Jane closed the refrigerator, turned around in the kitchen, and studied the apartment in a new way. Now it was a place that Christine had abandoned or been taken from. Jane knelt on the floor and examined the tile from the side, then eyed the carpet in the living room. She didn't see any stains or streaks from a big cleanup. Nothing in the apartment seemed to have been broken, and she couldn't see large footprints on the carpet. Whatever had happened here had been quiet and neat.

She walked into the bathroom. The electric toothbrush was still plugged in, charging. The razors, lotions, makeup, bubble bath, shampoo, and conditioner were all still here. She looked closely at the bathtub. It was clean and dry.

As Jane went back into the bedroom, she checked the windows, looking for one that had an open or damaged latch, but she couldn't find one. She went to the closet. The clothes Christine had picked out at the mall were all hanging on their hangers. The apartment looked as though Christine had left it to go out on an errand. Jane entered the second bedroom. The baby things were all still there. She moved to the living room again, found the telephone book in a drawer beneath the phone, and looked up the number of the hospital where Christine had been planning to deliver. As she dialed the number, dozens of possibilities crowded one another in her mind. Christine could have been admitted early because of complications, and been lying in bed to avoid a miscarriage. She could already have had the baby prematurely, or be in labor right now. She could have been subject to paranoid fear, decided the apartment wasn't safe and checked into a hotel. Christine could have met new friends and been invited to stay with them. She could have fallen down and broken a leg.

"University Hospital."

"Hello," said Jane. "I'm calling to find out whether you've admitted my niece, Linda Welles, as a patient. That's W-e-l-l-e-s. She'd be in maternity, a patient of Dr. Molinari."

"One moment please. I'll check for you."

Jane waited, holding her breath. The woman's voice had sounded warm and motherly. Maybe that was a good omen.

"No. I don't see her here."

"Is it possible she's been admitted and already discharged? I've just arrived from out of town."

"I'm sorry, but discharge information isn't on my computer. You said Molinari, right? If he's the admitting physician, you should probably check with his office. I have the number right here. Do you have a pen?"

"I have the number, thanks."

After a few rings, Jane got Dr. Molinari's answering service. "I'm the aunt of one of Dr. Molinari's patients, Linda Welles, and I need to have the doctor or his office call me as soon as possible about her. I'll be at her phone number." Jane read the number off Christine's telephone.

It was thirty-five minutes before the doctor returned her call. "Doctor, I'm Linda's aunt. I was with her when she first came to you, and we've talked a few times since then."

"Of course I remember you," said the doctor.

"I'm in town now to help her during the delivery and the first month or two with the baby. I'm at her apartment, and she's not here, and I'm worried. Is she all right?"

"I'm very glad you called," he said. "I haven't seen her for nearly a month. She skipped her last couple of checkups. My office has been calling and sending her reminder cards, but we haven't heard from her. I don't have her file here, but as you know, she could deliver any time now. Having regular checkups is essential to ensure her well-being and the health of her child."

"I know," said Jane.

"If it's a question of the fees or transportation, we can always work something out."

"No, there's nothing like that," said Jane. "I was calling because I thought she might have been admitted to a hospital. She had been talking about visiting another aunt before the baby is born, so she may have done it and forgotten to tell us. Thanks, Doctor. We'll be in touch."

"Good-bye."

Jane couldn't be sure exactly what had happened, but she knew she had to exhaust a few possibilities. She opened the telephone book again and made the same call to all of the hospitals in the area. There was nobody named Linda Welles in any of them. She called the police and asked if Linda Welles had been arrested or involved in an accident. She asked about the gray Volkswagen Passat, and was given four numbers to call to see if it had been towed. After three hours on the telephone, Jane ran out of numbers. She went outside, drove her SUV to the hotel, picked up her suitcase, and checked out. She went back on the interstate and headed west. When she reached a patch of highway with the traffic thinning as it moved away from the city, she took out her telephone and dialed the number of Sharon Curtis's house in San Diego. She waited while it rang, but no voice-mail system or answering machine took over. Jane drove faster.

As Jane drove, she remembered conversations, things she had told Christine about being Linda Welles. Christine had nodded and said, "I understand," or "Don't worry, I'd never do that," when she had told her of possible mistakes. Jane had tried to mention everything she could think of that might happen and how to respond to it. But the main lesson had been intended to instill the right attitude. Not being found was mostly accomplished by not wanting to be found. It involved cutting every tie to the past. It required not doing anything risky for a very long time, and making a consistent effort to avoid being easily visible. If Christine had been doing those things, then she should have been safe.

But Christine wasn't safe. If she'd detected danger and had to flee the apartment, she would have called Jane or found another way to let her know. She had been gone for at least three weeks, and maybe more, which meant she'd had plenty of time to send a letter. Her car was gone, and she could have driven to Amherst or Deganawida in two days and started over. But she had done nothing.

If Christine had planned even ten minutes

in advance to leave voluntarily there was no reason to leave her toothbrush, her good clothes, or any of the rest of her belongings. She had not run from here, either. If enemies had been at her door, she would have had to leave through a window, and she couldn't have relocked it. The apartment was still neat, with nothing out of place, so she had not been dragged out, resisting.

Suddenly, Jane knew exactly what must have happened. The four chasers had come to Minneapolis — how they had found Christine was unknowable for now — and made their way to her apartment complex. They had watched the building, and after a time, had seen Christine's car emerge from the underground garage and come out the driveway. She had driven somewhere by herself, probably at night. She had not been hiding long enough to pick up the knack some runners had of acquiring friends and allies quickly, so she had been alone. When Christine arrived at her destination — the parking lot of a supermarket or a shopping mall — conditions had been right.

In her mind's eye, Jane watched. The four saw Christine take a few steps from the gray Passat, then drove in quickly and stopped between her and her car. The two men held something over her mouth so she couldn't scream and dragged her into the car with them, while one of the women wrenched her purse away. The driver, probably the other woman, threw the car into gear and drove off. The woman with Christine's purse searched it, found the car keys, and drove the gray Passat off after the others. If it hadn't happened almost exactly that way, Christine would have had time to reach into her purse for the gun, the gray car would still be wherever she had left it, or someone would have had a chance to see and help her. The whole abduction would have taken no more than ten seconds, and probably closer to five.

Jane wished that she could get on an airplane and not have to drive the vast distance ahead, but putting herself in airports and planes would leave her at the other end unarmed and visible, and this time she couldn't afford either of those things. Jane stayed on the road for several hours at a time, trying to keep moving. She stopped only when she had to, and then only long enough to use the restroom, top off the tank, and buy food she could eat in the car.

As she moved west, the distances she could see began to extend ahead for miles, and the driving became a simple question of staying between two white lines and preventing her speed from increasing enough on the long, straight stretches to attract the attention of the police. In the late afternoon, when the sun sank low enough ahead of her to get in her eyes, she pulled over at a rest stop and slept two hours, until the sun was beneath the horizon and she could again drive into the darkness.

26

Jane drove across the border from Nevada into California at three A.M., her headlights making the phosphorescent markers on the black highway gleam. The slopes and curves in the darkness of the high desert made her feel as though she were above the world, swooping and climbing and banking. She kept the car above the speed limit, because the passing of time was making her anxious.

As she had driven across the country for the past three days she had felt a growing sense of impatience that was becoming unbearable. Coming into California made it seem that she was at the end of the trip, but she still had a long drive ahead of her. She would reach the heavily populated areas near the coast in the morning rush hour, so she tried to beat the other cars, pushing her speed higher.

At six A.M. when she smelled the ocean and then saw it at Dana Point, she knew she was nearly finished. If she drove much longer, she would be in danger of falling asleep. She made it as far as Capistrano, saw signs for motels, coasted off the freeway, and checked into the first one that didn't look as though it was part of some criminal enterprise. She brought her small suitcase inside, locked everything she could lock, took her gun out of her purse, checked the load and the safety, and put it under the pillow beside her where she could reach it instantly.

As she lay there drifting into sleep, old stories that her grandfather — her *hocsote* — had told her began to present themselves in her memory. In the stories there were people who lived alone, away from the long-houses and the communal fields. They built small shelters near isolated trails and pre-tended to offer hospitality to strangers who passed by. Sometimes the host would be a solitary man, sometimes a group of sisters, or just one lone woman who used her beauty to lure men to her house. But always, somewhere in the forest nearby, there would be a pile of victims' bones.

In the stories, a traveler would be out in the forest searching for a lost friend or a missing relative. While the lonely host was something much worse than he seemed to be, the searcher was much better, and he would find a way to outwit the man-eater. Eventually, Jane's grandfather always got to the part when the traveler saved himself and killed the evil one, then stood over the pile of victims' bones. Her grandfather would give an abrupt jump and yell, "Get up, quick! The tree is falling on you!" The bones would instantly reunite, and the revitalized victims would run in all directions to get out of the way.

Jane felt a moment of amusement as she remembered, and then an onrush of sadness. If only that could happen. She would begin her resurrections with her grandfather, partly because he had been forced to stay dead the longest, and partly because he had taught her the trick when she was a child. And then he could teach her other old tricks, so she could bring back her father, with his sharp black eyes that sometimes seemed shiny and wild like a crow's, and her mother, all milky white and fragrant, with sky blue eyes like Jane's. She and Hocsote would bring them back together, in one instant.

She fell into a deep, dreamless sleep. When she awoke her muscles felt half-paralyzed from long immobility and it was the middle of the afternoon. She had paid for two days in the motel because she had known she would not be out by noon. She got up slowly, but after she'd had a shower and dressed she felt strong and fresh.

The first thing she did was take out her cell phone and call Sharon Curtis's number. She had called at least once a day since leaving Minnesota, but had never reached her. One of the rules she had taught Sharon to follow in situations like this was never to leave a message for a runner, because there was no way to ensure that the right person would be the one who heard it. Apparently the warning had stuck, because Sharon had not left Jane a way to leave a message. Once again there was no answer. It was summer, and Sharon was a teacher, so maybe she had left town for the vacation. She hoped the reason was that Sharon was having something nice happen in her life. This year Sharon must be thirty-one. She had always been pretty, with her blond hair and thin figure, and by now, she probably had a boyfriend. Even if she moved in with somebody, Sharon would be the sort of woman who kept a second, secret place where she could keep a bag packed with a little money and the papers to document the second false identity Jane had bought her years ago.

Jane had always told her runners to beware

of vacations. Airports, resort hotels, and restaurants were places where people were recognized. But Sharon was a special case. There were only two men who wanted to harm her. She had known both of them so well that she could probably predict their movements accurately enough to stay out of their way.

But what Jane hoped for most was that Sharon was absent for a different purpose. She hoped that Christine had seen something that worried her in Minnesota and had simply come back to San Diego to seek refuge with her. Sharon would have the sense to take her somewhere and hide her.

Jane took the 5 freeway toward Encinitas, pulled off early, and drove to the neighborhood where Sharon lived. She remembered the way to the house, even though she had not been here in ten years. She took all of the usual precautions to be sure that nobody was watching the house from any of the nearby buildings or parked vehicles.

Jane parked two houses away and walked to Sharon's front door. She rang the doorbell and almost immediately heard the sound of footsteps inside, then heard the footsteps stop. She stood still on the porch for a few seconds while she was being recognized through the peephole. Then she waited a few more seconds while the streets and buildings nearby were being studied. She had taught Sharon these things. A person's closest friend could come to the door on an innocent visit and be followed by killers.

The door opened and Sharon stood there, smiling. She reached out and pulled Jane inside, shut the door and locked it, then hugged her tightly. "I can't believe it's you," she said.

"Hi, Sharon," said Jane. "Are you okay?"

"I'm fine, thanks to you. And how have you been?"

"Not so good right now. I'm afraid I've lost track of our mutual friend."

"Lost track?" Sharon seemed to turn a ghastly pale color. "Of Christine?"

"I set her up in an apartment in Minneapolis and said I'd be back just before the baby was due. I was there, she wasn't. Sharon, have you heard from her?"

"Oh, God. Yes. I did. It was about two months ago. She called me on the phone one night."

"What did she say?"

"I don't remember, exactly. It wasn't that she was in trouble or thinking she'd been found or anything. I'm afraid now that I might have done the wrong thing."

"What was the wrong thing?"

"I told her that if she wanted to survive she was going to have to give up things like calling her old friends on the phone. I said that running meant giving up her old self and her old relationships and trying to be somebody new. I warned her that Richard knew about me, so he could have had his hired criminals tap my phone and wait for her to call."

Jane said, "What you told her was true. It may even be what happened."

"But I should have done something different. Maybe I could have gone to visit her, taken her to another city for a few days just to be sure. She's barely twenty, and maybe when it finally came down to it, she couldn't cut herself off."

"You did."

"I wasn't pregnant."

"Sharon, this isn't your fault. It wouldn't have helped for you to rush off and join her in Minnesota. That's exactly what the people chasing her would want — to have you lead them to her."

"I know. It's what I told her. But if something has happened to her, I'll feel terrible."

"Has she tried to call you or e-mail you or anything after the one time?"

"I don't know," Sharon said. "After it happened the first time, I checked just about every hour so I could erase any message before someone else played it. Then I realized that wasn't good enough, so I unplugged my answering machine."

"Good. It also explains why I haven't been able to record a message when I called."

Sharon seemed to awaken from a kind of daze. "Oh, I haven't even offered you anything to drink. Please sit down somewhere, and I'll bring you something."

"No, let's talk," Jane said. "You were too polite to say it, but I'm sure you're wondering why I took the risk of coming here like this. I came because I thought you might have had contact with her. But I was also afraid that something might have happened to you. I think it's time now to make sure nothing does."

"What do you mean?"

"I want you to go away. I want you to go far from here — someplace pleasant and safe. I want you to stay away until school starts. I'll pay for your trip. Your house will have to be closed. There can't be some friend who comes to pick up your mail or water your plants."

"Well, I guess I can do that," said Sharon. "Yes, of course I can. I will."

"Good. I'll help you pack and turn things

off and lock up. Then I'll drive you to the airport and make sure you get on a plane."

"Where am I going?"

"How about the northwest? You can stay in Seattle or Portland and use it as a base to explore the area."

"Sounds all right," Sharon said. She went to a closet and pulled out a suitcase, then stopped. "It's bad, isn't it?"

Jane shrugged. "I don't know. She could be somewhere else, perfectly safe."

"But you don't want me to be here while you find out."

"No. I don't."

They stopped speaking and began the work of getting the house ready for an extended period with Sharon away. Jane went into the kitchen and began taking perishable food out of the refrigerator and putting it into a plastic garbage bag. It took Sharon only a few minutes to pack the things she needed and place her suitcase by the front door. By then Jane had taken the garbage out to her SUV and was going from room to room making sure all of the windows were locked.

Jane said, "I see some of the lights are on timers. Is there anything else we need to do here? No pets?"

"No. I just have to cancel the newspaper

491

and fill out a card to put a hold on the mail before we leave."

"All right. I'll see if I can get you a plane reservation."

The mood had turned somber. Jane used her cell phone to get the flight to Seattle while Sharon called the *San Diego Union-Tribune* to cancel the paper. While Sharon filled out the card for the postal service, Jane asked questions.

"Is there anyone you know of who might be putting Christine up?"

"No. She had friends here, but Richard would have known about all of them, and she knew — at least after I told her — that even calling them might put them in danger. If there is anybody like that it would have to be somebody outside San Diego, and it would have to be somebody that none of us knew about."

"Like me."

"Like you," said Sharon. She paused, then said, "I'd better take one last look around." Sharon went into her room and Jane could hear her for a few minutes, opening and closing drawers, moving hangers in the closet. After a time she came out to find Jane looking in the telephone book. "What are you looking for?"

"The Beale Company," Jane said. "I found

it. I didn't find Richard Beale's address, though, and I didn't bring it with me."

"I have it." She went to her kitchen counter and opened a small address book. After she copied an address, she handed it to Jane.

"Thank you." She looked at it for a moment, then said, "This was where Christine lived with him, right?"

"Yes. But I never went over there. When we talked during that time it was usually on the phone, or we'd meet at a restaurant. I thought it was sort of my responsibility as her old teacher not to act as though her situation was okay with me, or to get chummy with him."

"But he knew where you lived, right?"

"I'm sure he probably did." She smiled. "But I'm leaving, so it doesn't matter."

"Before you go, I'd like to borrow a spare key."

"Sure, but why?"

"If someone comes here to find you, I don't want their trip to be wasted."

27

Jane stood outside the wall of windows in front of the San Diego airport with the people smoking a last cigarette before their flights. She wore a wide sun hat and big sunglasses and held a lighted cigarette in her hand. Now and then she took some smoke into her mouth and blew it out. She watched Sharon until she was beyond the security barrier and walking down the concourse to board her plane. Then Jane turned her attention to the ticketing area long enough to be sure that none of the four people she had seen chasing Christine showed up at the last minute to board Sharon's flight. A minute after flight time, Jane threw away her cigarette and went inside to look at the television monitor to verify that Sharon's plane had taken off. Then she went to the parking lot and drove back to Sharon's house.

She was almost positive now that her

intuition about how Christine had been abducted from Minneapolis was correct. The four people Richard Beale had hired had stalked her there. Probably they had put her in an enclosed vehicle of some kind — Jane imagined a windowless van — and driven across half the country to bring Christine to Richard Beale. But that must have been three weeks ago, and finding Christine — and maybe the baby, too, by now — was not going to be simple. The next step for Jane was to find out where Beale was now.

In the late afternoon Jane drove to the offices of the Beale Company in La Jolla and studied the building from the street. It was a four-story rectangle with windows that had been tinted to an almost opaque black, so the building looked like a shiny black box. The place held a special attraction for Jane. If Beale had anything he wanted to keep secret, she was more likely to be able to find a way to get at it in his office than at his house. She was particularly interested in a list of the pieces of property that the company owned. If Beale was holding Christine, it would have to be in a place he could control absolutely.

Most businesses had some sort of video surveillance system. There would also be at least a halfhearted security service at night, an armed patrol that drove by looking for broken windows and unexpected lights. But most office buildings were cleaned at night by some kind of janitorial service, so it would be important that Jane be ready before then.

A little before six, Jane drove her SUV north to the area near Sharon's house in Encinitas. Earlier she had seen some stores that she knew would have the items she needed, and would be open in the evening. She began at a giant Sears store. She went to the men's clothing section and picked up a pair of navy blue pants and a matching shirt, a baseball cap that was only a half-shade darker blue than the clothes, and a dark blue bandanna. Then she went to the hardware section. There among the power tools she found packages of disposable dust masks that fit over a person's nose and mouth to keep dust from entering the lungs, and in the paint department a package of very thin rubber gloves.

She waited at Sharon's house until it was night, changed into her Sears clothes, and then drove back to La Jolla. She parked down the street from the Beale Company building and settled in to watch. At one A.M. she saw a white van pull into the parking lot beside the building. It was old, with some dents in the rear bumper, the sort that came from backing into posts in parking lots. The blue logo on the side of the van was a big outline of a hand, and the words said HELP-ING HAND JANITORIAL. Two young His-panic men climbed down from the van, went around to the back, and opened the doors. They pulled two boards out of the back and leaned them on the bumper to make a ramp, then steered a big industrial vacuum cleaner down, then a big floor buffer, and locked the van.

She watched them go to the front door, unlock it, and go inside. Now that it was dark out, she could look through the dark glass and see the janitors working in lighted offices. When they went into a room they would turn on the light, and that single square on the side of the black building would become transparent. First one of the men went from room to room emptying wastebaskets into a large plastic trash can on wheels. After he had done that he would take a rag and a bottle of glass cleaner to the desks and the windows. Coming along behind him, the second man ran the vacuum cleaner on the carpets and turned off the light. The two worked quickly, and Jane could follow their progress easily from outside.

When the first man went outside to wheel the trash can to the Dumpster, he stuck a doorstop in the front door to keep it ajar so he could get back in. While he was out of sight, Jane got out of her SUV wearing her work uniform, baseball cap, and dust mask. She went to the front door and slipped inside. Surveillance cameras were almost always mounted high, so she kept her head low as she hurried down the hall.

The two janitors had finished with the now-darkened interiors of the offices, so she hurried to one on the first floor, went inside, and crawled under the desk to wait. She heard the elevator doors open and close a couple of times in the quiet building as the men moved from one floor to another. Some time later she heard them return with the electric buffer and polish the lobby.

When Jane heard the sounds of the men moving their equipment outside, she waited a few more minutes, then got up and cautiously walked down the hall. Their van was gone, and she was alone in the dimly lit building. She could explore freely. After looking at the signs on a few doors, she found one off the main lobby that said, RICHARD BEALE, PRESIDENT. She looked the other way and saw the glass wall of the atrium, and in front of it, the receptionist's desk where she had seen Christine in the photographs on the Internet.

She opened the door to Beale's office and stopped. There were no windows. The office was the right size — a bit bigger than the others — and it had the right sort of furniture: large leather couches, a long polished conference table, and a big glass-topped desk with very little on it except a computer screen and a keyboard and a telephone. But it seemed terribly odd to her that the office of the owner of a prosperous company would have no windows.

She set the thought aside for the moment because there were things she had to do. She pushed a chair to the spot directly below the dome that covered the surveillance camera, used the blade of her pocketknife to pry the dark plastic dome off, then stopped again in surprise. The video cable for the camera had been disconnected. It had been unscrewed. Jane replaced the dome, got down, and moved along the walls looking carefully at every shelf or fixture to be sure there wasn't a buttonhole camera hidden somewhere. She found nothing.

Apparently Richard Beale had disabled the security camera himself. Now she had a better idea of what had made him pick the darkest, most closed-in office in his own company. He probably made deals in here with people like the ones he had sent after Christine. And Christine had said he was very careful that he not be the one to sign certain papers or have his name on certain deals. It wouldn't make much sense to videotape himself doing things that were illegal.

She began a methodical search of the room. She went through the files in the cabinet, plucking out the papers that seemed useful. The computer and the printer were turned on, and the printer had a copier function, so she copied the lists of buildings currently for sale or rent, the property tax files showing property the company had paid taxes on. Jane was particularly interested in addresses where land was registered in a name other than Beale Company. She worked quickly, scanning one paper while another was copied, leaving files opened so she could return each sheet to its place.

She found the articles of incorporation of the Beale Company and its subsequent filings with the Department of Corporations. The corporate papers were over forty years old, and the owners and officers were listed as Andrew and Ruby Beale. Richard Beale had signed for the past few years as the president of the company, but he was not listed as an owner, or even a stockholder. There were only two shares of stock, one owned by Ruby Beale and the other by Andrew Beale.

There was a personnel file for Richard Beale, so she checked to verify that his address was the one Sharon had given her. His salary was "as negotiated," and his payroll record showed he made about two hundred thousand dollars a year. He lived in a house in Del Mar owned by the company and drove a company car, a black Porsche. There were no personnel files for Steve Demming, Ronnie Sebrot, Pete Tilton, Claudia Marshall, Sybil Landreau, or Carl McGinnis.

When Jane had copied the records she wanted, she readjusted her dust mask and hat so she would not be identifiable on the surveillance cameras in the lobby, turned off the lights, and hurried out to the SUV.

Jane drove back to Sharon's house after two A.M., and made a careful search of the grounds and the surrounding streets before she went in. She had chosen to stay at Sharon's because she was hoping to surprise one or more of Richard Beale's thugs as they watched Sharon's house, but so far, she had seen no sign of them. She arranged blankets over some pillows to make Sharon's bed look occupied, then took a spare quilt and lay on the floor in the hallway leading from the kitchen to the living room with her two guns beside her where she could reach them in the dark. From there she judged she would be able to hear if someone broke in looking for Sharon.

Jane drowsed, then awoke suddenly and looked at the clock on the kitchen wall. It was almost three A.M. She had just fallen into a pleasant dream about Carey, then felt a panicky sensation, a fear that she was losing him. She stood, went out the back door of Sharon's house, and got into her SUV. She drove to the plaza where the big Sears store was, and parked beside the pay telephone she had seen in the afternoon. She dialed the number of the house in Amherst, New York, and put in enough coins for three minutes.

"Hello?"

"Hi. I knew it was six there, and you'd be getting ready for work. I couldn't relax until I talked to you."

"That's nice. I think it's nice, anyway. Unless you were dreaming about lawyers. Were you?"

"No lawyers. And it *is* nice. Your ears should be burning. And don't be alarmed if lots of other places are burning, too."

"You don't happen to be anywhere near here, do you? I could meet you somewhere — pick up a bottle of champagne and an orchestra on the way."

"I'm not near, but I wish I were. I just felt kind of desperate to say something."

"What is it?"

"That I'm sorry if things seemed a little hollow when I left home. I love you completely, and I will until I die. And probably when my heart stops, there will still be a few seconds before I lose consciousness, and I'll try to remember as many of the days I had with you as I can before my mind goes dark."

"Jane, are you in danger now?"

"No. Not at all. I'm just taking care of some things here. I called because I was afraid you were feeling as though I didn't love you enough. Or maybe I was feeling that I hadn't said it enough or said it right, or acted the way I wanted to."

"I'm glad you called. But I wasn't doubting you. I've been worried about you since long before . . . before the hospital benefit. But it was a normal family sort of worry. I knew you'd been having a hard time about the baby and everything, but I haven't found a way to be of much help."

Jane smiled. "I'm not your patient, Carey. You can't approach it that way. Just keep trying the other way. Something still might happen."

"It's a deal."

"And if nothing happens, I want you to know it doesn't change anything between us. You're it, the one I want. I have to finish what I'm doing right now, but after that everything will be the same."

"I would like it if you weren't out there taking risks."

"Don't worry. I'll be home soon. We'll talk then."

"That sounds terminal. Are you getting ready to hang up?"

"Yes. I want to say 'I love you' before I go, but I've just said it so many times you'll think I'm an idiot."

"Then let me be the idiot," he said. "I love you. Call again if you can, but I'll understand if you can't. Just come home safe."

"I will." She hung up, then got into her SUV and drove back to Sharon's house. She went in through the back door, settled into her spot in the corridor between the kitchen and the living room, and slept.

In the morning she drove past the Beale Company office in La Jolla again and verified that there was a black Porsche parked in the space marked RESERVED FOR RICH-ARD BEALE. Then she drove on.

Richard Beale's address was a house on the beach in Del Mar. Jane had been to Del Mar a couple of times about eight years ago. The beach at Del Mar was one of the prettiest inhabited places in the country. It had broad, white sand beaches that rose only slightly as they stretched up from the surf, and then tall groves of tropical trees that formed a curtain between the beach and the coast highway. The incredible blue Pacific was so enormous that having a few rich people living along its edge wasn't enough of a blight to be noticeable. The beaches were almost empty on a weekday morning, and most of the houses were low, sprawling structures that didn't irritate the eye.

She drove by the racetrack and then along the coast highway looking at street markers and mailboxes until she found the right number. From the road she could see only a tall wooden gate, a hedge, and a closed garage door. She kept going along the road until she reached a mall built on several terraces set into a bluff across the road from the ocean. There were restaurants, a few upscale shops, and a bookstore. Jane parked her SUV on a side street above the mall where she could drive it out quickly, then went to a restaurant and had a simple breakfast while she watched the highway and the stores. It was not out of the question that she might see the two men and two women who had been searching for Christine. If Christine was being held at Richard Beale's house, then Beale would need to have someone to keep her there. Jane went into a shop and bought a tank top, a pair of running shorts, and some sneakers. She changed into them in the dressing room, then put her clothes in the SUV and went jogging.

The beach access was a forty-foot gap in the trees where the asphalt of the road gave way to sand. Jane trotted across the wide, soft expanse of beach to the hard, wet margin where the long, slow swells hissed in. It was easier to run on the wet sand, and running along the surf gave her a chance to look at the area as she approached Richard Beale's property. The only person she passed was a platinum blond woman about fifty years old throwing a tennis ball into the surf for her German shorthair to retrieve. When Jane found Beale's house, she could see no signs of life on the ocean side of it, and there were no lights and no movement visible beyond the big picture windows. She could see no other windows open.

Jane looked up and down the beach, but she saw no faces at any windows in nearby houses. The woman and her dog were moving off down the beach in the other direction, so Jane decided to take the chance. She jogged up on the soft sand until her angle hid her from the houses on either side, and stopped at the oceanfront entrance to the house.

She could see the roof was bare, with no transmitter that would send a wireless signal to an alarm company, and when she peered in the windows she could still see no sign of anyone inside. She stepped around to the street side of the house, where there was a large yard with a swimming pool that had boulders and a waterfall. Attached to the house was a two-car garage. She tried the side door of the garage, found it unlocked, and stepped inside. The back wall had hooks on it to hold various tools. Jane selected a pair of long-handled hedge trimmers. She went back out, cut the telephone line where it came off the roof to the metal junction box on the side of the house, then returned to the garage and opened the main power switch at the circuit breaker box.

Jane made no attempt to hide the damage she made in her entry. She had decided that it would be best for her to let Richard Beale worry about who had been here to visit him. She used a cordless electric drill that had been plugged into a charger on the workbench to drill out the woodwork beside the doorknob, and picked up a crowbar. She knew that alarm systems usually had batteries that would give them enough power to work if the electricity was cut, so she was prepared for some noise. She pushed the door open and stepped into the house.

The frantic electronic beeping came from the speaker of the keyboard on the wall unit beside the front door, so she followed the sound and used her crowbar to pry the unit off the wall, disconnected the wires in the back, and restored the silence. She knew the system would be automatically dialing its internal modem to register the break-in, but the phone line was cut, so the call would never connect.

Jane stepped farther into the house. As she moved from room to room, she formed a sense of the place. It was designed and furnished for parties. There was a bar, lots of stylish, uncomfortable furniture and paintings with bold, stark lines in colors matched to the color scheme of each room — splashes of bright reds and yellows near the main entrance, calming down to sky blue and white near the beach side.

There was nothing homelike here. She stepped from room to room, searching for anything that would indicate that Christine had been living here, but there was nothing of Christine's. All the clothes in the closets were male. There were no toiletries of the sort that only women used. Jane looked farther into the house for hidden spaces. There was no locked door anywhere, and she paced a couple of interior rooms to be sure there wasn't any space between them that could be wide enough for a secret room.

She opened a closed door on the upper hall and found herself in a bright white room full of new baby furniture, baby clothes, toys, and equipment, but no sign that any of it had ever been used. Most of it was still in its original packaging. The crib mattress was still in a thick plastic wrapper.

Jane began another, more melancholy examination of the house. She searched for discoloration that might be an indication of the removal of blood from any of the floors, carpets, or furniture. She compulsively sighted along the walls and took down five paintings, trying to find a spot where blood might have hit a wall and trickled down behind a frame, or a spackle spot covering a hole where a bullet had entered the plaster.

Then she stopped and simply looked. The thought she had been evading was in the front of her mind now — that Christine was dead. It was more than a remote possibility. It was likely. Richard Beale was apparently the sort of man who would hunt his ex-girlfriend down and force her back to him. There had always been the chance that what he wanted was not to reconcile, but to be sure she retained nothing that could threaten his future — the baby, certainly, and also her knowledge of the particulars of his business, her memory of things he had done that would get him into trouble if they were revealed.

If he wanted her dead, he wouldn't necessarily have her killed in some distant city. The police there would try to identify her body and start trying to find out where she had lived and who she had worked for. But if he got Christine all the way back here, where he could take his time and control everything, he would be able to make her vanish. He had the whole Pacific Ocean at his back door.

Jane walked out the kitchen door to the garage, and then out the side door to the yard and back down to the beach. She reached the hard, wet sand at the edge, and began to jog. There were two young women in bathing suits a hundred yards down the beach. They had spread blankets on the sand and now they chatted while their two toddlers were busy digging with plastic shovels. As Jane passed, they diverted little of their attention from their children to notice her. It occurred to Jane that in a year or so, a young mother and child on the beach could be Christine and her baby, if they were alive.

For fifteen years, Jane had been telling her runners, "I'm not interested in helping you get revenge. If that's what you want, then go get it. But if you want to run, I'll teach you." But this time was going to be different. If Richard Beale had hunted Christine down, brought her and her baby back here and killed them, Jane would make sure he died, too.

28

As Jane drove along the coast highway and up over the hill to the freeway, she reminded herself that she had still found nothing that would prove Beale had caught Christine. It was still possible that something else had happened. Christine had spoken with Sharon on the telephone. Maybe she had called another friend, someone her own age. Christine might very well have gone to visit the friend and still be there. The fact that Christine's car was missing didn't necessarily mean the four kidnappers had taken it away from her. She could just as easily have driven it somewhere and still be using it.

Jane dialed the phone number of Christine's apartment in Minneapolis again and let it ring until the voice mail came on. Then she hung up, called Express Jet, and booked a flight to Santa Barbara, then called a car rental agency. In four hours she was on the plane in a chestnut-colored wig, feeling glad that she wouldn't have to wear it for a long flight.

When she reached Santa Barbara, she picked up a white Chrysler 300 at the rental agency and drove it northward on Highway 101. She checked into a hotel in Lompoc before she called the prison. She requested permission for Delia Monahan to visit Robert Monahan again on Saturday. When she called back to find out whether the visit had been approved, the official she was transferred to said she could come again at the same time as before.

She left for the prison an hour earlier than she had last time, stopped at various spots along the route, and studied every vehicle she saw, looking for any sign that Beale's crew was watching the road. When she reached the parking lot, she drove up and down the aisles, looking for the dark-haired woman who had followed her on the last trip. Then Jane drove another circuit looking for anyone at all who was waiting in a car, anything on a dashboard that could be a camera, or any other sign that the lot was under surveillance. She parked and made her way to the prison entrance to begin the long process of getting admitted to the visiting room.

The wait was not as long this time, possibly because she had shown up earlier than her appointment, or possibly because she had been here before and not caused any uneasiness among the guards. When the officer called Delia Monahan, she stood and followed him to the visiting room.

She could see the anxious look on Robert Monahan's face, and realized what it was. He was sitting on his side of the long counter expecting to hear that his new grandchild had been born. He stood up and held out his arms.

Jane gave him a brief hug to reassure the Visiting Room Officer that she was Delia, and that she had nothing in her hands that she was trying to slip to Monahan. They sat down and she said, "How have you been?"

"Not so hot, but it hasn't got anything to do with my daughter. Tell me about Chris and the baby."

Jane sighed. "You've got to stay calm and pretend that what I'm going to say isn't shocking. Can you?"

Monahan nodded.

"I went to stay with Christine a few days ago, and when I got to the apartment where I had left her, she wasn't there. Her car was gone and there were no signs of a struggle, but she'd been gone for a long time."

"How long?"

"The only one who had expected to see her was her doctor, and she hasn't been in for her checkups in a month. I think she may have been gone about three weeks."

"You said her car was gone. Could she have just driven it somewhere?"

Jane placed her hand on his forearm and looked into his eyes. "Believe me, I want that to be what happened. I just don't think it is."

"Why not? How can you know?"

"Last time I came to see you, a woman followed me away from the prison and up the road. I managed to lose her on the way through Lompoc, but each of us got a good close look at the other. I'm pretty sure she's one of the six people that Richard Beale hired to find Christine. There was no other reason for anyone to know who I was or that I was coming here. And there's certainly no other reason for anyone to follow me, except to find Christine."

Robert Monahan frowned. "I don't understand what you're saying."

"The woman wasn't here this morning when I got here, and neither were any of the others. Three months ago she was here, but today there's nobody here waiting for Christine or me to show up."

"Isn't that a good thing?"

"The only reason I can think of that they aren't here now is that they've already found her."

"Maybe you're wrong. Maybe they've just decided they've done all they could do here, so they're looking somewhere else. They've been here and talked to me, and maybe that persuaded them that coming here was a lost cause."

"Who talked to you?"

"Richard Beale's father. His name is Andy."

"When?"

"Not too long after you were here. He made a special request to the warden's office to be allowed in. They asked me if I would be willing to see him, and I figured, why not?"

"What did he tell you?"

"A lot. That Richard missed her and wanted to marry her. He said Richard had a ring with a three-carat diamond and all that. He wanted me to tell Christine I thought she should go back."

"You haven't had any chance to tell her that, have you?"

"No," he said. "I made it pretty clear that if she's hiding, I didn't expect that she would be visiting me here any time soon.

Maybe that was all it was. Maybe they waited for a month or so to be sure I was telling the truth, then went away and stayed away."

"I hope you're right," said Jane. "I hope they decided the whole enterprise was futile or too dangerous for them. After all, this place is filled with law-enforcement people, and the city cops are probably ready for trouble, too. Maybe they thought that even if they saw her they wouldn't be able to kidnap her here."

Robert Monahan leaned forward to study her. "Do you think my daughter is dead?"

"I hope she isn't," said Jane. "I think the people Richard Beale hired were supposed to bring her back to San Diego. I think that Beale wanted her — and the baby, if it was born by then — brought to him. I don't know anything about him beyond that. I know that Christine got lonely at one point. She made at least one phone call to a woman she knew in San Diego after I told her to stop communicating with anyone from the past. It's possible that the people Beale hired to find her were monitoring some of Christine's old friends and picked something up, or she left a message and they broke in and replayed it, or got the passwords and were routinely calling in to hear the messages. That's the kind of thing that professional chasers do — cops, and private detectives, too, if they think they can get away with it."

"You're telling me you think she made some little mistake like that? Some slipup and it killed her?" He knew there was no way for her to answer, so he looked down and put his head in his hands. "Jesus."

Jane said, "Tell me about Andy Beale."

"He's about sixty. He's big, and he looks as though he did some physical work in his time. Kind of tough-looking, but well dressed. When he talks he watches you for a reaction, and I get the impression that he's prepared to say whatever will give him the best one. He told me the things he knew would make me likely to want to please him — that he and his son had Chris's best interests at heart and that all Richard wanted was a chance to be a loving husband to her. But if he thought it would be more useful to say Richard was a kangaroo he would have said that instead."

"What did you tell him about Christine?"

"Nothing he didn't know already. That she didn't want to go back with Richard and that she wasn't likely to come here, either. You hadn't told me anything else."

"Right." She sat still for a moment, trying

to decide how to say the next part. "It's possible that when I leave here I'm going to find the four of them waiting outside to follow me to Christine. If so, I'll be very happy and I'll take them on quite a trip. But I honestly don't have much hope that's what's going to happen."

"I understand," he said.

"When I find out why Christine wasn't where I expected and what happened after that, I'll try to get word to you." She stood.

"Be careful," he said.

"Don't worry. I'll try very hard not to put her in danger."

"Or you," he said. "If anything happened to you, I wouldn't know where to start looking. All I've got is the address and number of your P.O. box in my memory."

She gave Robert Monahan a hug, then caught the Visiting Room Officer's eye and followed him to the door.

When Jane was outside the building, she walked slowly, scanning the lot. It was a hot, late-summer morning, and the sunlight glinted from every shiny surface of every car, and the distant parts of the lot melted into mirage lakes wavering in the glare. There was not a head in any car window to pay attention to her. As she approached her rental car, she was already sure that nobody was waiting. Wherever Christine was, Richard Beale was no longer curious about her.

29

Andy Beale's twenty-acre estate in Rancho
Santa Fe was in the tax rolls, but not in the
lists of holdings that were being offered for
sale, rental, or lease. It stood out in the tax
payments list, not only because it was
especially big and expensive, but because
no notation indicated what it was. At first
Jane thought it must be a parcel that was
being subdivided. She had seen lots of these
tracts in California — groups of little man-
sions, forty or fifty homes that looked like
miniature Tuscan villas. Every street was a
cul-de-sac, and the houses were all built
from the same three or four sets of plans, so
there was an illusion of variation. But then
she happened to see an internal memo
about a bid on a building site. It directed
that a copy be sent to Andrew Beale at the
Rancho Santa Fe address. It looked to her
as though it must be company property,
held ostensibly as an investment, but really

an expensive residence for the company's owner.

She looked at road maps to determine exactly where the house was, and then after lunch she drove out to see it. The landscapes of California were oddly familiar, like places in dreams. Every film, every television series, every commercial was filmed in some part of Southern California. People from the east like Jane came for the first time and stepped into places that had already been established in their memories. Rancho Santa Fe looked like landscapes in old movies. The road from the freeway began on a two-lane new black asphalt trail that ran among stunted live oaks and native brush. She had already learned that California roads like this always led to places where rich people lived — Malibu, Montecito, Hope Ranch, Rancho Santa Fe. It took millions to have a big house anywhere in Southern California, but to keep broad margins of land untouched around the whole community required people with great fortunes who were determined to maintain their exclusivity and quiet.

She began to see large rectangles of grassy land with the high white wooden rail fences that were the sure sign of horses, and then the horses themselves, smooth chestnut and brown bodies far off in grassy paddocks. It was hard to see any of the houses. In most cases only the mouths of the long driveways that led to them were visible — really no more than a gap in the trees with an iron gate across it, or a place where a long, unchanging wall suddenly fell back a few feet.

When Jane came upon the central square of the community, it was a mild surprise. There was a rustic post office, a brick structure that might be another public building, a couple of restaurants of the sort that were too good to post their names or even concede that they were restaurants. They simply looked like elegant residences built with broad entrances and tables in their gardens. Jane followed her map away from the square and up a long road with tall hedges on the left side and more oak trees and dry grass on the right.

When she reached the house it seemed to be nothing but a mailbox, two gaps in the tall hedge — one the size of a door and the other wide enough for a car — and, as she passed the bigger opening, a glimpse of brick pavement, a six-car garage, and the high, dark shadow of a house looming to the left of it. All she could tell about the building was that the main part was three stories tall and there were two one-story wings. Then she was past it, and the hedge was opaque. Down the road the hedge ended, and there was a long expanse of wall that seemed to belong to the next estate, which looked even bigger. There were other driveways farther along, and long stretches between them.

About two miles farther on, she turned around and drove back. This time she came at a slow, steady pace, looking for practical features — places where a car could be driven off the road and left without attracting any attention, barriers that might prevent a person from walking from property to property. She kept her window open and listened for the barking of dogs, the distant sounds of mowers or tractors that might give her an idea of the sizes of the estates.

She had memorized the way here from the freeway, but she kept checking her mirror so she would see what each landmark would look like if she came this way again. That was one of the tricks her father had taught her when she was very little. They would wander in the big state parks to the southeast of Deganawida, and he would let her lead the way back. He taught her that finding her way out of the woods was more important than finding her way in. He said that some people got lost because they never turned around to see what things were going to look like the next time they saw them.

When Jane returned to the freeway she kept going until she was back in Encinitas, in Sharon Curtis's neighborhood. She went to a sporting goods store and bought a racing bicycle with very narrow tires, a black helmet, and a tire pump. At a hardware store she bought a can of black spray paint. She put her bicycle, still in the carton, into the back of her SUV, drove it to Sharon's house, and carried it into the garage.

She took it out of its carton and completed the assembly and adjustments so it fit her perfectly. Then she took it to the back yard, set it on its carton, and spray painted all of its shiny parts a dull black. When the paint dried she sprayed Teflon lubricant on all the moving parts, rode the bicycle around the block once, and loaded it into the back of the SUV.

Jane went into Sharon's house, made a sandwich and ate it, set the alarm clock for midnight, and slept until it woke her. She dressed in black jeans, a black pullover, a black nylon windbreaker and gloves. She drove back toward Rancho Santa Fe. At this hour, the traffic was fast and sparse, so she got on the freeway and didn't have to touch her brakes again until the exit for Solana Beach. She drove until she found her way to the North Coast Repertory Theatre on Lomas Santa Fe Drive, parked her vehicle behind it, and rode off on her bicycle. She got off the main road quickly, rode in darkness up County Road S8 for three miles, turned onto Paseo Delicias, then La Gracia, and then La Flecha. There were no street-lamps on her route, and the roads were nearly empty.

Now and then Jane would hear a car coming along the road far behind her, and she would pull off the road into the entrance of a driveway or behind the end of a fence, dismount, and stay low and motionless. The car's lights would appear, and then the car disappeared around a curve or over a hill. The people in the cars were all on their way home now, probably from restaurants or shows or parties. Somewhere ahead where she couldn't see them, they probably turned off into one or another of the nearly hidden driveways and closed their gates.

The trip was just over four miles. Jane rode at an average speed of around twenty miles an hour, working her way up the gears when she had a downgrade to pick up more speed. She couldn't read street signs well in the dark, but she had memorized the curves of the roads and the distinctive landmarks.

Then she was there, beside the two openings in the tall hedge. She rode to the end of the hedge where the next estate began, lifted her bicycle over the low wall, and leaned it against the inner side so she could reach over and get it again, then swung her legs over the wall, took off her helmet and left it with the bicycle. She walked away from the road into the trees. Jane had no doubt that there would be surveillance cameras somewhere inside the Beale property trained on the two gates set into the hedge, but the Beales wouldn't have anything like that aimed into the neighbor's yard.

She moved patiently, stopping beside tree trunks to look and listen, then moving to the next spot she had chosen before she stopped again. The sun would not be up until a bit after five, and if she was on the road by four-thirty, she would be virtually invisible. She had four hours.

When she was at least a hundred feet from the road, she altered her course to the left, toward the Beale estate. She kept the move gradual, still stepping from one piece of cover to the next. She couldn't see anything on the Beale property. It seemed to be simply a great blackness, a place where seeing ended. She moved toward it.

There was another wall, this one at least ten feet high. She touched its rough surface. It seemed to be cinder block covered over with stucco so the surface would be even and featureless. When she stood beneath it and looked up, she could make out a slight irregularity near the top, as though there were bricks up there laid at an angle.

She walked along the wall for twenty paces looking for a way over, or even a handhold. It was not beyond imagining that there might be a gate. Neighbors didn't have to be strangers. Sometimes they built gates. At forty paces she gave up the idea of a gate. She looked the other way. She was now far enough from the road so she could see the front of the neighbor's house. Could there be a ladder somewhere? Even a long board would do, or a rope. She could have brought a rope. Why hadn't she realized this might happen?

As she walked on, Jane noticed one tree on her side of the wall seemed much thicker and nearer to the wall than some of the others. There was a thick limb that extended almost to the top of the wall. She quickly climbed the tree to the place where the limb branched away from the trunk.

She crawled out on it, listening and feeling for some warning that the limb wasn't strong enough to hold her. She could see over the wall into the Beale estate now. It occurred to her that she could simply sit here on the safe side of the wall and watch and listen. She could see the shape of the house from here. It looked huge. In the center part of the house the side wall facing Jane seemed to be all glass. There were sliding doors at ground level and big panes starting on the frame above them, and then a framework above that, so the room was three stories high. There were small, dim, bluish lights low on the walls of the gigantic room, like the safety lights in movie theaters. At the second-floor level, a walkway lit by the same bluish lights stretched across the room. On either end of the room the high part of the house extended thirty or forty feet, then dropped so the two wings were single-story extensions.

Her eye followed the wings, and she saw something that excited her. On the right wing, the back of the house, really, there were four windows with bars on them. She crawled out farther, clinging to the limb, and swung her feet to the top of the wall, eased herself forward for balance, and let go. She had no idea whether she would find anything on the far side of the wall that would get her back up here if she went in, but she knew she had to go. Caution was insanity now. Jane turned around and lowered herself until she was hanging from the top of the wall by both hands, then dropped. Her feet hit a layer of pine needles, and she rolled to break her fall.

She lay on the ground and looked around her for a way out. If this was where Beale was keeping Christine, then she would have to get her out, too. By now she would either have had the baby or be about as pregnant as a woman could be. Neither condition seemed good for wall climbing. Jane was in a small pine woods. She could see that on the ground, resting on the deep layer of pine needles, was a tree about fifteen feet long that had fallen some time ago. The boughs that stuck out from the trunk at intervals of a foot or so had only a few dry, brittle needles clinging to them.

She used her pocketknife to carve off the boughs on one side of the trunk, then lifted the lighter end of it and propped it on the rim of the wall. The remaining boughs made the trunk roll to keep the bare side up. The protruding stubs from the boughs were like rungs of a ladder.

Jane began to advance through the woods toward the house. She stepped almost to the edge of the trees and studied the buildings. To her left was the long back wall of the six-car garage. Directly ahead was the main house, and close to it on the right was a pool house.

Adjusting her course, she put the pool house directly in front of her to shield her from the main house. She crossed the lawn to the pool house and looked in through the arched doorway. She saw a counter with a kitchen sink, a wooden table and chairs, a bathroom with two showers, presumably for washing the chlorine off after swimming, and another archway leading to the pool. She moved past the arch, skirted the iron fence around the pool, and made her way up to the first of the barred windows.

Over each window was an iron grate like a flat cage, a single piece bolted to the house. She knew that was an arrangement that had been popular in the forties and fifties, but it had become rare — maybe against building codes — in recent years because it prevented an occupant from getting out in a fire. She stepped back and stared at the house. A lot of modernist architecture was far older than it looked. This place could easily have been built in the thirties, and the bars could simply be relics.

But to Jane the bars looked like a sign of

malicious intent. The old word *otgont* came to her. It meant more than simple evil. Witches — people who secretly had the power to cause disease and death — were *otgont.* It was potence, but it was also corruption, an unnatural degeneration from within.

She moved to the farthest window. In all the rooms in the wing the lights were off, so she had to peer in and strain her eyes to make out shapes. This one held an empty double bed, a dresser, a closet. The entrance to the bathroom was on her left. The small, high window in there had bars across it, too. She moved to the next window. The room was nearly the same, unoccupied but furnished. Jane kept moving along the side of the house until she reached the big room at the center. She stood perfectly still outside the glass wall and stared into the room. First there was a moving shadow, and then a figure appeared on the walkway above the room. There was a woman in a bathrobe and slippers moving sleepily from one set of rooms toward the other. She stopped and turned her head, as though she had to force herself to look down.

30

Ruby Beale saw the woman beyond the glass. She gave an involuntary shudder-jump, as all the muscles in her body tightened. It seemed to squeeze the scream out of her, so loud and high-pitched that she frightened herself, and her body dropped her into a crouch on the walkway. She involuntarily tried to curl up and be smaller as she stared down at the figure beyond the glass wall.

The woman was outside the glass, standing there without moving, her hands at her sides. She was all in black, and her hair was black, and Ruby couldn't make out her face with the moonlight behind her. She stood there staring at Ruby.

There were sounds of heavy, hurried footsteps on both ends of the hallway, and on her hands and knees, Ruby could feel the vibrations from the running men through the floor, and it scared her even more. Lights came on. It felt as though the walkway would be shaken loose. She looked back in the direction of her bedroom, and saw Andy running toward her in his pajamas, with a gun in his hand. From the other direction came Pete Tilton and Claudia Marshall, and both of them were carrying guns, too. The sight of so many guns did nothing to calm Ruby. Everyone was running, and all the guns seemed to be held in front of them and pointed downward, which was where she was.

They all converged and stood over her yelling at once. Andy was gasping, "Are you all right? What's the matter?" and other variations on the same theme, while the others were shouting, "What is it? What did you see?" Ruby looked over the edge of the walkway at the glass again.

The woman in black pivoted. Her silhouette was the same from the back, only the face was gone, and she walked into the dark in the garden. "There!" Ruby shrieked, and managed to point her finger. But the woman had dissolved into the night shadows.

Ruby said, "It's a woman — tall, thin, long black hair, dressed in black. She's out there."

"Sybil?" said Claudia Marshall.

"What?" It was Sybil Landreau, who had

come out of another room on the top floor.

Claudia turned to see her standing behind her. "It just sounded like you."

"I was asleep."

Ruby was agitated. "It wasn't her. I would have said 'Sybil,' not 'a woman.'"

Jane was running. She knew they would come out after her, and that what she had to outrun was the light. The only sounds in the darkness were the balls of her feet pounding the lawn and her lungs taking in deep breaths as she sprinted. As she approached the place where the grass melted into the stand of pine trees at the end of the property, she heard the sliding of one of the glass doors at the side of the building where she had been standing. She knew they had done the right thing — they had gotten someone outside in the dark who would now get into firing position — but she knew that the tactic would give her an extra five or six seconds at a full sprint. She ran hard, counting the seconds. She dashed past the first few pine trees and threw herself down.

The bright floodlights came on, an explosion of eye-searing glare, but she could see that two of them were outside holding pistols in two-handed stance, turning their bodies as they scanned the back yard for a target. After a few seconds one waved to the other and they turned away from each other to move along the two wings of the house and then continue around toward the front.

Jane knew that this was either her chance to get up and run for the wall, or their way of inducing her to try. She guessed it was a fake, and lay still. A second later they both spun and aimed their weapons down the lawn toward her. She could see beyond the glare of the floodlights mounted along the eaves of the house that there were two people half-hidden beside the sliding doors, staring out at the gardens, trying to act as spotters.

Jane stayed low and moved toward the left, away from the long featureless wall of the garage. She was almost sure that was where they would go to wait for her, thinking she must have come by car and needed to make it over the gate in the hedge to the street.

She found her pine tree lying at the foot of the wall, propped it up so she could climb it to the top, then pushed it back down so it would fall sideways. Then she dropped to the other side. She hurried to the road, lifted her bicycle over the low wall to the street, put on her helmet, mounted, and pedaled hard. She built up considerable speed before she passed the opening in the hedge where the gate was. The only sounds were the whisper of wind in her ears and a slight hiss of her tires on the pavement.

She kept going hard, building her speed as she went. By the time she had traveled two hundred yards, she judged she must be going at least forty miles an hour. Jane knew she probably couldn't go faster than that on this road until the first downgrade. But she was sure it hardly mattered. The people who were hunting for her had not seen her leave or heard a car engine, so they would assume she was still there.

Jane heard a new sound. It was the throaty, burbling sound of a motorcycle engine starting. She had underestimated the hunters. She couldn't outrun a motorcycle, but her bicycle still gave her advantages. It was silent. She could pull off and hide while the motorcycle went past, or find a path that was off the road and try to avoid roads entirely. In a couple of seconds the engine sound rose to a whine, and then a roar as the motorcycle came after her.

She could hear it gaining easily on her and saw the pavement ahead of her begin to glow from its distant headlight. Jane saw a street sign ahead, and she pedaled harder for it, then veered to the right and took the turn around the corner as fast as she dared and drifted almost to the left side of the road. She came upon a grove of stunted oaks, so she steered off the road into it, avoiding the trunks and raised roots until she could coast while she swung her leg over the seat and began to run with the bicycle. When she stopped her momentum fifty feet from the road, she dropped her bicycle in some high weeds and lay beside it.

She heard the motorcycle roar into the intersection, and looked in that direction, not raising her head, but staring through the weeds. There was the bright single headlight, the yellow motorcycle. Its helmeted rider was hunched forward over the handlebars, his legs bent so he held the motorcycle in a knock-kneed crouch. He had lost her, or maybe never caught sight of her, and just come this way because he knew she would be going in the direction of the freeway and the coast, not inland.

His single headlight turned in Jane's direction, and she ducked her head deep in the weeds, but he surged forward toward her hiding place only about thirty feet before he swung around, heading back into the intersection. He turned his motorcycle to the right so his light shone on the stretch of road he had been on before he'd turned, then rode a few feet up to the left, but didn't seem to see anything that way either. He came back along the road toward Jane. This time he seemed to have decided she couldn't have gone down either of the other stretches of road. He came along slowly, and as he approached, Jane saw the trees above her hiding place begin to glow brighter with his headlight.

The engine throttled back, so it was almost at idle again. Suddenly it grew much louder, and the motorcycle came off the road, over the shoulder, and into the grove, heading directly for Jane. She crawled behind a tree and stood, taking off her jacket. She pressed her body to the trunk of the tree, listening to the engine of the motorcycle and watching the beam of the headlight bouncing up and down on the leaves and upper branches of the oak trees around her.

She listened closely and watched the trees brighten more and more, and then stepped away from the trunk to face him. The man on the motorcycle was thirty feet away, moving toward her. As soon as he saw her he sped up, as though he intended to run her down. As he came toward her, Jane took two steps in one direction and then the other, as though she were transfixed, unable to decide what to do.

The motorcycle roared toward her, but she stepped aside at the last second and flung her jacket over his head and across his face. The motorcycle seemed to jerk as he tried to brake, then tried to turn it and lay it down. The motorcycle went ten feet past Jane into the trunk of an oak tree. The man was thrown over it, half-turned in the air, and hit the tree beyond it.

The motorcycle was still running, lying on the ground in front of the tree with its light on and the rear wheel still spinning and the engine roaring. Jane knelt there for a second and turned it off, then approached the injured man cautiously.

He was conscious, and Jane saw him try to move his right arm toward his jacket pocket, realize from the pain and immobility that it was broken, then try to reach across his body with his left. She saw the gun before he could get a grip on it, kicked his ribs, and snatched it out of his pocket. She held it to his head.

"You have one chance, and it's right now. What's your name?"

"Pete Tilton."

That was one of the names Christine had told her, so she accepted it. "Is Christine in that house?"

"No."

"Is she all right?"

"I'm not. I'm really hurt bad. Just call an ambulance and go. Nobody will come after you for this if you'll help." He tried to raise his head as though he wanted to sit up but couldn't.

"Is Christine dead?"

He moved convulsively, trying to catch Jane's legs in a side-kick and bring her down where he might be able to wrest the gun away with his left hand. Jane stepped backward and fired.

"What was that?" asked Ruby Beale.

"Probably nothing. A backfire," Andy Beale said.

"I haven't heard a backfire in twenty years."

On the couch in the great room, Andy Beale had his arm around Ruby. He said, "Sometimes, when people are under a lot of stress, it gets into their dreams. They can wake up enough to walk around, and still be dreaming."

Ruby took two deep breaths and blew them out through her nose. "It wasn't a dream, Andy. I saw her. And if you had just looked right away when I pointed, you would have seen her for yourself."

He spoke very gently. "You saw me order Pete and Steve and the girls to go out there to look around, and so far nobody has found any sign of her. They're all still at it, but as the time goes by, the chance gets slimmer. You know, sometimes — I'm not saying this is one of those times — we see things with our heads instead of our eyes."

She turned her whole body to face him. "Just what are you getting at?"

"There's no such thing as a ghost, Ruby."

"So. You did see her."

"No, I didn't."

"What do you think is crazier — to see something and admit it, or see it and tell yourself you couldn't have, so you didn't?"

Andy Beale thought for a moment, then shrugged. "When you're at that level, who cares? Take your pick."

She stood up and went to the elevator. "Sometimes you're a real jackass, you know?" She punched the button and the doors closed.

Andy Beale heard it going up to the third level, where the master suite was. He knew that it was probably his job to follow her up there and make a convincing apology for being insensitive. That was just another way of saying he was a jackass, and it only applied after the fact when she wasn't mad anymore. He knew what was required of him, but tonight he couldn't bring himself to do it just yet.

31

Jane was back in Sharon's house taking a shower by one-thirty A.M. She knew it was a good idea to wash thoroughly after discharging a firearm into a person, but that was all she allowed herself to think for the moment. It was not until she had finished the shower and was soaking in Sharon's tub that she allowed herself to turn her attention to what she had done to the man on the motorcycle.

The first conclusion she reached was that she didn't especially regret killing him. She had needed to do the same thing to other people several times in the past. Right after college, when she had started making the hunted disappear, it had not occurred to her that she would ever kill anyone. She was only going to help people who were in danger run away. It had been a simple, logical proposition for her. Saving a life could never be wrong.

But after she had helped a number of victims begin new lives, she began to realize that some time, one of the enemies would find his way to her. On the day it happened, she had not made a slow, reasoned decision to kill. Instead she had acted instinctively in a second, and then recognized that this, too, had been part of her original decision. The moment she invented the profession of preventing murderers from getting to their victims, she had already made it inevitable that one of them would try to kill her. Her only choice would be to die or kill him. The first time, and every time after that, she had chosen to kill.

Tonight Jane's feelings were complicated. She was tired, but she was also acutely aware that time was passing. From the day when she had arrived in Minneapolis and found Christine's apartment abandoned, she had been racing to find her. She had to keep trying every way she could, and to press every advantage. Tonight she had a slight advantage, and if she used it in time, it might cause some anxiety and confusion.

Jane dressed and went out into the night. She took with her the telephone number from Richard Beale's personnel file, and drove to Kearny Mesa. She stopped at a brightly lighted supermarket on Balboa. The pay phone was on the wall outside under the front window. She put in a few coins and dialed.

"Yeah?"

"Richard Beale?"

There was a brief, breathless silence, then "That's right. Who's this?"

"I'm not surprised you're awake. I suppose your parents called you."

"Who is this?"

"You know who it is, and you know I'm not going to tell you a name, so stop asking." Jane kept her eyes moving from the street to the supermarket parking lot. "The man who came after me tonight — Pete Tilton, right? — is dead. I want you to know I can do the same to the three you have left, to anyone else you hire, and to you. Tell me what happened to Christine."

"I don't know anybody named Christine."

"Tonight I told your friend he had one chance to answer, but he decided not to take it. This is your chance. Be sure you take it."

"You can't call people up and threaten them."

"Is Christine alive?"

"I don't know her."

"Good night, Richard. I'll see you very soon."

The telephone went dead. Richard Beale stood with the receiver in his hand until it began to make clicking noises and he remembered to press *End.* Had she been trying to trick him into saying something incriminating on a telephone and record it? What was she doing?

Demming had said the woman who had helped Christine was crazy. Crazy people weren't interested in going to court. A person who drove toward another car on a dark highway, perfectly willing to crash into it, was not anybody Richard Beale knew how to interpret. He was used to people who wanted something comprehensible, like collecting next week's paycheck.

Demming was just going to have to kill her. He should have already. It was part of the package. Demming's only purpose was to solve problems. Whatever the hell that woman was talking about with Pete Tilton, it didn't sound good. She certainly wasn't a problem Richard could tolerate.

Richard picked up his car keys from his dresser, looked at himself in the full-length mirror and ran his hand through his hair, then stepped to the doorway and reached for the light switch, but he thought better of it. If he came back an hour from now, he didn't want to walk into the bedroom and find that crazy bitch waiting for him in the dark.

He went downstairs to the kitchen and stopped at the new security door into the garage. He turned on the garage light, peered through the peephole, and made sure the garage was safe before he entered.

Richard got into his black Porsche, locked the doors, started the engine and shifted to reverse before he pressed the garage door opener. As the door rolled upward, he was already turned around in his seat, checking to be sure she wasn't in the driveway waiting for him. As soon as the door was up far enough for the Porsche's roof to clear it, he backed out quickly, pressed the button to close the garage, and drove off.

He had already told his mother he was on his way to the house in Rancho Santa Fe, or he might very well have changed his mind about going out there right now. The disturbance there and the phone call could easily be some sort of scheme to lure him out alone in the middle of the night. There was absolutely no doubt now that the woman was the one who had broken into his house. It wasn't just some coincidence that a burglar had chosen to hit the place today.

A simple thief was an impersonal threat, and had more reason to fear Richard than

Richard had to fear him. But a madwoman was a different thing entirely. Facing a woman who didn't care if she got killed was like facing somebody who was already dead. It made the hair on the back of Richard's neck stand up.

He turned off the freeway at Solana Beach and headed inland. The Porsche was made for this kind of drive, a winding road that was deserted at this time of night, where there were few lights or stop signs. Within minutes he was gliding up the road that led to his parents' house, and then he saw flashing lights far ahead — yellow and blue, but also some red ones that made the grayish leaves of the oak trees look as though they were on fire.

Richard slowed down in increments, downshifting until he was crawling along. Now he could make out cop cars and an ambulance, and people walking around on foot with flashlights. They were grouped around the last intersection before his parents' house, only about half a mile from it. More uniformed men and women were walking around in a stand of oak trees. The cars' headlights and the movable floodlights were trained to throw a steady glow of white light into the grove. The back doors of the ambulance were open, but the paramedics didn't seem to be in a rush.

Richard coasted past with his foot disengaging the clutch, partly to keep from drawing too much attention to himself. He saw Pete Tilton's bright yellow motorcycle lying in the brush under the trees. And not far from it he could see what looked like a sheet over a lump about the size of a man's body. It had to be Pete. Richard lifted his foot to release the clutch and gave the car a little gas, then shifted to second.

Farther on, he could see lights glowing through the hedge. He hoped the cops didn't wonder why everyone at the Beale house was up at this hour, but he supposed whatever had happened to Pete had been noisy. He picked up the other remote control while he was still many yards away, and held his thumb on the button so that when he turned in he didn't have to wait for the gate to open.

He parked in the middle of the paved area, got out of his car, trotted to the front door of the house, and touched the knob, but the door was locked. He took out his keys again and opened it, then froze. Across the foyer, Steve Demming and Sybil Landreau were leaning into the entrance to the great room, each showing only an eye, an arm, and a gun. As soon as they saw Richard they lowered their weapons, and Demming hurried to Richard and locked the dead bolt.

"Sorry for that," he said. "It sounded like your Porsche, but we had to be sure who was driving it."

"It's okay," Richard said. "I just drove by a bunch of cops looking over Pete's motorcycle in the woods down by the corner. It looked like a body beside it. What happened?"

Sybil Landreau said, "We don't —"

At that moment Claudia Marshall stepped out of the great room. "Oh my God," she wailed. "Pete, too?" She dissolved into sobs. Sybil glared at Richard as though he were to blame, put her arm around Claudia, and ushered her up the stairway.

"What's going on? Where are my parents?"

Demming said, "A while ago your mother got up and saw that woman who hid Christine."

"Saw her? Here?"

"She was outside the glass doors along the side wall of the house." Demming pointed. "At first we figured your mother had been dreaming. She said she saw this woman all in black, who kind of dissolved into the darkness. Of course we went to check it out and see if anybody was out there. We couldn't find anything, but Pete figured it was possible that she had been here and gotten away on foot. He figured if he went out on his motorcycle, he might be able to catch her before she got to her car."

"I guess he did," Richard said. "She says she shot him."

"She says?"

"I just talked to her. I was throwing on some clothes to come here and the phone rang. She called to tell me she'd shot him."

"Why?"

"She said she asked him where Christine was and he didn't tell her."

"Shit."

"She asked me, too."

Demming looked at him closely, as though he were wondering whether Richard understood what he had just said. "Did she say she was going to kill you, too?"

"Not in those words, but I guess so. And all of you."

"There! See?" Claudia Marshall was up on the first landing of the staircase. "We've got ourselves stuck in the brain of a psycho. You think she's going to try to find Christine for a while and then give up and go away?"

Demming shrugged. "You're probably right. Maybe we could arrange to make a trade."

552

"What?" Richard was confused.

"Claudia? What do you think? You're about the right height. We could get you the right wig, and we've already got Christine's clothes. This woman was probably with her when she bought them, and she'll recognize them as Christine's."

Richard said, "You think you can pass off Claudia as Christine?"

"Not forever. Just long enough to get Claudia close to her. Then Claudia puts her out of our misery."

"I'm in," said Claudia.

"We don't even have a plan," said Demming. "Don't sign on to be the bait until we at least have a plan."

"We'll think of something," Claudia said. "I really want to be the one who pops her. I'd like to be close enough when I do it to see the surprise on her face."

"Richard." The three all turned their heads to see Andy Beale standing beneath the arch into the great room. He was dressed now, wearing a pair of blue jeans that were stiff and dark-colored as though they had just come off the rack, a green flannel shirt, and walking shoes. To Richard, his father looked the way he used to look when they went to the mountain lakes for a week or two during the summers. It was a happy memory, because the lakes in the Sierras had all been too small to be choppy, and his parents had paid attention to him intermittently.

"I'll be right there," Richard called. He turned to Demming. "What are you going to do now?"

"We can't do much until the cops get Pete's body out of the woods and finish looking for evidence. I don't think that woman will be back before then. That means tomorrow night, I think."

Andy Beale called, "Take your time, Richard."

Richard hurried into the great room after him. Andy Beale sat down beside his wife on a couch along the wall beside the massive stone fireplace. All that stone and mortar shielded the couch from any shot fired from outside. Richard had to take the only seat left, a large leather armchair that he hoped made him hard to see from a distance. He was alarmed at the way his mother looked. The usual healthy plumpness of her face seemed to have been deflated. She was pale and her eyes were red, as though she had been crying.

"You okay, Mom?"

Andy Beale said, "It's not our favorite way to spend a night, but we plan to live

554

through it."

"You okay, Mom?" Richard repeated.

"I suppose so," she said. "It was a bit of a shock to look down and see her looking up at me in the middle of the night." She glanced at her husband. "Some people didn't think I really saw her. But your friend Mr. Tilton found her real enough."

"Yeah," Richard said. "I talked to her afterward. She called me up."

"She did?" Richard's mother seemed more interested in him than she had been in years.

"She wants Christine. She said that she asked Pete where she is, and he wouldn't tell her."

"Oh, my God," said Ruby Beale. "She keeps shooting people until somebody tells?"

"We don't know that," said Andy. "She wants Christine. She isn't after the baby. She doesn't even know we have him."

"Well," Richard said, "Steve says she won't be back tonight. She'll be scared of all the cops down the street. I guess I'll probably sleep here."

Andy said, "Tonight, anyway."

"What do you mean?"

"I think this will be our last night here, your mother and me. Tomorrow morning

I'll be in the office to take a look at the list of places the company has on the market and pick out a house."

"That makes sense," Richard conceded.

"Glad you think so. You'll be in charge of getting us packed up tomorrow and moved the next day. I'll want the trucks to arrive at eight in the morning the day after tomorrow. When it happens I'll need to have what's left of your little gang following the trucks from a distance to be sure that woman doesn't show up and go right along with us."

"Good idea," Richard said. "They might even get a chance to spot her and take care of her right then."

"Maybe," Andy Beale said. "But that's not why I'm doing it. This is chess. I'm moving your mother and little Robert out of any exposure to danger. That woman has found this house, so we'll castle. This square isn't any good to us anymore. I'd advise you to find a new place, too."

"I can move in with you until this is over."

"No, you can't."

"What do you mean?" Richard was shocked. "It'll make us all safer if we stick together and protect each other."

Andy Beale sighed. It was late, and he looked old and tired. "There are several reasons. One is that you've got to be out moving around accomplishing things, and that might attract her attention. I want this house emptied, cleaned, painted, and prepped for sale as soon as possible, and that means getting the crews lined up. I want the business running smoothly and I want it protected. Get some real security on the office and other key places, not just a few unarmed night watchmen. That's enough for now."

Richard was listening carefully. When his father stopped talking, he realized that he had been sitting there with his mouth open. He looked at his mother and saw that her eyes were wet. She looked away from him. He said, "You said this is chess. You're offering to sacrifice a piece, aren't you?"

"I never said that," said his father.

"But that's what you're doing. You're putting me in the open, where this psychotic woman will concentrate on me and leave you alone."

Andy Beale seemed to be weighing the idea, as though he hadn't thought of it before. Then he raised his head and met Richard's eyes. "Well, I suppose that's one way to look at it. An adult male usually takes whatever risks there are as a matter of course, and keeps his wife and babies and elderly parents safe. That's always been the way human societies have done things. But I suppose you probably have a new way."

"Suddenly you're old and weak, to be protected. Ten seconds ago you were ordering me around like a general."

"Right. And I will again. The other thing about this plan, Richard, is that it places responsibility for solving the problem on the person who caused the problem. That's you. All of this nonsense that we're trying to live through right now is because you were idiot enough to hire an underage girl and screw her until she got pregnant, but not man enough to keep her, even though she had no place to go and no money but what you were paying her. It seems to me that at the age of thirty-eight you can hardly expect your mother and father to get you out of this and risk the life of our grandson to protect you." He paused. "Now, is any of that unfair?"

"You know it is!" Richard caught himself and tried to control the volume of his voice. "It leaves out the real reason why any of this happened. It's that you two wanted a grandchild. It had to be this one, and no other. I could have had a half dozen other children if you could just have waited a couple of years. But no, it had to be Christine's baby."

This time Ruby spoke, her hand clutching Andy's arm to keep him quiet. "We did wait a year or two. Then we waited another year or two. We've been waiting for a grandchild since you were twenty-two years old. Sixteen years. Robert is the only chance we ever expect to have, and we're running out of time. It had to happen while we've got enough left in us to raise him, too."

Richard's shock had been growing, and now he realized he had forgotten to blink his eyes. He blinked them five times, and it made them water. "You're not behaving like he's my son. It's him instead of me. You're making him my replacement, aren't you?"

Andy said, "Isn't that what's supposed to happen? A man works in a business, has a child, and when the child grows up, the man steps aside and retires. It's natural, like the seasons or something. When you were old enough, I made you president of my company, and to the extent that I dared, I stepped aside. When Robert is ready, it's going to be his turn. Now we're going to bed. Be sure somebody with a gun keeps his eyes open so we live until morning."

He stood, and Ruby got up from the couch, too. They walked to the elevator and Ruby pressed the button. The doors opened, the two stepped inside, and the doors closed. Neither of them said anything more to Richard.

Richard walked to the couch and sat there for a few minutes, as though if he could see what they had been able to see, maybe he would understand. But he was too restless. He got up and walked to the stairs.

Demming sat on the staircase that led up to the walkway between the two wings of the house. The architect had apparently decided that the walkway with its Plexiglas sides and its hidden supports and the glass wall created enough of an illusion of openness. The staircase where Demming sat was hemmed in by chest-high walls with railings on them.

"What are you doing here?" Richard asked.

"Somebody's got to be awake, and the girls were tired. If that woman is crazy enough to break in tonight, the place she'll want to go is upstairs where everybody's sleeping. There are only two ways in, and I can control them both from here." He waited. "How about you? Going to bed?"

"Not yet. I wanted to talk to you."

"Something new?"

"Weren't you talking about a way to go out and get this woman, and not just sit here and hope you can shoot her in my parents' house?"

"That's a last resort. It's better to know where someone is going to be than to know where she is."

"You know she's going to come here?"

"You bet. This is where she thinks we're keeping everything she wants."

"She's winning, isn't she?"

"What?" Demming laughed. "Hardly."

"Come on," Richard said. "She's got us under siege. You're afraid to go outside. That's why you won't go look for her."

Demming took a deep breath, then let it out. "When we started, there were six of us to do the looking. We're down to three — two of them women, at that. Just be patient."

"Be patient so she can come and take her shot?"

"Sometimes you have to win in a way you didn't choose. It feels just as good. Look, I know you're under pressure. I was sitting here while your parents were talking. I heard."

"Be ready," Richard said. "I may have no other choice. If we can't solve this problem they really will cut me out of everything. I'll be out in the cold. I can't let that happen."

"Andy, and then Ruby, right?"

"Right. Him, then her, and then the baby."

32

Jane watched the trucks arrive at the Beale house in Rancho Santa Fe. There was no moving van, and there were no long trailers. These were four white, squared-off trucks with roll-down cargo doors and hydraulic lifts on the back, the kind used for delivering furniture or appliances.

At six A.M. Jane had parked her SUV far up the road beyond the Beale house and walked back inside the property lines and away from the road, then climbed another oak tree near the back fence so she could see the house clearly. The trucks arrived much earlier than she had expected. They were small enough to pass through the front gate and park in a row in front of the big garage, then back up to the house for loading.

Jane watched the doors and windows, until she was sure that none of the people she had seen at the house on her first trip were here. Then she turned her attention to the things that were being carried from the house.

Jane could tell from the start that this was not like any other moving day she had seen. It was more like the striking of the set of a play. Each truck held six men. They jumped down and went to work with the kind of relentless efficiency that meant there were no watchful customers around to see them. There was little wrapping or concern for breakage. They quickly hauled a lot of furniture out to the first truck, loaded it tightly, and closed its rear door. Then two men drove it away. The other four stayed, joining their comrades in packing cardboard cartons inside the house and moving them out to the next truck, where two men stood on the truck bed to stack them from floor to ceiling from the cab to the rear door. The two rolled down the door and locked it, then drove the truck off while the second group of four stayed to keep packing and loading. The men worked with the fevered concentration of thieves. They loaded one truck at a time, then sent it off and backed the next one to the door.

Finally she saw one of the items she had been waiting for, a large white wooden crib. The men didn't dismantle it or even remove the mattress. Two of them simply carried it out and set it on the truck bed, then went back for more. Jane saw a changing table, a stroller, a big toy box, another box that seemed to hold brightly colored decorations, possibly a mobile.

Jane climbed down from the limb where she had been sitting and walked to the SUV, then drove toward the freeway. She passed the Beale house and saw the next truck was filling up rapidly because of the excess of laborers, so she drove ahead and waited in a mall parking lot near the freeway entrance.

About ten minutes later one of the white trucks passed her parking lot and rolled up the ramp onto the freeway. Jane waited for thirty seconds, then went after it. She drove hard until she could see the truck, then dropped far back and merely watched for it to take an exit.

She followed the truck until it entered the front gate of a real estate development called Florentine Ranch. She could see from outside the tall fence that it was full of large new homes, all of them vaguely Mediterranean with tile roofs and white stucco sides. Each of them was placed on a lot so small that the sides of the houses shaded each other in the morning sun. She parked her car down the road a distance where there was a second gate that had no gate-house. She waited until a resident of the community coasted to the exit, opened the gate with a remote control, and drove out. As soon as the car passed she stepped inside.

It took her only a few minutes to find the right house. The first truck to arrive was leaving now, and the second was pulling up to the front to unload. As she walked along she studied the place. Its primary function as protection consisted of being different from the house in Rancho Santa Fe. It was the sort of place that only someone who had never broken into a house would think was safe.

She walked back to the gate where she had entered, found the button mounted on the wall for pedestrians to open the gate, pressed it, and walked out. As she drove back to Sharon's house she thought about the ways into the Beales' new home. There were two skylights on the roof that she could probably open, at least three windows on the sides of the house that she could unlock with a length of wire looped at the end, a set of French doors with very small panes of glass. She could tape one, break it without making much noise, reach in and turn the knob. There were certainly other ways she would discover if she came closer.

Jane went to a pay phone on a large plaza a few miles away from the development, and called Richard Beale's cell phone.

When he answered, she said, "Hello, Richard. It's me again. I've been to see your parents' new house."

"New house? What new house?"

"2952 Mona Lisa Terrace. It's a little cramped and kind of boxy. Not like the last one. I liked all that glass."

"I'll bet," he said. "This one will be a little harder for you, won't it?"

"Everything is good for me. The big one was better for looking, but this one is better for visiting. Nobody will see me until I'm inside."

"What do you want?"

"You know," said Jane. "I want Christine."

"You said that before. Why are you calling now?"

"I sensed that I wasn't really giving you your chance before. I called before you had time to find out that Derrick J. Smith really was dead. Did you know that was Pete Tilton's real name all along — Derrick J. Smith? It was in the paper."

"I don't know who you're talking about."

"Enough," said Jane. "I'm going to say it this time as clearly as I can. You and your employees kidnapped Christine. Until I have her, I'll keep doing whatever it takes to get her and her baby. I want to make sure you understand what I just said — whatever it takes. There are no limits, and I will never give up. When I leave, either she'll be with me, or every one of you will be dead."

Richard Beale's throat was so dry he couldn't swallow. His chest felt empty, as though it had been opened and everything had been scooped out of it. He didn't want to speak because he knew she would detect fear in his voice.

"Do you have anything to tell me, Richard? Last chance."

"Wait!" He held his breath. It took him a few seconds to get over the shock of what he had just done. He hadn't intended to say it, but he couldn't bear to let her hang up. He couldn't tell from her voice whether she really could kill him, but after listening to her he knew absolutely that she intended to try.

"I'm waiting, but not much longer."

"We can do this," he said. "We can solve it, make a deal."

She said, "There is nothing in the world that you can offer me except Christine and her baby. In exchange, I'll give you absolutely nothing. Does that sound like a deal?"

"Yes."

"Then I'm listening," she said.

"I want my life. That's all I'm asking for. You take Christine and the baby, and you leave me alone. Let me go on like it never happened."

"Tell me where she is, and when I have her I'm gone."

"Tonight. I'll bring her to the house my parents just moved out of, in Rancho Santa Fe. Let's say midnight. You call this number, and I'll release her."

"Why midnight? Why not right now, in daylight?"

"She's not here. She's in a resort hotel in Mexico, and it'll take hours to have somebody go down, pick her up, and bring her back."

"What about her baby?"

"The baby will be with her," he said.

"All right," she said. "If I see anyone there besides you, Christine, and the baby, it's off. If I see a weapon I open fire."

"How do I know I can trust you?"

"You wanted a deal. This is the deal. Still want it?"

"Yes."

Jane hung up. He was lying, of course. She drove back to Florentine Ranch, the gated community where she had seen the trucks unloading. After about an hour, she saw the first of the trucks returning to the new house where they had just brought the furniture. Richard must be moving his parents again, to a third house. That confirmed what she had suspected from the start. Richard was not assuming that Jane, Christine, and the baby would be leaving San Diego tonight. He was preparing for the possibility that Jane would still be nearby, alive and angry.

Jane waited for the rest of the trucks to arrive and begin loading up again, then followed the first truck as it left the gated enclave. It drove north all the way to San Juan Capistrano and up a long road to a new street that led to the summit of a hill. Jane waited for a few minutes, then drove up after them. She found the white truck being unloaded into a two-story stucco house. She memorized the address, then turned her SUV around and drove the way she had come. All the way back to the freeway she studied the route, because she knew that the next time she came here, it would be in the dark.

33

As Richard Beale spoke to his father on the telephone he paced from one end of his living room to the other. "You don't have to stay in San Juan Capistrano for long. I just need to have you and Mom and Robert out of here and safe until I'm sure this is over. You don't want that crazy woman climbing in your window some night, do you?"

Andy Beale said, "We're going to do what you ask this time, Richard. One more time we'll do things your way. But this had better solve the problem for good."

"You sound as though this is a big deal. I've already had them move your belongings out there. I don't know what difference it makes whether you're in Capistrano or San Diego."

He could hear his father's breaths coming out of his nose in snorts. "I worked a lifetime so nobody in this family would ever have to worry about money. Now I get to have some peace and do what I want for a few years before I die. I spent a lot of money on my boat, and I like taking it out on the ocean. It isn't saving the damn world or curing the clap, but I like it. If I'm in Capistrano, getting to the harbor and back takes two extra hours."

"Just put up with it for a few days, and then this will be over. Do something besides going out in the boat."

"How can you even be sure she found the other house?"

"She told me the address, and what she said made it clear she had been there to look it over."

"I thought your little gang was going to watch the move to be sure that couldn't happen."

"It's just one of those things. Steve was up all night, and the girls were up until at least four, and the movers got started early. By the time Steve and the girls were there, the first three trucks had already loaded and left. This time it will be safe."

"How the fuck do you know?"

"She was on the phone with me, and the second I hung up I called the moving people to go back out and move everything up to the Capistrano house. That way she won't know where you're staying."

Andy Beale sounded suspicious. "And you immediately thought of San Juan Capistrano, did you? It was the first place that came into your mind. You're not just moving me way up there so I can't keep an eye on what you're doing in the office, are you?"

"Jesus, Dad. Of course not." It was one of several reasons why Richard had chosen the Capistrano house, and directed the moving trucks there without clearing it with his parents first. He had been busy for much of the past month moving money to his own accounts and changing the ownership of certain pieces of property to Richard Beale Enterprises. He had covered the transfers in the books by making them trades of land he held — most of it in the desert — for land the Beale Company held along the ocean. He had done nothing illicit with the Capistrano property, so his father wouldn't get any mail from the county addressed to Richard Beale. But he genuinely didn't want his father to be able to come into the office on a whim and start noticing things.

His father said, "Just make sure there's nothing going on there that I'm not going to like."

"There isn't. You act as though I just drive by there once in a while to pick up a paycheck. I'm in there all day every day,

Saturdays included, and a lot of Sundays. Everything that happens there is on my desk in five minutes. Now look, I'm sorry, but I've got to go. There's a lot to do by tonight." He pressed the button on his cell phone to disconnect.

Steve Demming looked at him with suppressed irritation. "Are you ready to pay attention to this now?"

"I'm sorry," said Richard. "I've got to be sure I have the two of them where they're supposed to be, doing what they're supposed to do."

"I suppose you do. But you launched this operation before we even got a chance to set anything up, let alone practice. And this has to be perfect, or it isn't going to work. You've got to be prepared for the possibility that it won't."

"How the hell do I prepare for that?"

"We've got a couple of things. You can't have a weapon on you, so weapons will already be on the premises for you. I've put two in the house and two outside. They're loaded and the safeties are off. If you need one, you pick it up and pull the trigger. You can do that, right?"

"Of course I can. Where are they?"

"One is under the hose reel."

"Hose reel?"

"You know. The thing attached to the house that you crank to reel in the hose. It's in the garden at the back of the house. You reach into the middle of the hose, grab it, and you're ready to fire."

"I hope you're not expecting me to be the one who shoots her."

Demming said, "I'm not expecting you to be the one who shoots her. I just want you to have a couple of options — ways to stay alive — if something goes wrong."

"Where did you hide the other guns?"

"One is in the pool house in the cabinet under the sink. If you have to run for cover, the pool house is a good place, and the gun will be there for you. Another is in the house, inside the coat closet by the front door. It's taped to the wall above the door. You reach up, pull it down, and fire. The last one is in the guest bathroom off the great room, taped behind the toilet tank."

Richard cupped his hands over his nose and mouth and took a few deep breaths into them.

"Is something wrong?" Demming asked. "Are you dizzy or something?"

"A little bit," Richard said. "I'll be okay in a minute." He would have liked to breathe into a paper bag and stave off an anxiety attack, but his hands seemed to be helping.

He sat down on the white overstuffed chair beside him, then let his hands fall to his lap.

Demming said, "Don't freak out about this, Richard. We're going to handle every possibility. You and Claudia will be close to her, but Sybil and I will have you two covered from a distance. If trouble happens, you'll head in one direction and Claudia will head in the other. The woman will be standing by herself and one of us will kill her. What's wrong now?"

"The whole thing is just so unreal," said Richard. "I keep thinking, 'How the hell did I get from where I started all the way to this point?' I'm a real estate executive. All of this is like a bad dream."

"Forget that kind of thinking, because it will paralyze you. You're not going to have to do much, but you'll have to do something. I can't get you out of meeting her, because that was what you offered. If you don't show up, she'll know it's an ambush."

"It wasn't as though I wanted to offer her that. I had to do something right then, right at that moment, and I remembered this was what you and Claudia had been planning. She was on the phone getting ready to hang up, and I knew I had one chance."

Sybil Landreau's tall, skinny shape appeared in the hallway. "She's all set."

Demming said, "Let's see."

Sybil held out her right hand, and a woman stepped out of the guest room. She was pretty and small featured. Her eyes had been made up with shadow and eyeliner to make them seem bigger, and her tinted contact lenses made her irises blue. Her hair was shoulder length and chestnut colored, and it had a tendency to fall over one eye when she cocked her head. Her lipstick had been brushed on to imitate Christine's full lips. She walked with small steps, and she wore a pair of sweatpants and a hoodie.

"Oh, my God," said Demming. "You look exactly like Christine. Exactly."

"Think so?" said Claudia.

"Absolutely. You're right on the money. Don't you think so, Richard?" Demming's forced smile begged for the right answer.

"Perfect," Richard said. He smiled, too. "I mean you were perfect before as yourself, Claudia, but this . . . This is something."

Sybil and Claudia went back into the guest room and closed the door.

"She doesn't look like Christine," Richard said. "She's short, but she's not the same body type as Christine. What are we doing? Why say she does, if she doesn't? She's ten years older, and Christine gained thirty-five pounds in the pregnancy, at least."

"She'll be wearing padding, and that'll make her look fat," said Demming. "The wig is a perfect match for Christine's hair. She's the same height as Christine, and with the makeup, she's fine. You've got to remember it will be midnight, and there will only be a sliver of moon tonight. Once she's out of the house it will be like walking around in the bottom of a well. If the woman gets close enough to see the difference, Claudia will be close enough to shoot her."

"Jesus, Steve. I don't know about this. I don't think we should make her think she'll fool anybody. It could make her take chances."

Demming put his arm around Richard's shoulder. "We don't have a choice. You're the one who talked to this woman, and we're locked into giving her a Christine. Claudia is our only possible Christine. All we can do is make her feel confident and back her up."

Sybil Landreau reappeared and stood a few feet off, waiting. When Demming saw her he nodded. "Now we've got some more things to do before dark. We'll see you later." He and Sybil went outside, and in a moment Richard heard Demming's car accelerating onto the coast road.

Richard sat on one of the living room

couches, leaning back with his face toward the ceiling and his eyes closed. He didn't want to succumb to the fear, the shortness of breath, the throbbing in his head that made him feel sick. He knew that he needed to rest now, before the long night.

He heard something quiet, a swish, a rustle, and smelled perfume a half-second before he felt the lips against his. He opened his eyes just as Claudia's face pulled back a few inches. Her hair was blond again, and her eyes were brown.

"A sweet kiss, but a little short," she said.

"Are you making a fool of me?" he asked.

"No. You'll have to do that yourself." She lowered her head again and kissed him deeply, lingering there and letting her tongue tickle his lips and then slip into his mouth. They kissed for a minute or two. He put his arms around her and noticed that she had changed her clothes, too. She was wearing a light sundress held up by two thin straps. He moved his hand along her spine and verified that there was nothing under the dress. She tugged it back down and sat up, then looked out the large back windows at the ocean and squinted. "It's so bright. Come to the bedroom."

He got up and followed Claudia into the hallway. When she turned toward the guest bedroom where she had changed, he gently placed his hands on her hips and steered her into the master suite. He turned around to close the door and lock it.

When he turned back, she was kneeling on the bed, pulling the dress off over her head. She met his eyes. "Sex calms the nerves. I knew I could get you to help me out, Richard. You're such a whore."

34

Jane stood in Sharon's kitchen and fought the impulse to call Carey. After a few seconds she defeated the urge. If she told him she was calling because she might not be alive in a few hours, what would that accomplish? If she wasn't up to dying without tormenting him, then she had become a different person in five years. The only way to increase her chances of survival was to concentrate on what she had to do.

She went into the bedroom and laid out her black clothes and her running shoes, then went back to the kitchen table, checked the pair of Beretta M92 pistols, and loaded the two fourteen-round magazines. She took a shower, scrubbed in the bathtub, and then showered again to be sure she had washed off any trace of makeup, shampoo, or deodorant. She was going to be moving in the dark tonight, and she wasn't going to let a scent betray her.

Dressed in her black clothes, she returned to the kitchen for the small backpack and packed the kit she had devised for the evening. She had a spool of fifty-pound test monofilament fishing line, her razor-sharp folding knife, and the small plastic container of grease paint. She had bought a cell phone under the name Helen DeLong, and that was the one she placed in her kit. She had bought a battery-operated baby monitor and receiver and two thick chains with heavy padlocks.

Jane took her kit, her guns, and her bicycle to the garage and loaded them into the SUV. She knew she needed a safer place to hide her vehicle this time, so she drove to a hotel on the road to Rancho Santa Fe, rented a room, and parked in the parking structure where her SUV would not be visible. Then she put on her pack, took her bicycle out and rode it to the estate bordering the Beale house where she had climbed the wall on her earlier visit. She walked her bicycle into the oak woods off the road, left it in a dry creek bed, and covered it with leaves and fallen branches, then walked toward the Beale estate.

She came onto the estate by climbing the tree and using the overhanging limb she had used earlier. Before moving on, she found her half-stripped sapling and made sure it was in place in case she needed a ladder to reach the top of the wall again.

Once she had moved through the pine woods at the back of the Beale land, she crawled to the edge of the lawn to study the buildings. There was no sign that anyone was waiting. It was only three in the afternoon, nine hours early, but Jane wasn't sure yet that she was alone. She needed to reach the house without being seen. After she had waited an hour without hearing a sound from the house or seeing anyone pass a window, she decided it was time to move.

She stepped quietly along the back of the big garage, skirting the open lawn, and then walked to the back of the pool house. She didn't want to go any farther and leave the pool house behind her without first being sure no one had chosen it as the place to wait in ambush. She stepped to the doorway and peered inside, then slipped in and opened cabinets and drawers. She stared through each of the windows to determine what parts of the house and yard could be seen from there. She was almost ready to leave, when she opened the cabinet under the sink in the bar and found a gun. It was a .45 Glock, loaded, with a round in the chamber and the safety off. She took out the magazine, cleared the round, buried the magazine in the flower bed beside the pool house, and then returned the gun to its hiding place.

When she reached the side of the house, she stepped along it until she found the electric meter and circuit breakers. She could see the wheel in the meter turning very slowly, as though the only things still drawing current were the electric displays on the built-in appliances.

She opened her pack, took out her roll of monofilament fishing line, tied it to the master power switch beside the circuit box, and then ran it around a bar in the iron fence surrounding the pool, and finally along the side of the main house to the garden. She tested the line once by tugging it to turn off the power to the house, then went back to the box and closed the switch again.

The next step was to find a good way into the house. She approached the sliding door to the main room. Through the glass she examined the latch that locked it to the doorframe. She jiggled the door on its track. It was an expensive, well-fitted door: It wouldn't move from side to side. She tried grasping the handle and lifting the door straight up, and found that she could lift it nearly an inch. The wheels that held it on its track could be raised or lowered by adjustment screws recessed on the inner side of the door, and it was clear to her that nobody had adjusted them for years, so they had gotten very loose.

What she needed now was something she could use as a pry bar. There was nothing in the garden, but she remembered seeing a barbecue set in one of the drawers below the counter in the pool house. She went back and selected a big butcher knife. She returned to the sliding door, knelt, and lifted it again, pushed the knife into the space beneath it and moved it until she found the spring-loaded wheel under the door. She used the blade to hold the wheel up, and pushed the door off its track. Then she slipped the blade into the space she'd created between the door and frame, and lifted the latch. She lifted the door to set the wheel back onto its track, put the knife into her pack, and stepped inside.

She explored the interior of the house. The moving crew had taken everything that could be removed. The bare floors and walls made her footsteps echo as she went from room to room. On the ground floor there was a row of bedroom suites with bathrooms between them, and then at the end of the long hallway she came to one room that had a damaged wall.

The plaster had been dug away in two places under the window, as though someone had tried to burrow through the wall. Jane went to the window and looked out, then realized what it was. The holes in the wall were almost exactly in the places where the bars over the window were anchored. Somebody had been trying to remove the bars from the inside. Jane looked more closely and saw scratches on the plaster that looked like knife marks. These weren't part of some remodeling project. There were no drill holes or chiseled spots. Someone had tried to dig out of here with a knife — Christine.

It was obvious that Richard Beale had no intention of setting Christine free. The damaged plaster reminded Jane of the possibility that Christine was already dead. She might even be buried somewhere on this estate. She had been missing from her apartment in Minneapolis for about a month, and the plot of land around this house was huge. A girl like Christine, still weak from giving birth, would have been easy enough to kill, and then she could have been buried deep in one of the flower beds where the soil was soft and moist and free of stones and roots. They could have buried her and then transplanted a few flats of poppies and petunias over her. These were rich people. They could have had a crew plant a full-grown tree, or even cover Christine's body with a new section of driveway.

If Christine was dead, Jane knew, she would probably never find the body. San Diego had the Pacific Ocean to the west, and hundreds of miles of lonely deserts and mountains to the east. But she had seen the movers carrying a crib and boxes of toys. They wouldn't do that unless the baby was alive.

The second time through the house, Jane counted steps and judged angles, looking out windows to determine what could be seen and what couldn't from each of them. She studied the great room without its furniture, trying to detect hiding places. First she checked the inside of the fireplace, but found no guns. Then she checked the guest bathroom just off the big room, and found the second pistol. She unloaded it and taped it where she'd found it. She went into the garage, noticed a rope and a light stepladder, carried them out to two sections of the wall around the property that she had never visited, and hid them. She suspected that she might have to go over the wall again, and she wanted as many ways up and out as possible. Jane turned on the battery-operated baby monitor, climbed the shelves to the top of one of the built-in bookcases in the big room, and placed it there.

She took advantage of the waning daylight to study every part of the place. All the time while she worked, she was listening for the sound of someone else arriving. There was sparse traffic on the road beyond the high hedges. Each time she heard a car approach, she listened for the noise of the front gate opening. But there were only the calls of the birds in the surrounding groves of trees and an occasional flutter of leaves from a sudden warm gust off the desert. Jane unlocked several windows and two service doors on the wings of the house so she would be able to come in and out at will.

When everything was done, Jane went upstairs into the master bedroom, where she could see the grounds through windows on three sides. As she studied the estate, she picked out the places where Steve Demming might set up a sniper's nest to kill her, and calculated the angles from the house to the places where she could find the ladder and rope she'd left near the wall. She saw the hiding places she would have to check for enemies, and the false hiding places where a person would be more vulnerable rather than less: the low hedges near the house that would obscure a person but would make noise and reveal movement.

She waited, looked, and listened while the sun went down and the house gradually sunk into darkness. When it was eleven o'clock, she stood and put on her backpack, then looked out the windows again before she left the master bedroom. She went down the stairs at the center of the building and then walked from room to room in the dark, testing her memory of the distances and spaces. Then she went out to the garage and made her way across the broad brick pavement to the garden planted beside the front gate to hide the machinery that opened it. She sat down behind a tree near the gate.

At eleven-thirty the front gate began to glide to the left on its track. A black Cadillac Escalade drove in and stopped on the brick pavement in front of the garage where it was closest to the front door of the house. It was where Jane had expected the vehicle to park, shielded from the line of fire on three sides — the house, the garage, and the front hedge. Jane watched from her hiding place by the gate as car doors opened, lights went on, and people emerged. The driver was a man whom she had seen in

New York. He had to be Demming. He was tall, had light hair, and an athletic body that had thickened a bit in middle age. He wore a short-sleeved polo shirt with a sport coat over it, presumably to hide a gun. He went to the front door, unlocked and opened it, and stood guard there while the second man joined him.

The second man was also tall. His hair was dark, and he had a handsome face, smooth and a bit boyish. He had to be Richard Beale. She could imagine Christine being attracted to him. He stood on the porch just in the doorway while Demming went inside, presumably to make sure Jane wasn't in there waiting. Beale looked increasingly uneasy as he waited for Demming to return. When he did, Beale stepped in.

Jane remained motionless and looked hard, waiting for the next two, who were sitting in the back seat. The left rear door opened and there was the one with black hair she had seen outside Lompoc prison. The woman got out, held the door, and waited for the other woman to get out, then grasped her arm and hurried her into the house.

For the few moments while the second woman was visible, Jane strained to see her clearly. Her height seemed to match Christine's. She looked about thirty pounds heavier than Christine had been when Jane had seen her, and that would be about right. The hair seemed to be the same style as Christine's. Was that exactly what it would look like four months later? The dress was one that Jane and Christine had picked out at the Mall of America in Minnesota. There wasn't enough time. In the few steps between the car and the house Jane couldn't tell if was Christine or it wasn't.

Jane waited until she saw a light go on in the big central room, then stepped to the front gate across the driveway, took out the padlock and chain she had brought, wrapped it around the gate and its post, and locked it shut. Then she kept going to the pedestrian gate nearby and locked that one, too. She moved around the garage toward the back yard, where she could see through the big glass wall into the lighted room.

The four people looked lost in the emptiness of the big room. They drifted around in it, like fish swimming the perimeter of a bare aquarium. Jane could see no weapons on any of them, but she assumed they were armed. She moved into position in the garden a dozen yards from the back of the house, turned on the baby monitor she had kept, and watched the people in the house react. They must have heard the click.

"What's that?"

"Do you hear that, too?"

"It sounds like static."

"Where's it coming from — the ceiling?"

Jane said, "It's me. I'm here. We're going to do this quickly. Christine?"

A man's voice jumped in right away to preempt anything the woman would say. "What do you want us to do?" Jane guessed that they had rehearsed this in advance, trying to make sure that Jane didn't hear the impostor's voice.

"Let Christine walk out the glass door at the back of the house and onto the lawn. The rest of you, stand in the center of the room and keep your hands above your heads."

She recognized Beale's voice from her telephone call. "What do we do?"

There was a whisper. "She can hear."

The woman who was supposed to be Christine walked to the sliding door.

"Wait." It was Demming's voice.

The woman didn't stop. She opened the sliding door and stepped into the darkness. She began to walk out into the yard away from the house. She stepped past the rock garden where Jane crouched and onto the lawn.

Jane switched the monitor off and the woman turned around and took a step toward her. "Stop there."

The woman moved her head from side to side, and Jane could tell the woman was trying to see her better. Jane crouched in the shadows a few yards from her. The light from the glass wall of the house was behind Jane and illuminated the woman's features.

Jane said, "You're Claudia Marshall, aren't you?"

"No. It's me — Christine. Don't you even recognize me?"

It was awful to hear her mimic Christine's voice. Jane could tell that the woman had heard Christine talk recently, probably a number of times. Jane said, "I want you to tell me what happened. Is Christine alive?"

"Sure I am." The woman stepped closer again, but she was drifting to Jane's left. Jane could see she was attempting to step out of the light and make Jane easier to see.

Jane said, "Stop."

Then everything around Jane seemed to be in motion. The woman wearing Christine's clothes lifted the dress and pulled out a pistol. She managed to raise it toward Jane before Jane shot her. The woman fell backward onto the grass, a red spot in the center of her chest.

Jane dived to her left away from the glass wall just as shots from inside shattered the pane behind her. Jane rolled once, turning her body to face the house, and fired six shots through the glass at the figures in the big, empty room. She saw Demming go down, but she wasn't sure whether he had been hit or simply dropped to deny her a target. Sybil Landreau swatted the switch by the front door to turn off the lights, and disappeared in the blackness.

Jane had spent the afternoon making decisions about what she was going to do, and she executed the moves that she had planned. She crawled a few feet toward the side of the house, picked up the fishing line, and jerked it so the power to the house was cut. Then she ran along the house to the first of the windows she had left unlatched. She turned on the battery-operated receiver for the baby monitor again.

The voices were stage whispers. "Don't worry. We'll find her, and then get you to the hospital."

"I'm shot through the thigh, Sybil. If I lie here, I'm going to bleed to death."

"Come on, Steve. Tie it off with your belt while we take care of this."

"At least help me move out of the center of the floor, so if she comes back I'll have a chance."

"You're not thinking clearly. You're right where you want to be. She'll think you're dead, and you'll shoot her."

"Listen, Sybil. I really need to go."

"Quiet. Both of you." This time it was Richard Beale's voice. Jane could hear him walking, each step like a hammer blow on the hardwood. There was a click, then another, and the click-click-click as he tried to turn on the outdoor floodlights. "Shit! She cut the power."

Jane switched off the monitor and left it beside the house while she pushed the window open. She used both hands to raise herself to the windowsill, then slithered inside onto the floor and closed the window. She could tell from the dimensions of the room that this was a bedroom. She remained where she was with her gun aimed at the door and waited. When she hadn't heard anything for a few minutes, she rose and stepped to the door. She crouched low and looked down the hallway toward the central room. She could make out the shape of Steve Demming on the floor. She saw no movement, but that meant nothing, because lying still was not only the strategy Sybil Landreau had urged him to follow, but it was also probably the best way to slow the bleeding from his thigh.

She waited, but still heard no movement in the hallway from Richard Beale or Sybil Landreau. She left the bedroom and moved along the wall toward the central room. She heard a click from somewhere behind her, turned toward it, and dropped to the floor.

The muzzle flash blinded her for a half-second and the report was incredibly loud in the bare hallway, but the shot went over her head and pounded into the wall. Jane fired a round at the flash, and then two others below it, but she didn't think she hit anything. The hallway was deserted. Sybil Landreau had fired and then ducked into the last room off the hall, the one with the bars on the window.

Jane made a quick decision. She pushed off the wall and sprinted up the hall toward the room. She dashed along the corridor as fast as she could, switching pistols as she ran. As she approached the final door, she extended her right arm ahead of her with her finger on the trigger.

She saw a faint sliver of moonlight appear on the floor of the dark hall, then widen. She stopped and went flat against the wall as the face of Sybil Landreau appeared.

Jane fired, but the face was pulled back. The door slammed, and Jane heard the lock bolt slide into its receptacle. Jane moved across the corridor to the other wall, took ten more steps quietly, and stopped just past the wooden door. The doorknob was on the right, the hinges on the left. Jane knew where Sybil Landreau would be standing at this instant. She would have her back to the wall, close to the hinge side of the door, waiting for Jane to kick it in.

Jane aimed her pistol two feet to the left of the door and about four feet up from the floor and fired three rapid shots into the wall. Then she moved a few feet to the end of the hall. There was no return fire, no sound of movement from inside the room. Jane waited for a minute, then two minutes. She took three steps, brought her right leg up, and gave the door a hard stomp-kick just below the doorknob.

The wood at the doorknob splintered, and the door flew open. Jane saw Sybil Landreau sitting beneath the window, and fired. Sybil Landreau dropped her weapon and toppled to the side, inhaling with a raspy whistle and exhaling with a bubbling sound, as though her lungs were filling with blood. Only then did Jane realize the woman had already been wounded by her shots through the wall. Jane stepped close and picked up the gun Sybil had dropped, then knelt over her. "Where's Christine?"

Sybil smiled, her eyes burning with a sudden intensity. "Dead."

"The baby?"

"Dead."

"Who killed her?"

"You did, bitch."

Jane stood and moved to the door, stepped out, and then closed the door behind her to keep the hallway dark. She still had one more person to hunt. She moved to the bedroom where she had entered the house, went back to the window, and looked out.

Richard Beale was still somewhere within the house and grounds, unhurt. The place where he could hide and control the most space that Jane might cross was out in the back yard, but she couldn't see him. Jane stayed where she was for a few minutes, staring out the window into the dark and carefully identifying each unmoving shape, but she saw no sign of him. She quietly stepped out into the hall again.

Jane silently approached the central room, but didn't go in. She knew that Demming had been lying there waiting for her to come within range of his gun. She came to the end of the hall and looked across the big room at him.

He was still lying in the center of the

empty hardwood floor with his gun in his right hand. But now the pool of blood beside his leg had grown. His left hand was holding the end of a belt tightened around his leg above the wound.

Staying back in the shadows, Jane leaned into the room to try to spot Richard Beale. She heard the sound of a car engine starting outside.

Jane hurried back the way she had come, climbed out the window quickly, and dashed across the back lawn and around the far end of the garage. She saw the big black Escalade, then made out Richard Beale in the front seat. She ran along the garage behind the vehicle toward the blind spot on the passenger side. When she reached the back of the vehicle, he suddenly threw the Escalade into reverse and backed it toward her.

She dived to the side as the Escalade slammed against the garage door, bumping it inward and breaking the vehicle's left taillight. Jane stayed low and moved forward on the vehicle's right side, but Richard lowered the side windows and fired several wild pistol shots in her direction. Jane could tell some of his shots hit the inside of the car, the frame. Others splintered the front door of the house and broke a window somewhere behind Jane, but none of them were low enough to hit her.

Richard Beale shifted into drive. He was clearly not interested in chasing her down right now. He simply wanted to leave this place. He jerked the vehicle forward toward the front gate. Jane could tell he was pressing the remote control and waiting for the gate to open for him. The backup battery allowed the motor to engage, move the gate an inch or two until the padlock stopped it, and then begin to retract. Richard would press the button again, and it would move, stop, and reverse over and over.

Richard stopped the vehicle in front of the gate, jumped down from the driver's seat, and ran to the iron barrier. He stood there, half-hidden by the bulk of the black Escalade, tugged on the padlock, aimed his gun at it and fired a round, tugged it again, then ran to the smaller pedestrian gate, and found it padlocked, too.

Beale climbed back into his SUV, put it into reverse so he could swing it around, then backed it into the gate. The iron gate gave a musical sound as the chain snapped and the gate's wheels jumped off their track, but it didn't open. Jane moved toward the vehicle in the dark. Richard got out, stepped on the front bumper, walked over the hood to the roof of the SUV, and prepared to jump over the gate to the street.

Jane moved into position in the bushes a few yards from his vehicle, where she had hidden earlier. "Where is she, Richard?"

He turned toward her voice, trying to make out her shape in the darkness. "Sybil shot her. It was an accident. She was trying to get away."

"Where's the baby?"

"It died when she did. This was all for nothing." He turned toward the gate again.

"Richard! Don't!"

He jumped from the roof of the SUV toward the pavement on the outside of the gate, and Jane fired two rounds. As he dropped, the muscles in his legs turned limp and unresisting. When he landed he collapsed and lay still beyond the gate.

Jane stepped to the small pedestrian gate, unlocked the padlock and took off the chain, slipped out to the street and knelt beside Richard. She felt his carotid artery, but could detect no pulse. She saw that the side of his head was wet, looked more closely, and realized that one of her shots had passed through his temple. She moved to his feet, bent and grasped his ankles, dragged him inside the gate, and left him hidden from the street by the tall hedge.

She looked back at the huge, dark house,

and began to move to the area near the glass door at the back of the house. Claudia Marshall was lying on her back as she had last seen her. Her eyes were fixed, gazing sightless up at the sky, and her mouth had fallen open.

Jane stepped to the glass door and looked into the big room. Steve Demming was in exactly the same position as he had been in before. She quietly slid the door open and stepped into the hallway. She made her way down the hall to the room where she had left Sybil Landreau. She pushed the door open and stood back, but there was no sound or movement. Sybil was still lying on her side near the wall. Jane stepped in and touched the woman's throat, trying to find a pulse, but she was dead, too. Jane closed the door again and went up the hallway.

As Jane was walking across the living room toward the sliding door, she heard a sound. She whirled and aimed her gun at the man on the floor. "You're alive."

"Help me," said Steve Demming. His voice was strained and weak, but she could hear him.

"Toss your gun so you can't reach it."

He flipped his wrist and the gun slid a dozen feet on the bare floor. "Help me."

"You need to help me first."

"Get an ambulance. There are no phones in the house."

She understood. He had brought no phone because if he had made or received a call, it would prove where he was while Jane was being killed. "Tell me about Christine."

"I can tell you where she is."

"Her body?"

"No. That day, when she tried to get away, this house was already set up like a damned hospital. The Beales had brought a doctor from Mexico to deliver the baby, and a nurse to take care of it. They were still here a week later. And Ruby Beale is a nurse, too — retired. After Sybil shot Christine, they were all over her in five seconds. She's alive."

35

It was already nearly ten in the morning. The sun was bright and hot enough to burn off the protective haze from the ocean. The drive to the Mexican border seemed longer than Jane had imagined it. To her, San Diego had always seemed to be right on the border. But the wealthy parts where she had been spending much of her time had their faces turned to the north. Mexico was present only in the Indian faces of the people who worked in the restaurants and stood at the bus stops. Now, as she drove south on Interstate 5 and then through National City, Chula Vista, and Palm City, she began to see signs advertising attractions in Mexico and brokers who sold Mexican auto insurance to tourists. She pulled off at Palm Avenue and bought a policy. She knew she would never file a claim, but if she was in an accident she didn't want to be detained while the Mexican police sorted things out. A few minutes after that she reached San Ysidro.

Jane took her place in one of the seven lanes of cars waiting to cross the border. She read all of the signs and watched the movement of the cars on both sides of her, trying to be patient and calm because patience and calm were the things that customs agents on every border looked for. Jane had no experience at the southern border, but like most people in western New York, she had crossed the Canadian border frequently. This morning she was dressed in clothes that would make her identical to the hordes of female American tourists crowding the border. She wore a pair of expensive blue jeans, a long-sleeved white blouse, running shoes that showed she was expecting to be doing some walking, big sunglasses, and a baseball cap. She had her Alexandra Crowell identification in a worn wallet at the top of her purse, ready to show the customs officers.

The cars ahead didn't seem to be moving at all, but one at a time the ones at the row of customs kiosks changed. The people inching forward to the kiosks didn't seem worried, but they probably weren't carrying guns and ammunition and ten different sets of bogus identification. When she was given the wave to pull forward she took her turn with the Mexican officers. One of them came to her window.

Jane kept her face relaxed and blank, but looked at him attentively. He glanced at her for less than a second before he waved her into Tijuana and turned his eyes toward the next car.

Jane moved ahead. It had taken over two hours to get through the jam and into Mexico. She wanted to get out of the vicinity of the border, where the traffic was thick, but the traffic came with her and stayed with her — mostly in front of her — down Avenida Revolución. Mexico was crowded. The sidewalks were moving streams of people. There were hundreds of small stores and stalls and people selling everything — trinkets, textiles, leather, food. People who were obviously Americans elbowed one another to get closer to displays of brightly painted wooden objects. There were nightclubs, bars, and hotels, and in front of many of them, stalls that seemed to represent all of the great profusion of objects that existed and could be sold by one person to another.

As she made it onto Boulevard Agua Caliente the traffic thinned, and she dared to lift her eyes from the road to look around her more often. But as the sense of crowding eased, she was shocked by the sight of the endless hills on both sides, covered with the small cottages and shacks of poor people, most of them probably squatters, since it was hard to imagine pieces of land being cut into such small parcels. They went as far as she could see, and beyond.

By the time she was away from the border, many of the cars had pulled away onto Route 10 along the ocean toward Rosarito and Ensenada, and she felt a bit less hemmed in. But being on this side of the border worried Jane. Everything was unfamiliar and took extra seconds to interpret. She had seen not only policemen in the area close to the border, but also small contingents of armed soldiers at various corners, watching the passing cars. She wasn't sure what to expect of them. The crowds of people everywhere — half of them Americans — made her feel a bit less worried about standing out. Her long black hair might make an eye passing over a crowd include her with the Mexicans, but she didn't speak Spanish, so the impression was only of value if she kept moving and didn't talk.

She knew she was going to have a difficult time finding the building she was searching for, a hard time getting in, and a hard time getting out. As she moved along Boulevard Agua Caliente, she began to see some of the things Steve Demming had told her to look for. There were whole blocks of pharmacies. People who were obviously Americans, most of them elderly, came in and out carrying large shopping bags. There was even a charter bus parked on a side street with its motor running.

Now she moved into the part of the district that she had been watching for. There were medical and dental offices in every space of each block. There were signs offering lap band surgery, tummy tucks, breast and buttock implants, collagen treatments, botox injections, face-lifts, liposuction. The larger buildings were all called *clinicas.* Most signs were in a sort of English that had an otherworldly quality, with words that were cognates, not translations. There were buildings devoted to medical care that were called "spas." And beside a business offering a jumble of unrelated but major kinds of surgery would be an office offering "painless dentistry" and teeth whitening.

Jane found the address in the center of this wilderness of medical and cosmetic marketplaces. The four-story stucco structure looked like an apartment building jammed between a pharmacy and another medical center, but it had balconies that opened onto a view of another stucco wall two feet away.

She drove past and then around the area for a few minutes before she found a parking space in a lot beside a large market. She went inside and used American dollars to buy a few snacks and some cans of Coca-Cola. She put them into her SUV and began to walk.

She thought about her conversation with Steve Demming. The address he had given her seemed to match his description of the building and the district. But she still wasn't positive that he had given up hope of killing her.

She had knelt beside him in the dark house. "Why should I believe you?"

He said, "Because I don't have anything to gain by lying now. I want to live."

She heard the siren in the distance. "The ambulance. One last thing."

"I know. If you find out I lied, or that I warned anyone that you were coming, you'll kill me."

"I hope you believe that."

"I do."

Jane walked along the street behind Agua Caliente listening and looking, trying to get a sense of everything that was happening

608

around her. She went past dental offices, other places specializing in *"salud familiar."* Every place advertised that its doctor was board certified and everything cost less than half the U.S. price.

It took her a few minutes to walk to the Clinica Médica de la Mujer. She walked past and made a quick assessment. It had a staircase off the small lobby, and an elevator. There was a pretty young woman in a lavender skirt, matching high heels, and a white lab coat sitting at a graceful writing desk at the back wall. Near her sat a man in a set of hospital scrubs, but he was behind a solid counter that looked like a security station.

Jane never slowed down, and didn't attract any attention to herself. She kept going from one building to the next, shopping at stalls and watching the changes in the traffic and the movement of pedestrians. She had coffee in a nearby restaurant where she could watch the building through the front window but remain an undifferentiated part of the crowd. When she finished she walked to where she had left her car and drove off.

She spent the hours until dark exploring the city in the SUV. She took the road to Otay Mesa, where there was another border crossing, and studied the traffic there. When she judged it was late enough, she drove back to the Clinica Médica de la Mujer.

At midnight Jane climbed up the ladder at the back of the darkened pharmacy to the roof. It rose above the second floor of the Clinica Médica de la Mujer. She stepped close to the first balcony on the second floor of the Clinica, jumped the few feet between them, and climbed over the railing onto the balcony. She looked in the sliding glass door, and she could see there was a woman asleep in the bed.

She tried the door, and found that it was open a crack. Someone had been enjoying the cooler night air. Jane pushed the window open and stepped inside. She saw a tray on the movable table near the bed, picked it up carefully so it wouldn't wake the sleeping woman, and took it with her as she stepped out into the hall. If people saw her, their own minds would supply the explanation. The hall was empty.

Demming had told her that Christine was on the fourth floor of the building. She set the tray on the floor and stepped into the staircase near the end. She climbed to the fourth floor, walked down the hall, and looked in each of the rooms. There were no patients in any of them. When she got to the end of the hall away from the balconies, she saw a room with a solid door with a small double-glazed, metal-webbed window. It looked like a room for some kind of physical therapy or diagnostic equipment. But what caught her eye was that a key hung on a nail beside the door.

Jane moved close and looked in the window. There was a bed, and a patient asleep in it. She took the key and used it to unlock the door, then put it back on the nail so it wouldn't be missed, and slipped inside. She moved past the bed, and she could tell from the shape of the lump under the covers that it was a woman. She opened the blinds to let a little moonlight into the room. It was Christine. Demming had told the truth.

Christine was sleeping soundly, lying on her back, but Jane could see her chest rising and falling in a too-slow rhythm. Jane noticed that there was a medical chart on a clipboard hanging beside the door. She wasn't sure what it said, but there seemed to be a list of drugs and doses. The only one she recognized was diazepam. Valium. They must be giving it to her to help her sleep.

Jane went to the bed and touched Christine's shoulder. She didn't move. Jane shook her gently, then patted her face, but she didn't react. Finally, Jane lifted her to a sitting position and whispered in her ear, "Christine. Christine. You've got to wake up. You've got to be alert now and talk to me. Wake up."

There was no change. Christine was still limp and unconscious. Jane eased Christine down on the bed.

Jane pulled back the covers, then untied the hospital gown at the back of the neck, and looked under it. A fresh, clean-looking bandage stretched across Christine's upper chest from her left shoulder to under the right arm. Jane covered her again. Maybe the other medications were for pain. Bullet wounds were painful and took a long time to heal.

Jane searched the room and then the rest of the floor, looking for equipment that might help her get Christine out. There was no wheelchair, but maybe that was a good sign. If Christine couldn't walk, this was going to be difficult. There didn't seem to be a walker or crutches, either. Then she returned to Christine's room and tried again to wake her. Jane was acutely aware that time was passing. The clock on the wall said 2:14.

She heard the elevator arrive on the fourth floor, a quiet, sliding sound as the doors rolled open. She couldn't hear footsteps, but she was sure the staff must wear rubber-soled shoes. She went into the small bathroom, opened the shower curtain, stepped into the bathtub, and listened. She was right next to the corridor wall, so she heard a scrape as the newcomer lifted the key off the nail. Jane heard a louder sound as the key slid into the lock and rattled a bit when the door proved to be unlocked.

Jane stayed still. The person opened the door, stepped in, and let it close. Jane heard squeaky footsteps on the polished floor as the person stepped to Christine's bed. The person moved the rheostat on the wall up so the lights began to glow dimly. It was a woman's voice. "Christina," she said loudly. "Christina, are you asleep?" She waited a few seconds, there was a rustling sound, and then the woman set something on the table by the door and then went out again.

Jane listened while the woman locked the door. When Jane heard the elevator move again, she came out of the bathroom and looked at what the nurse had left on the table. It was a small tray with a pitcher of water, a plastic cup, and a small cup containing four colored pills. Since Christine hadn't been able to take her medicine, maybe the nurse would return soon.

Jane searched the area around the bed for a telephone or intercom, then for a button to summon the nurse. If there had ever been anything like that, it had been removed. Jane went to the window to see what was visible on this side of the building.

"What are you doing?"

Jane spun and looked down. Christine's eyes were open, gleaming with reflected light from the window.

Jane stepped closer. "I'm glad to see you're alive. They told me at first you were dead."

Christine seemed to be trying to sit up, but she was too groggy. She raised her head. "Jane?"

Jane touched Christine's arm. "I'm here. I told you I'd do whatever it took. Talk to me. Try to wake up."

She blinked, tried to raise herself. Jane lifted her to a sitting position. "Sybil shot me." She started to say something else, but she couldn't keep from crying.

"Your baby was born, wasn't it?" Jane said. "Is it here?"

"He's still in San Diego with Richard's family. They took him away." She sobbed. "His name is Robert. He's beautiful."

"Okay. We have to get you out of here. Can you walk?"

"Yes. Not at first, but now I can. They've been keeping me pretty doped up with painkillers and things, but there's nothing wrong with my legs. I just feel so tired all the time."

"Drugs are a good way to keep you from running to the police, but they can't be expecting to keep you in this place forever."

"It's a *clinica mujer.* A woman's clinic. The doctor who delivered Robert, and saved me, is a surgeon. He owns this place. Sybil and Claudia told me he's got big connections. There's a red-light district, all whorehouses and strip clubs. That's where the head nurse said I'm going."

"She sounds like a real delight."

"She is. But I know it's real. The nurse who takes care of me told me the doctor does a lot of work for the prostitutes. They have to get checked for STDs once a month, and there are a lot of breast and butt implants, tummy tucks, abortions."

"Don't even think about that. Try to wake up."

"She said that after he's done some surgery to hide the bullet scars and maybe some breast implants I was going to one of the houses. She said if I was good I'd get to stay there."

"If you were *good?*"

"She said there were places that I wouldn't like as much. And they're a lot farther from the border and harder to find, and there aren't any rules."

"We've got to get you out of here. You said you could walk. Do you think you could run if you had to?"

"Some. Not fast."

"Are the drugs wearing off now?"

"When the nurse came in I was already faking a little bit. I've been trying to get off the painkillers and sleeping pills, cutting down whenever I can. About half the time I palm them and flush them later."

"Great. Have you checked the possible ways out of the building?"

"They've wheeled me down to the examining rooms a few times, and I've looked. There's always a guard downstairs in the lobby. He has a gun, and there's another guy who kind of wanders. The windows in here don't open, but they seem to everywhere else. I think the only way out of this room is when the nurse comes with my pills."

"When will that be?"

"I didn't take them yet, so she'll keep coming until I do."

"All right. I've got a car — a blue Ford SUV — parked just around the block from here. The trick is to get from here to that. I saw the guard downstairs. You said there was a second guard somewhere. Do you know where his post is?"

"I don't think he has one. He seems to go on rounds like a night watchman. I've seen him look in to be sure I was here, or come in to lift something for the nurses. He has a uniform like a cop, and a gun in a holster. The other guy is always at the desk, even late at night. I don't know how often they change shifts or anything like that."

"Are there other women here who are being held?"

"Not that I know of. Since I've been here I've been the only one on this floor. But there are three or four other rooms, and they all have locks on the doors."

They both heard the elevator arrive again and the doors open. Jane said, "I've got to be out of sight. Your job is to not swallow any medicine." She stepped into the bathroom and behind the shower curtain.

They both heard the key in the lock. Christine pretended to be asleep. The door opened, the same nurse came in.

The nurse turned and looked behind her, but nobody was there. The nurse seemed to have a jumpy late-night sensation that there was movement somewhere beyond the corner of her eye. She shook her head and stepped to Christine's bed. "Christina," she said. "Wake up." She shook Christine gently, got no response, and then clutched Christine's left shoulder near the bullet wound.

Christine jumped and opened her eyes. "Ow! Are you trying to hurt me?"

"I'm trying to wake you. Take your medicine." She went to the table, poured water into the plastic cup and held it out to Christine. Then she held out the cup of pills.

"All right," said Christine. "You can go. I can take these by now without you."

"No you can't. I won't let you. I have to be sure you get everything you're supposed to." She folded her arms and stared at Christine.

Christine took the pills in her hand, brought her hand to her mouth, and gulped water, then held the cup out to the nurse.

The nurse seemed to reach for the cup, but then changed the direction of her movement and snatched Christine's other hand, twisted it hard, and held it.

Christine said, "Ow! What are you doing? Are you crazy?"

The nurse pried Christine's fingers open and revealed the pills. She gave a smirk. "I don't seem to be crazy."

"I don't need all those pills anymore. I'm

not in that much pain."

The nurse smiled. "Good. I'll tell the doctor that you're just about ready for your bed in the whorehouse."

"You're disgusting."

The nurse slapped her once, then turned away from her, a small smile forming on her lips, until she saw a woman standing behind her. She jerked, then took a step backward. "You don't belong here. Get out."

"Nobody belongs here," said Jane. "Christine, it's got to be now."

Christine got out of the bed and stood unsteadily a few feet off.

Jane refilled Christine's cup from the water pitcher and said to the nurse, "Now take the pills." Jane opened her jacket to show her the handgrips of the gun protruding from her belt.

The nurse put the pills into her mouth, lifted the cup, then hesitated. Jane glared at her, and she swallowed. Jane grasped both her wrists and made her open her hands. "Now I need your uniform. Take it off and lie on the bed."

The nurse said, "What if I scream?"

"You'll only live to do it once. No second breath."

The nurse looked into Jane's eyes, then stepped out of the light blue scrubs she was wearing and lay on the bed. Jane opened a drawer of the bedside stand and took out some adhesive tape. She raised the sides of the bed and taped the nurse's wrists to the two sides. Then she took out some cotton pads from the drawer and stuffed them into the nurse's mouth and taped it.

Jane helped Christine put on the scrubs, and then pulled off the nurse's sneakers and gave them to Christine. Jane watched Christine sit in the chair, then put them on and stand up, and it made her worry. She seemed weak and tottering on her feet. "This might not be easy," Jane said. "I'm sorry, but you'll have to do the best you can."

"Just get me out of here."

The nurse was not able to speak, but she was watching them intently. Jane took the gun out of her pocket and held it up where she could see it. "Don't make noise for one hour."

The nurse nodded and turned her face away.

Jane stepped to the rheostat and turned off the light, covered the nurse with the sheet, and took Christine to the door. She looked out the small window into the corridor to be sure it was clear, then pulled Christine out, closed the door and locked it. She thought about hanging the key on the nail so things would look exactly as they had. Instead, she broke the key off in the lock, then took the house key from the ring for her SUV, put it on the ring for the room key, and hung it on the nail.

She led Christine along the hall. Then she heard the elevator move again. Someone must have pushed the button on a lower floor, and now the elevator was going down to them. Jane pulled Christine into the stairwell and closed the door. She helped her down the stairs to the third floor, but she heard the sound of the elevator doors again. Someone had arrived on the third floor. Jane opened the door just a crack so she could see the elevator.

The doors opened and another nurse came out, this one younger. The rooms were all arranged around the outer walls, with a nursing station in the center of the floor. The nurse walked down the corridor to the nursing station and sat down behind the counter with another young nurse who seemed to be doing some kind of paperwork.

Jane closed the door the rest of the way and leaned close to Christine. She whispered, "There's a patient's room on this floor that's right next to the roof of the pharmacy next door. That's the way out, but now there are nurses. They weren't here before."

Christine whispered, "It was after two-thirty when we left my room. I don't know why they'd show up now. Maybe they kept somebody in the recovery room for a long time, then moved her here. What do we do now?"

"Go back up." Jane took her back up the stairs to the fourth floor, then went into an unoccupied room and looked out the window. "See? We're right above the room I wanted."

"What do you mean?"

"We don't have much choice. We've got to climb out this window and lower ourselves down."

"How?"

"Go to the next room and bring the sheets from the bed."

Christine went out, and Jane stripped the sheets from the two beds in the room. When she finished, Christine came back with another set. "Six sheets. We can roll them instead of tying the corners." Jane rolled each of the sheets and then tied them together. She looked up and saw Christine frowning. "What's the matter?"

"I'm not going to be good at climbing."

"That's the beauty of it. We're going down, not up. I'll tie you in and lower you."

"But what if —"

"No what-ifs. Either way you'll get down. All we're doing is slowing the trip." Jane folded the last sheet and wrapped it around Christine's body so the pressure was spread evenly. "Here's what you do. You go out the window and turn around to face me. Put your feet out and walk your way down. When you get to the third floor, push hard off the wall with your feet. When you swing out, I'll give you slack and you'll land on the roof of the pharmacy. Got the theory?"

"Yes."

"Then make it work."

"Jane, before I go, I want to say —"

"From here on, no sound."

She tied the loose end of the rope of sheets to the bed frame, tugged it tight, pushed the bed to the wall, and opened the window above it. She helped Christine climb from the bed to the windowsill, and then turn to go out on her belly. She had a pained expression on her face, which Jane hoped was only fear. Jane let her down slowly for a dozen feet, then looked over the edge at her. Christine still had her feet against the wall, and she was looking up expectantly, so Jane let her down at a steady

623

rate, the muscles in her back and legs straining. When Christine seemed to be barely above the level of the pharmacy roof, Jane waved.

Christine bent her knees and pushed off from the wall. When Jane could see she had swung out above the pharmacy roof, she let out most of the remaining sheet quickly, and Christine landed on her feet. She waved, then stepped out of the sling Jane had tied.

Jane climbed to the windowsill. As she turned to rappel down, she saw a man's face appear in the little window on the door to the hallway. Someone must have seen Christine descend past the third-floor window and called security. Jane let the sheet slide through her hands, going downward as quickly as she could. She felt something tugging on the upper end. He was untying her. She was still ten feet above the roof of the pharmacy, but she pushed off the wall to swing outward. As soon as she felt her momentum slow she let go.

A half-second later, the rope of bedsheets came free at the fourth-floor window. As Jane dropped to the pharmacy roof, the long white rope snaked down like a streamer and fell to the ground between the two buildings. Jane picked herself up. "Go."

"Where?"

"Over here." She pulled her to the edge of the roof. "See? That's the ladder. Grasp the two sides with both hands, then lower your feet to the first rung. Get down as fast as you can."

Jane looked up at the window, but the man was gone. She looked at Christine and saw she was making her way down tentatively, right foot down a rung, then the left foot to the same rung, then right foot down again. Jane could see she was having a hard time keeping her left hand from letting go.

Jane heard running feet coming along the street side of the pharmacy, then rounding the corner. Jane looked around her on the roof. All she could see near her was a small pile of five-foot two-by-fours that had been stored up here for some future improvement. She lifted one and stepped to the edge of the roof. She saw the guard running toward the back of the pharmacy where Christine was on the ladder. Jane held the piece of lumber like a spear and threw it straight down at him. The end of the two-by-four grazed the back of the man's head, hit his right shoulder blade, and knocked him to the ground, where he lay still.

Jane went down the ladder as quickly as she could, then grasped Christine's hand

and ran the other way around, between the two buildings toward the next street.

When they emerged, they could see Jane's SUV parked on the street, but there were three men in their twenties leaning against it, smoking cigarettes and talking. Jane said, "They may be harmless. Just stay out of sight for a minute while I find out."

Jane walked toward her vehicle with her keys in her hand. She pressed the button on the key fob, and the driver's-side door clicked to unlock. The men heard it and looked up to see Jane approaching. Two of them seemed to understand and stepped away from the car to the other side of the sidewalk, but the third, who had thick dark hair and a handsome face with big dark eyes, stayed where he was, leaning against the car, and grinned to reveal unnaturally white teeth.

Jane didn't smile back. *"Por favor,"* she said, and pointed to the door.

He stopped leaning, opened the driver's door as though he were helping her in.

Jane took a step toward it, but he quickly spun around and sat in the driver's seat. His two companions laughed. Jane reached into her jacket and produced the Beretta M92 pistol. She held it at waist level, so the man in the car was the only one who could see it. He was still smiling, but this time his mouth and his eyes didn't seem to belong in the same face. The smile was frozen. He said in English, "Just a joke."

"Get out of my car."

The man carefully got out of the driver's seat and stepped back across the sidewalk to join his two friends. He muttered something to them in Spanish, and they all backed away a few steps. Jane used those seconds to get into the vehicle, lock the doors, and start the engine. When she saw Christine emerge from the passageway ahead, she pulled forward and stopped in the street long enough to let her climb in.

As Jane pulled away, the uniformed security guard from the clinic arrived on foot, having run along the street instead of between buildings. His face was a mask of rage. He pulled his pistol out of its holster and appeared to take aim at Jane's back window, but then he seemed to recall that this was a very busy street even at this hour, with plenty of tall buildings to stop the bullet if he missed, pedestrians for witnesses, and probably policemen and soldiers listening for gunfire. Before Jane lost sight of the guard, a new white pickup truck arrived, and he climbed into it.

Jane made a quick turn and then another,

then drove down Boulevard Agua Caliente toward the bullfight ring, the racetrack, and the golf course, and away from the medical zone.

"You're going away from the border," Christine said. "San Ysidro is back that way."

"They're going to try to catch us," Jane said. "Most people cross at San Ysidro, don't they?"

"Yeah. It's the busiest border crossing in the world."

"Then it's where they'll think we're going. I'm going to try to cross at Otay Mesa."

"Okay, but I'm not sure if it's open at this hour."

"I drove almost to the crossing today while I was waiting for it to get dark. There are signs in English on the way. It closes for trucks at ten o'clock, but the passenger lanes are open twenty-four hours."

Christine was gripping the dashboard with both hands, staring ahead. Jane could see she was shivering.

"Believe me," said Jane. "I saw the signs."

"I'm just so scared," said Christine. "They're going to follow us."

"I'm sure they'll try. Do you remember what I taught you about firing a gun?"

"I think I do."

Jane took the Beretta out of her belt and held it so Christine could take it. "This one is different. See the little switch near your thumb?"

"This one?"

"Yes. It's the safety catch. If you slide it this way, the gun will be ready to fire. If you don't, it won't. It has fourteen rounds in the magazine and one in the chamber. You just keep pulling the trigger over and over until nothing happens. The brass casings eject to the right, and they come out hot."

Christine looked over her shoulder at the road. "I don't see the security guard."

"It's a precaution. When you're running you take every precaution before you think it might be necessary. We prepare for every threat we can imagine, remember? By the time there's a reason to prepare, it's too late. If they come up behind us, they'll try to run us off the road. Or they'll try to shoot me, because I'm the driver."

"What do I do about that?"

"If they pull up behind us, we'll do the same thing they're doing. I drive, you fire at them. You aim for the driver. But what you want to do is keep firing at the windshield. Any hit will make them lose their enthusiasm."

Christine sat in the passenger seat resting

the gun on her thigh and looking down at it.

Jane looked at her for a second. "If you have any doubt that you can do it, let me know now."

Christine shook her head. "No. No doubt."

Jane drove on. As they swung north again toward the Otay Mesa crossing, Jane saw the signs she remembered from the afternoon that said GARITA DE OTAY, and then the English one she had been looking for. It said the crossing was open twenty-four hours.

As Jane slowed to be sure the arrow was pointing in the direction she was going, she heard a sudden roar of an engine. She began to turn her head to see, but the movement was cut short. There was a ferocious jolt, a deafening noise, a giant hammerblow of steel on steel. The air bag exploded into her face, punching her backward into the headrest. An instant later there was the sound of glass and bits of metal bouncing on the pavement.

The car spun sideways, and as it rocked to a stop, Jane pulled her knife out of her pocket and punctured the air bag to get it out of her way. She stabbed Christine's air bag, too, and as it deflated she looked around her. Her SUV had been hit broadside by a white pickup truck, but Christine was still upright. "Are you hurt?"

"I don't think so."

Jane put her foot on the brake, shifted into neutral and then reverse, then stepped on the gas pedal and began to pull back. She could see that in the pickup truck that had hit her were two men wearing the same kind of security guard uniforms as the one at the hospital.

The man in the driver's seat interpreted Jane's maneuver and pulled forward to ram the side door of her vehicle, trying to stay with it and push it over. Jane reached for the pistol in her jacket pocket, but Christine's gun hand came up more quickly and fired four rounds into the truck's windshield. They could still hear the truck's engine as Jane's SUV roared backward to escape it, the front of the pickup scraping along the side of her vehicle as she cleared it. Then the unguided truck kept going, drifting ahead across the road and into an empty lot.

"Oh, my God," Christine whispered.

Jane threw the transmission into drive and headed south, away from the border. When she reached a junction with Route 10 she took it. The road looked, at least late at night, like a California freeway.

After a minute or two Christine said, "Could you see if that guy was dead?"

"The driver? Not sure," said Jane. "I hope so. He's not behind us, and that's all I care about right now."

"I just feel . . . weird. I didn't think about it. I just did it." She looked at Jane in the light of the dashboard. "You would have shot at them, right?"

"That's what I was going to do, but you were faster. Once I saw you still had the gun, I knew that what I ought to be doing was driving." Jane let the silence go for a time, then said, "You sure you didn't get hurt in the crash?"

"The air bag shook me up, but the seat belt went across my good shoulder, not the broken clavicle. I guess I was lucky the gun didn't fly into my face."

"You've been to Mexico a lot?"

"I grew up thirty-five miles from here."

"Have any ideas about how we can get across the border?"

"We could drive east, out of Baja, and try to get across the border somewhere else."

"East where?"

"I don't know. Calexico. Maybe Nogales, and cross into Arizona. Or even keep going and cross into Texas."

"We can't drive this car that distance. It's got too much damage. I haven't seen the outside of it yet, but I think it would attract attention at a border crossing." She looked at Christine. Beyond Christine was the black, endless Pacific. The moon hung above it, casting a silvery reflection on its surface.

"What are you looking at?"

"I'm thinking." Jane moved her eyes back to the road.

"Good, because we're going to hit Ensenada in a little while, and that's as far as we're supposed to go without stopping for a tourist card."

"I know," Jane said. "Let me ask you something else. There are a lot of cruise ships that stop in Ensenada, right?"

"Sure," said Christine. "All the time."

"The ships are huge, right?"

"Yeah. Thousands of rooms."

"They can't all be full, can they?"

Christine's eyes widened as she shook her head.

An hour later Jane pulled the SUV to a stop in the parking lot of a large *supermercado* near the harbor. She took her small suitcase with her clothes and the packet containing the false identification that Stewart had sent her and the cash she had brought. She took a rag from the back of the SUV and wiped the steering wheel, door handles, windows, trunk, and hood for fingerprints. Then she unscrewed the license plates and took them with her.

Jane and Christine walked to the beach. Jane kept watch while Christine slept on the sand for a couple of hours, until the air around them seemed to be lightening. Then the two women changed into clean jeans and blouses from Jane's suitcase and threw Christine's stolen scrubs into a trash can. Jane disassembled both of her pistols, removing the magazine, the slide, barrel, recoil spring, guide rod, slide catch, frame.

They walked to the harbor before dawn. As Jane went, she found places to put the pieces of the two weapons — the springs in a trash can, one slide in a storm sewer. The guide rods, slide catches, sears, and triggers went into a row of Dumpsters. She saved the most identifiable parts, the frames and magazines, until they reached the docks, then dropped them in deep water.

When it was fully light they made their way to the zone of resort hotels and went into what looked like the best one to order breakfast. When they had spent the early morning in a leisurely meal, Jane went to the concierge desk. She found a man there who seemed to be in charge and said, "Good morning. Do you speak English?"

"Yes, ma'am," the man said.

"I need to find a travel agent. Can you help me?"

"Certainly," he said. He reached under his counter and produced a glossy brochure, opened it to reveal a map of Ensenada. He used his pen to circle a rectangle that represented the hotel, then circled a spot one block south and four blocks east. He said, "We recommend Tours Riviera to our guests." He scribbled the name Tours Riviera. "Some of us have used their services ourselves."

Jane said, "I should mention that I don't speak Spanish."

"That isn't a problem, Señorita. Most of their customers are American."

"Thank you very much," Jane said. She handed him a twenty-dollar bill, mainly because of her relief that he had not demanded to know if she was a guest of the hotel.

He pocketed the money. "Thank you, Señorita."

Jane and Christine left for the travel agency at ten, and found the office open. The young woman who took charge of them at the door said her name was Estrella.

Jane said, "The reason we've come is that we'd like to change our travel plans. This is a last-minute idea, so tell me if it's not possible."

"Certainly."

"There are cruise ships stopping in Ensenada all the time, aren't there?"

"Oh, yes, especially at this time of year. There are Baja cruises, three-day, four-day, and five-day cruises that start in San Diego, Los Angeles, or Long Beach that stop at Catalina Island, Ensenada, Cabo San Lucas, and go back. There are fifteen-day cruises to Hawaii that stop here. Let me see what's in port now." She typed something into her computer and read off the screen. "The Carnival *Paradise,* Royal Caribbean *Monarch of the Seas, Diamond Princess,* Holland America *Zaandam.*"

"Are there ever any empty cabins when they reach Ensenada?"

"I would say there always are."

"Would it be possible for you to book us a cabin on one of them to go to one of the California ports?"

"I think so, but it might be an expensive way to get home. They usually sail from here around five or six o'clock in the evening and arrive in their American port at around six the next morning. So you won't see much."

"That's just fine," said Jane. She looked as remorseful as she felt. "It's a last-minute plan. We came down here by car with two men we didn't know as well as we thought we did. We're going home early."

Estrella looked at them sympathetically. "Say no more. You have your passports?"

"Yes." Jane reached into the side pocket of her suitcase and produced the ones she had received from Stewart Shattuck.

Estrella lifted her telephone, spoke rapidly in Spanish, and in a few minutes, the arrangements were made. "The price is prorated," she said. "It's a three-day cruise, and you will owe one-third."

"We'll take it," said Jane. She looked at her watch. "I wonder if it would be okay for us to go aboard the ship right away and get settled. I think we'd like to explore the ship a little before we sail."

"I think that sounds like a good idea," said Christine.

"Yes," Jane said. "I feel as though we've done everything here that we want to."

36

Ruby Beale was not a fearful or superstitious woman, but she had a bad feeling tonight, and it wasn't new. She had been feeling it, more or less, since she had looked down from the walkway in the great room of the big house and seen the woman staring in the window at her. There was a feeling that the curse had not yet worked all the way through her family and exhausted itself.

A minute after she had seen the woman Ruby had begun to resent the people around her, and the feeling had grown. She had seen something that other people had not seen, and they had not had the sense to realize what it was. Ruby had known. Anybody with any sense would have known. The black-haired woman in the all-black clothes could not have been easier to interpret if she had been a skeleton wearing a hooded robe.

The woman had been staring inside, choosing her way in. Ruby had sensed that she already knew a hundred ways in, as water would have, or air. It wasn't a question of Ruby being lucky and seeing her in time to stop her. It was more like being the one who saw something big and irresistible and destructive while it was still forming — like wind and waves beginning to churn, far out at sea.

Later that night she had thought to herself, Well, this would be the kind of thing that would happen, wouldn't it? Anybody in the world understood that if you did bad, cruel things to people, then some time the hatred you caused would take a form and come after you. Anybody would know, except her stupid son, Richard, who could feel nothing of the rhythms and balances of the world. Revenge was just a restoration of the natural balance. That was why people called it getting even.

They had heard her warn them about that woman, but none of them had believed it or even understood. In their hearts they thought Ruby was just an eccentric, spoiled rich woman, old before her time and scared witless by a five-second exposure to their world, the real world where people used guns to take things. They hadn't known her well enough to have the index to her mind. Even her husband, Andy, and her son, Richard, who both had good reason to know her, had not taken her seriously.

They hadn't seemed to remember that as a nurse she had seen more death than Steve Demming, Sybil Landreau, Claudia Marshall, and Pete Tilton combined. She had seen it arrive in ambulances and bloom in beds in intensive care and on operating tables. Some nights she had left the hospital and felt it plucking at her sleeve, trying to get her to turn around and stare into its face until she couldn't look away again. Death was what she had seen looking in the window that night.

Richard — poor, stupid Richard — had been the first one to actually say she was delusional. His hirelings had been lost from the beginning. They were people who had stopped making decisions. They just heard what the people who were paying them wanted, and thought about ways to oblige. That wasn't thinking. And over the years Richard had become worse than they were. He thought only about what he wanted, and listened only to people who told him reassuring lies.

And now the disaster had come. Since that night she'd had to guard against her own feelings about Andy, too. Ruby's alliance with Andrew Beale had been reasonable. They had lasted a long time, become prosperous and powerful, and she had not found her side of the bargain too hard, or his too easy. She knew that she had to be smart now and focus on the details — count her blessings, as her mother used to put it. She couldn't let herself start thinking too hard about the larger picture. She couldn't look at herself as a person who had come into the contract wanting one specific thing and being denied it. She had wanted to be the matriarch, the honored wife, mother and grandmother of a large and thriving family. She'd had other things, but not that.

Now Ruby was long past childbearing, and her only child had wasted his life and been shot to death. It wasn't really his life to gamble — not entirely his, anyway. Ruby was left with Andy, somehow robbed of their strength by time and all out of chances. When Andy was only one of many people in Ruby's life and she was distracted by lots of jobs and activities, she had been able to overlook, or at least not dwell on, his faults and failings. But now he was it. His faults soured big portions of her day. If he was what was left, the prize she got for all of her efforts on earth, why wasn't he better?

At one time she had thought the baby would be her prize, but he was not. Baby Robert was just a chance for a prize. He was a small, soft, unformed thing that might be coaxed to grow into a man, and that was hard. She would have to devote all of her remaining time and energy to the business of making Robert grow into something Richard never was.

Ruby sat in the unfamiliar living room of the unfamiliar house on the hill overlooking Capistrano. She hated it. The house was not well made like the one in Rancho Santa Fe. They had come here because it was supposed to be safe. But who said it was safe? Richard said it, because Demming had said it, and of course Claudia and Sybil had nodded their empty heads. They were all dead now. That's how much the lot of them knew about what was safe. Ruby had not forgotten that her husband, Andy, had acquiesced. He'd had the deepest contempt for Richard's judgment, but he had gone and agreed to the move anyway.

She listened to the baby monitor for a few seconds. There still seemed to be no sound coming from the baby's room. That was good. He was growing fast and was sometimes able to hold enough milk to keep him asleep until three or four o'clock in the

642

morning. She had let the baby nurse go home tonight, and she wasn't eager to heat up a bottle and trudge in there to feed him right now. She felt like going to bed.

Ruby wondered what was keeping Andy. He was supposedly going over some of the paperwork from the family business. She wouldn't be entirely surprised if it turned out that Richard had neglected his job while he had been trying to salvage his personal life. She stood up and walked down the hall to the dismal little square room where Andy had moved a desk and a lamp and a couch.

She came to the doorway and looked in. On the desk were about ten open files, some pens and pencils, and a calculator. Andy was lying faceup on the big leather couch with his hands at his sides. Gravity tightened his skin against the facial bones, and that gave his nose and cheeks that fragile bird-like appearance that dead men had at their wakes. She felt a moment of pain for him. He was an old man. He had worked so hard for forty years, and then let go. There was something particularly cruel about having begun to relax the muscles and the mind from all of that labor and stress, and then be dragged back into it again. No matter how much of a disappointment Richard had been, it was impossible for either of them to forget he was their son, and hard for them to take up the work he should have been doing.

"I know you're there," said Andy. "I'm just resting my eyes."

"You should rest. You don't have to punch a time clock. Does everything still seem to be a mess?"

He shook his head without opening his eyes, then sat up and looked at her. "The accounting wasn't actually the mess I thought it was."

"That's good."

"No, it's not. What I thought was carelessness was obfuscation. The little shit was stealing money."

"From us?"

"From the company. Whoever that is. Us, his child, even himself, I suppose. He formed a few corporations — Richard Beale this and Richard Beale that — and paid them."

Ruby stared down at the rug. "I'm sorry to hear that." She meant it exactly that way. It was something she would have been better off never knowing.

"Well, I guess it doesn't matter now that the girl is gone."

"Why would she matter?" She was irritated at him for telling her that her son

644

had robbed his own family, and now she was irritated at him for bringing up unpleasant, irrelevant memories.

He said, "You're forgetting about that marriage."

"That was a fake."

"The only thing fake about it was that the bride didn't actually say 'I do.' The witnesses signed the papers and they were filed to protect Richard's rights to the child."

"But that doesn't give her anything."

"In the state of California, she's his heir unless she says otherwise. Right now, half of whatever was in his name is already hers. When the death certificate is filed, the other half is, too."

"But he stole it."

"Some of it. Proving our dead son, the president of our company, was embezzling weakens the company, and weakens us. Nobody would lend money for projects, nobody wants to buy assets that might already have liens on them, and nobody's going to sign a contract with a company that doesn't even know if it's bankrupt."

"What are we going to do?"

"Nothing for now. Later, we'll have the boy, Robert, declared the sole heir of Richard and Christine. I'll have to go over it with the lawyers."

Ruby looked at the rug again. "Let them take care of it. We've got enough without it to raise Robert, haven't we?"

Beale nodded. Into the silence came a low beeping noise. He turned to look at the lights on the keypad on the wall.

"What's that noise?"

"The alarm system on this house sounds different. That's a perimeter breach. The motion detectors outside picked up movement. It's probably just a skunk or a raccoon."

"What if it's her?"

"Her?"

"That woman." Ruby was angry. "The one at the other house. The one who killed our son, for Christ's sake."

"Not very likely."

"It wasn't likely the first time."

Andy reached into the top desk drawer, took out a pistol, and inserted a full magazine into the handle. "I'll go check."

"Don't," she said. "I'm sure it's her. We've been here for three nights and there weren't raccoons before. Just come with me, and we'll stay with Robert — lock ourselves in."

Andy Beale kept the gun in his hand and followed her. He considered turning off the light in the office, but then he decided that if there was an intruder, darkness wasn't to his advantage.

As Ruby Beale walked quickly toward Robert's room, things began to occur to her. She hadn't heard the baby monitor for a long time. Usually there was some rustling or deep breathing or something, but she hadn't been hearing any of that. Ruby swung the door open and looked into the dimly lighted room. The baby monitor was unplugged. The window was open. Robert's crib was empty.

Jane Whitefield swung the black Cadillac into the last turn on the dark road and accelerated up the ramp onto the eastbound freeway. She glanced in the rearview mirror for a few seconds to be sure no headlights were following her, then passed a tractor-trailer truck and glided into the line of vehicles in the center lane, all traveling at high speed. Her car was already just one more set of taillights moving away into the night. She glanced in the rearview mirror again. From the shadowy silhouettes, she could see Christine was bent over, staring at Robert, his little body strapped in his new car seat. He already seemed to be asleep again, lulled back into slumber by the car's vibration and the quiet hum of tires on the road. As they passed an exit ramp, they came under a light. Jane sped up and got out of the glow, to be sure that Christine couldn't see her tears.

37

When Jane awoke it was already ten-thirty in the morning. She and Carey had stayed awake far into the night talking, and then made love while the fall wind blew leaves from the sycamore against the bedroom window. She sat up and looked for Carey, then put on her robe and went downstairs to search for him. He had said he had no surgeries scheduled. When she walked into the kitchen she saw his note on the table. "Morning rounds are at nine. I'll be home by one or two. Love you. C." Jane tied the sash of her robe, went out to the garage, and took four large plastic storage boxes from the top of the stack she kept there.

She carried them upstairs to the master suite, showered and dressed. Then she walked the few yards down the hall to the room she had allowed herself to think of as the baby's room.

She opened the upper two dresser drawers and took out the stacks of neatly folded baby outfits, the receiving blankets, the soft, hooded towels and washcloths, the tiny socks. From another drawer she took out the mobile she had bought to hang over the crib, the pictures she had selected for the walls, the sets of crib bumpers. Then she added the stuffed animals that had been so perfect when she had seen them in the stores that she had prudently brought them home for fear she would never find them again when the time came. Everything she had been saving for the baby went into the first three plastic storage boxes, and then Jane put on the lids and sealed them with duct tape.

The last item she carefully lifted from a hook on the wall. It was a *Ga-ose-ha,* a cradleboard. Jane had never made up her mind whether she would actually use it. It was a beautiful object, about two feet long and a foot wide, with the footboard and the protective bent wood bow above the place for the baby's head both carved in a diamond pattern. The fabric that was supposed to lace the baby in was black with bright beaded vines studded with white, red, yellow, and blue flowers. She had no idea how old it was. Her grandmother had told her once that her mother had put her in it and hung her to rock in the wind while she tended her garden on the Tonawanda reservation.

Jane wrapped the Ga-ose-ha in white tissue paper, set it carefully in its own plastic box, then sealed the box. It belonged in a museum anyway, she thought. Probably that was where it would end up.

She stacked the four boxes, carried them to the door at the far end of the hall, and climbed the narrow stairs to the attic. She switched on the light and took the boxes around the covered rack of winter clothes on hangers, and between four trunks full of antique china that some ancestor of Carey's had not been able to sell in his long-vanished general store. She set her four plastic storage boxes on the old leather couch with horsehair stuffing that had been stored in the attic since Carey's grandfather died. She took a last look, then went back down the stairs.

Jane went to the kitchen, poured some coffee into a silver thermos cup, screwed the top on, picked up her purse from the counter, and went out the door. She got into her white Volvo, backed out of the garage, and drove toward Deganawida.

On the Youngmann Expressway it took only about fifteen minutes to get to the small town beside the river, and another five to reach the stretch of old, narrow houses where she had grown up. As usual, Jane parked her car in the garage and rolled down the garage door to keep from being noticed. She went to the kitchen door because it gave her a chance to walk around to the back of the house and check for broken windows or jimmied locks.

She went into the kitchen and stood still for a minute, listening to the sounds of the house and smelling its familiar smells. Then she opened four windows and descended the stairs to the basement to return her remaining sets of identification cards to their hiding place. She returned to the ground floor and did some dusting, then rolled the vacuum cleaner from the front closet and vacuumed the floor. It occurred to her that on one of her next trips here she would have to wash the windows. The exact day didn't matter. There was no rush.

She carried the vacuum cleaner up the stairs to the second-floor landing, and rolled it a few feet toward the far end of the hall before the telephone rang. It made her jump, but then she realized that Carey must have finished his rounds early and guessed where she must be. She stepped into her old room, hurried to the nightstand beside the bed, and lifted the receiver. "Hello?"

"Is this the number where I can reach Jane Whitefield?" It was a man's voice, and she had never heard it before.

"Who's calling?"

"My name is Michael Schneider." The man waited through a moment of Jane's silence, then seemed to panic. "Please, don't hang up. This is urgent. I really need to talk to her, and in an hour it might be too late for me. I know this is the number because I've carried it in my memory for a long time in case I ever needed it, and now I do."

Two more seconds passed while Jane took in a deep breath and then let it out. "This is Jane Whitefield."

ABOUT THE AUTHOR

Thomas Perry is the author of the Jane Whitefield series and *Silence,* as well as the best-selling novels *Nightlife, Death Benefits,* and *Pursuit,* which was the first recipient of the Gumshoe Award for Best Novel. He won the Edgar Award for *The Butcher's Boy,* and *Metzger's Dog* was a *New York Times* Notable Book of the Year. He lives in Southern California.